Praise for
Adventurers Wanted: Slathbog's Gold

". . . a nod and a wink to classics like the *Lord of the Rings* and the game of *Dungeons & Dragons*."

—Bookspotcentral.com

"Entertaining . . . the series potential is limitless."

—Booklist

"A fantastic journey . . . the story reminded me a lot of *Eragon*, yet the reading is easier and quicker. Highly enjoyable, fast-paced, and full of adventure."

—SciFiChick.com

"The beginning of an epic fantasy series."

—Library Journal

Destry May 23rd/13 hope you

enjoy this Book

ADVENTURERS
✦ WANTED ✦

Love Grandma
Med.

BOOK ONE

ADVENTURERS
✦WANTED✦

SLATHBOG'S
GOLD

M. L. FORMAN

SHADOW
MOUNTAIN

First printing in hardbound 2009
First printing in paperbound 2011

Library of Congress Cataloging-in-Publication Data

Forman, Mark, 1964–
    Slathbog's gold / Mark Forman.
        p. cm. — (Adventurers wanted ; bk. 1)
    Summary: When fifteen-year-old orphan Alex Taylor sees an odd sign in a shop window and goes inside to investigate, he is sent on a quest to defeat an evil dragon, and in the process he confronts his fears and learns about his future and his past.
    ISBN 978-1-60641-029-5 (hardbound : alk. paper)
    ISBN 978-1-60641-681-5 (paperbound)
    [1. Fantasy.   2. Adventure and adventurers—Fiction. 3. Orphans—Fiction.   4. Wizards—Fiction.]   I. Title.
    PZ7.F7653Sl 2009
    [Fic]—dc22   2008030691

Printed in the United States of America
R. R. Donnelley, Crawfordsville, IN

10   9   8

For Ali,
who always believed

CONTENTS

CHAPTER ONE
ADVENTURERS WANTED

Alex and his friends gathered around the small opening, preparing for what they had to do. His eyes fixed on the darkness in front of him and a shiver ran down his back. The darkness didn't bother him, but the smell coming from the cave did. It was a nasty mix of rotten eggs and meat that had been left out too long, and it turned his stomach. Looking away, he tried to think of something happy, but nothing came to him.

Everything that had happened to him in the past few months seemed like a dream, a dream that was fast becoming a nightmare. They had reached the goal of their great quest. Alex had thought this day would never come, and for a moment he wondered why he was here.

"In we must go, or give up our quest," said Bregnest in a grim tone.

"To some this would seem foolish, but let us seek our fate and trust to luck," Skeld added, looking as serious as Alex had ever seen him.

Foolish, thought Alex. That was a good word for what they were about to do. Foolish or incredibly brave, he couldn't decide which. It didn't really matter though, because Alex knew he would go into the dark cave with his friends. He looked around at his seven companions and smiled, remembering how he had gotten here.

It had been a normal day when he had wished for a life different from the one he had known, a life of adventure. Yes, it had been a day like every other day he could remember—before he became an adventurer.

Alex had lived above the Happy Dragon tavern for as long as he could remember and there had been times when he'd enjoyed the sounds of the customers, the clinking of glasses, and the wonderful smells coming from the kitchen. The tavern was usually a happy place, but right then it was hard for Alex to think of anything happy.

"It wasn't even my fault," Alex said to himself as he clenched and unclenched his hands inside his jacket pockets, trying to work off his anger. If only he could run away from his life, run away to a place where no one would know him. He wanted to change his life, but he knew his wish was foolish and nothing would change. Frustrated, he walked faster than normal, ignoring the people and traffic around him.

It wasn't fair that he had been yelled at for breaking the glasses. His stepbrother, Todd, had tripped him as Alex was carrying the glasses to the kitchen. Todd hadn't meant to get him in trouble, or even to make him drop the glasses. He was always just goofing around. It was just Alex's bad luck that he got blamed when the joke went wrong.

Turning onto Sildon Lane, Alex slowed his pace and took a deep breath to calm himself. Todd was two years older than Alex, and as stepbrothers went, he wasn't all bad. The problem with Todd was that he was always doing things he shouldn't have been, or that he didn't really think through. It wasn't Mr. Roberts's fault that it looked like Alex was to blame for whatever happened. Todd was good at disappearing when things went wrong, leaving Alex to answer for what had happened.

Alex always called his stepfather "Mr. Roberts" or "sir" and Mr. Roberts was a busy man. He often didn't have time to listen to Alex's explanations of what had happened before he started yelling. Alex knew running the Happy Dragon was difficult work, and always being shorthanded didn't help Mr. Roberts's temper.

Alex paused and looked at his reflection in the dirty window beside him. His blue-green eyes looked back at him, and he could see the troubled look on his face. Smiling weakly at his reflection, he used both hands to flatten his ruffled, sandy-blond hair. He was being foolish and he knew it. But he couldn't deny he still felt unhappy and frustrated with his life and he longed for something different.

Alex shook his head to clear his thoughts as he continued to walk down the lane. He glanced at the shop windows as he passed them, not really looking for or seeing anything. He felt his anger burning out, just like it always did when he took time to think about things.

He knew that when he got back to the tavern, Mr. Roberts would apologize for yelling at him and Todd would apologize for getting him into trouble.

Mr. Roberts was a large man who shouted a lot, but never really got angry about anything. He had always treated Alex well enough, but he had never seemed like a real father, at least not to Alex. Even though he knew in his heart that Mr. Roberts and Todd would do anything for him, Alex felt alone in the world. And in some ways, it was the truth. His mother had died when Alex was only seven, and he had never known his real father. He didn't have any relatives, or at least none that he knew about.

Alex smiled as he remembered his mother, even though the memory made him sad. She had always told him that he could be whatever he wanted to be, if he just tried. Right now he wanted to be anything except the dishwasher at the Happy Dragon.

Alex stopped and looked back at the bookshop window he had just passed. It looked like the same bookshop he had walked by hundreds of times before, but there was something different about it today. Instead of the normal pile of dusty books in the window, there was a large, brightly painted sign with two words printed on it in large red letters

ADVENTURERS WANTED

Alex stared at the sign for a minute, forgetting his troubles. He wondered what the sign might mean and why it was in the bookshop at all. It looked out of place in the window. He moved closer to the glass and tried to look into the shop, cupping his hands around his eyes to cut out the afternoon glare, but he couldn't see anything. Puzzled, he looked back at the sign to see if he'd missed something. In deep blue letters the sign now said

ADVENTURERS WANTED
APPLY WITHIN

Alex stepped back and shook his head before looking at the sign again. The red letters were back, and he wondered if he'd seen the blue letters at all. He focused on the sign for several minutes without blinking, just to be sure, but the red letters remained unchanged.

Alex looked up and down the lane, wondering if anyone else had noticed the sign. The normally busy lane was oddly empty. There were several parked cars, and a few people walking at the far end of the lane, but nobody close. It was still early afternoon. There should have been dozens of people and cars crowding Sildon Lane.

Looking back at the window, Alex jumped when he saw the sign had changed for a third time, this time to shiny gold letters.

GREAT ADVENTURES
REASONABLE PRICES
APPLY NOW

Butterflies whirled in Alex's stomach. Something strange was happening; signs didn't change in an instant. There must be some reasonable explanation for what he was seeing. He moved closer to the window again, looking to see if there was some mechanical device that had changed the sign while he hadn't been paying attention. All he could see was the cardboard sign—a sign that changed every time he looked away.

Alex moved to the bookshop door. He looked up and down Sildon Lane once more, but even the few people he had seen before were gone. Taking a deep breath, and considering how best to ask about the sign in the window, he pushed open the door and walked into the shop.

"Good afternoon," said a happy voice as soon as the door had closed behind Alex. "Here to get an adventure, no doubt."

Alex looked around the shop to see who had spoken. He spotted a short, round, balding man standing behind a dusty, book-covered counter.

"No, I—" Alex began.

"Thought you might like to try being an adventurer," the man finished for him. "Excellent career choice I must say."

"N-no," Alex stammered. "I was just wondering—"

"Oh, not to worry," the man interrupted again. "We don't charge unless you're completely happy with the adventure. And our prices are very reasonable. In fact, most adventures build the cost right in, so there's no need for you to worry about payment at all."

"Yes, but—"

"Come along then," said the man with a laugh, turning away from the counter and walking toward the back of the shop. "We'll just get some information and see what kind of adventure we can find for you."

"I only wanted to ask about the sign," Alex said in a rush, afraid the man would interrupt him again.

"Yes, it's quite a good one, isn't it?" the man replied, smiling fondly at the sign displayed in the window. "I've only just put it up today, and you're the first one to notice it. Now, come along."

Not knowing what else to do, Alex followed the man through the blue velvet curtains that divided the back of the shop from the front. The man moved quickly and by the time Alex stepped through the curtains, the shopkeeper was already sitting behind a desk, shuffling through a pile of papers. He seemed to be looking for something special and ignored Alex completely.

Alex approached the desk and looked at the papers scattered across the desktop and the floor. He tried to read what was printed on them, but it was impossible because more papers kept flying everywhere as the man continued searching through them. Alex stood and waited for the man to say something.

"Here we are," said the man, pulling a single page from the pile. "Adventurers' Application. Exactly what we're looking for."

"Excuse me, sir," said Alex. "Who are you?"

"Who am I?" the man echoed. "Why, I'm Cornelius Clutter, of course."

"And you . . . sell adventures?"

"Of course I do," replied Mr. Clutter with a smile. "Didn't you say you saw the sign in the window?"

"Yes."

"Well, that says it all, doesn't it?"

"Yes, but—"

"I mean, it would be silly for me to put up a sign offering adventures if I didn't sell them, wouldn't it?" Mr. Clutter asked in a kindly voice. "No good advertising for things you haven't got, is it?"

"No, I suppose not."

"Of course not. That would be silly. And one thing Cornelius Clutter is not is *silly.*"

"No," Alex agreed, not wishing to offend Mr. Clutter. "But I'm not sure—"

"You're not sure if you're properly suited to be an adventurer," Mr. Clutter finished for him. "Well, not to worry, the application will sort that out. After all, you're already here, aren't you?"

"But—"

"No, no, don't worry," said Mr. Clutter, looking down at the paper in his hand. "Let's just see what we have once the application is filled out."

Alex looked around Mr. Clutter's office, feeling slightly nervous. He'd only wanted to know about the sign in the window, not fill out some application to become an adventurer, whatever that was. He was sure, however, that any objection he made would be brushed aside before he could get the words all the way out. He also felt certain that any answer of Mr. Clutter's would have nothing at all to do with his question.

"Have a seat then, mister? Mister? Mister what?" asked Mr. Clutter, looking at Alex and pointing to a large chair in front of his desk.

"Taylor," Alex answered, sitting down slowly. "Alexander Taylor. But I go by Alex."

"Ah, well, we'll jot that down," said Mr. Clutter, taking a pen from his desk and starting to write. "Now then, Mr. Taylor—or may I call you Alex?"

"Yes, please."

"Thank you. Now then, Alex, what is your age?"

"Fifteen."

"A bit young," Mr. Clutter said, scribbling on the paper in front of him and making a soft clucking sound.

"I'll be sixteen in two months," Alex added quickly, not liking the frown that had appeared on Mr. Clutter's face. "I turn sixteen at the end of October."

"Ah, well, that *does* make a difference. I find it's best to start a career early. So, any special abilities?" questioned Mr. Clutter.

"None that I know of."

Mr. Clutter nodded, writing something down. "We'll put you down as untested then."

"Yes, I suppose so," Alex replied. He didn't know what Mr. Clutter meant by "special abilities" or "untested," but he didn't dare ask any questions.

"Ah, yes, now a more difficult question," said Mr. Clutter, the corners of his mouth twitching as he tried not to smile.

"Would you have any problems traveling with female adventurers?"

"What?" Alex asked, blushing at the question.

"Well, as I'm sure you know, there have always been female adventurers," Mr. Clutter said quickly. "And many of them have found a great deal of success. It's just that, well, some male adventurers don't think the ladies belong—if you know what I mean. A bit silly if you ask me, but people can be silly about things like that."

"No, I don't have a problem with female adventurers," said Alex.

"Right," Mr. Clutter went on without waiting for Alex to say anything more. "Do you believe in brownies, dragons, dwarfs, elves, fairies, ghosts, goblins, griffins, pixies . . ."

Mr. Clutter continued to read names from the paper and Alex listened closely as the list went on and on. He wondered how long it would be before Mr. Clutter ran out of breath. Alex had never heard of most of the things on the list before, and those he did recognize, he didn't believe in anyway. After several minutes, and what seemed like hundreds of names, Mr. Clutter appeared to be winding up.

" . . . Sea serpents, skin changers, trolls, werewolves, and wraiths?" Mr. Clutter took a deep breath and looked at Alex.

"Well," said Alex, feeling uncomfortable. "I—"

"We'll just put yes on that one, shall we?" Mr. Clutter interrupted. "Not to worry, not to worry, most people don't know half of the creatures listed."

"No, I suppose not."

"And we'll put yes down on number seven as well. Everybody says yes to number seven."

"Number seven?"

"And let's see. We should put down unknown on magical ability and resistance to curses."

"I—"

"And yes to willing to learn magic," Mr. Clutter continued happily, marking the page in front of him as if Alex wasn't there. "We should put no to affiliated with dark creatures. And no to evil intent."

"Does anybody say yes to evil intent?" Alex asked, more to himself than Mr. Clutter.

"It's better to be safe than sorry," Mr. Clutter replied, looking up from the page. "We have to ask, it's on the form."

"Oh," Alex said, surprised that Mr. Clutter had answered his question directly.

"Any experience with weapons?" Mr. Clutter asked suddenly. "You know—sword, ax, bow. Anything at all?"

"No," Alex answered, confused.

"Ah, well," said Mr. Clutter, looking back to the paper on his desk. "Not a problem, not a problem at all. Lots of first-timers don't have any experience with weapons."

"Are there many first-timers?" Alex asked, not terribly surprised when Mr. Clutter didn't answer.

"That about does it I think," said Mr. Clutter, standing up. "If you'll just sign here at the bottom, we'll see what we can do about finding you an adventure."

"Yes, well," Alex began as Mr. Clutter forced the pen into

his hand and pointed to the place where he should sign. "I don't—"

"I'm sure this seems very fast," said Mr. Clutter, tapping the page in front of Alex. "It's just that I know of an adventure that's about to begin, and if we get your application to them quickly enough, they may take you along."

"Oh," was all Alex could think to say. He paused, then signed his name in the spot next to Mr. Clutter's finger.

"Excellent," said Mr. Clutter, taking the pen and looking over the signed application. "If you'll follow me, I'll see if I can arrange an interview immediately."

Confused by everything that was happening, and a little breathless because of Mr. Clutter's way of talking very fast, Alex considered running for the door. He was curious, however, and the idea of adventures had caught his interest. And although he didn't believe in magic, he thought perhaps he *could*.

Alex followed Mr. Clutter out of the room and down a long, wood-paneled hallway. There were several doors on either side of the hallway, but Mr. Clutter led Alex straight to the door at the far end.

"If you'll just relax in here for a few minutes," Mr. Clutter said, opening the door for Alex, "I'll see if I can arrange your interview."

Alex was about to say, "Thank you, but I really have to be going," but he never got the chance. Mr. Clutter shut the door and was gone. Alex was alone in a large room with a warm fire and several comfortable-looking chairs. Two small tables with large silver lamps on them had been pushed against one wall of the room, and there was a large window on the back wall. Alex looked around, but there was nothing more to see.

"This is complete madness," Alex said to himself as he started pacing around the room. *Mr. Clutter must be mad, or maybe worse,* Alex thought as he continued to circle the room. *I'll just make some excuse to get out of the shop and go back to Sildon Lane, that's all.*

Making his way to the window at the back of the room, Alex looked outside absently. He was trying to think of an excuse to leave, but what he saw outside the window made him forget everything. The view was not of an alleyway or a back-yard, but of a snow-covered countryside. Rubbing his eyes to make sure he was seeing clearly, Alex looked closer. The view did not change like the sign had. He could see people moving around a small cluster of houses. Outside the window, it had started to snow and, try as he might, Alex couldn't find an explanation for what he was seeing. After several minutes of staring out the window, Alex moved to the fireplace and dropped into a large leather chair, dazed.

He had almost convinced himself that Mr. Clutter was simply crazy. Yes, it would have been nice to believe in magic and adventures, but there really were no such things. Alex was starting to wish he had never come into the bookshop.

Suddenly the door opened, shaking him from his thoughts. Mr. Clutter had returned, and two people were following him.

"Now then," Mr. Clutter began in a businesslike tone. "This is Mister Alexander Taylor, but he goes by Alex. He has applied for an adventure, and naturally I thought of you gentlemen."

Alex's eyes grew wide as he saw the two people who had followed Mr. Clutter into the room. The first man was barely five feet tall, with wide shoulders and short legs. He wore large leather boots and a blood-red shirt. His beard reached to just below his belt. The second person was close to six feet tall, with long, silver-blond hair and a happy, almost glowing, face. His clothes seemed to be all different shades of green, but Alex couldn't tell what they were made of. As he looked at the two strangers, Alex realized that these were not normal people at all.

"Hmmm," said the short one, looking at Alex. "Not had many applicants lately, have we?"

"Well, no," Mr. Clutter admitted in an apologetic tone. "However, this young man seems willing, and I'm sure he would be an excellent addition to your adventure."

"Really," the short man replied, turning to look at Mr. Clutter. "Would you say that if *you* were going on *this* adventure, Clutter?"

"Well, my adventuring days are over," replied Mr. Clutter, stammering slightly but continuing to smile. "But Alex seems an excellent choice for a first-time adventurer. You've seen his application, and applications are almost always right."

"Would you bring us some tea?" asked the second man in a clear, musical voice.

"Yes, of course," said Mr. Clutter, turning to go. "I'll bring it right along then, shall I?"

"Give us a few minutes," replied the second man with a slight smile. "We need to ask some questions first."

Mr. Clutter was out of the room without another word,

leaving Alex alone with the two strangers. The men seemed not to notice that he was staring at them as they moved two chairs closer to the fire and took their seats. There was an uncomfortable minute of silence, and Alex wondered if he should say something.

"Well," the man with the musical voice began, "I suppose introductions are in order. My name is Arconn. I am, as you may have guessed, an elf of the house of Dalious, hailing from the great forest lands of Delanor."

Alex couldn't have said anything if he'd tried. He had no idea what the "house of Dalious" was or where the "lands of Delanor" were, but he had noticed that Arconn, though looking normal enough, had oddly pointed ears.

"I'm Thrang Silversmith," said the short man. "Son of Thorgood Silversmith. From the land of Thraxon."

"I . . ." Alex started then stopped.

"You are Alexander Taylor," said Arconn. "We've seen your application, so if it's all right with you, we'll call you Alex."

"All right," Alex managed to reply.

"He's not sure what to make of us, I reckon," said Thrang with a short laugh. "Thinking we're just a couple of strange men, he is."

"Oh, no," Alex said quickly.

"Don't worry 'bout it," Thrang continued, waving off Alex's words. "Most first-timers don't know what to make of their new companions."

"I suppose not," said Alex. "I'm not at all sure about any of this."

"That is an excellent place to start," said Arconn happily.

"It is?" Alex asked.

"'Course it is," Thrang answered in a more serious tone. "Not being sure leaves your mind open to all kinds of things, don't it?"

"I suppose it does," Alex admitted.

"Well, then, we're looking for an eighth person to join our adventure," said Thrang. "Clutter says you might be our man."

"Yes, well I—"

"I think he will do nicely," said Arconn. "Not too sure of himself, but willing."

"Needs to be outfitted," said Thrang, stroking his beard. "Be no good taking him dressed like that."

"Dressed like what?" Alex asked, looking down at his clothes.

"You're hardly dressed for an adventure." Thrang laughed.

"I wasn't planning to go on an adventure," Alex answered defensively. "I wasn't planning any of this."

"The best ones never do," said Thrang.

"May I ask, then," said Arconn in a slightly concerned tone, "why did you come here?"

"What?" Alex asked.

"How did you enter Mr. Clutter's shop, and more important, *why* did you enter Mr. Clutter's shop? It's not as if just anyone can get in, after all."

"I saw a sign in the window," Alex replied. "The sign seemed to change every time I looked at it, so I thought I'd ask about it in the bookstore."

"I see," said Arconn, leaning back into his chair. "And do you think anyone else noticed the sign?"

Alex thought. "Sildon Lane was strangely empty when I noticed the sign. I was going to ask someone in the street if they noticed the sign changing, but when I looked around, there was nobody there."

"'Course not," said Thrang in a matter-of-fact tone. "That's because you weren't really there either."

"What do you mean? Of course I was there. If I wasn't there, how could I have seen the sign?"

"An interesting question," Arconn said in an understanding voice, "as not many people ever see the sign, and fewer still ever ask about it."

"I'm sure I don't know what you are talking about," said Alex, not liking the way the conversation was going. All of this talk about people not seeing a sign that was in plain view concerned him. "I really should be going," he continued quickly. "Mr. Roberts will be looking for me soon, and—"

"He won't be looking at all," said Arconn calmly. "Because, in fact, you haven't been gone long at all."

"But I have," Alex insisted. "It must be an hour or more since I left."

"He don't understand," said Thrang, looking amused. "He don't know what we're on about."

"No, I understand," said Alex. "But I really should be getting back. I have a lot of work to do at the tavern—"

"Let me explain," said Arconn, cutting Alex off and

motioning for him to sit down in a chair. "I promise, you won't be late getting back to your work if you'll just listen."

Alex sat down on the edge of his chair, not sure he really wanted anything explained to him. Since entering the shop, every time he'd managed to get a question answered things seemed to make less sense.

"We are adventurers," Arconn began.

"He knows that much," Thrang interrupted. "You've got to tell him why he won't be late getting back to work."

"Of course," said Arconn. "But I want to go step-by-step, so he will understand exactly what is happening."

"Oh, fluff," said Thrang, blowing air out of his mouth loudly. "You're telling him like he was a child. Just give it to him plain and let him think it over."

"Very well," said Arconn. "I suppose you're right."

Alex's eyes moved from Thrang to Arconn. He thought he should just leave, but part of him—the part that wanted to believe in adventures and magic—made him stay to hear what Thrang and Arconn had to say.

"The first thing you need to know is about magic," said Arconn. "The sign in the window is a magic sign. That's why it seemed to change every time you looked away from it."

"Magic?" asked Alex.

"Don't interrupt," said Thrang, making himself more comfortable in his chair. "Jus' listen to everything, then think it over."

"You saw the sign because the sign called to you, or showed itself to you, if you like," Arconn continued. "And you didn't walk into a bookshop, you walked into Clutter's Adventure Shop."

Alex leaned forward, feeling he should say something, but a stern look from Thrang stopped him.

"When you entered the shop, you passed through a magic gateway," Arconn said. "Gateways are a bit difficult to explain, as they only open when they are needed, and then only for certain people. Only a true adventurer could see the magic sign and pass through the gateway, so you must be an adventurer, even if you don't know it."

Alex shifted in his chair but didn't say anything. None of this made any kind of sense to him, but strangely, he found himself wanting, even trying, to believe what Arconn was saying.

"Time as you know it doesn't matter here, because no matter how long you stay on this side of the gateway, you'll never be late for anything on the other side of it. When you go on an adventure, time is real enough, but that's only time where you *are*, not where you came from," Arconn continued.

Alex thought for a minute. Arconn's explanation was clear enough, but still, Alex couldn't believe that time could be different here.

If he accepted the idea of magic, and the simple fact that a dwarf and an elf were sitting in front of him made magic seem possible, then it all made sense. The trouble was, even if he wanted to believe in magic, that didn't make it real.

"When you go on an adventure, time passes normally," Arconn said. "You get older, grow larger, everything. Then, when you complete the adventure and return through the gateway, you return to the way you are now."

"That's right," Thrang said with a smile. "Wouldn't do to get home and be years older than when you left, would it? Being gone for only a few seconds and aging several years would be hard to explain to anyone."

"Yes, I suppose it would," Alex admitted.

"And when you go on another adventure, you can choose what age you want to start at," Arconn added. "Of course, you have to choose from the ages you were in a previous adventure."

"What?" Alex asked.

"It's simple," Thrang answered. "Say you was on a ten-year adventure. By the time you get done, you'd be twenty-five. You can't go back home being twenty-five—not if you left at fifteen only a few seconds before. So when you get back, you magically return to the age you were when you started. Then later you go on another adventure, but you don't want to start at twenty-five and get older, and you don't really want to start at fifteen again. So you can choose to start somewhere between the two—like twenty."

"Oh," said Alex, nodding his understanding. It made sense the way Thrang and Arconn explained it, but part of him still felt like he should be getting back to the Happy Dragon.

"If you're willing to accept the fact that there's magic involved, everything else is easy," Arconn finished with a smile.

"It does make things simpler," Alex admitted.

For several minutes Alex sat quietly and thought about

what Arconn and Thrang had said. It all made sense—*if* there was such a thing as magic. If not, then he would be very late getting back to work and in for a real scolding.

"Just bring the tea in, then, shall I?" Mr. Clutter questioned, pushing the door open and stepping into the room. "Nice bit of green tea and some cakes."

"That will be fine," replied Arconn, without looking away from Alex.

Alex watched Mr. Clutter as he carried a large, silver tray into the room. It was easier to watch Mr. Clutter than to think about magic and gateways and adventures because then he didn't have to decide if he believed in any of it.

"Come on, then," said Mr. Clutter, looking at one of the tables next to the wall.

To Alex's amazement, the silver lamp on the table jumped onto the second table and the first table walked awkwardly into the empty space between Alex, Thrang, and Arconn.

Rubbing his eyes in disbelief, Alex felt completely numb. The table started to spin as he watched it, and right before his eyes it changed. What had been a small, rectangular table was now a large, round table. Mr. Clutter sat the tea tray on the tabletop without a care.

"How's it going, then?" Mr. Clutter asked.

"Just fine," replied Arconn. "We've been explaining things to Alex."

"Explaining?" asked Mr. Clutter, a slight note of concern in his voice.

"He don't know nothin' 'bout magic or adventures, you great pelican," said Thrang in a disgruntled tone.

"Doesn't know about adventures or magic?" Mr. Clutter repeated, glancing quickly at Alex. "But the sign . . . the gateway. I assure you, gentlemen, only a true adventurer could have passed through the gateway."

"That may be true, Clutter," replied Thrang. "But the fact is, this boy knows nothin' 'bout being chosen or adventures or anything."

"Doesn't know about being chosen?" Mr. Clutter looked confused. "Well, then, how did he get into the shop?"

"We will call that a lucky chance," said Arconn. "Thank you, Mr. Clutter. We'll serve ourselves."

Mr. Clutter left the room, scratching his head and mumbling to himself. It sounded to Alex like he didn't believe what Thrang had said, and was sure that everybody knew about adventures and magic.

"Tea?" questioned Arconn, filling a large cup and holding it out for Alex to take.

"What?" said Alex, still dumbfounded by the moving table.

"Have some tea," said Thrang, holding out his own cup for Arconn to fill. "A bit of tea and a cake or two and you'll feel much better."

"No, thank you," Alex said, distracted. All the talk about magic and time being different and gateways and signs that other people couldn't see had his head spinning. He didn't know what to make of any of it, though he had to admit that it was exciting.

"Have a cake then," said Thrang, pushing a large plate full of cakes toward him. "Always better to think on a full stomach."

Alex smiled weakly and took a cake from the plate. He didn't feel hungry, but it gave him something normal to think about. Thrang and Arconn didn't say anything at all as they drank their tea and ate several cakes.

Alex stared at his uneaten cake for a long time. He wished he'd never entered the bookshop to ask about the sign, and he wondered how he was going to get back to the Happy Dragon.

Thinking about everything he'd heard and seen so far, Alex had to admit that there *must* be magic, because he'd seen the table move on its own and change its shape. Plus he was sitting with a dwarf and an elf, which was something he'd never expected to do. He still had no idea what his new companions meant by his being chosen, but he decided not to worry about it right then because his head was starting to hurt.

CHAPTER TWO

MR. CLUTTER'S BACK DOOR

S o," said Thrang, setting his teacup down and wiping his mouth with his shirtsleeve. "What do you think, Alex?"

"I'm not sure," said Alex.

"Excellent," said Arconn. "Shall we discuss the contract?"

"Contract?"

"Adventurer's bargain, if you prefer, or agreement if that suits you," replied Thrang. "After all, we can't go on an adventure together without a bargain."

"Oh, I see," said Alex with a nod, though he didn't see, not really. He hadn't really expected his wish for a different life to come true, but somehow it had. Now he had to decide if he was willing to accept the new life he was being offered.

But what if this isn't real? Alex wondered. Maybe it was all some big joke, or some kind of game that he didn't know about. What if it was one of those TV shows that played jokes on people and filmed them looking foolish? There was a chance, however, that it *was* real, that everything he'd been told was true, and that he could go on a grand adventure. If there was even a tiny chance for a real adventure, Alex wanted to be part of it.

"All right," he said decisively. "Let's talk about the contract."

"Let's see," said Thrang, taking a large piece of paper out of his shirt pocket. "First, we should discuss compensation for time spent."

"Compensation?" Alex questioned.

"How much you get paid for the adventure," replied Thrang, unfolding the paper, holding it close to his face and squinting his eyes. "After all, it's no good going on an adventure unless there's some hope of getting paid for it."

"I suppose not."

"As a first-time adventurer, you are entitled to one share in twenty of the primary treasure, once it's recovered," Thrang began. "In addition, you may receive bonus treasure as the leader of our company sees fit. Any small or magical items you find on your own are yours to keep. Any magical item that chooses you as its owner is, of course, yours."

Thrang paused for a moment to take a deep breath before plowing on.

"All secondary treasure recovered is to be divided equally among the company. Extra items—that is to say, items that can't be divided equally between the members of the company—go to the leader of the company, who may then give those extra items as bonus treasure to anyone in the company whom he feels has earned them. Also, in the event that you recover treasure alone, it will be divided equally between the members of the company. Normally, an extra share of the secondary treasure is given to the adventurer who found it.

"The leader has the last word about how treasure is divided. At times, the honor of dividing treasure may be given to a member of the company. Single victory against an enemy is always a reason for the victor to be given such an honor. In most cases, the single victor will also receive any treasure that cannot be divided equally. This follows the standard rules set out in the *Adventurer's Handbook*."

Alex sat motionless, listening to Thrang, his thoughts spinning. What did he mean, "one share in twenty of the primary treasure," and, "magical items" that might choose him as an owner? How could an item choose him?

"He's confused," said Arconn, noticing Alex's puzzled look. "The idea of treasure hunting and adventures hasn't sunk in yet. It is completely new to him."

"What?" questioned Thrang, lowering his paper slightly to look from Arconn to Alex. "How do you think we pay for the adventure if we don't collect some treasure along the way or at the end?" Thrang demanded.

"I've never thought about it," answered Alex. The idea of looking for treasure seemed odd, but Alex had to admit it made as much sense as anything else he'd heard so far.

"You see, Alex, each adventure has a goal," Arconn explained. "And it usually involves some kind of treasure or payment."

Alex nodded. "What's the goal of this adventure?"

"Jumps right to the point, don't he?" said Thrang, smiling happily. "Got a good head for this, I can see it now."

"Our goal," Arconn replied, ignoring Thrang's comments, "is to kill a dragon and reclaim the treasure in its hoard."

"Not just any dragon," Thrang interrupted. "We're goin' after Slathbog the Red."

"And dragons are bad?" Alex asked, sure he already knew the answer.

"Most dragons are evil, if that's what you mean," said Arconn. "Of course, there are a few dragons that are decent enough, but normally, yes, dragons are considered bad."

"And we're going to kill this Slatsbog?"

"Slathbog the Red," Thrang corrected. "Yes."

"And take his treasure?"

"'Course," replied Thrang with a grunting laugh. "No good killin' a dragon and then leavin' the hoard lying about for anybody who wants it."

"May I ask," Alex said, looking from Arconn to Thrang and back again. "Whose treasure is it?"

"It's Slathbog the Red's treasure," answered Thrang, looking surprised by Alex's question.

"I don't mean now," Alex said quickly. "I mean, whose was it before the dragon took it? He had to take it from someone, didn't he?"

"The treasure of Slathbog has been collected from many places," Arconn explained. "Slathbog has been hoarding treasure for several hundred years."

"At *least* several hundred," Thrang added.

"Won't the people he took the treasure from want it back?" Alex asked.

"Common law clearly states that whoever kills the dragon gets the hoard. It's on page fifty-seven of the *Adventurer's Handbook*," replied Thrang in a businesslike tone. "'Course that don't mean others won't try to steal it from us. There's always someone lookin' for easy treasure, but that's part of the adventure, isn't it?"

Alex rubbed his eyes. The idea of killing a dragon and taking its treasure sounded dangerous to him. It didn't matter that he'd never seen a dragon and had no idea what a real dragon might look like. More troubling was the thought that if they did manage to kill the dragon and collect its treasure, other people might try to take the treasure from them. For the moment, Alex had completely forgotten that he didn't really believe in dragons or magic because somewhere in the back of his head, a small voice whispered, *It might all be real, you know.*

"Don't worry about losing the hoard," said Arconn in a reassuring tone. "Killing the dragon will be the hardest part of this adventure. Getting the treasure home will be easy, once we have it."

"Of course," said Alex. "But I can't help thinking that we'll just be doing the same thing the dragon did."

"What's that?" Thrang questioned.

"Well, the dragon killed people and took their treasure. Now we're going to try to kill the dragon and take the treasure from him," Alex replied in a thoughtful tone.

"Yes, I see what you mean," Arconn agreed with a nod. "But there is more to it than just killing Slathbog and taking the treasure."

"Much more than that," Thrang added quickly. "We're on a quest and that makes all the difference."

"A quest?"

"We're not going after the dragon merely to get the treasure," Arconn explained. "Our quest is to kill Slathbog the Red. He is evil, which is reason enough to try to destroy him, but there is even more to it than that. In time, Slathbog will decide that he doesn't have enough treasure. He will start to think that he hasn't destroyed enough cities or eaten enough people. Eventually he will leave his lair, looking for a new one—a new one where he can hoard more treasure and kill more people. That's the way it is with evil dragons I'm afraid, and the only way to stop them is to kill them."

"So this Slathbog," Alex said slowly. "He's destroyed several cities and killed lots of people?"

"At least five cities that I can name," answered Arconn in a serious tone. "There may be more as Slathbog may have been called something else long ago. So to stop his evil forever, we must try to destroy him."

"I see," said Alex thoughtfully.

"If you agree to this quest and accept the bargain, you need to sign the contract," said Thrang, pointing at the paper in his hand.

"May I ask a few more questions first?"

"Yes, of course," said Arconn.

"How many of us will be on this adventure?" Alex thought twenty would be a small number to attack a dragon, especially one like Slathbog the Red.

"Eight, as I said before," answered Arconn without saying anything more.

"Do we know how to kill a dragon?" Alex asked hopefully. "I mean, is there a special way that dragons are killed?"

"There's lots," Thrang answered enthusiastically. "But none of them are one hundred percent effective. There's always some risk when goin' against a dragon—that's why so few adventurers ever do. Powerful creatures, dragons, and magical as well."

Alex thought about Thrang's answer for a minute before asking his next question. The fact that he didn't believe in dragons was lost in the flood of questions that the little voice in the back of his head was asking.

"If only eight of us are going, why are there twenty shares in the hoard?"

"Said he had a good head for this." Thrang laughed.

"Shares are given to each adventurer based on experience and special skills," answered Arconn. "First-time adventurers get one share, experienced adventurers get two, the leader gets three. A wizard would also get three."

"Do we have a wizard?" Alex asked hopefully.

"No," said Thrang, stroking his beard. "Couldn't find one available. Mind you, there aren't many wizards around these days, and very few of them ever go on adventures."

"That's only sixteen shares," said Alex, quickly thinking the numbers through.

"Well, one share goes to Clutter for setting up the adventure," Thrang said. "And one goes to the Widows and Orphans fund, which is normal for most decent adventurers. Then there's a share set aside to pay expenses the group might have while on the adventure."

"That's nineteen," said Alex, not sure why he was so interested in how the treasure was divided. He felt certain that the dragon would be keeping all of the treasure, and he and his new companions would be coming home empty-handed, if they came home at all.

"There's an extra share for whoever kills the dragon," said Thrang with a grunting laugh. "If more than one adventurer is in on the kill, they split it up."

"Oh," Alex managed to say as thoughts of dragons raced through his head.

"'Course there's other places to get treasure along the way," Thrang added happily. "Always the chance of runnin' into goblins or bandits, maybe even a troll, isn't there? That's where the bit about secondary treasure comes into play."

Alex didn't like the sound of goblins, bandits, or trolls.

"Before you decide, there are a few other things you should know," said Arconn. "In signing this document, you pledge to do all you can to help the company achieve its goal. You promise to never desert the company for any reason. You agree to take orders from the company's leader, and if worse comes to worst, you promise to return the belongings of the other company members to their families or heirs."

"Oh," said Alex. "It's just . . . I mean, the thing is—"

Arconn was looking at him, and something in his look made Alex stop talking.

"Alex," said Arconn in a soft voice. "Fate has chosen you to go on this adventure. It is your destiny to become an adventurer. If you throw away this chance, you will regret it for the rest of your life. You may not understand everything we've said, or even believe it, but it is all true."

There was a sudden spark in Alex's chest, and an odd electric pricking in his fingers and toes. He felt a real desire to go on this adventure. He didn't understand why, but it felt right in a way that he couldn't explain, not even to himself. All of his short life he'd wanted to do something different, something exciting. He'd never had the chance until now, and he knew that Arconn was right and that he would regret it if he didn't go.

"All right, I'll go," said Alex, taking the paper from Thrang and signing his name to it. "What's the worst that could happen?"

"You don't want to know," replied Thrang with a snort of laughter.

"Perhaps not," Alex admitted, handing the paper back to Thrang. "Now what?"

"Now we go to Telous," said Arconn, his eyes gleaming. "The adventure begins."

Alex followed Thrang and Arconn as together they made their way back to Mr. Clutter's office.

"All settled then?" Mr. Clutter asked, looking up from his desk as the trio entered the room.

"Signed and ready to go," Thrang answered, handing Mr.

Clutter the paper Alex had signed. "Need you to file that for us, if you would."

"Right you are," said Mr. Clutter. "You'll be on to Telous then?"

"Yes," said Arconn, looking over his shoulder. "Through the wardrobe?"

"Oh, no," Mr. Clutter answered, his smile fading. "Someone tried to bring a bummblehog through there earlier today; it's quite a mess."

"Bummblehogs don't like wardrobes," said Thrang, nudging Alex with his elbow. "In fact, there isn't much that bummblehogs do like."

Alex wondered what a bummblehog was, but decided he might be happier not knowing. He looked around the room, and for a moment thought about running for the door, a last desperate hope to escape before it was too late. But he knew he wouldn't run. Nobody had forced him to sign the Adventurer's Bargain; he'd done that on his own. And now that he'd agreed to go, part of him was really looking forward to it.

"Out the back door if that's all right," said Mr. Clutter, his smile returning. "It'll put you just outside of Telous and give young Mr. Taylor a chance to see the town."

"Very well," said Arconn, walking to the far side of the room. "Thank you for the tea and your help, Mr. Clutter."

"Not at all, not at all," replied Mr. Clutter with a laugh and a wave of his hand. "Always happy to help."

"Off we go then." Thrang nudged Alex with his elbow

again. "No sense hangin' round here when there's an adventure waitin'."

"No," Alex agreed. "I suppose not."

Alex followed Thrang, joining Arconn by the wall. He couldn't see any sign of a door. Without a word, Arconn reached out and knocked three times on what appeared to be a solid wall. To Alex's surprise, the silver outline of a door suddenly appeared exactly where Arconn had knocked.

"See you when you get back," Mr. Clutter called, turning back to his desk and shuffling through papers once more.

Arconn pushed on the silver outline and the door swung open to reveal a sunny green field and a bright blue sky. Alex stared in amazement as Arconn stepped through the doorway. Thrang laughed at the stunned look on Alex's face and nudged him forward. Nervously, Alex followed Arconn through the door and into the field. He turned just in time to see Thrang step through the doorway. The silver door faded behind him, disappearing with a small pop.

"Going to be a nice day," said Thrang, stroking his beard thoughtfully. "Clear mornings like this are always good for adventures."

Alex didn't say anything, stunned by the sudden change in their location. He wasn't sure what to think, and he wondered what he'd gotten himself into.

"I know it seems strange the first time," said Arconn in a reassuring tone. "You'll get used to it after an adventure or two."

"Let's go," said Thrang, starting off across the field. "Bregnest will be waiting."

"Bregnest?" Alex questioned as he hurried after Thrang.

"Silvan Bregnest, the leader of our adventure," said Arconn.

Alex didn't ask any more questions as they walked through the open field. He felt strange and out of place. Walking with a dwarf and an elf was new to him, and he wasn't sure how or what he should be feeling. Any worries he'd had were fading fast, however, and the longer they walked, the happier he felt about his decision.

A small town came into view ahead of them as they left the field behind and started down a stone-paved road. Alex guessed that the town must be Telous and he looked around curiously.

Alex's first impression of Telous was that everything looked extremely old. The town wasn't shabby or run-down—it was actually well-kept and clean—it just *felt* old. The stone buildings along the road all looked as though they had been standing there for ages. The smell of woodsmoke filled the air, and the morning sun quickly warmed the stones beneath his feet.

Alex's eyes moved wildly as he walked through the streets of Telous. The signs in the shop windows advertised all kinds of things he'd never seen in any shop at home. The people on the street were dressed much like Thrang and Arconn—in brown and green clothes made for the rugged outdoors—nothing at all like the people in Sildon Lane who usually wore suits and ties.

"We'll find Bregnest at the Swan," said Thrang, pointing to a large building ahead of them. "I suppose the others will be there too."

The Golden Swan was three stories tall and stood alone in the center of Telous. It had white walls and many windows, each with emerald-green shutters and trim. Alex thought the building looked friendly and inviting. A large golden swan with emerald eyes hung above the main entrance of the tavern. Alex wondered if the swan was made of solid gold.

"Best tavern in Telous," Thrang commented to Alex with a smile. "And the favorite of most adventurers."

"It's very impressive," Alex managed to say as they walked through the main doors.

Alex and Arconn followed Thrang into one of several small rooms on the right-hand side of the building. The room was brightly lit by the sunlight streaming in through the windows and the several lamps that hung from the ceiling.

"Thrang," a voice called from the far corner of the room. "About time you got back."

"Not easy findin' our eighth man," replied Thrang. "Lucky we was able to find anyone at all."

"Times aren't what they were," said the man in a serious tone. "But we needed eight for the job. Who have you found?"

"This is Alexander Taylor," said Arconn, as they crossed the room. "He goes by Alex, and this is his first adventure."

The man looked at Alex, his eyebrows rising. "I'm not too keen on taking a first-timer on a trip like this."

"He was referred by Mr. Clutter," said Arconn. "The Oracle did say eight, and now we are eight."

"All the same," said the man, as he stood and took a step toward Alex, "I'd be happier if he had some experience."

"We couldn't find no one with experience," said Thrang, his voice a little tight. "We're in a rush, and he was available. Besides, he's already signed the Bargain."

"Very well," replied the man, stretching out his hand to Alex. "Silvan Bregnest."

"Pleased to meet you," Alex replied, taking his hand and shaking it.

"Clutter referred you then, did he?" Bregnest asked, returning to his chair.

Alex nodded cautiously.

"He's a good judge, normally," said Bregnest. "Hasn't been wrong in more than four hundred years."

"And he wasn't wrong then, not really," said Thrang, signaling for a barman to bring him a drink.

"Perhaps not," Bregnest agreed.

Silvan Bregnest looked like a serious man to Alex. He was tall and lean, with gray eyes that shone brightly with an inner light. Most of his long, black hair was pulled into a neat ponytail at the back of his neck, but there was a single narrow braid hanging down either side of his face. He appeared to be a rugged man, tough and hardened by time and travel, and Alex felt a little uneasy standing under his gaze.

"Where are the others?" Thrang asked, taking a large mug from the barman. "They'll be wantin' to meet young Alex here."

"They went to check on the horses," said Bregnest, turning his attention away from Alex. "They should be back anytime now."

"We'll need to get Alex outfitted," said Thrang in a matter-of-fact way.

"Andy can take him," replied Bregnest. "We need to talk." His eyes flicked to Alex and back to Thrang, who grunted into his mug.

For several minutes there was silence, except for the sound of Thrang drinking from his mug and the fire burning in the grate. Arconn sat beside Bregnest, calmly looking out the window.

Alex, not knowing what else to do, remained standing. He was just beginning to think that he should sit down as well, when a noisy group entered the room behind him.

"We're ready to go," a tall blond man called across the room to Bregnest. "Just need our eighth man and we're off."

"We have eight," replied Bregnest, standing and nodding toward Alex. "This is Alexander Taylor," he said. "He goes by Alex, and this is his first time out."

"Skeld, son of Haplack," said the blond man, grabbing Alex's hand and shaking it vigorously. "Glad you're with us."

"So am I," Alex managed to say, surprised by Skeld's introduction.

"If you'll allow me," said Bregnest, pushing Skeld to one side. "Alex, I'd like you to meet your other companions on this adventure."

Skeld stumbled slightly as Bregnest pushed him again, but he continued smiling. He looked both strong and happy, and Alex liked him instantly.

"This is Tayo Blackman," said Bregnest, indicating a dark-haired man who was standing behind Skeld. Tayo nodded slightly to Alex but did not offer his hand. Alex thought Tayo's face and dark eyes looked extremely sad.

"This is Halfdan Bluevest," Bregnest continued, pointing to a young-looking dwarf. "As you might guess from the look of him, he's Thrang's cousin."

"A pleasure," said Halfdan as he bowed to Alex.

"And last but not least," Bregnest said. "Anders Goodseed. We all call him Andy."

"A great pleasure," said Andy, nudging Halfdan in the ribs as he too bowed to Alex.

"The pleasure is mine," Alex managed as he remembered his manners and bowed slightly.

"So, we're off today then, are we?" Skeld questioned with a smile.

"Alex needs to get outfitted first," replied Bregnest, moving back to his chair. "Andy, go with him and get him set up, will you."

It was more a command than a question, and Andy bowed slightly to Bregnest before turning to Alex and motioning for him to follow.

"We should be able to get everything he needs," said Andy. "What about payment?"

"Tell them I'll stand good for it," said Thrang, lowering his mug and winking at Alex.

"Very well," replied Andy, starting toward the door.

"And Andy," Thrang called after them. "Make sure to get him a decent bag."

"Of course," Andy answered.

———◆◆▶———

After Alex and Andy had left the room, the others gathered around Bregnest. They were undertaking a dangerous adventure and there were several things they needed to discuss. Not least among their concerns was the selection of Alex as the eighth member of their company.

"He's very young," said Tayo, looking at Bregnest grimly. "He's not trained, and he's unprepared for what lies ahead."

"He comes highly recommended," Thrang replied, watching Bregnest over his mug. "And he's large for his age."

"His hands are well-callused so he knows how to work," Skeld commented thoughtfully. "Dragons are difficult though, and his size and willingness to work won't help much. We can teach him some basics on the road, of course, but with two so young, it will be hard."

"It would be hard with experienced warriors," Halfdan added. "I don't see how we can succeed as we are."

"What do you say, Arconn?" Bregnest questioned, his gaze settling on the elf. "Do you have an opinion on this?"

"A feeling more than anything else," replied Arconn, turning away from the window for the first time since he'd sat down. "A feeling that I find hard to voice."

"Will you try?" Bregnest persisted.

"I feel we are fortunate to have him with us," Arconn

answered in a slow and thoughtful tone. "I cannot say why, but I feel that it will be good both for him and for us."

"Elves often feel things that others cannot," said Bregnest, almost to himself. "Yet I also feel that this is for the best, and I am glad that Alex is our eighth."

"Something the Oracle told you?" Skeld asked, his eyebrows rising.

"What the Oracle says to a man is for him alone to know," replied Bregnest with a half-smile. "As you know well enough, Skeld."

Skeld laughed and signaled for the barman to bring drinks for them all.

"I knew you would not answer straight," Skeld said with a mischievous smile on his face. "And I know how it annoys you when I ask."

"And you will have your fun," said Bregnest. "But enough of this. We will go with what—and who—we have, and hope for the best."

"Excellent," said Thrang, taking another mug from the barman. "Let's drink on it."

"Drink on it indeed, master dwarf," Bregnest chuckled. "But not as much as you may like. The road ahead will be long and hard, and we start early in the morning."

CHAPTER THREE

MAGIC BAG

A lex followed Andy into the streets of Telous. He was relieved that Thrang had offered to pay for what he needed because he didn't have any money of his own. He wasn't even sure what kind of money was used in Telous, and he hadn't thought to ask.

"First time?" Andy asked.

"Yes, it is," replied Alex, a little ashamed of his answer.

"You're lucky," Andy said, taking no notice of Alex's tone. "Most first-timers go on really dull adventures. This one sounds very exciting and should be great fun."

"Fun?" Alex wondered why anyone would think trying to kill a dragon would be fun.

"It's better than my first," said Andy. "My first adventure was incredibly dull, and we didn't find much treasure at all."

Alex looked closely at Andy for the first time. He was tall and blond, perhaps twenty-five years old, but his baby face made him look younger. He seemed happy to be on an adventure, or perhaps he was just happy. Alex decided that he liked Andy, and that Andy would be the one he'd ask about things he didn't understand.

"I'm a little surprised that Arconn and Thrang picked a first-timer," said Andy as they walked into a shop. "But I suppose they know what they're doing."

Alex wanted to say he thought Arconn and Thrang had made a huge mistake, but kept that to himself. It was obvious Andy had a great deal of respect for Arconn and Thrang, and Alex didn't want to anger his new companion by saying something stupid.

As the day went on, Andy led Alex to several shops around Telous. After each of their stops, Alex was carrying more and more packages, many of which he didn't even recognize. Andy helped Alex carry his new things, and tried to answer some of Alex's questions as they went.

Alex, struggling to carry all the packages Andy had purchased for him, wondered how he would be able to carry everything with him on the adventure. There were shirts and pants and blankets, two new pairs of boots, cooking pots, a tent, and several other camping items. He was also worried that Thrang would be upset about the amount of money they'd spent. Andy kept shopping however, unconcerned about the number of items they were buying or the prices.

"We've spent an awful lot of money," Alex said as he struggled to keep ahold of his packages. "I don't want to take advantage of Thrang's goodwill."

"We're almost done," said Andy, shifting some of the packages he was carrying from one arm to the other. "Thrang offered to stand good for you, so don't worry."

"But I'm sure he didn't know we'd be spending so much,"

Alex protested. "And I can honestly say I don't know how much we've spent."

"You don't know how much we've spent?" Andy asked in a puzzled tone.

"I don't know anything about the money here," Alex admitted.

"What do you use at home, then?"

"We have metal coins, but we also use paper money."

"Paper money?" said Andy, the smile on his face showing he thought Alex was joking.

"It's true," Alex insisted. "We don't use gold or silver coins at all."

"It's easy—one gold coin is worth thirteen silver coins. Didn't the adventurer who took you to the Oracle explain about money and treasure?" Andy asked.

"I didn't go to an oracle."

Andy stopped dead in his tracks. "Then how were you chosen as an adventurer?"

Alex explained about seeing the sign in the shop window and what had happened at Mr. Clutter's shop. He was happy to go over all the details again for Andy because it helped him get things straight in his own mind as well.

"No wonder Thrang and Arconn asked you to join us," said Andy, sounding impressed. "I've only heard of two other people seeing the sign and that was years ago."

"That's strange," said Alex. "The sign was in plain view, anybody could have seen it."

"I doubt that," said Andy with a laugh. "The sign may

have been in plain view for you, but I doubt that anyone else—even another adventurer—would have seen it."

"Why?" Alex questioned.

"I'm not sure I can say," answered Andy. "It might have something to do with magic, or maybe it was your fate to see the sign when you did. Whatever the reason, I'm sure it was good fortune that you saw it."

Alex thought about Andy's answer, but he wasn't sure what to think. He shook his head and pushed Andy's explanation to the back of his mind for now, more worried at the moment about Thrang and the money they'd spent. He told Andy his feelings but he just smiled at Alex's concern.

"I guess you don't know much about dwarfs," said Andy as they started walking again.

"No, I don't," Alex admitted.

"I know a little, and I'll tell you this," said Andy, catching a package as it slipped out from under Alex's arm. "Dwarfs are careful with their money. They're not cheap or miserly or anything like that, but they're careful just the same."

"And we're spending Thrang's money quickly," said Alex.

"What you need to understand is this," Andy continued, taking no notice of Alex's comment. "If a dwarf offers to stand good for you, he expects you to spend freely."

"I don't understand," said Alex, trapping a package under his chin.

"Once he's offered to stand good for you, he'll expect you to take advantage of his offer," Andy explained. "It would be

an insult to him if you didn't buy everything you needed—and
the best of everything you needed at that."

"An insult?" Alex wondered out loud as they entered
another shop. "I would insult Thrang if I didn't spend as much
of his money as I could?"

"You're not spending as much as you could," Andy
laughed, piling Alex's packages in the corner of the shop.
"You're not spending like there's no tomorrow, or buying more
than you need. You're just spending as much as you need on
what you need."

"But it seems to be a lot."

"And it is," Andy agreed. "But if you don't have the best of
everything you need, Thrang will take it as an insult."

"But can he afford what I need?"

"As long as you spend it on what you need, Thrang would
happily let you spend all the gold in his bag—down to the very
last coin," Andy replied. "And between you and me, I don't
think we could spend everything in Thrang's bag in a lifetime
of trying."

"That's crazy," said Alex, stacking packages on top of the
pile Andy had made.

"It may sound crazy to you and me, but that's how dwarfs
are," Andy replied, turning to look for the shopkeeper.

Alex thought about what Andy had said, but it still didn't
sound right. Thrang had been extremely generous, and Alex
couldn't help feeling he was taking advantage of the dwarf.

Knowing that every gold coin was worth thirteen silver coins didn't help at all.

"What will it be then, gentlemen?" asked a round shopkeeper in square glasses. "Something in a deluxe model with a pool? Or maybe a nice garden?"

"Nothing so grand, master bag maker," replied Andy. "My friend needs a top quality bag, but hardly a pool or a garden."

"Ah, yes," the shopkeeper said, looking at Alex. "Something in a three- or four-room model I should think. That's always the best place to start. You can add on later as you need to."

"Okay," said Alex slowly.

"Sorry, Alex," said Andy, noticing the confused look on Alex's face. "You've never seen a magic bag before, have you?"

Alex shook his head.

"Do you have a demonstration model that my friend and I can look at?" Andy asked the shopkeeper.

"Oh, yes," the shopkeeper replied. "I have a lovely four-room model that you can look at right over here."

Alex and Andy followed the shopkeeper to the back of the shop. On a table was a leather bag with a long strap attached to it and silver fastenings at the top. The bag was about twice as long as it was wide, and Alex thought it looked like a postman's bag.

"Standard passwords," said the shopkeeper, nodding to Andy, before leaving to help another customer.

"Right," said Andy. He turned to Alex. "All you have to do is pick up the bag, open it, and say 'enter.'"

"What?" Alex asked.

"Just do it," Andy laughed. "It will be all right."

Alex hesitated for a moment before reaching for the bag. The leather was soft and flexible, but the bag appeared to be empty. He was sure this must be some kind of joke, but he couldn't see what the joke was.

"Go on," urged Andy. "I'll be right behind you."

"Enter."

Everything went dark. Alex felt like he was dropping from a high place and spinning slightly as he fell. Then, as quickly as the feeling started, he felt himself come to a sudden stop. He could feel a stone floor under his feet, but everything was still dark.

"Lights," Andy's voice said from the darkness next to him.

Several lamps sprang to life, and Alex could see he was standing in a large square room made of stone. The room was empty except for a doorway in one wall.

"Sorry about that," said Andy, moving toward the doorway. "I thought the lamps would be burning. If I'd known they were out, I would have come first."

"Where . . . where are we?"

"In the bag," Andy replied happily. "Let's see the other rooms."

"Wait. What do you mean, in the bag?"

"We're in the leather bag on the table," said Andy, as if there was nothing strange about his answer. "It's a magic bag after all. What did you expect?"

"I . . . I don't know," said Alex.

"I'll try to explain," said Andy, motioning for Alex to follow him into the next room. "You can tell by how much gear you already have that we will have a lot of things to carry with us on this adventure. But there are only eight of us to carry it all, right?"

"Right," Alex answered.

"And we'd need a lot of horses to carry all of our gear and supplies if we were going to carry it the normal way," Andy continued.

"Yes, I suppose so," Alex agreed.

"That would attract a lot of attention, wouldn't it?"

"I suppose it would."

"So instead of all that extra attention and the extra work of taking care of so many horses, we use magic bags," Andy concluded with a smile.

"I still don't understand," said Alex.

"What's not to understand? A magic bag lets you carry all your gear in a very small space. And believe me, it makes life a lot easier."

"I'm sure it does, but how does it work?" Alex questioned.

"It's magic," laughed Andy. "It's like Arconn always says, 'If you're willing to accept the fact that there's magic involved, everything else is easy.'"

Alex had never really thought about magic, or at least not real magic, and he wasn't sure how he felt about it. He had seen the table at Mr. Clutter's move and change shape, but that wasn't really the same as this, was it? Looking around the stone room, however, he had to believe there was magic.

"Not a bad size," said Andy as they walked around the different rooms. "If we have one room modified to expand as needed, and add a little furniture, you should be good to go."

"Expand as needed?" Alex asked.

"If we manage to get the hoard from Slathbog, your share wouldn't fit into just these four rooms," Andy answered with a laugh. "If half the tales of Slathbog's treasure are true, you'll need twice as much space just to get started."

"And magic can make one of the rooms bigger as it fills up?" Alex asked, trying hard to understand.

"Exactly," said Andy. "You can use the other rooms to keep your things in. You'll probably collect a lot of things as we travel."

"Okay," said Alex, still a little unsure about how the magic bag worked.

"Don't worry," said Andy. "We'll get you set up, and I'll show you how to work the bag until you get the hang of it."

"Does everybody in our group have a magic bag?"

"Of course. Most adventurers do. I have a five-room bag that my father gave me. I'll have to show it to you sometime. Of course you should be careful who you show your bag to," Andy cautioned. "And you shouldn't share your passwords with anybody, not if you can help it. Well, except your heir, of course."

"Passwords?" Alex asked.

"Like when you said 'enter' before," replied Andy. "That's the standard password to get in, and there's a different one to get out—'exit.' You'll want to use something different for your own bag of course, so not just anyone can get in and out of it."

Alex decided it all made perfect sense, as long as he accepted the fact that magic was involved. He still had his doubts, but they were fading fast.

"Ready to go then?" asked Andy.

Alex nodded, his thoughts cluttered with the idea of real magic.

"I'll just put out the lights before I go," said Andy. "Then listen carefully so you'll know the password to get out of the bag."

"All right," said Alex nervously. "But if I'm not out in a minute or two, come back and turn the lights on."

Andy's laugh was full of kindness and good humor and it made Alex like him even more.

"Dark," said Andy, and all the lamps went out. "Exit."

Alex waited in the darkness. He wasn't sure if Andy was still there or not. He listened carefully, but could only hear his own breathing. Deciding he was alone in the bag, he took a deep breath.

"Exit."

As quickly as Alex had entered the bag, he was out of it again. He was standing in the brightly lit shop, the soft leather bag in his hands. He looked at Andy, a little surprised by how easy it had been.

"Neat little trick, isn't it?" said Andy.

"Very neat," Alex agreed. "But how do you get things in and out of the bag without going in yourself every time?"

"You hold the bag next to the thing you want to put in and tell the bag where to put it. When you need something, you ask for what you want and it'll come out. You don't normally have to specify where things are when you're taking something out, unless you have more than one of something. You can practice tonight with your packages."

Andy went to find the shopkeeper, leaving Alex alone with the magic bag. Alex quickly looked around to make sure nobody was watching him, and then he looked into the top of the bag to see what was there. The bag was completely empty, and Alex's doubts about magic started creeping into his mind once more.

After several minutes of discussion and a little debate on price, the shopkeeper wrote Alex's name in a large black book. Alex held the bag while the shopkeeper read something in a language Alex didn't understand, waving his hands over Alex and the bag.

"It's a good thing they bind the bag to you," said Andy, putting Alex's packages into the new bag. "That way you can't lose it, no matter what."

"Can't lose it?"

"Not unless some powerful magic is used against you," Andy said. "The bag will either stay with you, or stay where you put it, no matter what. Unless of course you're dead."

"Oh," Alex said in reply. His head felt stuffed with information, and he was afraid he was running out of time to do any serious thinking.

"There you go," said Andy, handing Alex his new bag. "All your gear is inside and ready to go."

"Thanks," said Alex. "Will we be sleeping inside our magic bags as we travel?"

"Of course not," said Andy in a surprised tone. "Why would we do that?"

"It seems to me that we'd be safe and comfortable inside our bags," said Alex.

"Safe until you come out in the morning and find a bunch of goblins standing around you," replied Andy. "How could you warn the rest of us if there was trouble?"

"I didn't think of that," said Alex.

"If you were alone, you could sleep in your bag, I suppose," Andy went on. "But when you are with a company, it is best to camp as a company. We'll all be there if trouble shows up, and it helps to build fellowship as well."

"Yes, of course," said Alex. "It was a foolish question. It's just that . . ."

"What?"

"Well, we don't really have magic where I come from," said Alex. "I mean there are people who do things they call magic, but it isn't real. I don't know anything about real magic, and I don't know anything about adventures either. I'm starting to think I don't know very much about anything at all."

"Don't worry," said Andy, slapping him on the back. "You'll learn quick enough as we travel. We all know this is your first adventure, so everybody will help explain things to you. As far as not knowing about how magic works, not many people really do. Just accept that it *does* work and try not to worry about the *why*."

"All right," Alex replied. "I guess I'm ready to go then."

"Not quite," said Andy, leading him down a narrow road, away from the Golden Swan and the center of Telous. "You still need a weapon. And I know just the place."

"A weapon?"

"You can't go on an adventure without one," said Andy. "No telling what we might run into on the way. And there's always the dragon at the end of our journey as well."

"I . . . I suppose so," Alex agreed nervously. "But I don't know how to use a weapon. I mean, I've never had to, and Mr. Roberts would never allow—"

"It's all right," Andy interrupted. "Mr. Blackburn will know what weapon suits you best. There will be time for you to learn how to use it on the road."

"Yes, but I—"

"It will be all right," Andy said again. "You need a weapon if you're going on this adventure, it's as simple as that."

Alex could see that Andy was right. He thought about the different kind of weapons he knew about as they walked toward the edge of town and wondered what kind of weapon he, or anybody, could use to kill a dragon.

"Blackburn's Smithy," said Andy, pointing to a fair-sized building that stood a short distance from the rest of the town. "One of the best smithys you'll ever see."

Alex didn't reply because this was the only smithy he'd ever seen. He could smell coal smoke as they walked toward

Blackburn's and hear the ringing of hammers on steel. A new burst of excitement filled him as they entered the building, pushing all of his worries to the back of his mind.

"And what can I help you lads with?" asked a large, bald man in a leather apron as soon as Alex and Andy had closed the door. "Looking for something special, are you?"

"My friend needs a weapon," Andy replied. "First time on an adventure, so he doesn't know what suits him."

The bald man eyed Alex and rubbed his chin. "Got any money?"

"Thrang Silversmith will stand good for him, Mr. Blackburn," replied Andy.

"Thrang sent you, did he?" Mr. Blackburn walked toward Alex and Andy. "Well, then, we'd best measure and see what's needed."

Alex felt out of place and nervous, but the feeling of excitement kept growing inside of him. He was amazed and dazzled as he looked around the smithy. The walls were covered with an incredible variety of weapons and armor. There were swords and axes of all sizes. Bows, spears, crossbows, hammer-shaped weapons, and knives hung on the walls. There were strange curved weapons with blades, metal disks that looked like Frisbees, solid-looking plate armor, shiny chain mail, metal-covered gloves, and several other things Alex had never seen before. He wasn't sure everything on the walls was even a weapon, but he didn't have time for a closer look because Mr. Blackburn started giving him orders.

"Hold your arms out," said Mr. Blackburn. "Out to the sides. Now in front. Stand up straight. Now—feet apart."

Mr. Blackburn gave Alex a series of orders to stand in different positions and poses. After each one, Mr. Blackburn would take a measurement and jot down his notes on a small pad. This went on for several minutes, and Alex's excitement was beginning to fade before Mr. Blackburn was done giving him orders.

"Interesting," said Mr. Blackburn, walking away and leaving Alex with one foot in the air and one hand on top of his head. "Oh, you can relax now."

Alex let his arms drop to his sides and resumed his normal stance. Being measured for a weapon seemed odd, but he didn't know anything at all about weapons so he didn't say anything.

"Very interesting," said Mr. Blackburn again, scribbling on his notepad. "Not seen one like this in years."

"Like what?" Alex asked nervously.

"Oh, nothing to worry about," Mr. Blackburn replied. "Just that you measure different than most."

"Is that a problem?" Andy asked, the slightest sound of concern in his voice.

"No, no problem," said Mr. Blackburn, taking a large book from a shelf on one side of the room. "Not a problem at all."

"What type of weapon should we be looking for?" Andy questioned, looking more than a little concerned.

"Just a moment," said Mr. Blackburn as he flipped through the pages. "Want to make sure before I say."

Alex looked questioningly at Andy, but Andy only

shrugged in reply. Andy's concern, though, made Alex more nervous as he waited to hear what Mr. Blackburn would say.

"Ah," said Mr. Blackburn at last, snapping the book shut. "Just as I thought."

"What is?" Alex asked.

"According to the measurements, you'll do well with most any weapon you choose," answered Mr. Blackburn. "Book says you'll do best with a sword or an ax . . . or a staff."

"A staff?" Andy jumped in surprise.

Alex looked from Andy to Mr. Blackburn and back, wondering nervously what the big deal was about a staff.

"That's what the book says," answered Mr. Blackburn, putting the book back on its shelf. "Book's never been wrong neither."

"He's not trained for a staff," Andy said quickly. "We'd better look at swords. Maybe an ax or two."

"As you wish," said Mr. Blackburn. "If he's not trained for a staff, it'll do no good looking at them."

"What's so special about a staff?" Alex asked.

"Staffs are a wizard's weapon," said Andy, a look of wonder on his face. "Only a wizard can use a staff, and there aren't many wizards around these days."

"That's a fact," said Mr. Blackburn, nodding. "I haven't sold a staff in ages out of mind."

"That can't be right," protested Alex. "I'm no wizard. I can't even do a card trick right."

"Be that as it may be," said Mr. Blackburn, shrugging. "Measurements don't lie, and the book's never been wrong."

"We'll just look at the swords and the axes," Andy said again.

"As you wish," Mr. Blackburn said.

Mr. Blackburn showed them dozens of finely made swords. He took great pleasure in pointing out the special features of each sword, and he insisted that Alex hold each one to get a feel for the balance. Alex felt a little awkward because he'd never held a sword before and some of them were surprisingly heavy. Others didn't feel right in his hand, though he wasn't able to say why.

Mr. Blackburn also showed them several large axes, each with a different shaped head. Once again Alex held them all and tried to decide what an ax should feel like. After what seemed like a long time to Alex, Mr. Blackburn stopped bringing new weapons for him to look at.

"Made a choice then?" Mr. Blackburn asked politely.

"I don't know," Alex answered. "They are all so well-made that it is difficult to choose," he added quickly for Mr. Blackburn's benefit.

"You've got to choose something," Andy urged. "And if you don't hurry, we'll be late for dinner with the others."

Alex closed his eyes for several minutes, thinking. He wasn't thinking about which sword or ax to pick though, but about wizards and staffs. He was certain Mr. Blackburn's book was wrong about his being able to use a staff. Finally, he took a deep breath and opened his eyes.

A sword with a blue-black blade seemed to stand out from the others as the room came back into focus. The sword had elegant gold inlay on the hilt, and Alex thought he could almost read something written in the gold, but he blinked and the words disappeared.

"I'll take this one," said Alex, picking up the sword.

"A fine choice," said Mr. Blackburn with a smile. "Not one of mine, but still a fine piece of work."

"It's not one of your swords?" Alex asked, liking how the hilt felt in his hand.

"No, but it's an excellent piece of work, that's for sure," Mr. Blackburn replied. "This sword was sold to me by an adventurer, much like yourselves, but he couldn't tell me anything of its history."

"And you're sure it's a good sword?" Andy questioned in a serious tone.

"Good as any I've ever made," Mr. Blackburn admitted. "Maybe better. But I'll ask you not to repeat that."

While Andy and Mr. Blackburn discussed the price of Alex's new sword, Alex examined every inch of the sword. Mr. Blackburn's price seemed high to Alex, but Andy seemed to think it was fair and agreed to pay in Thrang's place.

Mr. Blackburn brought the sword's scabbard to Alex and bowed slightly as he handed it to him. The scabbard, like the sword, was inlayed with gold. Once again Alex thought he could make out words mixed in with the swirls of gold, and once again when he blinked, the words were gone and only the golden swirls remained.

Alex put his new sword in its scabbard and, with Andy's help, he managed to get it inside his magic bag. They both thanked Mr. Blackburn for his help, and then they walked back into Telous.

Alex couldn't stop thinking about his new sword, a sword with a mysterious past. Mr. Blackburn had made it sound like a sword's history was important to know and it bothered Alex that his sword had no history, or at least none he knew about. He also thought it seemed a little odd that he had chosen the sword after closing his eyes and thinking about wizards.

At the back of Alex's mind, the strange little voice was talking again. Mr. Blackburn had said he could use a staff, and that meant he could use magic. The idea of using magic and being a wizard excited Alex's imagination, though he knew almost nothing about magic—other than it actually worked—and even less about wizards. His thoughts circled endlessly in his mind, before he decided finally that it was pointless to worry.

"Get everything you need?" Thrang asked as soon as Alex and Andy entered the Golden Swan.

"Everything," Andy answered, handing Thrang the bundle of receipts he'd been collecting. "Hope we didn't go too far."

"Or damage Master Thrang's hoard too much," Skeld laughed from behind Thrang. "But that would take more time than you two had."

"Your tongue does more damage than anything else," said Thrang, glancing over his shoulder at Skeld. "Though it looks like these two tried very hard to break me," he added with a wink and a grin.

"I'm sorry," Alex started.

"Not at all, not at all," said Thrang before Alex could add

anything more. "As long as you got what you needed, there's no damage done."

"I don't know how I'll ever be able to repay you," Alex managed to say, but Thrang simply waved his hand and laughed.

"It's nothing," said Thrang, tucking the receipts into his belt. "Your friendship is payment enough."

Alex saw Bregnest come down the main staircase and Andy walk quickly to his side. Andy leaned close and whispered something to Bregnest. He glanced at Alex, his eyebrows raised, and then nodded to Andy. Alex suspected Andy was telling Bregnest what Mr. Blackburn had said about his being able to use a staff. He wondered what Bregnest would think, and more important, what he would do.

"Come on then, dinner's waiting," said Skeld happily. "Best eat well while we can."

Alex followed Skeld down a hallway toward the back of the Golden Swan with Thrang at his side. Alex wasn't sure if he should thank Thrang again for his generosity or not. He decided not to say anything more, mostly because of what Andy had told him about dwarfs.

At the end of the hallway, they entered a dining room with a huge table that barely fit inside. The other members of the company were already seated and waiting for them, talking casually about the upcoming adventure.

"Now we are eight," said Bregnest, taking his place at the head of the table between Thrang and Arconn. "And before we are overcome with food and drink, I would like to say a few words."

"Food first, talk after," Skeld said loudly, sliding into his own chair and motioning for Alex to take the seat to his right.

"You'll eat and drink too much to listen," Bregnest replied with half a smile. "And then you'll complain that I never told you anything."

"I'll complain anyway," Skeld laughed merrily.

"Be that as it may," Bregnest continued. "First of all, I would like to formally welcome our eighth member. As he has just joined us today, and this is his first adventure, he may not know all of our ways. I ask that each of you help him and be patient with him."

The rest of the company voiced their agreement to Bregnest's request. Alex doubted that he knew *anything* about the ways of adventurers and he wondered if he'd ever be able to learn everything he needed to know.

"One of the first things you should know, Alex, is this," said Bregnest, his face serious and his tone stern. "As we have all signed the Bargain for this adventure, there will be no secrets kept in our group. We will all depend on each other throughout this adventure and so every member of this company has the right to know anything and everything to do with it. And that includes knowing things about each other that may affect the success or failure of our adventure."

Bregnest was watching Alex closely as he spoke, perhaps judging how well Alex took in what he was saying.

"With that in mind, I feel it important to share some

information I have learned about Alex," Bregnest continued. "It seems that the distinguished Mr. Blackburn measured Alex for his weapon and found that he is well suited for all types of weapons. That alone would mean we have been very lucky in our eighth man. What is of more importance to our current adventure, however, is the fact that Alex is exceptionally suited to use a staff."

Bregnest paused to let the information sink in with the other members of the company. Alex felt extremely uncomfortable with everyone looking at him. He still thought Mr. Blackburn must be wrong about the staff, but he said nothing.

"Knew it all along," said Thrang, tapping the side of his nose with his finger. "Something special about that boy. I said as much to Arconn just this morning."

"Of course, Alex is not trained, though there is some value even in having an untrained wizard with us," said Bregnest. "Perhaps, when we return from this adventure, we can find a wizard for Alex to apprentice with. For now, there is no time."

"Practical experience is the best teacher," said Thrang, smiling at Alex. "And Arconn and I can each teach him a thing or two while we travel."

"Then let us toast our adventure and wish for luck," Bregnest concluded, ringing a small golden bell.

As soon as the bell had sounded, servants appeared carrying silver pitchers. They filled a mug for each of the adventurers, placed the pitchers on the table, and left the company alone.

"What is this?" Alex asked Skeld, who was already raising

his mug. Though Mr. Roberts ran a tavern, Alex had never been allowed to drink anything stronger than soda.

"It's only a honey cider," Skeld answered with a smile. "Don't worry, it's not strong enough to muddle your wizardly wits."

"To the adventure and for luck," said Bregnest, lifting his mug.

"To the adventure and for luck," the rest of them repeated as they all stood up.

To Alex's surprise, the cider tasted sweet and slightly fruity.

"Not half bad, is it, your wizardliness?" Skeld laughed and they all sat back down.

"No, it's not," said Alex with a smile. "It's very good, in fact."

"Be careful," said Tayo, who was sitting across the table from Alex. "It may taste sweet tonight, but if you drink too much of it, your head will pay come sunrise."

"And if the sun doesn't rise, you've nothing to worry about." Skeld laughed and took another long drink from his mug.

Bregnest rang the bell a second time. As before, servants instantly appeared, this time carrying large trays of wonderful-smelling food. Alex was stunned by the variety of the food he saw on the trays. Mr. Roberts was a good cook, and Alex had always had plenty to eat, but no meal he'd ever had compared to the meal he ate at the Golden Swan that night. Alex tried everything on the table twice, and a few things three times.

Skeld continued to tease him about being a wizard, and while the idea still troubled Alex, it was hard to worry too much with Skeld laughing at his side.

As the evening wore on, Alex listened closely as the others discussed the upcoming adventure. They all seemed to know a great deal about where they were going and what they might run into as they traveled. Alex even managed to ask a few questions, once his second mug of cider was gone.

"So when we ride through the great arch, we're suddenly in a different land?"

"Yes, and it is there that our journey actually begins," Tayo answered.

"But if the arch is magic, why can't we ride through it and be at the end of our journey? You know, close to where the dragon is," Alex questioned, more to himself than the others.

"Because the arch of each land is in a fixed location," Arconn explained.

"And dragons don't like staying too close to an arch," Thrang added. "Dragons don't like visitors—unexpected ones least of all."

"I see," said Alex, feeling slightly sleepy. "And I suppose we'd like to be unexpected?"

"Well, if we *are* expected, old Slathbog will give us a warm welcome, that's for sure," said Skeld with a grin.

"Then Skeld might get his wish to die in battle," Halfdan commented, looking over his mug at Skeld.

"You want to die?" Alex asked in concern.

"Nobody wants to die," replied Skeld, his grin faltering just a little. "But if death is my fate, I'll not run from it."

"I don't understand," said Alex.

"No wonder, with all that cider in you." Skeld knocked his

mug against Alex's. "This is not the time to speak of death, but only of success."

"Success," Tayo repeated, lifting his mug as the others followed in the toast.

Bregnest stood and lifted his mug. "A final toast to friendships, new and old."

"Friendships, new and old," the rest of them repeated and drank.

As they left the dining room, Alex felt a little lightheaded and wondered if he'd drunk too much of the cider after all.

"Don't worry," said Andy, coming up beside him. "The cider here at the Golden Swan is charmed, and you won't have to pay for it in the morning like Tayo said. I hope you don't mind my telling Bregnest, you know, about what Blackburn told you. I knew he would want to know, and like he said, we have no secrets."

"That's all right," Alex replied as they walked down the hallway. "I should have told him myself, but I still think Mr. Blackburn made a mistake."

"This is our room," said Andy, opening a door. "You should probably practice with your bag for a bit before you go to sleep."

Alex did want to practice using his new magic bag and he asked Andy to explain again how they worked, listening closely to the instructions. For about thirty minutes, Alex practiced going in and out of his bag several times before he changed the passwords to something he knew he would remember. He wanted to tell Andy what the new passwords were, but Andy wouldn't hear of it.

"Passwords should be secret," said Andy in a firm tone.

"What about no secrets in the company?"

"That's for things that might affect the whole company and the adventure."

Alex didn't press the matter, deciding that Andy knew what he was talking about. He took out a set of his new traveling clothes from his bag. Laying the clothes on a chair, he put the magic bag down carefully beside them. He was pleased with his magic bag, and his doubts about that, at least, had faded completely.

"Tomorrow's a big day," said Andy, climbing into a large bed on one side of the room. "A new adventure to begin, and who knows how it will end."

"Do you think we'll succeed?" Alex questioned, climbing into his own bed.

"Only fate knows our end," Andy replied. "Like Skeld, I'll not run from my destiny."

"Are you and Skeld from the same country?" Alex asked, thinking how alike the two men seemed to be.

"The same land," Andy answered, turning down his bedside lamp. "Skeld, Tayo, and I all come from Norsland."

"Will you tell me about your homeland sometime?" Alex asked, turning down his own lamp. "I mean, if you don't mind."

"Happily," Andy replied. "But for now, sleep is more important for both of us."

"Good night then," said Alex, pulling his covers up.

Andy didn't answer and he already seemed to be asleep. Alex felt tired, but his excitement and wonder kept him awake for some time. His fears about returning to the Happy Dragon and Mr. Roberts had completely vanished from his mind. Now his thoughts were on this adventure he'd somehow stumbled into, and he wondered what new things he would learn tomorrow.

Without noticing, Alex fell into a deep sleep, dreaming of the adventure to come. It was a restful dream, full of fun and good friends. He saw great mounds of treasure, and magical items that made him laugh. As he slept, his dreams shifted from treasure and fun to something darker, something he thought he knew but could not name.

Alex woke with a start, sitting straight up in bed and staring into the darkness around him. His heart raced and cold sweat covered his face. He had seen something in his dream, something terrifying. Whatever it was, it had tried to reach out to him, tried to get hold of him. The dream had been so real. Even as he considered what he might have seen, the fear was fading from his mind and the cold inside of him was slipping away. Slowly Alex's heart stopped pounding in his ears and he lay back on his bed. It wasn't long before he was asleep once more, and all his fears and thoughts of darkness were lost in a dreamless sleep.

CHAPTER FOUR
THE GREAT ARCH

The next morning Alex awoke with his bed shaking under him. At first he thought it was his stepbrother, Todd, trying to shake him awake. He rolled over. He had been having a wonderful dream about adventures and magic and he didn't want the dream to end.

"You'll be late for breakfast," said Andy, pulling on his boots and stamping his feet on the floor. "If you don't hurry, you won't get anything at all."

Alex jumped out of bed, remembering that this wasn't a dream. He *was* on an adventure, and there just might be magic. With a rush of happiness, he pulled on his new clothes. He knew Andy was joking about not getting any breakfast, but the adventure started today and he didn't want to miss any of it.

Alex walked to the basin and washed his face and hands. The cold water washed away any desire he had for more sleep. His dreams had faded from his memory, and the thoughts that had troubled him the day before had vanished as well.

"Bring your bag with you," said Andy, standing at the door. "We'll be leaving as soon as we're done eating."

Alex put his old clothes into his magic bag as fast as he

could and pulled the bag's strap over his shoulder and head. He looked around the room to make sure he hadn't forgotten anything, and then followed Andy into the hallway. They made their way back to the dining room where they had eaten the night before, and found Arconn waiting for them.

"Where is everybody?" Alex asked in concern. "We're not too late are we?"

"Not late at all," replied Arconn, ringing the golden bell. "Though you're not as early as you might have been."

Servants once again appeared at the sound of the bell, bringing breakfast for Alex and Andy.

"The others have gone to collect the horses," Arconn said, taking a piece of toast. "You'll have time to eat before they return."

Alex and Andy didn't waste any time, but started piling eggs, bacon, and fried potatoes on their plates, and eating at full speed. After several minutes with only the noise of their utensils, Andy broke the silence.

"The others were up early," he said, spitting bits of toast on the table. "I thought we'd all eat together."

"The others have many concerns," said Arconn. "They are less in need of sleep and more in need of doing."

"Did they sleep at all?" Andy asked, pushing his chair back from the table and looking at the dark window. "It's not even daybreak yet."

"We've all slept," Arconn replied, smiling. "And daybreak isn't far off."

"How far away is the great arch?" Alex questioned, pushing his own chair back.

"Two hours' hard ride," answered Arconn. "But we should get there in about four hours. Perhaps a little more. I doubt we'll pass through the arch until after our midday meal."

"And Bregnest still needs to give us final instructions," Andy added, looking at Alex.

"Final instructions?"

"What to do if you get separated from the group, or lost, or something," Andy answered. "You know, just in case."

"Or in case you run into trouble that the company needs to know about," Arconn added.

"Aren't we all traveling together?" Alex asked in alarm.

"Yes, we are," said Arconn with a slight laugh. "But you never know what might happen on an adventure. It's best to be prepared."

"If you're finished, Alex," Andy said, "we should probably head to the stables."

Alex swallowed the last bite of his breakfast. "I've never ridden a horse," he said, sounding more nervous than he would have liked.

"Don't worry," said Andy, patting Alex on the shoulder. "Bregnest picked good horses. I don't imagine you could fall off unless you really tried. Maybe not even then."

"Yes, but—"

"He's quite right," said Arconn, standing up. "Bregnest is a good judge of horses as well as of men. You have nothing to worry about."

Alex was worried, though, even with Arconn's reassurance. He'd never been up close to a horse, not because he'd never had the chance, but because they scared him. They were big and seemed to know things about people. Alex remembered when Todd had been bitten by a horse. Somehow the horse had known Todd was up to something he shouldn't have been. Alex remembered the look in the horse's eyes and he had stayed clear of horses ever since.

"These are for you," said Arconn, handing Alex a package as they walked to the front of the Golden Swan. "I thought they might be useful."

"Thank you," said Alex, slightly puzzled. He thought about all the gear he and Andy had bought the previous day and wondered what they could have forgotten.

Opening the package, Alex found two books. The first was a thin book bound in black leather. *Adventurer's Handbook* was written on the cover in silver letters. The second book was much larger and its binding was made of something Alex didn't recognize. There was nothing written on the cover of the second book, and when he opened it, Alex saw that the pages were covered in strange markings he couldn't read.

"What is it?" Alex asked.

"It is a book of magic," Arconn answered in a serious tone. "It will teach you many things you may need to know on this adventure. However, it will teach you only a small part of what you will need to know if you want to be a wizard."

"But I can't read the writing," Alex said softly, not wanting to offend Arconn.

"I don't imagine you can," said Arconn, a smile returning to his face. "But in time you will learn how to read this book, and I will help you as much as I can."

"But you're not a wizard," said Alex without thinking. "I mean, you said before that—"

"You are correct." Arconn laughed. "I am not a wizard and could never be one. But that doesn't mean I don't have some magic of my own."

"I'm sorry, I didn't mean—"

"It is all right," Arconn said. "You have much to learn, and your words have not offended."

"Thank you," Alex said again, not knowing what else to say. He looked at the books once more before putting them in his magic bag.

"And you don't need to look so worried, Master Goodseed," Arconn added, looking at Andy. "The others know I have given this book to Alex."

"I wasn't worried," Andy protested. "I was just curious about the magic bit."

"Be careful of your curiosity," Arconn warned. "Magic in the hands of those without the gift is often harmful, both to themselves and to others."

"I know it well," said Andy, bowing slightly to Arconn, a dark shadow crossing his face.

"Here come the others," said Arconn, stepping into the road. "It's time for the adventure to begin at last."

"Courage, master wizard," Skeld laughed, holding the reins

to an extra gray horse. "You need not fear so common a thing as a horse."

"I'm not a wizard," Alex replied, embarrassed that Skeld could see how nervous he was.

"She is a kind animal," Skeld said with a friendly smile. "She'll carry you far and to good fortune."

Alex looked at the large silver-gray horse in front of him, a touch of fear running down his back. The horse in turn looked at Alex, her clever eyes watching him cautiously. Alex stepped closer and put his hand gently on the horse's neck.

"She is called Shahree," said Bregnest, riding up to Alex. "It means 'great heart' in the ancient language of Alusia."

"Shahree," Alex repeated softly.

The horse shook her head up and down, looking at Alex with what he could only describe as happiness. Alex felt a surge of confidence, though he wasn't sure why. Legs shaking only slightly, he climbed into the saddle and tried to make himself comfortable.

"And so we begin," said Bregnest, starting down the road.

Alex and his companions formed two lines behind Bregnest and Arconn. Thrang and Halfdan rode in front of Skeld and Tayo, while Andy rode next to Alex at the back of the group. They followed a well-traveled road that led them south out of Telous. Green fields flanked the road on both sides, and a pair of low stone walls divided the road from the fields.

Alex's fear of riding soon vanished as Shahree carried him gently on her back, and after a few minutes, he managed to make himself comfortable in the saddle. He watched as the landscape slowly changed from well-kept fields to open meadows. The stone walls continued long after the fields were left behind, but they finally ended in two large posts at the roadside.

"We're leaving the lands of Telous," said Andy, pointing to one of the posts.

"What land are we entering now?" Alex asked.

"This is free land," said Andy. "It belongs to no one, though the people of Telous come here often to hunt."

"Hunt what?"

"Wild game," Andy laughed. "This land is too tame for anything more than deer and rabbits."

"Oh," said Alex, annoyed by how little he knew.

There was little talk as they rode along, the road slipping away beneath them. The large meadows changed to tree-covered hills with smaller meadows between them. Several small streams crossed the road, but none of them were very deep.

After riding for what seemed like a long time, Alex could see two large hills ahead of them on the road. A large and ancient-looking tower stood on top of each hill. Alex wondered what the towers might be for, and as they continued to move toward them, he felt sure that they marked the great arch. His excitement grew; he wanted to see the magic arch that would let them pass into a new land.

"We'll eat here," said Bregnest, as he dismounted from his

horse. "Fill all your water bags and containers. It may be several days before we find good water again."

Alex climbed off Shahree with a bit of trouble. He was not used to riding, and his legs felt wobbly once he was standing again. Shahree stood still for him, giving him a look that said, "I understand, and it's all right." Alex patted Shahree's neck softly and thanked the horse under his breath.

Following Andy to a nearby spring, Alex retrieved the many water bags Andy had insisted he buy. Yesterday, Alex had thought Andy was mad to insist on so many water bags; today, Alex was glad he had them.

After he'd filled his water bags and stored them in his magic bag, Alex walked stiffly back to the others. They were gathered around a small fire, sitting quietly and watching as Thrang cooked their meal.

"Final instructions while we eat," said Bregnest, accepting a plate of food from Thrang. "Then we will arm, and divide some food between us. Am I correct in thinking that we all do not have food in our bags?"

"All but two have food enough," Skeld laughed, nodding toward Alex and Andy.

Alex hadn't thought of buying food while he and Andy were shopping the day before. Andy hadn't taken him to any shops to buy food, though now it seemed like an obvious thing to think of. Now it was too late, and Alex had no idea how much food he would need for himself, let alone the other members of his company.

"I think there will be plenty for all," said Bregnest with a smile. "It will be a good thing for each of us to have some food in our bags. You never know what might happen on an adventure. Having a little extra food in your bag might make the difference between finishing the quest and starving to death.

"First, however, the final instructions," Bregnest continued. "We have all signed the Bargain and know what is expected if any or all of our company should fall. We have also agreed, except for our eighth man, that if any are lost, we will try to find them. The time limit on this search will be thirteen days, as specified in the *Adventurer's Handbook*."

"Do you agree to this, Alex?" Arconn asked as Bregnest paused.

"Yes, I agree," answered Alex.

"Very well then," said Bregnest, his tone remaining serious. "After the thirteenth day of searching, the lost person or persons are free to do what seems best to them. If they wish to continue the adventure to its end or return to Telous, none here will say anything against their choice."

Alex accepted his own plate from Thrang. The instructions seemed sensible, but he hoped he would not need to remember them later. He wondered how he would ever be able to find his way back to Telous if he got lost.

"Finally, I wish you all luck," said Bregnest with a smile.

"Luck," the rest of the company said loudly.

They finished eating in silence; soon Thrang stood to collect the plates. The rest of the company began producing packages of food from their magic bags and giving them to Andy and Alex.

"Thrang and Arconn will keep the freshest things," said Skeld. "They've got ice rooms in their bags."

"Ice rooms?" Alex questioned, looking at Andy.

"Rooms that stay cold," Andy answered. "I thought about ordering you one, but I didn't want to go too far with Thrang's gold."

"A useful room," said Thrang, as he playfully threw a package of food at Skeld. "You'd be wise to get one if you ever have the chance."

"When Slathbog's hoard is ours, I'll get one," Skeld replied as the package bounced off his head.

The exchange of packages went on for some time, and Alex wondered if he would have room in his bag for everything. With some difficulty, he managed to store everything where he thought he would remember.

"Time to arm ourselves," said Bregnest. "We do not know what lies ahead. We should be ready to meet whatever we find."

Alex carefully retrieved his new sword from his bag. Once again he thought he could see words mixed in with the gold swirls on the scabbard, and once again they vanished when he blinked. Andy showed him how to attach the scabbard to his belt and helped him arrange the straps so they looped over his head and shoulder. Alex felt uncomfortable with a sword at his side and hoped his discomfort didn't show too much.

The rest of the company armed themselves as well. Bregnest strapped a sword to his side and slung a larger, two-handed sword across his back. He also had a round shield with a bright-red dragon's head painted on it, which he attached to his saddle.

Arconn carried a longbow with a quiver of black arrows on his back and a long knife at his side. Thrang carried a large double-headed ax and a short sword. He also had a steel helmet with gold and silver inlays, which Alex saw him return to his bag. He looked fierce, even without his helmet, and Alex was glad he was a friend. Halfdan was equipped much the same as Thrang was, though he didn't look quite so fierce. Tayo, Skeld, and Andy all carried heavy swords and shields, though Tayo also carried a long spear and Andy looped a fair-sized ax on his belt.

"Quite a collection," said Andy. "Now you see why you needed a weapon."

"Yes," said Alex. "But it feels awkward."

"You'll get used to it soon enough," Andy replied. "It's best to have a weapon handy when you go into wild lands. You should be able to pick up a good knife or perhaps an ax to go with your sword as we travel."

"So where is the great arch?" Alex asked, his voice lowered so only Andy could hear him.

"Right in front of you," Andy replied in surprise.

"I don't see an arch," Alex protested.

"Well, it's not really an arch. It's only *called* the great arch. The two towers and the hills are the base of the arch and the sky is the top."

"Oh," Alex replied, feeling a bit unhappy. He'd expected a

grand arch of finely cut stone, but what he saw was something almost common.

"It is time," said Bregnest, looking around the group to make sure everyone was ready. "We have a long road ahead of us, and a quest to complete."

They all climbed back onto their horses. Alex managed it with more confidence than he'd had that morning, and he gave another grateful pat and thanks to Shahree. Falling into line behind Bregnest and the others, Alex followed the road between the towers on the hills and into his adventure.

CHAPTER FIVE
THREE-LEGGED TROLL

Once the company had ridden between the hills that marked the great arch, Alex noticed a change in the landscape. There were no green fields or meadows along the road ahead of them; everything looked brown and dead, like open fields after a long winter. The air was colder on this side of the arch as well, and the thin clouds dimmed the sunlight.

"Springtime is slow to come in Vargland," said Tayo, as he rode in front of Alex and Andy. "It will be at least a fortnight before anything green appears."

"Vargland?" Alex questioned.

"That's where we are now," replied Andy. "We have passed through the arch into Vargland and its wilderness."

Tayo grunted. "Tame enough here," he said over his shoulder. "Not many wild things live near an arch."

"Why is that?" Alex asked.

"Good magic, maybe," Tayo replied.

"Do many people come to Vargland?"

"Not so many in recent years," Tayo answered, as he looked at the land around them.

"I'm surprised there isn't a town or village closer to the arch," said Alex.

"Not many people live near an arch," said Skeld with a smile. "Maybe that's good magic too."

"More good sense than good magic," said Tayo.

"Why's that?" Alex questioned.

"There have never been a lot of people in the north of Vargland," answered Tayo. "And just because the great arch is here doesn't mean a lot of people travel this way. If you were a trader, you could make a better living in the south and not have to face the dangers of these wilder lands."

The sun was low in the western sky when Bregnest finally halted the company for the night. The wind that had started blowing late that afternoon grew in strength, and the clouds that had followed them all day were growing darker. The smell of rain filled the cold air as they made their camp, and there were distant flashes of lightning. Skeld and Tayo attended to the horses while the rest of the company set up the small tents they had brought with them. Alex thought it would probably rain before morning, maybe even snow with as cold as the wind felt.

"Here now, Alex," said Thrang, waving Alex closer. "I'll teach you a bit of magic you'll find useful on the road."

"All right," said Alex in an uneasy tone. He knew the others thought he had magical powers, but he still thought it had to be a mistake.

"Right then," said Thrang briskly. "Now, watch closely.

Inferno!" Thrang commanded, one hand pointing at the small pile of wood he'd gathered.

A branch burst into flame. The fire quickly spread to the rest of the wood, and Alex could feel the heat on his skin.

"Now pay attention," said Thrang to Alex. He pointed at the fire once more. *"Quench."*

As quickly as the flames had appeared, they vanished and the branches were left cold and burnt. Alex put his hand near the pile, but there was no heat at all, and no smoke rose from the branches.

"Good to know how to put out a fire quick if enemies are near," Thrang explained with a smile. "Now you try."

Alex scratched his nose as he looked from the branches to Thrang and back again. He knew nothing would happen if he tried to copy Thrang's magic, but he also knew Thrang was eager for him to try it just the same.

"Inferno," said Alex loudly, pointing at the pile of branches.

Nothing happened.

"Oh, you need to think of fire," Thrang said. "And I mean *really* think about it—the heat, the smell, the sound. Focus all of your thoughts on the fire when you give the command."

Alex wondered for a moment if Thrang was toying with him. But seeing the sincere look on his new friend's face convinced him that it wasn't a joke, so he took a deep breath. He thought about the fires at the Golden Swan—how they looked, how they felt—and tried again.

"Inferno!" Alex commanded.

As soon as the word had left his mouth, the entire pile of branches burst into flame. Thrang staggered back, slapping out several sparks that had jumped from the fire into his beard.

"Well done!" Thrang exclaimed, smoke rising from his beard. "Though maybe next time, you should concentrate on a single branch, not the whole pile."

"Sorry," said Alex, amazed by what he'd just done. "I wasn't sure it would work."

"'Course it works," Thrang replied with a grunting laugh while continuing to check his beard for sparks. "Now try to put it out. Just think of a plain pile of branches, or a cold pile of ash this time."

Alex scratched his nose again and thought about the branches without any fire. He was surprised and a little pleased he'd managed to copy Thrang's magic on his first real try.

"Quench."

The flames flickered for a moment and went out, a large cloud of smoke rising from the wood. Alex staggered slightly, feeling dizzy. Thrang caught Alex by the arm to steady him.

"Well done indeed," said Thrang, slapping Alex on the shoulder. "Most people can't even get the flame to flicker on their first try."

"Why was it harder to put out the fire than it was to start it?" Alex asked.

"Always harder to put out a fire," said Thrang. "Fire's an adventurer's ally most of the time. It's hard to give it up."

"I see," said Alex thoughtfully. "And why was I dizzy?"

"All magic has a price," Thrang answered. "Even something

as simple as starting and putting out a fire. As you practice, your powers will grow stronger and you won't even notice the price for such simple magic."

"Can anyone learn to start fires with magic?"

"Not if they don't have magic in them to begin with," Thrang replied. "Halfdan doesn't have any magic at all, so he could think about fire and say the word for years and nothing at all would happen."

"You have magic," said Alex. "Does that mean you could become a wizard if you tried?"

"Ha," Thrang laughed. "I've got a bit of dwarf magic in me, but not near enough to be a wizard. Not if I worked at it for the rest of my days would I be able to do magic like a true and trained wizard."

"If you two have finished playing with that pile of wood, you might light it for the evening and leave it burning," said Skeld as he walked toward them. "Or did you intend for it to blink off and on all night?"

"Perhaps we should light you instead," Thrang replied in a serious tone, though he was smiling.

"Can you light other things, besides wood?" Alex asked, interested by the idea.

"Hmm, what?" said Thrang, distracted by Skeld. "Course you can, what do you think? Though it's harder with some things than others. Dry branches are the easiest."

Thrang took a step back from the pile of branches, protecting his beard with his hand. "Go on then," he said.

"Inferno," said Alex, this time concentrating on a single branch instead of the whole pile.

Again the flames appeared, but this time only on the branch he intended. The fire quickly spread to the other branches, and once more Alex could feel the warmth of the flames. Alex watched the fire grow, pleased with both his new ability and the fact he hadn't felt as dizzy as when he'd put the fire out.

"That may be handy come morning," said Bregnest, walking up to the fire. "Smells like rain, but the wind promises snow."

Bregnest was right about the rain, which started falling softly as they ate their evening meal. By the time they had finished eating, the fire was smoking and flickering out. They sat and watched the embers fade as the rain fell, not ready to go to bed but with little else to do.

"Best put some blankets on the horses," said Tayo when the last ember of the fire turned black.

Without speaking, they all walked to where the horses were tied. Alex took a heavy blanket from his magic bag and gently placed it over Shahree's back. Shahree shook her head and looked at Alex in a grateful sort of way, as if to thank him. Alex patted her neck and wondered why he had ever been afraid of horses.

———◆◆◆———

Waking with a start, Alex saw Skeld's laughing face above him.

"Time to be up, my friends," Skeld laughed loudly. "And here's a little something for you," he added, throwing a bit of snow into the tent.

"Get out!" Andy shouted, his normal happy expression replaced by a look of pain.

When Alex sat up he understood Andy's pained expression. His whole body ached, and his legs felt like they might fall off. Slowly he pulled on his pants, but his boots seemed like too much work.

"I've never felt so sore," Alex said, looking at Andy, who was pulling on one of his own boots and trying desperately not to fall over while doing it.

"It's the riding," Andy replied. "It will take a few days to get used to it."

Alex nodded but said nothing. The only part of his body that didn't hurt was his head, and he thought talking too much might change that. Slowly, he pulled his boots toward him and tried to slip them on.

"Here is a pretty sight," Skeld laughed, as Alex and Andy emerged from their tent. "It seems they've aged a hundred years in just one night."

"Oh, shut up," Andy snapped grumpily.

Several inches of wet snow covered the ground, but the clouds had blown away during the night, a pale line of them just visible across the eastern horizon.

"Here," said Thrang, walking up to Alex and Andy and holding out a canteen. "Take a sip of this, but no more than a sip."

Alex took the canteen from Thrang, sniffed it, and sipped a little of the liquid. He felt the cool liquid slide down his throat, but didn't taste anything strange and handed the canteen to Andy. He tried to ask Thrang what was in the canteen, but the words wouldn't come out of his mouth. As soon as he had swallowed, all his pains had disappeared.

"Ancient dwarf remedy," Thrang laughed, seeing the look on Alex's face. "Takes the soreness out of muscle and joint. It'll take a few days for us all to get used to traveling again."

Alex looked at Andy, who grinned. Stretching carefully, Alex found that Thrang was right—his aches and pains were completely gone.

"Thank you," said Alex. "That really does the trick."

Thrang bowed slightly and then laughed. He walked off to the campfire as he sipped from the canteen.

"That's some remedy," said Andy, carefully stretching. "I'll have to get some before my next adventure."

"Or always travel with a dwarf," laughed Skeld.

They packed their tents, shaking off the snow, as Thrang prepared breakfast. Thrang made Alex practice starting the fire and putting it out again before he started cooking. He seemed to be pleased that Alex had picked up the bit of magic so quickly, and Alex couldn't help feeling a little proud of himself as well.

"The more you practice, the better it'll work," said Thrang with a wink.

When they were ready to ride, Thrang had Alex put out the fire once more. The *quench* command worked well in the wet snow, and there was little smoke from the fire. Alex felt slightly dizzy again after putting the fire out, but not as much as he had the night before.

With the fire out, they climbed onto their horses and set off along the snow-covered road, riding south as the day grew brighter around them. They continued to travel south for three more days. Each day they stopped at midday to stretch their legs and eat a little, and every time, Alex would practice with the fire before Thrang started cooking the meal. Alex's control improved rapidly, and after a few days, he was able to put out the fire without any smoke at all. The dizziness had passed completely now that he had used magic several times.

"You've picked that up fast," said Thrang as they ate their midday meal on the fourth day. "Some people practice for weeks and still leave behind a trail of smoke."

"Do you really think I could become a wizard?" Alex asked, happy with his success.

"If you choose to be," Thrang answered. "Though not everyone with the gift wants the responsibility."

"Responsibility?"

"Where there is power, there is an accounting for it," Thrang replied and fell silent.

Alex thought about Thrang's answer while he ate. Yes, power had to be accounted for, but he wondered who did the accounting.

The road turned easterly that afternoon, and Bregnest took a map from his bag and examined it closely with Arconn as they continued to ride. Bregnest seemed pleased with the progress the company had made in the four days they'd been in Vargland, though Alex had no real idea of how far they'd traveled.

"We'll camp early tonight," Bregnest announced when they stopped by a stream later that day. "This water is good, and we should refill our water bags."

They set up camp between the stream and a grove of trees growing close to the road. The wind had picked up again, but the sky was clear and the late afternoon sun was warm. Thrang asked Alex to start their campfire, but didn't have him put it out as he normally did.

"You've got the hang of it," said Thrang when Alex questioned him. "Now fetch me a large pot of clean water from the stream."

Alex took the large iron pot Thrang had pointed to and walked to the stream. The full pot was heavy, and he had to pay attention to where he was walking so he wouldn't spill the water all over himself.

While Alex and the others were setting up camp and taking care of the horses, Arconn took his bow and disappeared into the woods. As the sun was slipping out of the sky, Arconn returned with two rabbits and three birds that were almost as big as turkeys.

Thrang took the rabbits and birds from Arconn and quickly prepared them for cooking. The rabbits were added to the pot on the fire, while the birds were skewered on long poles and propped over the flames to roast. It wasn't long before Thrang had a wonderful rabbit stew ready for them to eat. The birds continued to roast, filling the air with a mouthwatering smell.

"You're a master cook," said Skeld, bowing to Thrang. "It is a wonder your people let you go on adventures when you cook so well."

"If you think this is good cooking, you should visit the halls of my people," Thrang laughed with a pleased look on his face. "I am only a fair cook in my own land."

"Then perhaps our next adventure should be to your land." Skeld laughed happily, filling his bowl with more stew.

The company was merry that night, and there was plenty of talk and stories of past adventures. Even Tayo, who normally didn't say much, told them part of the tale of his first adventure. Both Alex and Andy listened to all the stories, fascinated and entertained. Though Andy had been on one adventure before this one, he said that he had no stories to tell.

"Have you all traveled together before?" Alex asked between stories.

"No, not as a group," answered Thrang.

"Tayo and I have been on a few adventures together," said Skeld. "And I think all of us—except for you and Andy, of course—have traveled at least once with Bregnest."

There was a general agreement with what Skeld said, and then some talk about who had traveled where and with whom in the past. Alex tried to keep track of it all, but there were too many jokes and bits of stories mixed in with the talk. In the end, all he knew for sure was that Thrang and Arconn had traveled together many times, Skeld and Tayo had traveled together, and Bregnest had been on too many adventures to count.

Finally, when the fire was burning low, they went to their tents, tired and happy after their fine meal and long talk. The wind was still blowing, but gently. The full moon rose, covering the ground with a pale light. Alex feel asleep, peaceful and relaxed.

◆ ◆ ◆

Alex felt a hand on his shoulder, shaking him awake. Struggling to open his eyes, Alex was confused to see Tayo in his tent. It was still dark outside and there was a grim look on Tayo's face. He motioned for Alex to stay silent. Alex nodded and pulled on his boots, following Andy out of the tent. The rest of the company was already gathered around the cold ashes of their fire, speaking softly.

"The horses have broken away," Tayo said in a whisper. "Something has spooked them into flight."

"Whatever it is, it hasn't come close to the camp," said Thrang. "There are no tracks or any other signs to be seen close in."

"Should we wait for dawn to seek the horses, or go now?" Arconn questioned, looking at Bregnest.

"They could be far away by dawn," said Bregnest, looking at the trees where the horses had been tied. "We should look now, but in pairs."

Alex volunteered to go with Andy to look for the horses, but the others were against the idea.

"You are both young and have little experience," Skeld commented. "Perhaps you should remain here, in case the horses find their own way back."

"Good idea," said Thrang in a heavy whisper. "They are good animals and will try to return if they can. And as nothing has come close to the camp, you should be safe enough."

"Agreed," said Bregnest, looking at Alex and Andy. "You two remain here and keep your eyes open. We will look for the horses and return. I don't think we will need to look far, perhaps a mile at the most. If you need us, call out loudly. Arconn will hear you."

Alex, unhappy about staying behind, wanted to argue, but the look in Bregnest's eyes told him it would be pointless. Remaining silent, he and Andy watched the rest of the company walk away toward the trees.

"Should we light a fire?" Alex asked in a lowered voice.

"Best not," Andy replied. "If something is out there, a fire might draw it to us."

"What do you think might be out there?"

"Goblins, maybe," said Andy. "Or maybe a troll."

"You couldn't just say robbers, could you?" said Alex, bumping Andy's shoulder in fun.

"Bandits or robbers would have attacked the camp before taking the horses," said Andy. "Trolls or goblins are more likely to steal the horses for food and leave us alone."

"Trolls and goblins eat horses?" Alex asked in a worried tone.

"Goblins do," said Andy. "I don't know about trolls, but I've heard they'll eat most anything."

The two of them stood looking into the darkness without speaking for what seemed like a long time. The light from the full moon gave the nearby trees a strange, shiny look and cast long, dark shadows across the ground. Alex's ears started to ring as he strained to listen for any sound at all, but all he heard were the branches moving in the soft breeze, the trees creaking gently, and the water running in the stream beside them.

"How long do you think they'll be?" Alex whispered.

"Depends on what they find," Andy answered quietly. "Though I don't think it will be long. We should have set a watch, but I'm sure Bregnest didn't think we'd run into trouble so soon."

They fell silent again, listening and swaying slightly from side to side. Time seemed to be moving slowly. Alex didn't like waiting at camp, though he knew it was probably for the best. He rolled his head around on his neck to fight off sleep, and halfway through the roll, he heard a sound. Freezing, he strained to listen. He heard the sound again: the frightened whinny of a horse.

"Did you hear that?" Alex asked.

"Yes."

"What should we do?"

"I don't know," said Andy nervously. "It sounds troubled."

The frightened whinny came a third time as Andy finished speaking. It was a scared and lonely sound. It sounded to Alex like a desperate call for help.

"Stay here," said Alex, turning to follow the sound.

"What are you doing?" Andy asked in alarm.

"I'm not sure. I . . . I just feel that I have to go."

"We were told to stay here," Andy protested, grabbing Alex's shoulder. "We should do as Bregnest said. He is the leader."

"I know," Alex answered, pulling free. "But I have to go, I can't explain why."

Alex felt desperate, and he was determined to go, no matter what. Following the distant sound would mean leaving the post Bregnest had assigned to them, breaking an important rule of adventurers.

"Go," said Andy after a moment of thought. "If you run into trouble, call out or light a fire and I'll come. If you find the horse, return as fast as you can."

Alex nodded and started off along the stream. He didn't know why he had to go into the darkness alone, but something inside him knew he had to get to the frightened horse. The feeling was stronger than his fear of breaking the rules and upsetting Bregnest. Something in the terrified and lonely whinny of the horse called out to him, and Alex knew that the only thing that mattered was finding the horse, and fast.

He moved quickly along the bank of the stream in the darkness. The ground was mostly clear and the moonlight reflected off the large rocks and bushes in his path, making them easy to see and avoid. Alex tried to move as quietly as he could. He had never seen a goblin or a troll and he hoped he wouldn't be seeing either of them tonight.

Alex heard the whinny again. It was closer now, and off to his left. Leaving the stream behind, he moved deeper into the trees, stopping to listen. He heard nothing, so he moved forward, trying to head in the same direction as the whinny. He climbed a small hill and stopped to listen again. There was a sound of movement in front of him: hooves stamping the ground nervously.

Moving cautiously, Alex tried to stay silent. He had no idea what he might run into, and he didn't really want to think about the options. Putting his arms out in front of him, he was able to keep the small tree branches from slapping his face and poking him in the eyes. He moved as fast as he dared in the darkness under the trees, worried about every little noise he made. Soon the trees began to thin, and he could see moonlight filling an open clearing in front of him. His eyes, accustomed to the darkness beneath the trees, could see clearly across the open ground.

On the far side of the clearing stood Shahree, stamping her hooves in fear. About halfway across the clearing was a massive figure—ten feet tall, five feet wide, and with long arms and oddly bowed legs. Alex's mouth went dry, certain he was seeing a troll for the first time.

The troll was closing in on Shahree, a huge club raised over its small, round head. It was clear that Shahree was afraid to run into the darkness under the trees, and the troll was using that fact to trap her.

Alex could see Shahree's terror, and her helpless fear filled him with an anger he had never felt before. Even though he had only known the horse for a few days, he already felt a great fondness for her. He wouldn't let this troll kill her.

"Over here!" Alex shouted, jumping out of the trees without thinking. "Over here, you stupid troll!"

The troll turned away from Shahree. It spotted Alex moving into the clearing and lowered its club slightly. The troll tilted its head to one side, as if considering how dangerous Alex might be. Then, without any warning, the troll charged. The creature was faster than Alex would have thought possible for something so large.

Before Alex could stop it, the huge club came down, missing him by inches and shaking the ground under his feet. Alex staggered backward, tripping over an unseen rock and falling to the ground.

The troll grabbed Alex by his left leg and lifted him up until they were face to face.

"Run, Shahree!" Alex yelled. "There is nothing in the darkness to fear. Run, and find the others."

The troll, apparently understanding what Alex had said, turned to look at Shahree. The horse whinnied loudly, and without hesitation, she bolted into the darkness under the trees. The troll made angry sounds that Alex thought might be curses, and when it looked at Alex again, anger burned like tiny flames in its eyes. Alex wondered if the troll would club him on the spot, but then the troll lowered its arm to its side—Alex's head almost hitting the ground—and started off toward the far end of the clearing.

Swinging along upside down and helpless, Alex knew he

was in trouble, but he had no idea what to do. His sword hung at a strange angle to his body and he couldn't draw the blade. His friends were far off and scattered, looking for the lost horses, and it was unlikely anyone would hear him if he yelled for help.

Looking at the troll's heavy leather boots gave Alex an idea, an idea he almost lost when he noticed the troll was wearing three boots—three boots for the troll's three legs. Putting aside his surprise, Alex pointed his finger at the boot nearest him and called out.

"*Inferno!*"

Three things happened almost simultaneously: the boot burst into bright red flames; there was a deafening roar as the troll stamped madly to put out the flames; and Alex was dropped on his head.

Rolling away from the troll's burning, stomping foot, Alex rubbed his head. He hadn't expected to be dropped quite so quickly, and he felt lucky the ground was soft and damp. Scrambling to his knees, he saw the troll had almost put out the flames on its burning boot and was turning around to look for him.

"*Inferno!*" Alex called again, focusing on a different boot.

The second boot burst into flames and the troll howled even louder than before. The troll stormed around the clearing, trying madly to douse the flames in its boots. A stream of angry sounds flowed from the troll, and this time Alex was sure they were curses.

Alex knew he couldn't kill the troll by lighting its boots on fire, and in its rage, the troll might simply ignore the flames and rush him. For a moment Alex considered running, but he didn't think he could outrun the troll, even with its burnt feet.

Stepping a little further away from the troll, Alex drew his sword. The sword's edge shone like blue flame in the pale moonlight, but he didn't have time to appreciate its beauty. Alex watched for an opportunity to strike as the troll continued to curse and stomp around the clearing.

Seeing his chance, Alex summoned his courage and leapt forward, swinging his sword with all his strength. He thought he was close enough to hit the troll, but the blow seemed to miss completely, and Alex spun around, falling with the force of his own swing.

The troll's screaming and howling convinced Alex that he had managed to injure it after all, but he feared he hadn't done much damage. He scrambled to his feet, ready to strike again. A strange heat was growing inside of him, but he didn't have time to wonder what it might mean.

To Alex's surprise, his first swing had completely removed one of the troll's three legs. Off balance, the troll lifted its club and swung wildly. The club caught the edge of Alex's sword, knocking it out of his hand.

Alex reached for his sword, but he could see the club coming down again. He rolled away to escape being crushed by it. He tried to get back to his feet again, but the troll was right on top of him, its curses filling the air. Alex managed to roll away a second time, but as he did, he hit his head on a large, sharp rock. His eyes blurred as he struggled to get up, and he could see strange flashes of light in front of him. Something warm and wet ran down the side of his face, but Alex didn't have time to think about it.

He was in more danger now than he had been before. The troll had him cornered, and Alex couldn't get to his sword. He looked up at the troll as he tried to clear his vision. Its eyes were burning with rage and its club was raised, ready to strike the fatal blow. Alex wondered what it would feel like to be squashed by the huge wooden club.

"Quench!" Alex yelled in desperation, his hand pointing at the troll's body.

Alex closed his eyes, waiting for the club to fall, but nothing happened. Opening one eye, he looked up. The troll was still there, but it wasn't moving. Its mouth was slack and its eyes had lost their burning anger.

Alex staggered to his feet and hurried to retrieve his sword. He wasn't sure how or why, but the quench command had frozen the troll in place. He leaned on his sword, dropping to one knee as he gulped in the cool night air, wondering what he should do next.

"Alex!" Arconn's voice called loudly. "Alex, where are you?"

"Over here," Alex called back, his voice weak and shaking. "I'm here."

Arconn, Thrang, and Bregnest came crashing into the clearing, their weapons raised and ready for battle. The three of them stopped as soon as they spotted the frozen troll. They looked from the troll to Alex and back again.

"What have you done?" Thrang asked in wonder, his eyes fixed on the troll.

"I quenched his fire," said Alex, wiping the blood off his face. "At least, I think that's what I did."

"What—?" Bregnest asked without lowering his sword.

"Is Shahree all right?" Alex interrupted. "Did she find you?"

"She is fine," said Arconn, moving to Alex's side and examining the cut on his head. "She told us where to find you. She is helping the others find the rest of our horses."

"She told you?" Alex asked.

"We elves can speak to many animals," Arconn replied. "She knows what you did for her, and she will not forget the debt."

"I had to," said Alex, feeling tired and shaky. "I mean . . . I . . . I couldn't let that . . . that thing just kill her."

"Tell us exactly what happened," said Bregnest, his eyes fixed on the troll. "We should know all before deciding on a punishment."

"Punishment?" Alex tried to stand up, but he couldn't manage it.

"You left your post and put yourself and the company in danger," Arconn said, gently pushing him back to the ground. "This is a serious matter, even if all turns out well. Tell us everything—what you thought, what you felt—as you undertook this task."

Alex took a deep breath and gathered his thoughts. He told them how Shahree's terrified whinny had called to him, and how he felt that he *must* follow, even though he knew he shouldn't leave the camp. He told them that Andy was against him leaving, and how he had gone anyway, following a feeling he couldn't explain. He told them everything as calmly as he could, and when he finished, the others remained silent for several minutes.

"It is not yet harmless," Bregnest finally said, breaking the silence and pointing at the troll with his sword. "Though dawn's light will finish the job you started."

"We should check its pockets before it turns to stone," Thrang commented. "Might be worth the trouble."

"Turns to stone?" Alex questioned.

"Trolls turn to stone in sunlight," Thrang answered. "And what's in its pockets will turn to stone as well."

"Check them," Bregnest said to Thrang. "I'll be ready if it moves again. Though I doubt it ever will."

Thrang cautiously approached the troll and reached up to pat the large pockets. He drew his short sword and cut the bottom out of each pocket, letting the contents fall to the ground. Moving quickly to retrieve everything that fell, he hurried away from the troll once more.

"Have to wait for daylight to see what there is," Thrang commented, squinting at the pile of items in his hands.

"Dawn will be here soon," replied Arconn. "And punishment should be decided before it arrives."

"Very well," said Bregnest, looking grim. "As punishment for disobeying orders, Alex, you forfeit your extra share of any treasure found with the troll or in its lair. You will still receive an equal share, as agreed upon in the Adventurer's Bargain, but even though you defeated the troll in single combat, you will not have the honor of dividing this treasure."

"All right," said Alex, relieved. He had worried he'd be sent back to Telous and not allowed to go on. "I know it was wrong to leave the camp," he added quickly to cover the sound of his relief. "I just felt I had to."

"This may seem a small punishment to you," said Bregnest sternly. "However, it is a dishonor to lose your extra share. You do not know all the ways of adventurers yet, nor do you understand how much value we place on honor."

"I may not understand," Alex answered, standing up, "but I feel that I did what I had to do."

"And it has turned out well," Arconn added.

"Yes, yes it has," admitted Bregnest with a slight smile. "So there will be no punishment other than what I have said. After all, few adventurers would take on a three-legged troll alone. You have proven your courage and worth this night, my friend."

"Thank you," said Alex, bowing to Bregnest.

"Arconn, bring the others here when they have found the horses," said Bregnest, his eyes turning to the troll once more. "We should search the troll's cave as a company."

CHAPTER SIX

THE TROLL'S CAVE

Alex wiped the troll's blood off his sword and sheathed it as he waited with Thrang and Bregnest. He felt tired and drained, but proud at having defeated the troll.

The eastern sky was growing light when Arconn finally returned to the clearing, followed closely by the rest of the company. It seemed that Arconn had already told Alex's story to the others, and they arrived, excited to see the frozen troll.

"Not a bad night's work," Skeld commented, looking at the troll and its missing leg. "Don't see many like this one, do we?"

"Three legs," said Tayo as he stood beside Bregnest.

"What do you mean? Isn't that normal for trolls?" Alex asked.

Skeld burst into laughter and the others smiled as well. When Skeld regained control of himself, he looked at Alex. "Do you know about the birds and the bees?" he asked in a tone that made him sound like a schoolteacher.

"Yes," Alex replied.

"Well, trolls don't," said Skeld, laughing madly again.

Alex looked to Thrang for an answer.

"Trolls aren't like other creatures," Thrang explained with a smile. "Trolls molt."

"Molt?"

"They shed their skins, but not like a snake. When trolls molt, they divide into two different trolls."

Alex looked at the other members of the company, thinking that this was a joke, but they all nodded in agreement with what Thrang had said.

"It's in the handbook," said Andy. "You should take more time to read it."

"I suppose I should," Alex admitted. He hadn't even looked at the handbook since Arconn had given it to him.

"Now watch," said Thrang, looking to the east. "You'll see something that not many have."

Alex and his companions watched as the sunlight moved to where they were standing in the clearing. Even Skeld became quiet as the light inched closer to the troll. When the first ray of sunlight touched the troll's uplifted arm there was a sharp cracking sound, like ice splitting, and the troll's skin and clothes changed from green and brown to light gray stone.

"That's what happens to trolls caught in sunlight," said Thrang in a satisfied tone.

"That's incredible," said Alex in amazement.

"Most adventurers know that sunlight will turn trolls to stone," said Skeld, chuckling to himself. "But getting them into the sunlight—that's the hard part."

"Enough talk," said Thrang. "Let's see what it had in its pockets."

They all gathered around the objects Thrang had retrieved in the darkness: a fair-sized iron key, a suitcase-sized coin purse, and half a dozen leather bags.

"The key will be to its cave," said Thrang, handing it to Bregnest. "We'll have to look for that."

"And well worth looking for," Arconn added.

"Let's see now," Thrang continued, opening the giant coin purse and pouring the contents onto the ground.

Alex gasped as the gold and silver coins spilled out at Thrang's feet. He had never seen any treasure in his life and this pile seemed huge to him.

"Most trolls carry only a small part of their wealth with them," said Tayo with a grim smile. "If this is a sign, the cave should hold a fair amount."

"Let's see what these might be," said Thrang, reaching for one of the leather bags and untying the knotted cord that held it closed.

Thrang slipped his hand inside. Alex took a deep breath as Thrang pulled out a handful of large, dark red rubies. Out of the second bag, Thrang withdrew some incredibly green emeralds. The third bag contained more rubies, while the fourth and fifth bags were each full of shiny white diamonds. Alex couldn't believe how much treasure the troll had been carrying.

"It seems our adventure has already made a profit," said Skeld, slapping Alex on the back and smiling.

Thrang's hands trembled with excitement as he untied the

cords on the last bag. Alex watched him closely, wondering what new treasure this last bag would hold. Thrang looked into the bag for a moment, a puzzled look on his face. Then he held out his left hand and dumped the bag's contents into it: a single golden ring set with a large black stone.

"Something special 'bout this," said Thrang, looking at Bregnest. "No troll would carry a ring. Not unless it was something special."

"That's true," Bregnest agreed. "So hear now what I say about the division of this treasure. As a single victor, Alex would normally have the honor of dividing this treasure as well as an extra share. Because of Alex's punishment for leaving his post, I will divide this first treasure evenly between us, with one exception. This ring is unknown, but may have magical powers. According to our agreement, it belongs to Alex." He looked sternly at Alex. "I would advise leaving it in its bag, however, until you find an oracle who can tell you exactly what it is."

Thrang placed the ring back into the leather bag and handed it to Alex. He accepted the bag with a bow, but made no move to put it into his magic bag with his other belongings. Part of him wanted to look at the ring again, but he decided to follow Bregnest's advice and kept the bag closed.

"I would say that these gems are an uncommon treasure, as trolls seldom carry gems with them. Though Alex has lost his extra share in this treasure, these should go to him for his victory over the troll," said Bregnest with a smile. "He may choose to share them or to keep them for himself."

"Share them, please," said Alex as Thrang held out two of the bags to him. "It is only right that we share these."

"You are most generous," said Bregnest. "We will do as you ask. So then, eight equal shares and all odd numbers to the victor."

"To the victor," six voices agreed.

Alex wasn't sure what Bregnest meant by "to the victor" but he soon learned it meant that any items that couldn't be divided into eight equal shares belonged to him. In the end, Alex received seven rubies, six emeralds, three diamonds, five gold coins, and two silver coins more than anyone else.

Once the treasure had been divided, Skeld said, "Let's find the home of our stone friend. If he carried this much treasure with him, a fair hoard awaits us in his cave."

Arconn took the lead, and they followed him across the clearing and up the hill beyond. The deep imprints of the troll's leather boots had left a clear trail that was not difficult to follow.

"You've done a good night's work," said Thrang, walking next to Alex. "Even if the cave is empty, we've more than paid for our adventure with this treasure."

Alex wondered if he should offer to pay Thrang back for the items he'd bought in Telous, but then he remembered Andy's comments about dwarfs and their money and he decided to remain silent, at least until he understood a little more about dwarfs.

"An impressive first victory," said Andy, coming up on Alex's other side.

"I was lucky," Alex replied.

"Lucky or not, it's still remarkable," Thrang commented.

Alex shook his head. "I was too angry and foolish to see the danger."

"You may have been many things, but not foolish," said Thrang in a serious tone. "You followed your instincts and did what your heart told you. And you used magic to defeat your enemy."

"It was luck," Alex insisted. "I really didn't have time to think about it."

"Luck is a good thing to have," said Andy, as they climbed the hillside. "Maybe better than magic, in some ways."

Alex considered what Thrang and Andy had said. He still had mixed feelings about magic, but he was glad that he had some luck.

The sun was well up when they came at last to a flat, open space on the side of the hill. Alex looked back down the path they had climbed, and he could see their tents far off in the morning light. He hoped Shahree was all right and had been able to shake off her fear from the night before.

"Going to take a bit of looking," said Halfdan as they moved into the clearing. "Looks like this troll was careful."

"What do you mean?" Alex questioned.

"Look at the ground," said Tayo. "The troll's tracks have vanished."

Alex looked around the clearing and Tayo was right, the boot tracks they had followed up the hillside were nowhere to be seen.

"Its lair must be close," said Skeld.

"Spread out," said Bregnest. "Look for anything that seems out of place."

Alex walked a few paces, but he didn't have any idea what to look for. There were no boot prints leading to the troll's lair, and as far as Alex could tell, this was just an open space on the hillside.

"A bit higher on the hillside would give the troll a better view of the land below," said Halfdan.

They climbed up the hill, looking for any sign of the troll. Alex watched the ground, but there was nothing to see. He glanced around at his companions and saw that Thrang had stopped and was looking up at the branches of a tree.

"Here's the door," called Thrang, pointing at a moss-covered boulder that stood between two trees. "Better hidden than most troll's lairs."

"I don't see a door," said Alex as he looked at the boulder.

"That's because you don't know what you're lookin' for," replied Thrang. "Look up at the branches. See how some of them have been broken off?"

"Yes," replied Alex.

"Now, look at the boulder. What do you see?" Thrang questioned.

"It's just a moss-covered boulder," said Alex.

"Ah, but what side is the moss growing on?" Thrang asked.

"Um, the south side?" Alex guessed.

"Moss grows on the north side of boulders and trees," said Thrang. "Or at least it does here in the north of Vargland."

"So why is there moss on this boulder?" Alex questioned.

"Because the troll uses it to hide his door," Thrang answered with a grunting laugh. "I'd guess the keyhole is hidden in the moss."

"Stand ready," Bregnest ordered, the key in his hand. "There may be another troll inside."

The rest of the company all moved back a little, spreading out in a half circle around the doorway. Alex was a little nervous, believing his victory was more luck and anger than anything else and he didn't want to meet a second troll so soon.

Bregnest pushed the key into a small crack that Alex had not seen and turned it once. There was a loud click, and with some hard pulling, Bregnest managed to open the door to the troll's cave.

A terrible smell filled the air as the door swung open—rotten fish and old socks mixed with dirty dishes that had been left to soak for too long. Alex thought for a moment he was going to be sick. He pulled his shirt up over his nose, but it did little to block the smell.

Thrang ignited a large dead branch that was lying nearby and carefully stepped into the doorway.

"It's all right," he said in a tone that sounded both relieved and happy. "The cave isn't deep, and there aren't any trolls."

The rest of the company followed Thrang into the cave, wary and alert. The foul smell was stronger inside the cave, and Alex began to feel a little dizzy.

"Step outside," said Arconn, seeing the look on Alex's face.

"You've had a long night, and the smell might be too much for you."

"I should stay with the company," Alex replied in a determined tone.

Arconn nodded in response and said nothing more.

Once they were all inside the cave, Thrang lit the several lamps that were scattered around the single large room.

Alex's feelings of sickness were forgotten once the lamps were lit. He was stunned and amazed by what he saw in the troll's cave. He'd never imagined so much gold and silver could be in one place at one time.

Along the back wall of the cave were two huge black cauldrons, big enough for a man to sit in, and both of them were overflowing with coins. Next to the cauldrons were several piles of leather bags, all neatly tied at the top, just like the bags the troll had been carrying in its pockets. Alex looked at everything, his mouth hanging open in disbelief.

"You've done well, master wizard," Skeld laughed loudly, but he suddenly stopped.

Alex followed Skeld's gaze to the opposite wall. Hanging there on wooden pegs were what looked like seven magic bags. Broken weapons were scattered on the floor beneath them. The bags looked almost exactly like Alex's own bag, though a bit more worn. Alex's mouth snapped shut as he realized what this discovery meant. The others looked at the bags as well and their happiness with the treasure changed to sorrow for the lost adventurers who had once owned these bags.

"Take them outside, Skeld," Bregnest commanded. "We will not leave them in this evil place another moment."

Skeld carefully took the bags from their pegs and carried them out into the sunlight. His cheerful face was grim and slightly pale with sorrow.

"Alex," Bregnest continued. "Gather wood and start a fire. We will eat in the clearing while we remove the treasure."

Alex nodded. As he left the cave, the others began hauling the treasure into the sunlight. By the time Alex had gathered a large stack of wood and had a fire burning, his friends were covered with sweat from their heavy work. In the sunlight there seemed to be even more treasure than Alex had thought and he was surprised when he reentered the cave and saw the mounds of treasure that remained.

"Let's eat before we continue," said Bregnest, nodding to Thrang. "It's been a long night for us all and the food and drink will do us good."

Alex and his friends gathered around the fire, sitting in silence as Thrang cooked their meal. Skeld began looking at the recovered magic bags while they waited. He put his mouth to the top of one bag and spoke softly into it, but nothing happened.

"What are you doing?" Alex asked.

"It's possible an adventurer has survived inside his bag," answered Skeld, taking another of the bags and lifting it to his mouth. "If they have, I'm telling them it's safe to come out now."

Alex wondered how long someone could survive inside a

ADVENTURERS WANTED: SLATHBOG'S GOLD

magic bag. Considering that his own bag had four rooms and a fair amount of food and water, Skeld's actions seemed to make sense.

"It's a fool's hope," said Halfdan, watching Skeld speak into the bags. "If any adventurer was inside his bag, the bag would be where he left it and not here."

"Of course," said Skeld, laying down the last bag on top of the others. "But it's better to hope than to despair," he said, a touch of color returning to his face.

They ate their meal in silence, too tired and sad for conversation. When they finished eating, they returned to the cave, and once more started hauling treasure into the sunlight. It was heavy work, but the labor distracted them from the foul smell that hung in the air.

It was well after midday before the cave was empty and the treasure stacked in the sunlight. Alex and the others were exhausted from the work and the lack of sleep, and they all dropped to the ground to rest for several minutes. The piles of treasure had grown enormous in Alex's eyes. He wondered if Slathbog's hoard was bigger than this, and if so, how they would ever move it.

After catching his breath, Bregnest stood up and walked to the pile of magic bags they'd taken from the cave. He looked at the bags sadly for several minutes before he spoke.

"It is customary that the one who recovers an adventurer's bag returns it to the heir of the lost adventurer," said Bregnest, looking at Alex. "These were recovered because of your victory over the troll, and so the honor and burden falls to you.

However, as you are a new adventurer, I will carry this burden for you if you wish."

Bregnest hesitated for a moment and then continued. "Any reward given for the return of these bags will be yours, of course, as it was by your valor these bags were recovered."

Alex hadn't considered what they would do with the seven magic bags. He wanted to do what was right among adventurers, and he suspected it wasn't to duck his responsibility and let someone else, even Bregnest, carry the burden.

"You are very kind," Alex said after a moment of thought. "But I will keep the custom and return the lost bags. Any reward should be shared among the company, however, as all profits from this adventure should be."

"Well spoken," Bregnest replied with a smile. "You have learned a great deal in a short time. The honor of carrying the bags remains with you."

Bregnest handed the bags to Alex, bowing low as he did so. Alex returned the bow and carefully placed each of the magic bags inside his own. He had no idea how he would ever find the adventurer's heirs, but he was pleased to know he had given the correct answer.

"Now to happier matters," said Bregnest. "A fair amount of treasure to divide among the eight of us."

They all cheered and Bregnest put each member of the company to work sorting the piles of treasure. He also repeated that all odd numbers were to go to Alex, which made Alex blush slightly as the others cheered again.

By the time they'd divided the treasure and stored it in

their bags, the sun was sinking in the west. Tired and happy, they made their way back down the hill to their camp by the road. They were completely worn out when they finally reached their tents, and all they could think of was sleep. Instead of preparing another meal, they ate leftover stew from Thrang's pot and the roasted birds Arconn had shot the day before.

While everyone else ate, Alex slipped away from the fire. He wanted to check on Shahree and make sure she was all right. Shahree whinnied loudly as he approached, a sound that was much happier now than it had been the night before. Alex gently rubbed the horse's neck and let her nuzzle his shoulder.

"You did well, my friend," Alex said softly. "You found Arconn and told him where I was. Thank you."

Shahree whinnied again, nodding her head up and down as though agreeing to what Alex had said.

Alex looked into her eyes, and he could see for himself how grateful she was that he had saved her.

"It's all right," said Alex with a smile. "I may not be able to understand you like Arconn does, but I know exactly what you mean."

"Alex," said Bregnest as he came up beside Shahree.

"I'm sorry I broke the rules," Alex blurted out. "I know everything turned out well, but I'm sorry I forced you to punish me."

"A small matter," said Bregnest.

"But . . ." Alex started, then stopped. He wasn't sure he

could put his thoughts into words, or at least not into words that Bregnest would understand.

"I know," said Bregnest with a smile. "You were right to do what you did. You followed your heart and did what you knew was the right thing to do. Knowing when to trust yourself is far more important than any rule. And a great deal of good may come from your actions."

"What good?" Alex questioned. "I mean, I'm glad the troll was destroyed and that Shahree is all right. I'm happy we were able to find the other horses and claim the troll's treasure, but what other good can come from that?"

"You forget the seven lost bags," said Bregnest. "You've done a great thing, recovering those bags. You have the chance to help many people when you return the bags to the heirs and families of the lost adventurers."

"I don't know how I'll ever be able to do that," said Alex. "I don't even know how I'll find out who owned the bags to start with."

"The bag maker in Telous will be able to tell you who the bags belonged to," Bregnest replied, resting his hand on Alex's shoulder. "He should also be able to tell you who the heirs are and where they might be found."

"Oh, I never thought of that."

"You are learning quickly," Bregnest said, "and I'm glad Thrang and Arconn asked you to join our adventure."

"Thank you," said Alex, humbled and pleased at the same time.

"Come now, let's join the others," said Bregnest. "Though

I don't think there will be much talk around the campfire tonight."

"I am rather tired," said Alex as they walked back to the campfire. "I don't remember ever feeling as tired as I do right now."

It had been a long day, and Alex was happy with how things had worked out. He smiled as he closed his eyes, hoping that Bregnest was right and that a great deal of good would come from returning the lost magic bags.

That night they all slept soundly with only the sound of the stream to break the silence. If any wild creature passed the camp, it went unnoticed. They slept late into the following morning, and then slowly ate the breakfast Thrang prepared. With a final cheer for their good fortunes and Alex's victory over the troll, they rode away from what the company had dubbed the Troll's Stream.

CHAPTER SEVEN

THE WHITE TOWER

The Troll's Stream was soon left far behind as Alex and his companions followed the road to the east. The weather grew warmer as the days passed, and the fields and forests became greener. They didn't meet anyone as they traveled, and to Alex's relief, they had no more encounters with trolls or anything worse. Bregnest insisted they keep a watch at night, however, and he had them draw marked stones from a bag to decide which watch each of them would take. Alex was happy when he drew the first watch, as it seemed to be the best to him.

Early one day, they came to a fork in the road, and Bregnest had them stop and gather around him. One road turned sharply to the south, while the other continued mostly east, bending slightly to the north.

"Which road shall we take?" Bregnest questioned.

Alex knew Bregnest wasn't really looking for an answer; he just wanted to hear what each member of the company had to say.

"The south road will be better," said Halfdan, without

commitment. "But there are many people that way, and the road to our final goal will be longer."

"East and north lies the White Tower," Arconn commented, looking into the distance. "It might be wise to seek the Oracle."

"The wait at the tower may be a long one," said Thrang thoughtfully.

"But worth the time spent," Tayo answered him.

"And when has waiting ever been troublesome to a dwarf?" asked Skeld with a laugh. "It will give you time to grow back your beard, though our young wizard burnt off but little of it."

"It would be pleasant to see the White Tower," Andy commented softly as the others laughed at Skeld's jest. "The Oracle may help us in our quest."

"Only if she can use a sword," Skeld laughed.

"What do you think, Alex?" questioned Bregnest.

Alex's companions had become extremely interested in his opinions since his victory over the troll. It didn't seem to matter how many times Alex told them he'd just been lucky. They simply saw his luck as part of his magical powers, and laughed whenever he expressed his own doubts.

Alex knew from reading the *Adventurer's Handbook* that the south road was considered the safer road. There were many cities to the south as well, and he thought it might be nice to see how the people of this land lived. In his heart, though, he wanted to see the White Tower of the Oracle.

"I think the south road would be safest, but the east road

would be wisest," Alex answered. "And I would like to try to speak to the Oracle if I can."

"Even if you have a chance to speak with her, the Oracle may not tell you what you wish to hear," said Arconn in a thoughtful tone.

"Just the same, I'd like to try," Alex replied more boldly.

"As would I," Bregnest added. "So east we will go, and hope the Oracle will agree to speak with us."

Alex fell back into line beside Andy as they started forward again.

"How far is the White Tower from here?" Alex questioned.

"It depends," Andy replied. "Some say the tower moves. Others say it is hidden, so only those who the Oracle wishes to speak with can find it."

"What do you believe?"

"I believe we will find it," Andy said.

"I hope so," said Alex.

"Why is that?" Skeld asked, looking over his shoulder at Alex.

"It would be good to see some people," Alex said. "Even if we don't get to talk to the Oracle, it would be good to see a city or town as we travel."

"Adventures aren't about seeing cities or people," said Tayo.

"No, I suppose not," replied Alex. "I just thought . . ."

"Thought what?" asked Skeld as a smile spread across his face.

"I thought there would be more than just riding and camping," answered Alex.

"Ready to fight another troll, are you?" Skeld asked with a laugh.

"No, nothing like that," said Alex, laughing as well. "It's just that seeing new places and meeting new people would make things more . . ."

"Adventurous?" offered Andy.

"Yes," said Alex.

"Adventures aren't all about excitement and finding treasure," said Tayo with a slight smile.

"Most adventures can be very common, even boring," laughed Skeld.

"What's so funny?" Halfdan questioned, slowing his horse to ride beside Skeld.

"Alex doesn't think our adventure is very exciting," Skeld answered happily.

"Excitement? Bah!" said Halfdan. "We don't need more excitement. We'll have enough of that when we face Slathbog."

"Too much perhaps," Tayo added in a grim tone.

"That's not what I meant," Alex protested, but then he saw Halfdan wink.

"Don't worry," he said. "There will likely be plenty of excitement before we're all safe at home once more."

Alex let the subject drop, trying to understand his own feelings about excitement and adventure. All this travel did seem very—as Skeld had said—boring. Still, he was in a new land, learning new things, and not cleaning up or washing dishes at his stepfather's tavern.

They rode east for two more days, stopping only at midday

for a meal and then riding until it was almost dark. The warm weather meant they could simply sleep on their blankets under the stars. Alex enjoyed sleeping in the open, because each night one of his friends would tell a story about a previous adventure.

On the first night after the crossroad, Thrang told of how he'd joined an adventure to capture a dangerous sea monster. With great excitement and some vigorous demonstrations, Thrang explained how the monster had almost gotten away, but was captured in the end. His descriptions of how the monster acted amused them all, and when he finished his story, Alex and the rest of the company cheered.

The next night, Tayo told of an adventure to rescue a young prince who had been wrongfully imprisoned. And though his tone was not as animated as Thrang's, Tayo's story was still cheered at the end.

"He rules his kingdom still," Tayo concluded in a satisfied tone. "And remembers his friends when they visit."

Alex wondered about Tayo as he prepared for bed that night. He thought it was strange that Tayo always seemed to be in a dark mood, seldom showing any sign of happiness beyond a smile and rarely laughing or joking like Skeld and Andy. Alex thought some deep sorrow must be in him, or perhaps he simply worried too much.

On the third morning from the crossroad, Alex heard a strange dinging noise. He thought he must be dreaming, but when the sound came again, he sat up, rubbing his eyes and wondering if his friends were playing a joke on him.

Something dropped onto his legs. He looked down at his

blankets and blinked. Standing on his blankets was a strange-looking creature. It was the size and shape of a bowling pin, but bright yellow, with a red strip zigzaging around its middle. It had a single bird-like leg.

"Um, Thrang?" Alex called in as normal a tone as he could manage. "What's this?"

"What's what?" Thrang asked, turning away from cooking breakfast.

"This," Alex replied, pointing.

"Oh, that," said Thrang, smiling as he hurried over. "It's a geeb, of course. Well, a bottle-necked geeb to be exact. Wonderful creatures."

"So they're not dangerous?" Alex asked, his surprise replaced by curiosity.

"No, they're messengers," Thrang replied. "Good ones too because they've got a bit of magic in them."

"More magic?"

"'Course they can only answer yes and no questions," Thrang continued. "When they honk it means no, and when they ding it means yes."

Alex nodded his understanding without looking away from the geeb.

"Watch," said Thrang, turning to the geeb. "Do you have a message for our company?"

"Honk," the geeb replied, its head transforming into the shape of a small bicycle horn.

"Are you just visiting then?" Thrang questioned.

"Honk."

"Then do you have a message for a person in our company?" Thrang asked.

"Ding," the geeb replied, its head changing into a small bell.

"Do you know who the message is for?"

"Ding."

"Excellent," said Thrang. "Is the message for Bregnest, our leader?"

"Honk."

"Very odd," Thrang muttered. "Is the message for Arconn the elf?"

"Honk."

Thrang scratched his head. "Well then, can you find the person who the message is for?"

"Ding."

Thrang looked at the geeb for a second before continuing. "Have you already found the person your message is for?"

"Ding."

"Your message is for me?" Alex asked in surprise.

"Ding! Ding! Ding!"

"But I don't know anyone who'd send me a message," Alex said, looking at Thrang. "Everyone I know who'd know anything about geebs is here."

"Never mind that now," said Thrang. "Ask the geeb to give you the message."

"May I have the message?" Alex asked.

"Ding."

A thin hole like a mouth appeared in the middle of the geeb and a long envelope emerged, flopping into Alex's hands.

"Thank you," said Alex.

The geeb remained standing on Alex's legs.

"Is it waiting for something?" he asked.

"Payment, of course," said Thrang.

"How do I pay a bottle-necked geeb?"

"Oh, they'll take silver or gold coins," Thrang answered. "But they prefer gems if they can get them."

"Gems?" questioned Alex.

"Ding!"

"Yes, gems," said Thrang. "Geebs know a fair price for any gem you may give them. If the gem is worth more than you owe, they'll give you back the difference in gold and silver coins. Try it."

Alex retrieved a small emerald from his bag and held it toward the geeb, who simply stood on its leg and waited.

"Toss it up," Thrang instructed, amused by Alex's puzzled look.

Alex tossed the emerald in a high arc, and the geeb jumped off Alex's legs and caught the gem in midair.

"Ding," the geeb sounded as it landed back on its single leg. The geeb bent down for a moment and Alex saw six gold coins and three silver coins on the blanket.

"I told you. A fair price," Thrang laughed.

The geeb remained motionless while Alex collected the coins and put them in his bag.

"Now what?" Alex questioned, assuming the geeb would leave once it had been paid.

"Are you waiting for an answer?" Thrang asked the geeb.

"Ding!"

Alex looked at the envelope in his hand. Carefully he opened it and removed a single folded piece of paper. Looking once more at the geeb and Thrang, he began to read.

> *Master Alexander Taylor, Esq.,*
> *Please accept this invitation for yourself and your company to dine with me on your arrival in two days' time.*
> *Awaiting your reply.*

At the bottom of the note was a drawing that looked like a tower with some strange writing next to it. Alex showed the letter to Thrang, who seemed stunned.

"What's all the noise about?" Andy asked as he rolled over in his blankets.

"Best reply quickly," said Thrang, handing the letter back to Alex. "Do you have paper and pen?"

"Yes," said Alex, reaching for his magic bag. "But who's the letter from?"

"The Oracle herself," said Thrang, in a tone of wonder. "Didn't you see how it was signed?"

"What are you two talking about?" Andy questioned again.

"Here," said Alex, handing him the letter he'd just received.

Retrieving his writing things from his bag, Alex looked at Thrang. "What should I say?"

"Just say you're happy to accept her invitation, and you're sure the rest of the company will accept as well," Thrang answered. "And don't forget to sign it."

Alex wrote as carefully as he could.

I am pleased to accept your invitation and am confident the rest of the company will accept as well.

Alex Taylor

"How's that?" Alex asked, handing his note to Thrang.

"No, that won't do," said Thrang, looking it over. "Doesn't sound right."

"This came for you?" Andy interrupted, holding the Oracle's letter and looking as stunned as Thrang had.

"Yes," said Alex.

"Arconn," Thrang called. "We need your assistance."

"How may I be of help?" Arconn asked as he walked into camp carrying two large rabbits. Laying the rabbits next to the fire, he moved toward Thrang and Alex.

"Read this," said Thrang, snatching the letter from Andy's hand and giving it to Arconn.

"Impressive," said Arconn with a smile. "It's not often that one is invited to dine with the Oracle. And to include the entire company . . ."

"Include the entire company in what?" asked Bregnest as he walked into camp carrying several water bottles.

"It seems our young friend is better known than we thought," replied Arconn, passing the note to Bregnest.

Bregnest's eyes widened as he read the note. Then he

carefully refolded the paper and handed it to Alex. "Best make a reply."

"That's what we're trying to do," said Thrang, sounding put out. "I thought Arconn could help as he's best with letters."

"Pleased to assist," said Arconn, taking Alex's writing things and thinking for a moment. "Let's put it like this."

I am honored at your favor and pleased to accept your kind invitation. I am confident my companions will feel as honored and pleased as I do.

Your servant,

"Now sign the bottom 'Alexander Taylor, Esq.'" Arconn handed the pen back to Alex.

"I knew an elf would have the right answer," said Thrang with a smile. "Always clever in language, the elves."

"You are most kind," said Arconn, bowing to Thrang.

"Now what do I do?" Alex asked, as he carefully folded the note and placed it in a new envelope.

"Here, let me," said Thrang, taking the envelope. Turning to the geeb, he held the envelope carefully by one edge. "Please take this reply to the Oracle," he said to the geeb. "And if you require payment, please deliver the note and return. We will be happy to pay you."

"Ding," the geeb sounded and accepted the envelope from Thrang.

With Alex's reply accepted, and Thrang's instructions understood, the geeb hopped off Alex's legs and, with a slight popping sound, it vanished into thin air.

"Remarkable creatures," said Thrang happily.

At breakfast that morning, Thrang told Tayo, Skeld, and Halfdan the news of Alex's message. The three warriors had been taking care of the horses when the note had arrived, and they insisted on hearing the entire story with every honk and ding in place.

"Seems our young wizard's made quite a name for himself," Skeld teased. "First he single-handedly kills a three-legged troll, and now he's been invited to dine with the Oracle."

"We're *all* invited," Alex corrected.

"Yes, but the message came to you," Tayo commented in his normal somber fashion. "Which I think is odd. I would have expected it to come to Bregnest, as our leader."

"It is of small concern who the message came to," said Bregnest, waving off Tayo's comment. "I think it is odd that we were all asked to join the Oracle for dinner."

"I've never heard of such a thing," commented Halfdan, without looking up from his plate. "Must mean something special."

"It is odd, but not unheard of," said Arconn, winking at Alex. "And as far as it meaning something special, well, who can say?"

"I don't know what to think," said Alex.

"Well, I think it's wonderful," said Andy, slapping Alex's shoulder.

"As do I," Thrang added, putting his cooking pots away. "And it's a sign of good fortune as well."

"Only time will show our fortunes," said Tayo, standing up and looking down the road to the east.

"And it is time we were on our way to seek them," Bregnest added. "At the very least, we will have a grand meal."

———— ◆◆▶ ————

As they traveled that day, Alex thought of the Oracle's note, wondering why it had been sent to him and not to Bregnest or one of the others. There was no special reason he could think of for the Oracle to be interested in him. Ever since Mr. Blackburn had said he could use a staff, Alex's friends all thought of him as a wizard in training, but Alex had his doubts. He knew he had some magical ability, but he still knew so little about magic. Surely not enough to interest an oracle.

"Have you read about the Oracle and the White Tower?" Andy questioned as they rode along.

"A little," Alex replied. "The *Adventurer's Handbook* said there are many oracles, but the Oracle of the White Tower is one of the best known. I haven't finished reading everything yet."

"They say she is a thousand years old," Andy said in a thoughtful tone. "Though many things are said, and few there are who can say what is the truth."

"What do you want to ask the Oracle?" Alex questioned, lowering his voice so the others wouldn't hear. "I mean, if you don't mind my asking."

Andy thought for a moment before he answered, a look of inner struggle on his face. "I would rather not say. Not that I doubt you to keep my thoughts, but because I doubt myself in speaking them," he added quickly.

"Fair enough," said Alex with a smile to ease Andy's troubled look. "I should not have asked."

"Each man's question is private and personal," said Andy, returning Alex's smile. "Difficult to explain to anyone but himself."

There was little talking as they traveled that day. They ate their midday meal quickly, and it seemed they all were in a hurry to move on once more. When they camped that night, they remained restless and eager.

"It seems we would all rush to the White Tower," Skeld laughed, as much at himself as the others. "Even I would give up sleep if I thought tomorrow would come sooner."

"It will come soon enough," Tayo replied glumly. "Though I fear it may not bring what we hope for."

"Always a worrier," Skeld laughed. "Your wisdom may be sound, my friend, but you're always a cloud of darkness."

"And I am seldom disappointed," Tayo answered with a slight smile.

"Enough," Bregnest interrupted. "We must start early tomorrow."

As the others rolled themselves in their blankets, Arconn remained seated next to Alex by the fire, humming softly to himself but not speaking. When Alex woke Thrang for the next watch, Arconn's strange humming remained in his ears and he fell asleep thinking about the happy tune.

The next morning, the eastern sky was still black as they

quickly ate their breakfast and started off. They rode faster that morning than normal, and with each bend of the road or small hill they passed, they looked forward in hopes of seeing the White Tower.

The road became more rugged as the day passed, and the path twisted between hills that slowly grew larger on either side of them as they traveled. Alex thought it was well past midday when Bregnest suddenly stopped in the road.

"My friends, we have arrived," Bregnest said over his shoulder.

As they gathered around Bregnest, Alex and the others could see a great white tower standing in a wide, open valley below them. Pure white walls ran out from the tower, encircling lush orchards and gardens around its base. Beyond the wall, on the southern side of the tower, was a small city made of sand-colored stone.

Bregnest led them down the hills and into the valley, following the road toward the city. As they drew nearer, a rider came racing toward them from the direction of the tower. He carried a large green banner with a white tower in the middle of it.

"Are you the party of Silvan Bregnest?" the rider asked politely, reining in his horse.

"We are," Bregnest answered.

"Well met, Master Bregnest," said the horseman with a slight bow. "The lady of the tower bids you welcome, and asks that you and your companions follow me to the tower gardens. There you will be given accommodations for your stay."

"We are honored," said Bregnest, bowing his head slightly to the messenger.

"Then come, honored guests," said the horseman, turning his horse toward the tower. "The gardens are not far, and all has been made ready for your arrival."

They left the road and followed the horseman without speaking, all of them looking up at the massive tower in front of them. When they passed through a large gate in one of the walls, Alex noticed a strange tingling feeling in his hands and feet, but he quickly forgot about it as they entered a vast orchard full of sweet-smelling blossoms.

As they emerged from the orchard, the horseman halted in front of four white buildings that looked like small houses compared to the enormous tower next to them.

"The lady of the tower asks that you rest here," said the horseman, nodding toward the buildings. "You will find all that you require in the west houses. If you need anything, ring one of the gongs and it will be brought to you."

"What of our horses?" Bregnest asked.

"The westernmost house is a stable," the rider replied. "Refreshments have been laid out for you in the second house. The third house is for bathing; the fourth, for sleeping."

"The lady is too kind," said Bregnest, bowing once more.

"You will be summoned for the evening meal when the sun touches the western hills." The horseman nodded once and rode away toward the tower.

"The lady shows us a great kindness," said Arconn as the company rode toward the first house.

"Indeed," Bregnest agreed. "I wonder why we should be so favored."

"Because of our young wizard friend, of course," Skeld laughed, climbing off his horse and looking into the stable. "This is finer than many inns I've slept in," he added.

"Yes, but you'll sleep anywhere," Thrang replied with a laugh of his own.

They all laughed at Thrang's comment as they led their horses into the stable.

"You should be comfortable here, Shahree," said Alex, patting the horse's neck. "I don't know much about stables, but this looks like a first-class one."

Shahree whinnied loudly in agreement and stepped out from under her saddle as Alex lifted it from her back. She was a clever horse, and Alex was quick to tell her so. Putting aside the saddle, he quickly brushed her down, then hurried out of the stable to join the others in the second house.

The second house was a simple, massive stone pavilion. The front was completely open, the view overlooking the courtyard and the gardens beyond. Heavy wooden panels were folded like an accordion at both sides of the opening to cover the front of the house in cold or stormy weather.

As Alex entered the second house, an overwhelming mixture of smells greeted him. A banquet had been laid out for them on three large tables. Eight comfortable-looking chairs were placed around a smaller, fourth table in the center of the room, waiting for them to arrive.

"The Oracle knows the way to a man's heart," Skeld commented, piling food on his plate.

"The way to your heart is no great mystery, Skeld," said Tayo, looking happier than Alex had ever seen him.

The food on the tables, as Alex found out from his friends, was from many different lands. Alex tried so many different dishes, he had trouble remembering what any of them were called. He was a little worried about some of the food however, because he wasn't sure what it was made of and Skeld kept joking about what the ingredients might be.

Some of the food was easy to identify, and the taste of even simple things like potatoes or peas seemed more intense to Alex. There were all kinds of meat and vegetables that Alex had never seen before, and several kinds of fresh, warm bread. Sweet, sour, spicy, and even smoky flavors turned up in the different dishes—each new flavor better than the last.

"If this is refreshment, what will dinner be?" questioned Thrang, refilling his mug with some aged red ale that he seemed to enjoy.

"I doubt it will be so grand as this," Arconn replied with a knowing smile. "It is said the lady eats little. I doubt so many foods will be brought to her table."

They left the banquet behind them, moving into the third house—the bathhouse.

The company entered a room with several small changing rooms inside it. Each of the changing rooms had a stack of clean, white towels, as well as a place for Alex and his friends to put their things. On the far side of the room was another doorway, leading to a room with a dozen enormous brass tubs. Low walls separated each of the tubs for privacy, but still allowed the adventurers to talk to each other while they bathed. Eight of the tubs were already filled with steaming water.

"A blessing indeed," said Skeld as he dove into the tub nearest the door, splashing water everywhere.

"The water is meant to stay in the tub," growled Thrang, whipping water out of his eyes.

Alex thought the hot bath was even better than the meal. The hot water was wonderful and he couldn't remember the last time he'd felt so clean and comfortable. He made a mental note to add a bath to his magic bag as soon as he had a chance.

Clean and full, they left the room with the brass tubs and returned to their clothes. There was a moment of stunned silence when they re-entered the first room. Next to each companion's dirty travel clothes was a fine new set of clothes waiting for them. New leather boots were waiting as well, shining from fresh polish.

"The Oracle's kindness continues," said Arconn, looking at a sky-blue shirt that was sitting by his things.

"Why does the lady favor us so?" Tayo questioned, looking at his new silver-gray shirt. "We have done nothing worthy of such honors."

Alex dressed in a dark green shirt that fit him perfectly, and his new belt had a bright silver buckle on it. He pulled on his new boots, and looked at himself in one of the large mirrors near the entrance of the building.

"A proper adventurer," said Skeld from behind him. "And a perfect fit all around."

"It seems strange," Alex commented, looking at Skeld in the mirror. "Are oracles normally so kind?"

"At times," Skeld replied. "Though perhaps not so often as some would hope, and rarely so generous as this."

"The ways of oracles should not be questioned," said Thrang, pulling on a dark red shirt. "If there's a reason for this kindness, we will learn it soon enough."

"Whatever the reason, we seem to have won the lady's favor," said Bregnest, pushing Skeld away from the mirror so he could look at himself.

When they finally left the bathhouse, the sun was already moving to the west. Alex and his friends walked into the sleeping house where they found eight large beds ready and waiting for them. Each of them chose a bed, and Alex noticed that the others put their magic bags and weapons on their beds. Alex did the same, though he wasn't too happy about leaving the magic bag behind.

"It's tradition," said Thrang, seeing Alex's look. "The bags are for travelers, not guests, and weapons are for warriors, not friends."

Alex nodded, then followed Thrang out of the sleeping house into the shady courtyard where they waited to be summoned. They did not have to wait long; as soon as the sun touched the western hills, a young woman appeared from the tower.

"My mistress bids you welcome," she said in a voice that

sounded like falling water. "She asks that you follow me to the dining chamber of the tower."

"We are honored," replied Bregnest, bowing to the young woman.

The rest of the company followed Bregnest's example and bowed. The young woman seemed pleased and smiled as she turned back to the tower.

Bregnest led the company as they followed their guide into the tower. On entering the tower, they ascended a wide, stone staircase that looked polished and new. Alex wondered how old the young woman was and how she had come to work at the Oracle's tower. He felt the strange tingling in his hands and feet again and guessed that he was feeling the magic of the tower.

At the top of the stairs, their guide turned to the right and, after a short walk, the company entered a large room with a round table in the center. On one side of the table stood a high-backed silver chair that was flanked by eight plain, wooden chairs.

"Master Bregnest," said the young woman, indicating the wooden chair directly to the left of the silver one.

The woman continued calling each of the company by name and indicating which seat they should take. Lastly, she asked Alex to take the chair on the right of the silver chair.

"My mistress will join you shortly," said the woman, bowing to the company and departing.

"You are highly honored," Thrang said to Alex, sitting down on Bregnest's left.

Alex didn't understand what he meant, but he remembered

how the company had been seated around Bregnest at their dinner in Telous. There seemed to be some meaning to the seating arrangement then, and there was now as well, but Alex didn't know what it was.

"Welcome, honored guests," a warm, friendly sounding voice said.

A tall, dark-haired woman stood in the doorway, her bright blue eyes moving around the table to look at each of them. She wore a pure white dress edged in silver, and a wide, happy smile. The adventurers stared, dumbfounded, as the woman gracefully crossed the room and took her place in the silver chair.

"Please, be at ease," said the woman. "I am Iownan, Oracle of the White Tower. I welcome you here, and I thank you for joining me."

"It is our great pleasure," Bregnest managed to reply as he started to rise from his chair. "The honor is truly ours."

"You are most kind, Silvan Bregnest," replied the lady with a smile. "Please, be seated."

"May I introduce my company?" Bregnest asked as he returned to his seat.

"I know them all," replied Iownan. "I have watched as you have traveled in this land, and I know of your quest."

"You know much, great lady," Bregnest stammered. "And we are in your debt for the kindness you have shown us."

"You need not be so formal, Master Bregnest," Iownan replied. "This is but a dinner party. Tonight I am simply your host, not the Oracle."

"Your pardon, lady," said Bregnest, inclining his head. "Though I must say, we have felt somewhat troubled by your kindness. We have done nothing to deserve your generous gifts."

Iownan laughed happily before she replied. "I have shown you a small kindness, though some would think it great."

She clapped her hands and several servants carrying trays entered the room. The table was quickly filled with an assortment of food and drink, and Iownan laughed again as she looked at the company.

"I hope you see something you like," said Iownan. "It's not often my cooks have reason to prepare such a meal."

"Lady," Bregnest stammered, "we are overcome with your kindness."

Iownan smiled and invited them to help themselves to whatever they liked. Though the company had eaten a great deal earlier in the day, they each made an effort to at least sample everything on the table.

Alex noticed Iownan herself ate little of anything.

"Don't worry about me, Master Taylor," said Iownan, looking Alex in the eyes. "I will not go without. Please, have some more."

Alex was impressed with Iownan, and it seemed that all his friends were as well. They all took great pains to show proper respect, remaining silent whenever Iownan spoke.

"You are excellent guests," Iownan commented when the trays had been picked clean. "I hate for this evening to end, but end it must. Before you rest, though, I will answer the two questions that you all would ask."

Alex and his friends straightened in their seats as Iownan spoke, looks of wonder on their faces.

"The first is why my invitation was sent to young Master Taylor, instead of Master Bregnest," she said, smiling at Alex. "This was because Master Taylor has the power of a true wizard in him, though he doubts it himself. And a wizard, even one untrained, should always be given respect."

Alex's face flushed red as Iownan spoke, and he looked down at his napkin.

"You need not feel shame or embarrassment here," said Iownan, reaching out her hand to lift Alex's chin. "You are among friends and what I say is true."

Alex continued to blush as he looked at Iownan, but now he didn't feel embarrassed at all.

"The second question," she continued, looking around at the company, "is what I would ask of you in return for my kindness."

Iownan paused for a moment before continuing. Alex noticed that his friends looked worried. He wondered what Iownan would ask of them.

"Ask what you will, great lady," Bregnest said sincerely. "If it is within our power, we shall do it."

"You speak before you know what I would ask," said Iownan in a thoughtful tone. "I will not hold you bound to this now, nor will I speak of what I will ask until a later time.

Be content to know that I will ask, and I believe you will do as I ask for friendship alone."

"You are most generous, lady," replied Bregnest. "Your counsel is your own. We will await your request."

Iownan smiled. "Go now and find your rest. I will speak with each of you tomorrow as the Oracle of the White Tower."

The company stood and bowed as Iownan left the room. For a moment, Alex thought the light in the room seemed to dim behind her.

"My lords," said a young man from the doorway. "I am Rothgar, and the lady commands I should see to your needs this evening."

"The lady is most kind," said Bregnest, nodding to Rothgar. "Though I feel that sleep will be our only need this night. I thank you for your kindness, and the lady for sending you."

"As you wish," Rothgar replied with a bow. "I will guide you to your rest."

They followed Rothgar down a corridor for some distance, then turned left, climbing a flight of stairs. At the top of the stairs, they turned right and suddenly found themselves outside the tower entrance.

"But we went upstairs when we entered," said Alex, looking up at the tower in puzzlement.

"The inside of the tower changes," Rothgar replied. "The rooms and corridors never remain the same for long."

"Ingenious security," said Thrang. "Anyone not trained in how the tower moves would soon be lost."

"That is true, Master Silversmith," said Rothgar. "Though that is perhaps the simplest protection the tower employs."

Alex and his companions said goodnight to Rothgar and returned to the sleeping house. They were tired after the long day and there was little talk as they prepared for bed. One by one, they put out the lamps and went to sleep.

The others were soon snoring softly. Alex's body ached for sleep, but his eyes would not stay closed and his mind was full of questions. Finally, he gave up and climbed out of bed and pulled on his new clothes. Quietly, he walked to the entrance of the house and slipped out into the moonlight. He thought Rothgar might be there, but the courtyard was empty and quiet.

Alex walked to the stable to check on Shahree. The moonlight was bright, and he had no trouble seeing his way. Inside the stable, several lamps were still burning. Alex wondered why they had not been put out.

"Well, Shahree," said Alex, patting the horse's neck. "Have you eaten as well as the rest of us?"

Shahree nuzzled Alex's shoulder affectionately but made no sound. Alex leaned against her neck, rubbing it gently, but said nothing more. His mind was buzzing with questions and he desperately tried to make sense of them.

"You show this horse great kindness," a voice said from behind him, "though once you feared her."

Alex spun around, surprised that he was not alone.

"There is a great bond between you two," continued Iownan, smiling at him from the stable door.

"I have grown to trust her," Alex stammered, unsure of what to say or how to act.

"And she puts great trust in you as well," Iownan replied, walking over and patting Shahree's forehead. "I am surprised that such strong feelings have grown so quickly between you and this noble steed."

"Perhaps need has quickened the growth," replied Alex.

"Perhaps." Iownan continued to rub Shahree's forehead. "What keeps you from your sleep?"

"I have so many questions. I was trying to make some order of them," Alex answered.

"And some doubts as well?" Iownan's blue eyes seemed to look right through him, but they were soft and kind.

"Yes," said Alex, looking away.

"Do not be troubled," said Iownan, stepping away from Shahree. "You will find the answers you need, in time."

"And if the answers are more than I can bear?" Alex asked, voicing his greatest fear before he could stop himself.

"Then you will break," Iownan answered in a matter-of-fact tone. "Though I believe you are much stronger than you think."

"I doubt it," said Alex, turning away again from Iownan's gaze.

"As do all who have not been tested," replied Iownan with a kind smile. "You will have trials, that much is certain. How you deal with your trials . . . only time will tell."

"Can't you see the future?" Alex asked.

"The future is not yet written. I can see only possibilities and advise on the best way to make them come to pass—or not come to pass, as the case may be."

"But I thought an oracle could—"

"See the future of men and tell them what will be? No, there are none who have that power. As I said, I see possibilities. Nothing more."

Alex stood quietly, thinking about Iownan's words. He had hoped to find some answers at the White Tower, but now he wasn't sure he would find them anywhere.

"I feel so confused," said Alex softly, though his mind felt more restful since Iownan had entered the stable. "I just don't know what I should do."

"Come," said Iownan, taking his hand and leading him out of the stable. "You need your rest. We will speak again tomorrow."

At the door to the sleeping house, Iownan let go of Alex's hand. He suddenly felt weak and tired. Stumbling slightly, he found his way back to his bed, managing to get undressed before falling into a deep and peaceful sleep.

CHAPTER EIGHT

ORACLE

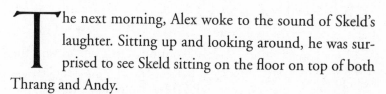

The next morning, Alex woke to the sound of Skeld's laughter. Sitting up and looking around, he was surprised to see Skeld sitting on the floor on top of both Thrang and Andy.

"What's going on?" Alex asked, swinging his legs out of bed and reaching for his clothes.

"Just a bit of fun," Skeld replied.

"Fun for some," Thrang grumbled, pushing Skeld off.

"You are too grim, Thrang," said Skeld, still laughing as he picked himself up off the floor. "You ponder the future and forget the day."

"I have not forgotten that we will each see the Oracle today," said Thrang in a serious tone.

Alex smiled and pulled on his shirt. He couldn't help but like Skeld; the big warrior was always laughing and joking. Stamping his feet into his boots, Alex hurried to follow his friends into the courtyard. Arconn stood next to the doorway, watching Alex as he approached.

"You were up late," Arconn commented. "Were you troubled in the night?"

"Too many thoughts," said Alex. "The night air helped calm my mind."

"And did the lady help as well?" Arconn asked, smiling at the stunned look on Alex's face.

"How did you know?" Alex questioned in a low voice.

"I see many things others do not," replied Arconn. "I was surprised to see her follow you to the stable, but perhaps I should not have been."

Alex stared at Arconn. He'd been sure his friends had all been asleep when he'd gone to the stables the night before.

"It is a small thing," Arconn continued, turning toward the doorway. "Your heart has been lightened and your thoughts are more clear. Because of that, I am happy for you. What happened is between you and the lady. Perhaps I should not have said anything."

"I'm not angry," Alex said at last. "I just didn't think anyone knew."

"As I said, it is a small matter," said Arconn. "Now, of greater importance, is breakfast."

Alex grinned. Arconn's words had been something of a shock, but he was glad his friend had seen him, though he didn't know why.

"Look out!" Alex heard Skeld yell just before a clump of oatmeal landed on his cheek. "Oh, not quick enough," Skeld laughed.

"Enough of your foolishness, Skeld," said Bregnest in a loud voice. "We will each see the Oracle today. It won't do for us to be covered in food."

"My apologies, master wizard," said Skeld, bowing to Alex and offering him a napkin. "My aim was off—I meant to hit Arconn."

"Enough!" commanded Bregnest. "Your jests drive all thought from my mind."

Skeld returned to his breakfast without comment, though he winked at Alex as he sat down. Alex was troubled by Bregnest's stern words; he seemed to be in a dark mood this morning, as if some great weight was pressing down on him.

Alex and his friends ate their meal quickly and quietly. It felt to Alex like they were all waiting for bad news—bad news they knew would be coming soon.

"My apologies, Skeld," Bregnest said softly as they were finishing their meal. "I am troubled by what the day may bring."

Skeld bowed to Bregnest, accepting his apology.

Alex was nervous. Last night, he'd felt at ease around Iownan, but today, she would speak to him as the Oracle. He wondered how different she would be. He hoped that, as the Oracle, she would answer some of his questions.

"You'd best collect your ring," said Thrang as they walked toward the tower. "The Oracle should be able to tell you what it is and if it has any magic in it."

Alex had forgotten about the ring in his magic bag, and he hurried back to the sleeping house to retrieve it. When Alex returned to his companions, Rothgar was waiting. He held a tall silver lamp that looked out of place in the early morning sunlight.

"The Oracle will speak with you individually," said Rothgar in a somber tone. "First, she will speak with Master Bregnest. Then, she will call the rest of you in turn. I will remind you all that what the Oracle says to each of you is for you alone. You may, in time, wish to share her words with others, but I would urge you to do so only with those you trust completely."

Bregnest stepped forward and bowed to Rothgar. Rothgar returned the bow, and then led Bregnest into the tower without another word.

"Have you spoken to many oracles?" Alex asked Thrang.

"A few," Thrang replied. "Though none as well-known as the lady of the White Tower."

Alex felt nervous and excited, like he was waiting to see the dentist on Christmas morning, only better and worse at the same time.

"Relax or you may pop," said Skeld, jabbing him in the ribs. "You should not worry before the ax falls."

"I'm just excited," said Alex with a weak smile.

After some time, Rothgar appeared again, carrying his silver lamp. Bregnest did not return with Rothgar, which added to Alex's nervousness.

"The lady asks that Master Goodseed come next," said Rothgar.

Alex watched as Andy and Rothgar exchanged bows. Without looking back at the company, Andy followed Rothgar and soon disappeared from view as he entered the tower.

"Where is Bregnest?" Alex questioned.

"In the gardens I should think," Arconn answered. "It is customary not to rejoin your company until all have spoken with the Oracle. Then, none will enter with expectations that may not be met."

Alex thought about Arconn's words for a moment and decided that they made sense. If Bregnest had returned to the company unhappy, the rest of them would believe the worst and expect bad news from the Oracle. However, if Bregnest returned happy, they would all expect good news, and that might not be the case either.

"What kinds of things will the lady tell us?" Alex asked Arconn.

"It is not the lady you see today," Thrang replied instead. "Today she is the Oracle."

"So what kinds of things will the Oracle tell us?" Alex persisted.

"An oracle's words are often vague," said Tayo. "Seldom are they simple to understand."

"And they are often misunderstood," Halfdan added. "Sometimes an oracle's words mean nothing until much time has passed."

"And sometimes they truly mean nothing at all," said Skeld with a grim laugh.

"You don't believe in oracles?" Alex asked.

"I don't disbelieve," Skeld answered. "The future is not yet written, so none may know what it holds. The Oracle gives guidance, but seldom a clear answer."

Alex remembered what Iownan had said to him the night

before, and he smiled at Skeld's reply. He thought Skeld might understand oracles better than any of his other friends.

It wasn't long before Rothgar reappeared, this time asking that Halfdan follow him. As the sun rose slowly into the sky, each member of the company was called into the tower. Tayo, then Skeld, and then Thrang, until only Arconn and Alex were left waiting.

"Is there some meaning in the order we are called?" Alex questioned, his nervousness almost unbearable.

"If there is, only the Oracle knows it," answered Arconn. "Though it is often thought best to be first or last to see an oracle."

"Why is that?"

"First is considered a place of honor, usually reserved for a leader or a king," Arconn answered slowly, considering his words. "Last is considered a place of respect, reserved for the wise, or wizards, or even other oracles."

"Have you spoken to many oracles?"

"Many more than our friend Thrang," Arconn replied with a laugh. "Perhaps more than all the others as well, though I seldom seek oracles for my own reasons."

"Then why do you seek them?" Alex asked.

"Mostly, as now, because the company has come here. You must remember that I am of the elder race and our fate is not the same as men or dwarfs."

"The elder race?" Alex questioned.

Before Arconn could reply, Rothgar appeared, though this time without his silver lamp.

"The lady asks that you join her, Master Taylor," said Rothgar, bowing low.

Alex returned his bow and followed Rothgar into the tower, not looking back at Arconn as the others had not looked back at him. He thought it odd that Rothgar had bowed to him first instead of waiting as he had for the others.

Rothgar did not speak as he led Alex down a corridor and up a long, spiral staircase. Alex was glad he had not been called last because that would mark him as a wizard for sure in his companions' eyes. As much as he liked Skeld, he was getting a little tired of his constant jokes.

He followed Rothgar up another staircase, sure they were high up in the tower. He wondered why Rothgar had been carrying the lamp before because the staircase was well-lit by windows placed at regular intervals. Eventually, they reached the top of the staircase and Rothgar stopped, turning to face Alex.

"I cannot lead you further," said Rothgar. "Climb the stairs at the end of this corridor. The Oracle awaits you at the top."

Alex wondered if this was normal, but Rothgar started down the stairs before he could ask. It seemed strange that Rothgar would leave him alone, but then he wondered if perhaps there was some greater meaning he didn't know about. It seemed to him almost everything surrounding the Oracle had some meaning he didn't understand.

At the end of the corridor, Alex climbed the stairs, counting as he went, trying to distract his worried thoughts. When he reached three hundred and sixty steps, the stairs ended. Alex stepped forward into a small, dim room.

"You wonder about many things," said Iownan's voice from in front of him. "You look for reasons and answers, yet find none."

"That is true," Alex replied.

"Why do you look?"

"So that I may understand."

"Will understanding help you?"

"I . . . I don't know."

"What is the one thing you wish for above all else?" asked the Oracle as she pulled back a curtain and let sunlight fill the room.

Alex blinked in the bright light. The figure standing before him looked like Iownan, but somehow he knew she wasn't the same person who had spoken to him last night in the stable. He knew he stood before the Oracle of the White Tower. Alex swallowed hard.

"I don't know."

"Surely there is something you hope for." She pulled open another curtain.

"To do well," Alex answered.

"To do well at what?"

"At whatever needs doing," said Alex, confused.

"And that makes you wiser than most," said the Oracle with a smile. "But you doubt your ability to do well. You think of yourself as a small matter."

"I am a small matter," said Alex. "I'm not special."

She shook her head. "You have been measured as a wizard.

You defeated a troll. Even now, your magic bag holds seven others that you have won back from a dark place."

"I think Blackburn made a mistake," said Alex in a shaky voice. "And I was just lucky when I fought the troll."

"And was it also luck that brought the great sword into your hand?"

"What great sword?" Alex questioned.

"The sword you carry," she replied. "Ask your friend Arconn to look at it. He will know it for what it is."

"But even that was luck," Alex protested. "I closed my eyes and picked it from a pile of swords."

"You may wish to call it luck, but is not luck a magical thing?"

"I don't understand," said Alex. "What are you trying to say?"

"I told you that I see possibilities," replied the Oracle. "In you, I see many, though you do not see them yourself."

"What possibilities? I'm nobody. I just walked into a book-shop and the next thing I knew, I was here."

"Not just anyone could walk into that shop, Alex, as I'm sure your friends have told you," she answered. "Not just any-one could be chosen as the eighth member of Bregnest's com-pany. And not just anyone could have so much luck."

"What are you saying then? That I *am* a . . . a wizard?"

"I will speak plainly so you will understand," she replied, the smile leaving her face. "This is not the normal way for an Oracle, but as you are young and know little of adventures, I will risk plain speech."

The Oracle paused for a moment as if thinking.

"I see in you many things—kindness, loyalty, courage, honor. You have the ability to be a great wizard, if you wish to be one, or a great warrior, if that is what you seek. You can be both or neither, depending on the choices you make."

"And what would you advise me to be?"

"I would advise you to follow your heart and not let your mind get in the way," answered the Oracle, the smile returning to her face. "If you follow what your heart tells you, in time, you may become both a wizard *and* a warrior. Perhaps something more than both."

"I will try," said Alex.

"Yet your doubts remain," she commented thoughtfully. "Perhaps that is good, as doubts often help keep pride in check."

"You know many things," said Alex as he thought about the Oracle's words. "You know my feelings and doubts, and still you tell me I can be a wizard and a warrior. I would not doubt your words, so I will try to do the best I can."

"It is well then," said the Oracle with a nod. "Now, you have something else to ask about."

"I do?"

"The ring you carry in your pocket," she reminded him. "You wish to know what it is."

"Oh, yes," said Alex, taking the gold-and-black ring from his pocket and holding it in his open hand.

"I cannot say what this ring is," replied the Oracle. "But I would tell you not to lose it, or sell it. And do not wear it—at least not until you know what it is."

"You *cannot* say, or *will not* say?" Alex questioned.

"I see you are already thinking like a wizard," she replied happily. "Let us say for now that I *cannot* say."

"As you wish," said Alex, bowing to the Oracle.

"Now you should go," she said. "Rothgar will meet you to guide you to the gardens."

Alex turned to leave, but as he started down the stairs he heard the Oracle call after him.

"Remember—doubts may check pride, but too much doubt will keep you from doing what must be done."

Alex thought about the Oracle's words as he descended the three hundred and sixty stairs to the corridor. Though she had given him much to think about, his thoughts no longer troubled him as they had before, and he was grateful that she had spoken so plainly to him.

At the end of the corridor, Rothgar was waiting as the Oracle had said he would be. Alex followed him down another staircase, and after several turns and more stairs, Rothgar led him into a garden. He bowed, then departed without saying a word.

Alex looked around the garden expecting to see the rest of the company, but he was alone. This didn't bother him, because he wanted some time to think about what the Oracle had said. He walked deeper into the garden, looking at the different plants and flowers that grew everywhere. Soon he heard the sound of falling water, and following the sound, he found Arconn sitting next to a large fountain.

"Your meeting with the Oracle went well then?" Arconn asked politely.

"Yes," said Alex, then stopped short. "Shouldn't you be speaking with the Oracle now?"

"I have no need," replied Arconn. "As I told you before, I am of the elder race."

"What does that mean, exactly? If you don't mind my asking," said Alex.

"We elves are the eldest race of thinking creatures—except perhaps for dragons," Arconn answered, looking at the falling water in the fountain. "We came first to all the known lands, though in some lands we have been forgotten."

"And why don't you need or want to speak with the Oracle?" Alex asked.

"Oracles are for mortals," replied Arconn, turning his attention back to Alex. "Though I have spoken with many, it has been only to gain wisdom, not to learn about myself."

"You are not mortal then?"

"You know nothing of elves," said Arconn with a laugh.

"Well, no," Alex admitted. "You're the first elf I've ever met."

"I will try to explain," said Arconn, looking back at the fountain. "Elves are not mortal as you think of it, though we can die. We do not grow old or sick, but we may become tired of life and choose to fade away. There are also a few of my race who have chosen to live and die as mortal men, though for most of my race, life is too pleasing and we choose to remain as we are."

"I think I understand," said Alex.

"Then we should join the others," said Arconn, standing and moving away from the fountain. "Though I doubt they've waited for us before eating."

Alex felt hungry as soon as Arconn mentioned food. He hadn't eaten since breakfast, and now it was well past midday.

"Do the others know that I was last?" Alex asked with some concern. "I mean . . . I didn't want to be last because . . ."

"Because I told you the last to see the Oracle was considered a wizard," Arconn finished for him. "Yes, they know you were last, but then they already know you are a wizard—or at least that you may become one. Even if you have doubts, the others believe what Blackburn and Iownan have said."

"My doubts are less than they were," said Alex.

"That is good," said Arconn, putting his hand on Alex's shoulder. "Doubts can hold you back when need calls."

"There is one other thing," said Alex, stopping again. "Iownan—I mean the Oracle—said I should ask you about my sword. She said it was a great sword and that you would know about it."

"Then we shall look at it this afternoon, after we have eaten, and I will tell you what I can," said Arconn.

CHAPTER NINE
THE PROMISE

Alex and Arconn found the others in a much better mood than they had been that morning. Even Tayo smiled as they entered the feasting house to join the company.

"At last," said Skeld, lowering his mug. "I thought you'd have to go hungry. Andy has been eating everything in sight."

"No, I haven't," Andy protested, spitting bits of food and throwing a hunk of bread at Skeld.

"There is more than enough," said Thrang, raising his mug as if to toast Alex and Arconn. "The lady's kitchens have left us wanting for nothing."

"Perhaps too much of your red ale," Skeld laughed, launching the bread Andy had thrown at him in the direction of Thrang's mug.

"It is a fair vintage," Thrang replied, slapping the bread away.

Alex and Arconn helped themselves from the three tables that were once again covered with food.

"You seem more at ease than you were this morning,"

commented Thrang, looking closely at Alex. "Did the Oracle tell you what you wished to hear?"

"Yes," replied Alex.

"It is not your concern," said Bregnest sternly to Thrang. "You know that the Oracle's words are private."

"Forgive me," said Thrang, smiling ruefully at Alex. "Perhaps Skeld is right—I've had too much ale."

Alex simply smiled, bowing his head slightly to accept Thrang's apology. He was happy, and the thoughts that had troubled him for so long now seemed distant. For the first time in a long while, he felt at peace.

Alex and Arconn ate their meal while the rest of their companions joked and picked at what remained on their plates. They spent their time talking happily, not worried about what tomorrow would bring. There was no reason to rush, and they were all relaxed.

"We should look at your sword," said Arconn as the company walked out into the afternoon sunlight. "Though I should tell you, my knowledge of swords is small."

"The Oracle said you would know about this one," Alex said, turning toward the sleeping house.

"Then bring it out into the sunlight," Arconn called after him. "It is too fine a day to be indoors."

Alex entered the sleeping house and picked up his sword. He remembered how easily the blade had passed through the troll's leg, as if his own effort was unimportant, and the strange heat he had felt during the fight. Picking up the scabbard, he saw that the inlayed swirls of gold still seemed to spell something, but he still couldn't make out what the words might be.

Leaving the sleeping house, Alex saw the others had gathered on the shady side of the bathhouse. Carrying his sword in both hands, he approached Arconn, who was laughing at one of Skeld's jokes. Arconn's laughter stopped as soon as he saw Alex's sword and his eyes widened in surprise.

"You recognize it then?" Alex asked.

"I do," said Arconn, his voice slightly higher than normal. "Though I never thought I would see such a weapon again."

"Can you tell me about it?" Alex held out the scabbard as the others gathered around to get a better look.

"I . . . I can," Arconn answered slowly. "Draw the blade so that I will be correct in what I tell you."

Alex drew the sword from its scabbard and held it up in the sunlight. The gold inlay flashed like fire in his hand, and Alex heard Arconn catch his breath.

"A well-made weapon," said Thrang, looking from the sword to Arconn and back again. "Looks like elfin work, though better than anything they've made in many years."

"Indeed it is," said Arconn, regaining his speech. "The Oracle was wise to have you ask me about it. Please, return it to its scabbard."

As Alex obeyed, Arconn looked at Andy. "You bought this at Blackburn's? He sold this to you?"

"Yes," Andy answered, looking worried. "He said it wasn't one of his swords, but that an adventurer had sold it to him.

He said it was as good as anything he'd ever made, maybe better."

"Better indeed," said Arconn with a laugh. "This sword is the one the elves call Moon Slayer. The name is written on the scabbard, though in the ancient language of the dark elves."

"Dark elves?" Alex questioned, concerned.

"Not evil elves as you might think," Arconn clarified. "They were called dark elves because they loved the earth. Mining ore and making wonderful things with it was their passion. They loved it as much as the dwarf races do, perhaps more."

"Not more," Halfdan stated in a defiant tone.

"At least as much then," said Arconn, bowing slightly to Halfdan.

"You speak of them in the past," said Skeld. "Are they no longer to be found?"

"Most of them were destroyed long ago," replied Arconn, sounding troubled. "The few who were left were scattered. Now most have faded away, overcome by the sorrows of the mortal lands." Arconn's eyes returned to the sword. "Men, goblins, even dwarfs, desired weapons and armor made by dark elves, as there has never been any better. Dragons hated them because not even their scales could protect them from a dark elf blade. The dark elves were wise, however, selling little of what they made. When they did sell a weapon, it was only to trusted friends."

"Do you know any more about this sword and its history?" Bregnest asked.

"Moon Slayer was the sword of many great warriors, but I'll not trouble you with their names and deeds," replied Arconn. "I also know that whatever price Blackburn asked it was nothing compared to the sword's true value. Indeed, in the elfin kingdoms, a treasure as great as a dragon's hoard would be given for such a sword."

"Then you made a good bargain," said Alex, looking at Thrang. "You paid for this sword, and I cannot claim it as my own."

Thrang looked at the sword and then at Alex. He seemed a little nervous, almost afraid, when he spoke.

"The sword is yours," said Thrang, his hand automatically stroking his beard. "I have no claim on it. You have chosen it— or perhaps it has chosen you. I offered to stand good for you, that is all. I won't go back on my word."

"You show great wisdom, Thrang Silversmith," said Arconn, nodding to the dwarf. "This sword chooses its own master, and it is clear it has chosen Alex."

Alex felt pleased that such a famous sword would choose him as its master. He hoped he would be able to live up to the ancient tradition of the sword, though he still had some doubts about his skill as a warrior.

"For as long as you carry Moon Slayer, you will find honor among the elves," Arconn said. "Keep it well, and it will keep you."

"Thank you," said Alex, bowing to Arconn. "You have told me a great deal. I see the wisdom of the Oracle in having me ask you about my sword."

"As do I," Arconn replied, glancing up at the tower.

Alex returned the sword to the sleeping house, though he was reluctant to leave it there. He placed it carefully beside his magic bag, then quickly rejoined his companions.

"A warrior *and* a wizard," said Skeld, slapping him on the back and grinning broadly. "You've come a long way in a short time, little brother."

The others laughed at Skeld's comments and so did Alex. He knew he was not a wizard or a warrior—at least not yet—but somehow, he knew he would be both someday.

As the shadows started to creep across the courtyard, Rothgar appeared, carrying a large book. He bowed politely to Bregnest before addressing the group.

"The lady Iownan asks for your forgiveness, as she cannot dine with you this evening. She asks also that I deliver this book into Master Taylor's hands. She thanks you for your kindness and bids you all a good evening."

When he finished speaking, Rothgar bowed to Alex and handed him the large book. The others crowded around Alex as Rothgar departed as quickly as he had appeared.

"Another gift from the lady? You must have made a great impression," said Skeld, looking over Alex's shoulder.

Alex waved him off but didn't say anything. The fine leather cover of the book was blank and he wondered what it might contain. He opened the book slowly and a note slipped out from inside the front cover.

My Friend,

Please accept this gift. It will aid you on your future journeys. I'm sure you will find it useful.

Iownan

Alex handed the note to Bregnest, who read it out loud while Alex examined the book more closely. The pages were covered with tight, spidery writing and there were drawings of different plants and animals, many of which Alex did not recognize.

"The lady calls you friend," Tayo commented, sounding impressed. "It is a great honor for an oracle to call you friend."

"What's the book then?" asked Thrang, pushing toward Alex.

"I'm not sure," said Alex, looking up. "I can't read what's written in it."

"What?" said Thrang in surprise. "You don't know how to read?"

"I can read," Alex protested. "But the writing in the book is like the magic book that Arconn gave me."

"It's elfin," said Arconn, looking over Alex's shoulder. "This appears to be a book of herb craft and healing potions."

"Elfin?" Alex asked in wonder. "Is the magic book written in elf too?"

Arconn smiled at Alex's question and looked at the note that Bregnest handed to him.

"The other book is a magic book, one not written by elves," replied Arconn, handing the note back to Alex. "Though many people use elfin letters in their writing because

166

it is easier to express your true meaning with them. You have not looked at the magic book for a long time now, have you?"

"I haven't really thought about it," said Alex, feeling ashamed that he had neglected Arconn's gift.

"Then we shall make time from now on," said Arconn firmly, patting Alex's shoulder. "I will teach you the elfin letters so you can read this book and the magic book as well."

"You are most kind," Alex replied with a bow. "I am in your debt."

"Not at all," said Arconn, returning the bow.

Alex took his new book back to the sleeping house. Carefully, he tucked Iownan's note inside the front cover, and then thumbed through some of the pages.

"You are eager to start then?" questioned Arconn from the doorway.

"Yes," replied Alex, looking up at Arconn. "I have a lot to learn."

"As do we all," said Arconn. "Shall we begin?"

"Yes, please."

For the rest of the evening Arconn sat beside Alex in the sleeping house teaching him the elfin way of writing. By the time Thrang called them to join the rest of the company for dinner, Alex had already learned the names and shapes of most of the elfin letters as well as how the letters joined to form words.

"You've done well," Arconn beamed at Alex. "I have never seen a man take to the elfin language so quickly. Most humans have great difficulty with the ways of elves."

"It seems natural," said Alex. "It's like this is something I already know and only need to remember."

"I'm not sure I understand," said Arconn in a thoughtful way.

"And I'm not sure I can explain," replied Alex. "It's like when I first saw my sword. I thought I could read something written in the swirls of gold, but when I blinked it was gone. What you're teaching me now is like that, only different."

"Then let us hope what you learn today is not gone tomorrow," said Arconn with a laugh.

Alex followed Arconn out of the sleeping house to join the rest of their companions in the second house. It was almost dark, but the moon was rising in the east. Alex looked up at the tower as they walked and wondered why Iownan could not join them. He felt sad and a little troubled that she could not be with them.

After eating another grand meal, Alex walked to the stables while the others headed to the sleeping house. Bregnest was telling them about his first adventure, but Alex wanted to see Shahree.

Shahree whinnied as Alex entered the stable and moved toward him in her stall. Alex stroked her forehead gently with his fingers but did not speak. He gazed into the horse's eyes, remembering how they had once scared him. Now he found comfort in those eyes, the comfort of a trusted friend.

Alex hoped Iownan would appear in the stable again, but she did not. After several minutes of waiting and thinking, he patted Shahree's neck and said goodnight to the horse. He walked out into the moonlight and looked up at the White Tower. Alex knew he and the others would soon leave this place and the thought made him sad.

Returning to the sleeping house, Alex found Arconn telling a story about the ancient elves. Alex listened closely and when Arconn would speak a name in the elfin language, he thought—or rather felt—he knew what it meant, though he could not explain the meaning in words.

Alex went to sleep that night with the elfin words in his mind, dreaming of things from the distant past.

The next morning as they were finishing breakfast, Bregnest stood to speak to the company. He had a stern look on his face, but he seemed happy just the same.

"Tomorrow we will depart," he said. "The parting will be a sad one, but our adventure and our quest are still ahead of us."

"Sad for Thrang and his loss of ale," Skeld commented, elbowing Thrang in the side.

"Sad for us all, I think," said Tayo. "It will be long before we eat such fine meals in such fine surroundings again."

"So eat while you can. I won't cook so much or so well on the road," said Thrang, laughing softly.

The day was warm and sunny and Alex walked in the courtyard and the nearby gardens. That afternoon, Arconn sat with him in the gardens, teaching him more of the elfin writing in his new book. Alex almost asked about the magic book he had ignored for so long, but then Arconn began teaching him to speak the elfin words out loud.

As darkness filled the courtyard, Rothgar appeared and again asked them to forgive Iownan for not joining them.

"My lady will see you in the morning," said Rothgar. "She wishes to speak to you all before you depart."

"We will await the lady's arrival," Bregnest replied with a deep bow.

Alex and his friends were subdued but happy that night at dinner. Skeld told them a story of when his company had been surrounded by bandits and almost killed. With a great deal of luck and a very clever plan, they had managed not only their escape, but also to capture many bandit horses as well. Alex's thoughts were not on Skeld's story, though he pretended to listen and managed to smile and laugh at all the right places. He was thinking of the road ahead of them and the troubles they might meet. He knew little about this wild land and less about adventures, but he knew enough to be concerned.

Once more after the evening meal, he went to the stables to see Shahree. Once more, he hoped Iownan would appear and talk to him. Once more, she did not. Alex thought about Iownan and her kindness as he rubbed Shahree's forehead. He thought of her words at their first dinner in the tower, and he wondered what it was she would ask them to do.

There were no stories that night in the sleeping house, and little talk. Everyone was busy checking their bags and making sure everything was ready for their departure in the morning. Bregnest rang the gong and asked the girl who appeared to bring him paper and pen. The girl bowed and departed, returning quickly with the requested items. Alex wondered why Bregnest had asked for something to write with, but he didn't ask.

Before the sun was up the next morning, Alex and his friends had gathered in the second house. Breakfast was waiting for them when they entered and they ate quickly and with little talk. Alex knew he was not the only one who would be sorry to leave the White Tower behind. When they finished their meal, Skeld, Tayo, and Halfdan went to the stables to saddle all the horses, while Alex and the others returned to the sleeping house to make sure nothing had been left behind.

When they exited the sleeping house, Iownan was waiting for them in the courtyard with her servants behind her, each one holding many parcels. She smiled kindly at them all, bowing slightly first to Alex and then to Bregnest. Alex blushed at the honor as he returned Iownan's bow. Iownan waited as Tayo, Skeld, and Halfdan brought the horses from the stable and joined their companions.

"We have brought you some things to take with you," said Iownan, waving her hand toward the servants. "I would not have you depart without improving your store of food as your journey may be a long one."

"You are most kind, lady," replied Bregnest with a bow. "We find great sorrow in leaving."

Iownan nodded. Her servants came forward and gave each member of the company several neatly wrapped and labeled parcels. Alex put his in his magic bag as quickly as he could, his eyes returning at once to Iownan.

"The road ahead may be cold as there is no guarantee that you will reach your goal before winter," said Iownan, still smiling. "So we have also prepared warm clothing and blankets."

"Your kindness is too great," said Bregnest with another bow. "We have not words to give thanks."

Iownan nodded once more. More servants came forward and more parcels were given to each member of the company.

"Now I will answer your question," said Iownan, her smile fading. "Though it troubles me greatly to ask such a thing of my guests."

"Ask what you will, great lady," said Bregnest. "If it is in our power, we shall do as you ask."

"You are very kind," Iownan replied, a weak smile returning to her face. "This is what I would ask of you all: that you return to me a lost treasure of the White Tower."

"What treasure of the tower has been lost?" Bregnest questioned in surprise.

"Long ago, there was a stone in the high places of the tower. It was not a gem; it was a crystal of clear stone, like glass, and it was stolen from the tower." Iownan looked pained as she spoke. "The stone is now hidden in Slathbog's hoard, so I ask that you return it to me, if your quest is completed successfully."

"If any of us remain alive when Slathbog is defeated, we shall return the stone to you," said Bregnest, dropping to one knee as he spoke. "This I pledge on my life and my honor, as leader of this company."

"Your pledge is great, Silvan Bregnest, and I know it to be true. But I will not hold any man to another's pledge and so must ask that each of you make his own pledge. If any of you feel you cannot make this pledge, I will not force it on you."

Arconn dropped to one knee beside Bregnest. "I shall pledge as Bregnest has. I will do as you ask."

The rest of the company followed Arconn's example, each kneeling and pledging that if they were still alive when Slathbog was dead, to return the crystal to the White Tower. The pledge took on more meaning for Alex as he said it out loud, and he saw once more Iownan's wisdom.

"True friends, you give me great hope," said Iownan, smiling at them. "Though there is great sorrow in our parting, ride now, and know my hopes and good wishes go with you."

Alex found himself unable to reply to Iownan's words. A strange feeling of joy was in his heart, along with a deep sorrow as well. The company mounted their horses without speaking, and each of them bowed to Iownan as they rode past.

Alex and his companions rode east toward the rising sun. They soon left the orchards and gardens of the White Tower behind, but they didn't look back. Alex's sorrow diminished as he rode, and only the joy of Iownan's kind words and smile remained with him.

Bregnest halted the company at the top of the first hill they came to, looking back at the White Tower before it was lost from sight. In soft voices, Alex and his friends each repeated their promise to Iownan, then turned away and rode on.

CHAPTER TEN

MAGIC SWORD

———◦◦◦|◦◦◦———

The road grew worse as Alex and his friends continued east. Grass and weeds grew over the path in several places and there were no bridges over the streams they had to cross. Alex thought the road hadn't been ridden over for a hundred years or more.

The day was clear and the sun grew hot as they traveled; it seemed the heat of summer would soon replace the pleasant warmth of spring in Vargland. Alex looked up at the clear sky, considering how far they still had to go. He had already traveled further on this adventure than he had ever gone in his life.

They camped early that first night away from the White Tower, finding a sheltered place a short distance off the road. There was less laughter now than there had been, but they all remained in good spirits.

"We should keep a watch again," said Bregnest as they ate their evening meal. "These wilder lands have many dangers."

"That is true," Thrang said. "Though I doubt we'll find any trouble so close to the White Tower."

They agreed that keeping a watch would be a good idea, and Bregnest marked eight stones and placed them in a bag for all members of the company to draw their watch as he had done before. Alex, with his normal luck, drew the stone marked for the first watch, which made him happy.

As the others prepared for sleep, Arconn remained by the fire with Alex. He asked Alex to bring out his books so they could continue their lessons. Alex was happy to do so since the book that Iownan had given him was turning out to be interesting, now that he could read parts of it. Arconn also insisted he try to read from the magic book, even though it was much harder to understand, even with Arconn's help.

"The book of magic is written with letters similar to the elfin," Arconn explained, "though they are not exactly the same. You will need to learn both. Learning the one will help with the other."

"Do the words mean the same thing in both books?" Alex questioned.

"At times they do," said Arconn as he considered the question. "But magic words are not elfin in nature. They are more difficult to speak and read, but also more powerful."

"There is power in the words?" Alex asked.

"All words have some power, whether written or spoken," Arconn replied with a soft laugh. "You know this already, as do all who can read or speak, but perhaps you have never thought of it that way before."

"Words have power to communicate and to tell us what things are," said Alex, thinking hard.

"Yes, that," Arconn agreed. "But words can do more than explain what things are. Words can give us knowledge and understanding. They can tell us of things as they once were, as they should be, or even as they might be."

"And that is power?" questioned Alex.

"Understanding and knowledge are the beginning of all power," answered Arconn. "It is late, and your watch has passed. Go sleep. We will continue tomorrow."

Alex left the fire and sat down on his blankets. He considered Arconn's words about understanding and knowledge. He wondered what Arconn meant by "should be" and "might be." He didn't see how understanding what something might be could be magical. Arconn's lessons were not nearly as simple as Thrang's *inferno* and *quench* commands had been. Alex's questions and the magic letters continued to bounce through his mind as he slowly fell into a deep sleep.

The next morning, Alex woke early, his thoughts about magic vanishing in the night, but Arconn's lessons continued. As the company rode, Arconn would occasionally ride to one side or the other and climb off his horse. When he caught up to the group again, he would stop next to Alex and Andy. He would hand a leaf or twig or a seed to Alex and ask him to identify it. Most of the items Alex recognized from studying Iownan's book. When Alex could not tell Arconn what an item was and what it was used for, Arconn would simply smile and place the item in a leather pouch that hung from his saddle. Alex knew Arconn would bring these items out again when he had read more and could identify them.

By the end of their third day away from the White Tower, the weather turned wet once more. Low clouds filled the sky, and the wind picked up from the west. The road led them more to the south, though their main direction remained east.

"Summer rains are coming," said Tayo as they ate their dinner.

"At least it's not cold," Skeld replied with a laugh. "Though wet is wet, no matter the temperature."

"Wind and rain are allies to bandits," Bregnest commented thoughtfully, scanning the area around their camp.

The hills they had been riding through were small and had spread out. The small meadows had grown into wide open fields with only a few clumps of trees and small hills between them.

"We should stay alert," Bregnest continued, returning his gaze to the company.

"Alert and quiet," Thrang added, glancing at Skeld.

That night, Alex had a hard time reading as he sat beside the fire with Arconn. His mind was occupied with thoughts of bandits and the trouble that could mean. Arconn seemed strangely watchful as well, as if he were waiting for something. He would gaze into the darkness for long periods of time as Alex read aloud, seeming to pay no attention to what Alex was saying.

"Are there really bandits this close to the White Tower?" Alex asked as he finished his reading.

"We are far from the tower now," replied Arconn, his eyes fixed on the darkness. "Bandits have little respect for anything, even an oracle."

"Will they try to kill us?" Alex questioned nervously.

"Perhaps. Though I think they would try to steal our horses first. A company on foot is easier prey."

"Andy said bandits would attack first and steal our horses later," Alex commented, remembering Andy's words at the Troll's Stream.

"Andy has little experience with bandits. Though at times they will attack first and steal later."

Alex stood beside Arconn and looked into the darkness, but he couldn't see anything at all. He listened as hard as he could, but all he heard was the wind moving through the nearby trees.

"Perhaps we should build the fire up."

"That would draw them like moths, if there are any about," said Arconn. "Take your rest. Your watch has passed and mine is just beginning."

Alex did as Arconn said, putting his books back inside his magic bag as he moved to the tent he and Andy shared. They had been sleeping under the stars, but with the threat of rain, they had set up their tents as a precaution. Alex looked back at his friend before entering the tent; Arconn remained still and silent, gazing into the darkness.

They followed the road for several more days, seeing no sign of anyone or anything as they went. Each night, Arconn would teach Alex, who was learning quickly; Arconn seemed happy and impressed with his progress.

"Soon you will be able to read elfin as well as any man, and better than many elves," said Arconn with a smile as Alex put his books away.

"You are a good teacher," Alex replied.

Arconn did not reply, his eyes turning suddenly from Alex to the darkness around the camp. Alex followed Arconn's gaze, but he could see only darkness.

"What is it?" Alex questioned softly.

"Perhaps nothing," replied Arconn, his gaze remaining on the darkness. "Perhaps something. I have felt for several days that we are being watched."

"Should I wake the others?"

"No," said Arconn. "The danger is not close. Not yet."

Alex felt nervous and tense as he lay down on his blankets. Anticipation filled his mind and he found it difficult to sleep. He pulled his sword closer to him, letting his hand rest on the hilt. The cold metal seemed to ease his worries, and slowly he fell into a fitful sleep.

A hand covered Alex's mouth and he jerked awake, wanting to cry a warning to his friends. His hand gripped tightly around his sword.

"Stay quiet," Thrang's voice whispered. "Trouble's close. Pull on your boots and come outside. Quickly."

Alex could hear Andy moving in the darkness, but his eyes would not focus. He pulled on his boots and rubbed his eyes, trying hard to shake off sleep. Fastening Moon Slayer to his belt, he followed Andy out of the tent. He could breathe better in the open air, but he was still having trouble seeing. Clouds filled the sky, hiding the moonlight, but he could make out the gray outlines of his companions standing near the cold fire pit. As quietly as he could, Alex moved toward them, his senses becoming sharper with each step.

The wind had died down, allowing a strange silence to settle over the campsite. Alex could hear trees creaking softly in the light breeze, but what he focused on was the sound of horses in the distance, moving slowly from side to side.

"They will come soon," whispered Thrang. "Be ready."

Alex and his friends spread out, forming a line in front of their camp. Thrang was next to him on his right, Andy on his left. To Thrang's right stood Halfdan and then Bregnest, but there was no sign of Tayo, Skeld, or Arconn. Alex gripped his sword tightly, worried about his friends.

"Where are the others?" Alex asked nervously, keeping his voice lowered.

"Close," Thrang replied, lifting his ax to a fighting position.

Alex followed Thrang's example and drew Moon Slayer from his side. The blade shimmered black in the darkness, a hint of blue running down the sharp edges. Alex felt a strange heat growing inside him as he held the sword and waited for battle. It was the same heat he had felt when he fought the troll, though he hadn't noticed it then. A powerful desire to rush into battle grew in his chest and mind, but he resisted it, thinking it was just his nerves.

Suddenly the sound of horses grew louder, moving fast, no longer shifting from side to side but coming straight toward the camp.

Alex felt his stomach tighten, knowing that any moment he would have to fight and kill if he wanted to stay alive.

From out of the darkness, the dim outline of men on horses appeared, and Alex heard a terrible yell from the bandits as they charged. Alex and his friends raised their own battle cry when the bandits came into view. Alex saw some of the horsemen turn quickly to ride away, surprised to see an armed company ready to fight, but the rest charged forward wildly. Alex stood firm with his companions, afraid, but ready to meet the charging bandits and his fate.

The noise of steel meeting steel filled the air around him, followed by the groans of wounded and dying men. Alex side-stepped a charging horse, swinging Moon Slayer at the rider's body as hard as he could. He didn't think to strike a second time, but quickly looked for another enemy to fight. A strange madness filled his mind as he wielded his sword, a madness that drove him recklessly into the battle. To Alex, his movements felt natural but strangely alien as well. There was no time for him to think even if he'd been able to focus his mind. He had to attack the bandits if he wanted to stay alive, and he did attack. Without hesitation, without thought, and without fear, Alex rushed into battle as a great happiness and a deep sorrow filled his heart and mind.

The bandits quickly changed their minds about the attack and turned their horses to flee. They let out another scream as they tried to make their escape. Skeld, Tayo, and Arconn were waiting for them, ready to attack them from behind. Again

ADVENTURERS WANTED: SLATHBOG'S GOLD

there was the sound of steel on steel as more bandits fell from their horses.

Alex rushed toward the remaining bandits he could see, slashing at them as they tried to break away. He felt a great heat inside his body as he attacked, swinging his sword wildly at everything on horseback. His movements were quicker now, and he could see his enemies clearly in the darkness, as if some strange light illuminated them. Running forward, Alex fought to stop the bandits from escaping, cutting down any who came near him.

As quickly as it had begun, the battle was over. Alex spun around, wildly looking for more bandits, but there were none left. The heat inside him began to cool quickly, and as it cooled, darkness clouded his vision.

"Are you all right, Alex?" asked Arconn, standing at a distance. "Is the heat leaving you?"

"Yes," replied Alex, suddenly feeling tired and weak. "What . . . what happened to me?"

"It is the sword," said Arconn, stepping a little closer. "Its power entered you, its master."

Alex didn't reply but looked down at the sword in his hand. The sword's edges gleamed bright blue, as if tiny flames raced up and down the blade. It looked beautiful in the darkness, and Alex felt a surge of fierce pride that Moon Slayer was his sword.

"You didn't tell me this would happen," said Alex, his eyes turning to Arconn. "I mean, having the power of the sword enter me."

"I wasn't sure it would," replied Arconn with a slight smile. "I have heard stories, but I have never seen it happen. At least, not until tonight."

"We all saw it," said Andy, coming up beside Alex. "It was amazing. If I hadn't seen it myself, I'd never have believed it."

"What did you all see?" Alex asked, fear growing inside of him.

"A strange, pale light," Bregnest replied softly, watching Alex closely, a look of wonder on his face. "Like you were glowing. Not like a lamp, but like a beam of moonlight in the darkness."

"Indeed he was," said Thrang, looking from Alex to Bregnest. "I've heard stories too, but never thought I'd see something like this."

"What does it mean?" Alex asked in a troubled voice.

"The fire of a great warrior was lit inside of you this night," replied Arconn. "The sword has chosen its true master, and now we all know why the sword was named Moon Slayer."

"But I'm not a great warrior," Alex protested.

"Tell that to the bandits," said Skeld with a grim laugh.

Alex looked at the ground in surprise. Around him lay the bodies of the bandits he had killed. A spark of fear ran through him as he realized what he had done. Without thinking, he had rushed into the charging bandits and killed them. How many had he killed? He wasn't sure.

What troubled Alex most was that now that the battle was over, he felt nothing toward the dead bandits. He had simply done what he had to do. There were no feelings of guilt or sorrow or even happiness. There was only the knowledge that he'd done what had to be done—he'd killed the enemy. The whole battle seemed like some half-forgotten dream.

"This can't be," said Alex, looking at his companions helplessly.

"It is," said Arconn in a kindly voice. "It is part of what you are. You cannot change what you are any more than you can change the sun or the sky. You can only accept it, and learn to use your gifts wisely."

Alex took a deep breath and let out a sigh. He knew Arconn was right and that the warrior inside him was a part of his true self.

"What now?" Alex asked, wiping Moon Slayer on the grass and returning it to his side.

"We'll wait for daylight," said Bregnest. "Then we'll search the bandits for anything of value."

"Isn't that stealing?" Alex asked with a weak smile.

"They're dead," Skeld laughed. "And they are bandits."

Alex knew the bandits would have killed them and stolen their things if they could have. He also knew from reading the *Adventurer's Handbook* that bandits fell into the same group of evil creatures as goblins and trolls. It wasn't stealing, but Alex didn't like the idea of searching the dead bodies.

Thrang relit their campfire and they gathered around the flames to wait for dawn. Thrang cooked breakfast, muttering to himself about Alex's moonlight glow. He seemed amused by the evening's events, even if Alex wasn't. When the eastern sky started to grow light, Skeld and Halfdan rode off in search of the bandits' horses.

The darkness slowly changed to a dull gray as the sun came up behind the clouds. The air smelled like rain as Alex and his companions returned to the dead bandits. Alex wished it would rain and wash away the smell of death and the color of blood. He felt strange, going through the pockets of the dead bandits, but the others didn't seem to mind at all. They placed everything of value they found, including weapons, near their fire pit. Then they piled the dead bandits downwind from their camp.

"Slim pickings," commented Thrang, tossing a bandit onto the pile. "Bandits never have much of value."

"Then why bother?" Alex asked, struggling to drag a body to the pile himself.

"You never know," replied Thrang, helping Alex toss the dead bandit onto the pile. "You might find something wonderful from time to time. Besides, every little bit helps to build the fortune."

Once they had piled the bodies, they gathered wood and put it on top of the stack. Thrang ignited the piled wood with his *inferno* command, standing back to watch as the flames spread. Alex watched with Thrang as the fire consumed the dead men, and then he turned and walked back to the campfire. He tried not to think about the bandits burning a short distance away, but it was difficult not to. It was one thing to kill a troll and have it turn to stone, but this was something else.

"Not much," said Bregnest, separating the small pile of

treasure into eight smaller piles. "Though the horses will bring a fair price in Techen."

"Techen?" Alex questioned.

"A small city, four or five days' ride from here," Bregnest answered. "I hadn't planned to stop there, but if we have horses to sell, it will be worth it."

"And we might be able to get some information about Varlo and the lands around it," added Thrang.

"Varlo is the resting place of Slathbog," explained Arconn before Alex could ask. "It was an ancient city, and very rich. Which is why the dragon came there, of course."

"How much do we know about Varlo?" Alex asked.

"Little more than what Arconn has just said," Thrang replied. "We do know there was a great castle, its foundation set deep in the mountain's side."

"And deep in the mountain is where the worm will be hidden," said Tayo in a grim tone. "He's not likely to leave his hoard above ground."

Alex knew almost nothing about dragons and what they would or would not be likely to do. The *Adventurer's Handbook* said little about dragons and nothing about Slathbog. He wondered how much more his companions could tell him about dragons, certain he would need all the information he could get before facing Slathbog.

Skeld and Halfdan returned with a string of twenty horses. The horses looked well cared for, which surprised Alex. He thought they would be unhealthy and uncared-for creatures, judging by what he'd seen of the bandits who had been riding them.

"We found these easily enough," said Skeld with his normal smile. "The others have run further than we cared to follow."

"Anything in the saddlebags?" questioned Thrang.

"We haven't looked," Halfdan replied, glancing back at the horses. "Thought it best to come back with these than wait around for an arrow in the back."

"You mean there are more bandits out there?" Alex asked in a concerned tone.

"If there are, they are few," Bregnest replied. "And after last night's events, they'll stay well clear of us."

Skeld and Halfdan dismounted and began taking the saddlebags off the captured horses. To Thrang's delight, the contents of the saddlebags more than tripled the amount of treasure they had to divide. Alex hesitated, thinking that the bandits were men after all and not monsters.

"Don't trouble yourself over them," said Tayo, watching Alex's face. "Once a man becomes a bandit, he is no longer truly a man."

"I don't understand," said Alex.

"They become wild and cruel," said Thrang, taking notice of the discussion. "Bandits don't care about nothing but stealing and killing. In most lands there's a bounty on them. They're nothing more than a plague to all people."

Alex nodded his understanding and took his share of the

treasure, trying to forget his misgivings about the bandits being men.

"We'll ride to Techen," said Bregnest as they prepared to depart. "If the rains hold off, we should make it in four days."

"And if the rains come, it will be five or six," Skeld replied. "And the horses won't look so good when we try to sell them."

"Then I expect you to take care of them," answered Bregnest with a smile. "And if they don't fetch a fair price, you'll make up the difference to us all."

Skeld laughed loudly and Alex wondered if anything ever dimmed his happy mood. Skeld's endless happiness made Alex's heart feel lighter so he was glad that Skeld was with them.

The rains held off for two days as the company rode toward Techen and they made good time both days. The morning of their third day, though, the rain started falling, building into a terrific downpour before midday. Alex and his friends moved slowly along the muddy and slick road. The rain continued as they stopped to camp for the night.

"At least we can eat without getting any wetter," Skeld laughed, shaking his head like a dog.

The company's mood had darkened slightly because they were all soaked to the skin and unhappy about it. The muddy road had slowed their progress as well, and Bregnest said he thought it would be at least two more days before they reached Techen.

"Remember, when we reach Techen, we are trading horses. Nobody is to speak of our goal to anyone," warned Bregnest.

"I will make a few inquiries about Varlo and see if there is anything I can learn."

The company agreed with Bregnest's plan, though Alex thought eight adventurers turning up and trading bandit ponies was sure to attract interest from the people of Techen. If anyone knew anything about Varlo, they would quickly suspect that Alex and his friends were headed there.

"Perhaps they will," agreed Arconn when Alex spoke his mind that night during his watch. "But many adventurers come and go on different quests and most ask about Varlo."

"If they're on a different quest, why do they ask?" Alex questioned.

"For future reference," replied Arconn. "Every adventurer dreams of one day seeking a dragon's hoard, as that is one of the richest quests an adventurer can go on. So, many will ask, but few will ever attempt the challenge."

"Is it really that dangerous?" Alex asked.

"It won't be easy," answered Arconn. "Though nothing of importance ever is. Bregnest is following a dream of his own, and a prophecy. Both will help us, I think."

"Prophecy?"

"Yes, but it is not mine to speak of," said Arconn. "We will discuss what I know of dragons tomorrow night during your watch. Though I know little enough, I may know as much as any other."

"May I ask you something else?" Alex questioned.

"You should rest, your watch has passed," said Arconn.

"It's about my sword," said Alex. "About the feelings I had when we were fighting the bandits."

"Ah, I wondered how the sword might affect you," said Arconn. "Many emotions are bound to the magic of your sword. Tell me, what did you feel?"

"It is hard to explain, but while I was using the sword, I felt almost like laughing out loud and crying at the same time."

"And after the battle?"

"I didn't really feel anything after. I just . . . well, I just knew that I'd done what was needed. I didn't feel happy or sad or anything."

Arconn looked into the darkness beyond the fire. "The elves who made your sword took great joy and pride in their work, yet they also had great sorrow because they were forced to create weapons of destruction. The magic they put into your sword holds both their joy and their sorrow. So when the magic enters you . . ."

"I feel their emotions as well," said Alex.

"Yes. I would guess the joy was greater, as the sword was being used to destroy evil. Still, it is a terrible kind of joy, one tempered by much sorrow."

"Yes," said Alex. "It was a terrible joy."

"Do not be troubled, Alex," Arconn went on. "The emotions will always be there, but I think, in time, they will not trouble you so much."

"Thank you for telling me what you know," said Alex, bowing to Arconn and then making his way to his tent.

The next morning dawned bright and clear. The clouds

had drifted away during the night, and the sun came out to dry the waterlogged land. They made good progress that day, but as night crept across the land, there was still no sign of Techen.

That night during his watch, Arconn told Alex all he knew about dragons, which was more than Alex would have guessed.

"Forgive me for saying so, but you seem to have great respect for dragons," said Alex, as Arconn finished speaking.

"Indeed I do," said Arconn with a slight smile. "They are powerful and magical creatures; some of them are very noble. It is said in some lands they are friendly to other races. Still, they are all dragons at heart."

"And what does that mean?" Alex asked.

"As with all people, they are what they are," replied Arconn, shrugging. "They have their own nature, and that is to be a dragon. Most dragons are considered evil because they lust for treasure and never seem to have enough. Some, however, have overcome that lust, or perhaps never had it. Those few dragons are very wise." Arconn's voice dropped to a whisper. "One last thing you should know about dragons: Never look a dragon in the eye unless you are sure you are stronger than it is."

"Why?" Alex asked, wondering if anyone could really be stronger than a dragon.

"Dragons are magical. They have powers of their own that only they understand. If you look them in the eye, they can capture you in a spell."

"Can the spell be broken?"

"It is said that once the dragon looks away, the spell will be broken," replied Arconn. "Though I've never heard of anyone escaping a dragon once he had gazed into the dragon's eyes."

Alex considered everything Arconn had told him about dragons. He wondered what might be seen in a dragon's eyes, and if it would be worth the risk of looking.

That night, Alex dreamed about dragons and the mysteries hidden behind their eyes. He dreamed that he could look into a dragon's eyes without fear, but before he could look, it was morning, and time to ride on.

CHAPTER ELEVEN
TECHEN

It was almost noon the next day when Alex and his friends reached the city of Techen. It was not a large city nor was it a fair city to look at. Most of the buildings were short and brown, their walls cracked and bulging. The tallest buildings Alex could see were several towers built into the wall around the city. The towers were twice as high as anything else, and Alex was amazed they could stand so tall when they looked so close to falling down.

"It's not much to look at," said Andy, riding next to Alex. "But if half the tales are true, the stop will be worth it."

"Why?" questioned Alex.

"They say a feast in Techen is worth two in any other city," Andy replied with a smile.

"It would have to be something special to make up for the city's appearance," Alex commented in a lowered tone.

"The food is supposed to be incredible," Andy continued, taking no notice of Alex's comment. "They say that this is where most of the really great ideas in food were started."

"And Master Goodseed would know a bit about food,"

Skeld laughed happily from behind Alex. "I've noticed he never gets enough of Thrang's cooking."

Skeld and Halfdan had been riding at the rear of the company, leading the bandit horses they had captured. Andy turned around quickly to reply to Skeld's comment, but both Skeld and Halfdan were already laughing too hard to hear anything he had to say.

Alex smiled to himself but managed to keep from laughing as well.

He noticed Andy's attention focus on the city as they approached the main gates, and he tried to see what Andy found so interesting there.

"Hold," a voice commanded from the gate. "State your names and business."

"Silvan Bregnest and company," Bregnest replied loudly. "We have come to sell horses, if there are any here who would buy."

"Indeed, yes, there are. We'll have a look," answered the voice.

A small door in the main gate opened and a short man with a round, good-natured face stepped out. He wore a black uniform with dark green edging on the cuffs and collar, and two rows of shiny brass buttons running down the front. Alex thought the man looked a little old to be a guard.

"These are not wild horses," said the man, looking at the horses behind Skeld and Halfdan. "These are bandit horses."

"You speak truly, sir," said Bregnest, climbing off his own horse and walking toward the man in uniform. "We were attacked some days ago by bandits and captured these after the attack."

"Well, then, that is something," the man replied, looking closely at Bregnest. "I count twenty horses and only eight of you. How many of your company were lost in the attack?"

"None," answered Bregnest. "We were fortunate; the bandits did not take us unaware."

"Indeed," said the man, a look of wonder on his face. "Most fortunate I should say, and very lucky as well."

"Perhaps so," Bregnest agreed. "Now, may we enter your fine city to sell these horses?"

"Oh, yes," the man replied quickly. "My apologies, Master Bregnest. We have seen few travelers of late, and travelers with bandit horses to sell . . . well, that is something unheard of in years. I'm quite sure the magistrate will want to meet you."

"We will be pleased to meet the magistrate," said Bregnest with a slight bow. "But first we will need a place to stable these horses. Can you name where we can get a fair price?"

"Oh, yes, yes indeed," the man beamed. "Tantic's would be your best bet. Old man Tantic has a fine stable and is a good judge of horses. He also keeps a pleasant inn next to his stables so you and your companions can find a place to rest as well."

"And where might we find Master Tantic and his inn?" Bregnest asked politely.

"Up the main street and left at the square," the man replied. "Tell him Bartholomew the gatekeeper sent you. I'm sure he will be most helpful."

"Our thanks," said Bregnest, bowing slightly before returning to his horse.

Bartholomew called for the main gate of Techen to be opened. The few guards present watched as the company rode through the open gates, and then they quickly closed the gates.

"I'll let the magistrate know you're staying at Tantic's," Bartholomew called after Bregnest. "I'm sure he'll be along directly to see you."

Bregnest led the company up the main city street to the square. Alex thought the buildings looked even worse close up than they did from a distance. He was beginning to think Andy had been joking when he'd been talking about the excellent food because everything in Techen looked rather shabby and dull. He was about to say something to Andy when the smell of something delicious reached his nose.

"It seems the stories are true," said Andy with a wide smile, before Alex could speak.

"Yes, it does," Alex quickly agreed.

Alex let his attention settle on the wonderful smells filling the air. He had never smelled anything like it before, and his opinion of Techen went up with each new scent that reached his nose. He detected fresh bread and honey, roasted meats, spices, and surprisingly, chocolate. Alex tried to enjoy each individual scent, but with so many in the air it wasn't easy to do. For a moment he thought he could smell caramel, but it was soon lost to a wonderful blend of maple syrup and sausages.

Alex hardly noticed when the company turned left at the

square and made their way to Tantic's inn and stable. The yard around the inn seemed deserted however, and the stable was empty. Alex realized the only people he had seen in Techen were the gate guards and Bartholomew. Even the square had been empty as they rode past.

"Very quiet for so large a town," commented Halfdan. "You'd think there would be someone about."

"The people of Techen are suspicious of strangers," said Skeld, his smile as bright as ever. "All the horses will make them more suspicious of us."

"Hello, there!" a man called from the inn. "And what may I do for you?" Alex thought that the man's tone of voice sounded like someone welcoming unwanted relatives who turned up unexpectedly and needed a place to stay.

"Perhaps a great deal," said Bregnest. "Can you direct me to Master Tantic?"

"Indeed I can," replied the man curtly. He was a short, balding man who looked a great deal like Bartholomew the gatekeeper. He wore a dark blue coat and black pants with high black boots. "And who might you be, and what reason might you have to seek Tantic?"

"I am Silvan Bregnest. The gatekeeper Bartholomew informed us that Master Tantic might be interested in buying some horses from us."

The man looked from Bregnest to the horses behind Skeld and Halfdan. "Bandit ponies, I should say. They seem to have lost their masters."

"Indeed they have," replied Bregnest with a smile. "So we thought we should find them a new master."

"There is wisdom in that," said the man with a slight smile. "Well then, if that's your business, I'll speak more plainly. I am Tantic, and I am interested in buying horses. However, the day is growing warm and this is not the place to discuss business."

"Then perhaps your inn is a better place," Bregnest suggested. "We would spend the night, if you will have us."

"Very well then," Tantic replied, his tone becoming friendlier. "You'll have to stable your own horses. The rest can go in the corral there." Tantic motioned to the corral next to the stable, walking over to unlatch the gate.

"I suppose you'll want to sell the saddles and trappings as well," said Tantic, looking over the bandits' horses.

"If that is acceptable," answered Bregnest, dismounting and giving his horse's reins to Arconn. "We have no need for saddles without horses."

"No, of course not," Tantic agreed, swinging the wooden gate of the corral wide open. "What would you want with saddles and no horses? Common sense you'd want to sell the saddles as well."

Tantic watched the horses closely as Skeld and Halfdan led them into the corral. He seemed pleased with what he saw. He closed the gate behind Skeld and Halfdan, and then stood looking over the horses. Alex and the rest of the company dismounted and led their horses into the stable while Bregnest remained with Tantic by the corral.

Inside the stable, they found the stalls were empty, though there was a good supply of hay and oats. They quickly unsaddled their horses and made their way back toward the stable door. Alex lingered behind, making sure Shahree had plenty of food and water.

"A fine-looking animal," said a thin, reedy voice. "Would you consider selling her?"

"Not for any price," replied Alex, turning around to see an old man standing behind him.

"Then you are wise," said the old man. "I see there is a bond between you two, and she would not willingly take another master."

"You see much," said Alex, feeling uncomfortable under the old man's gaze.

The old man walked toward Shahree's stall, moving slowly, his left leg dragging a little behind him as he moved forward.

"Tell your leader that I have information," whispered the old man to Alex, looking over his shoulder to make sure they were alone. "I will speak with him, if he will allow it."

"Information?" Alex could see the old man was excited and nervous. "What kind of information?"

"About Varlo," the old man replied, looking over his shoulder again. "Information that may prove profitable."

"I will tell him," said Alex carefully. "However, I can't say if he will speak to you or not."

"I will come tonight, after you have eaten," said the old man. "When the locals have left the inn, I will speak with your leader."

"As I said," Alex replied, turning to close Shahree's stall. "I don't know if he'll talk to you or not."

There was no reply to his words. When Alex turned around, the old man was gone.

Alex left the stable, worried by the old man's words. He found the others waiting for him just outside the inn. Tantic and Bregnest were deep in conversation about the horses, and Alex knew he would have to wait before he could tell Bregnest about the old man.

"It's true we have few horses these days," Tantic said as Alex approached. "The city guards have taken most of them. They think they can catch the bandits if they have horses of their own."

"And they have not been able to catch the bandits?" questioned Bregnest.

"They don't know the land as well as the bandits do," Tantic replied, spitting in the dirt. "And they don't ride or take care of their horses as well either."

"Then we have done a service to Techen," replied Bregnest in casual tone.

"A great service," Tantic agreed. "Though the magistrate will be suspicious of it. He won't like the fact that you've done what his guards could not. I doubt he'll offer you any reward."

"But we were not chasing bandits. They came to us," said Bregnest with a smile.

"True enough," Tantic admitted, leading them all into the inn. "Still, the magistrate will not be happy about it. He'll be even less happy when he finds out I've already bought the horses from you."

"Then we must settle on a price," said Bregnest in a more businesslike tone.

Tantic rubbed his chin, muttering numbers to himself. He seemed lost in his own thoughts, taking no notice of Bregnest or the rest of the company for several minutes.

"I'll give you twenty-five gold for each horse," said Tantic, a satisfied look covering his face. "Though I'll tell you straight, the magistrate will pay me at least thirty."

"Twenty-five for each horse?" Bregnest repeated, his tone uncommitted. "And for the saddles and trappings?"

"Twenty-seven for all then," Tantic answered quickly. "And room and board for the night as well."

Bregnest considered the offer for several minutes, watching Tantic closely, but the innkeeper did not fidget or change his offer.

"A fair price," Bregnest agreed. "Shall we have a drink to seal the bargain?"

"Indeed, yes, my friends," said Tantic, a broad smile on his face. "And a second drink to the magistrate's unhappiness."

Alex followed the rest of the company into the main bar, his thoughts still on the old man from the stable. He wanted to talk to Bregnest right away, but knew he would have to wait.

"The bargain," toasted Tantic, lifting a glass.

"The bargain," Bregnest and the rest of the adventurers repeated, raising their own glasses.

Alex swallowed the liquid from his glass, and his throat

began to burn. The drink was something he had never tasted before, and for a moment it took his breath away. His throat tightened and he had to struggle for a minute to catch his breath.

"To trouble for the magistrate," said Tantic, raising his glass a second time.

Alex was unable to repeat the words because he couldn't seem to find his voice, but he did manage to raise his glass.

"A strong brew," said Skeld, slapping Alex on the back.

"Yes," Alex managed to reply with a cough, his eyes watering.

"You should be more careful when you don't know what's in the glass," said Skeld, laughing happily.

Alex nodded. He set his glass down and left the rest of the drink untouched.

"You seem troubled," said Arconn, stepping up to Alex's side. "And by more than the strong drink."

"I need to speak with Bregnest," replied Alex, lowering his voice. "There was an old man in the stable. He says he has information."

"Hold your thoughts," said Arconn. "I'll let Bregnest know, and we'll find a quiet place to talk."

Bregnest collected their payment from Tantic and turned to face the company. As he turned, Arconn spoke softly into his ear. Bregnest nodded but didn't look in Alex's direction. He moved to a round table near a large fireplace and sat down. The rest of the company spread out around the main room, taking seats and ordering drinks for themselves.

Bregnest called them to him one at a time to give them their share of the payment, calling Alex last of all. As Alex approached Bregnest he noticed that Arconn remained seated next to Bregnest.

"Here you are," said Bregnest, pushing a pile of coins toward Alex. "Sixty-seven gold and six silver. Not bad for so little work."

"It seems a fair price," replied Alex, taking a seat and putting the coins into the small pouch he'd bought in Telous.

"What do you have to tell me?" Bregnest questioned, leaning toward Alex and lowering his voice.

"There was an old man in the stable," Alex reported. "He said to tell you he had information about Varlo, and that it would be profitable for you to listen."

"It seems our adventure has been guessed by at least one," Arconn commented softly.

"And profitable information is seldom free," Bregnest added. "What more did this old man have to say?"

Alex thought for a moment, trying to remember the exact words. "He said he would come tonight, after we had eaten and the local people had left the inn. He said he would come and speak to you, Bregnest."

"Did he call me by name?" Bregnest asked, concerned.

"No," Alex replied quickly. "He said he would speak to the leader of our company. I tried to tell him that I didn't know if you'd talk to him or not, but he didn't seem to care."

"Well, then, we can do nothing but wait," said Arconn.

"We will wait," Bregnest repeated. "And tonight we will see what this old man has to say."

"He will want money, of course," Arconn said flatly, echoing Bregnest's own words. "Information is almost never free."

"We will hear what he has to say before we agree to pay for anything," replied Bregnest, a stern look on his face. "For now, let's see what Tantic has for a midday meal."

Tantic had a great deal for the company's meal, and Alex was pleased that his nose had not lied to him earlier when he had smelled such wonderful things cooking. He was surprised the food looked as good as it smelled, and tasted even better.

"It is only simple Techen cooking," said Tantic in an apologetic tone. "We don't often serve a midday meal, though tonight there should be a fair crowd. And if you had arrived on a feast day, well . . . If you really want to experience Techen food, you should visit on a feast day. But it has been some time since we've had a proper feast day."

"The food is most excellent," said Bregnest. "A blessing on your ovens, we shall all spread their fame."

Tantic seemed pleased with the praise and bowed to Bregnest and the rest of the company before leaving them to their meal.

As Alex and his friends were finishing their meal, the city magistrate appeared in the doorway. He was a tall, thin man dressed in dark green robes. He had a gold chain hanging around his neck and an annoyed look on his face. His face grew tight with anger when he learned that Bregnest had already sold the horses to Tantic, but he managed to control his feelings and the tone of his voice.

"No law against that," said the magistrate stiffly. "And if you did indeed kill a number of bandits, we should be grateful to you."

"You are very kind," replied Bregnest in his most businesslike tone.

"Yes, well, it is no small thing," the magistrate continued. "The city guards seem unable to do anything about the bandits, who have ruined our trade with the south. Perhaps the city should hire you and your company to hunt down the rest of these troublemakers."

"A noble task," commented Bregnest, as if considering the offer.

"So you would be willing to take the job?" the magistrate asked hopefully.

"Sadly, we have other business to attend to," answered Bregnest. "However, we will happily remove any bandits we encounter along our way. Though I suspect they will avoid us in the future."

"Perhaps, when your business is completed, you will consider my offer further," replied the magistrate, returning to his stiff manner.

"Indeed, yes, we will," replied Bregnest. "It would be a great honor to work for the city of Techen."

The magistrate smiled thinly, nodded to Bregnest, and without another word, left Tantic's inn.

"To work for the city would be an honor, but to work for *him* would be a curse," commented Thrang in a low voice.

Alex agreed with Thrang's assessment, remembering Tantic's comment about how the city guards didn't take care of their horses. His feelings about horses had changed a great deal since the start of his adventure, and the thought of mistreating a horse made him more than a little angry.

There were several hours before the evening meal would be served, so Alex, Andy, Skeld, and Halfdan left Tantic's inn and wandered back to the main square, which was now full of people selling various items from small tables.

The people of Techen reacted in different ways to Alex and his companions, and Alex noticed that all of them seemed a little nervous. Some of the people were anxious for Alex and his friends to approach their tables, hoping to sell them something, while others pretended not to see them at all. This second group would watch them closely when they did approach one of their tables and would not speak unless spoken to.

Alex and the others each bought a few small items, more from boredom than from need. Alex purchased a small folding knife he thought would be useful, as well as a notepad so he could practice writing his elfin letters. He noticed Andy bought a few small pieces of jewelry, and he guessed they were souvenirs or gifts for his friends back home. It didn't take long to browse the small market and they soon wandered out of the square, heading back to Tantic's inn.

"A strange city," commented Halfdan, as they walked past the squashed mud houses. "Not a tree or a bush to be seen."

"And what would a dwarf know about cities?" asked Skeld, a wicked smile on his face. "I've heard you all live underground in vast, dark caves."

"Dwarf caves are not dark," retorted Halfdan, pushing Skeld into one of the mud walls lining the street. "Even dwarfs long for the wind in our faces and a bit of green now and then. If we enter the dwarf realm of Vargland, you will see you are wrong about our cities."

"I shall make a point of visiting your country, whether we enter the dwarf realm or not," said Skeld, laughing loudly.

They returned to Tantic's inn and found the others waiting for them. It seemed there was nothing to do in Techen but wait.

CHAPTER TWELVE

ERIC VON TEALO

Later that afternoon, Tantic asked if they would like to see their rooms. Alex and his friends followed the innkeeper to the back of the inn, where they entered a large suite of rooms. The main sitting room had several chairs, a few small tables, and a large fireplace. Two short hallways led from either side of the room into two smaller bedrooms with two beds each and a small table with a lamp.

"I hope this will do," said Tantic, as he showed them around the suite. "We seldom have one company take an entire apartment, but you seem to fit perfectly."

"This will do nicely," replied Bregnest with a slight bow.

"About your evening meal, then," Tantic began. "Will you want a private room, or would you prefer to eat in the common room? The common room will not be crowded tonight as we have so few visitors these days."

"A private room would be best," said Bregnest. "We have several things to discuss, and I would not want to trouble your other guests."

"A kind gesture," replied Tantic. "You know we Techens are often shy of strangers, though I doubt they would be put off by your company. At least, not once they know about your victory over the bandits."

"You are most kind," answered Bregnest, bowing slightly once more. "Perhaps we will join your guests after our meal."

"As you wish," said Tantic, returning the bow.

The company ate their evening meal in a dining room well away from the common room of the inn. Tantic promised to bring them something special, and when the food arrived, everything looked and smelled wonderful. Alex was hungry, but he was too worried about when the old man might arrive and what he might have to say, and couldn't enjoy the food.

"You worry too much for one so young," said Skeld, jokingly. "You should learn to let things be and to take things as they come."

"Ignore him," commented Tayo, sitting down next to Alex. "He never worries about anything and so he never plans for anything."

"I plan," replied Skeld with a laugh. "I plan to have as much fun as I can before I cross the wall."

"The wall?" Alex questioned.

"The wall between this life and the next," said Tayo, his face twisting slightly as though he felt a pain. "We should not speak of it."

"It's there for all of us poor mortals," Skeld said, no longer laughing. "Worrying about it won't make it go away."

"Neither will laughing at it," answered Tayo, and he fell silent.

"I'm sorry I asked," Alex said in a lowered voice to Tayo.

He knew Tayo seldom laughed, but he'd never seen him quite this way before. "I did not mean to trouble you."

"It does not matter," replied Tayo, though his pained look remained. "Perhaps Skeld is right and I do think too much on this thing."

Alex didn't reply, leaving Tayo to his own thoughts.

As they ate, Bregnest told the rest of the company about the old man who had approached Alex in the stable. He asked Alex to tell the story and repeat everything the old man had said. After Alex had finished, they were all silent for several minutes.

"Why does he want to come when no one is around?" Thrang questioned.

"Perhaps he does not wish to be seen speaking to us," suggested Arconn.

"And perhaps he's not a simple old man," Tayo added.

"We won't know what he is or what he knows until he chooses to tell us. For now, we will wait," Bregnest said.

"Should we go to the common room for a drink?" Halfdan asked in a hopeful tone. "It might make the old man more comfortable."

"Perhaps," said Bregnest. "However, I think we should wait for our visitor in our rooms. I will ask Tantic to send us something to drink, so don't look so sad, Halfdan."

"The spiced ale is very good," said Halfdan, smiling sheepishly.

They finished their meal in silence. Alex poked at his food, having lost his appetite, worried that waiting in their rooms might be a mistake. What if the old man couldn't find them? Alex didn't want to look foolish in front of his friends if the old man didn't show up at all.

As they left the dining room, Bregnest went to find Tantic, and Alex and the others moved slowly toward their rooms at the back of the inn.

It wasn't long before Bregnest returned, followed by servants carrying several pitchers and mugs. Halfdan grinned and claimed a mug of dark Techen beer. As the servants departed, Bregnest took a seat near the fireplace, his eyes fixed on the flames, a troubled look on his face.

Alex sat in a chair across from Bregnest, worried the old man wouldn't come. He almost jumped out of his chair when there was a soft knock at the door a short time later. Alex looked at the door, then at Bregnest, unsure of what he should do. Bregnest smiled slightly at Alex and motioned for Arconn to open the door.

Arconn politely showed the old man into the room, offering him a chair near Bregnest. The old man moved slowly, looking at each of the company in turn as he walked through the room. He seemed unsure of himself, as if he had been summoned here instead of it being his own idea to come.

"All of you then," said the old man, taking the seat Arconn had indicated. "I suppose you know your own ways."

"But we do not know yours," replied Bregnest, his eyes never leaving the old man. "Will you tell us why you wish to speak to us?"

"I'm sure you know," the old man answered, laughing

slightly. "First, tell me your names. And if you will, a drop of ale would be most welcome."

"The ale first," said Bregnest, motioning to Halfdan. "But perhaps you should give your name first, so we will know what to call you."

"Thank you kindly," said the old man, taking a mug from Halfdan and drinking deeply. "I see you have some wisdom. I am called Eric—Eric Von Tealo."

"That is not a Techen name," Bregnest replied in a thoughtful tone. "I am Silvan Bregnest, leader of this company. If you wish, I will name my companions, but it seems a small matter."

"As you wish, Master Bregnest," Eric replied, raising his mug in a toast.

"Will you tell us what business you have with us?" Bregnest questioned.

"Oh, yes," Eric replied. "I have quite a tale to tell, and I think you will be happy to hear it—even if it does come from a poor old man like myself."

"Old I can see," said Bregnest with a smile. "Poor, I cannot judge. I think, however, that you wish to be less poor before your tale is told."

"You have a keen eye," Eric answered, a sly grin on his face. "Perhaps some arrangement can be reached?"

"I would not pay for goods before I see them," said Bregnest in a stern tone. "However, I will make you this offer. If your tale rings true and has any value, I will pay you five gold coins. Sufficient payment, I think, for even the best of stories."

"Five from each man who hears my story would be closer to the mark," countered Eric. "Though perhaps my story is of no value and I should go about my own business."

"Free drink is payment enough for stories," snapped Halfdan, rising from his seat.

"Halfdan," said Bregnest sharply. The dwarf sank back to his chair.

"The dwarf has no patience," commented Eric, still smiling slyly.

"And mine will grow short," replied Bregnest. "Tell your tale, old man. If there is value in it, we will pay five gold coins each for the hearing. If not . . . well, the free drink will be your payment."

"Very well," replied Eric. "Perhaps a touch more ale then, to wet my throat in the telling."

Halfdan refilled Eric's cup, a look of anger and dislike on his face.

"To begin with, you are correct, my name is not Techen at all," Eric began. "My family is from Varlo, though none of my family now living has ever seen that fabled city. It was my father's, father's, father who last saw the great city and it was in ruins then. It was my grandsire of many generations ago who last saw the city when it was fair."

Eric paused, his eyes half-closed in deep thought or memory. For several minutes the only sound was the soft crackling of the fire in the grate, and then Eric continued.

"It was this ancient Von Tealo who served in the great city as one of its most trusted guards. It is from him that my information comes, though my great-grandfather found that his story was true.

"I will not tell the whole story of the days before the dragon came to Varlo, as the tale is too long and has little to do with my own. I will say that my ancestor was living in the heart of the great castle when the evil arrived.

"Though he did not see the beast himself, my ancient father soon learned of the worm's arrival. He was deep inside the castle on the king's business and his first thoughts were to find the king and fight the monster, but fortunately for myself that was not to be. For as news of the disaster came, so did the survivors of Varlo. They were white with fear, and even the bravest of them were shaken and confused. It was from them that my ancestor learned of the king's death."

Once more the old man fell silent. Alex saw a look of anger cross his face, but it vanished as Eric sipped his ale.

"With his master dead and so many terrified people looking to him for guidance and protection, he knew the course he had to take," Eric went on. "He knew that escape from the castle into the city would be madness. The dragon would surely kill them all if they went through the main gates, so he took a different path."

"And it is this path that you wish to tell us about?" Bregnest questioned.

"Forty pieces of gold seems a small price to pay for the path to the dragon's hoard," replied Eric.

"You test my patience," said Bregnest coldly. "You ask for payment before the goods are seen."

"Not at all," replied Eric. "I simply wish a fair price for showing you the way to great wealth."

"The way to wealth is a small matter when its protector is so great," answered Bregnest. "You may show us a path that leads to our doom, and that is of no value at all."

"Perhaps doom is all there is," Eric said calmly. "However, I will not ask for payment unless you find success."

"Very well then," said Bregnest, his tone softening slightly. "If your path leads us to success, we will each give you fifty times the price we pay for your story."

"A small amount from such a hoard," complained Eric.

"You may know the path, but we will have to face the evil at its end," replied Bregnest. "Fifty times five from each of us is all I will promise."

"Perhaps, if you find success, you will feel more generous," Eric offered.

"I have no doubt we will," Bregnest agreed.

"This other path then," Eric continued. "This other path that lead my ancestor to safety was hidden far beneath the castle, where few had ever gone. It was only by chance my ancestor knew of it at all, but that is another story for another time.

"In the deepest part of the castle there was a great hall and at the end of this hall was a spring. The spring was large, creating a fair-sized stream of water. A channel was cut for the water to flow in so the hall and the castle above would not be flooded. At the end of this channel, a tunnel emptied the water out of the mountain. The tunnel leads from the great hall to the meadows on the southern side of the city. There was at one time a stone path cut into one side of the tunnel so the ancient kings could go to the open fields beyond the city unseen."

"If there was a spring beneath the castle, the dragon would have blocked it up years ago," interrupted Bregnest. "And failing that, he would have blocked the tunnel."

"The men of Varlo once tried to block the spring and failed," said Eric. "And if the dragon blocked the tunnel, the castle would even now be flooded. However, when my great-grandfather last saw the city—a little more than a hundred years ago—the tunnel was not blocked."

"Much can change in a hundred years," said Bregnest in a thoughtful voice. "Why did your ancestor return to Varlo?"

"He hoped to win the city back," answered Eric with a sad look on his face. "He thought he could drive the dragon out and restore life to the land of his fathers."

"A secret entrance once used is no longer a secret," said Bregnest grimly.

"Perhaps not, but it is still better than the front gate," Eric answered. "The opening to the tunnel is not as easy to access as it once was, that much I know. When my great-grandfather returned to Techen, he told us what he'd seen. The dragon had piled great rocks over the tunnel's mouth—not to block the water, but to block anyone trying to enter. The water flows freely out from under the rocks, but if a man wanted to enter the tunnel, he would have to swim under the rocks, against the current of the water."

"A near-impossible task," said Bregnest, a stern look on his face. "What value is a path we cannot enter or use?"

"As you said, much can change in a hundred years," Eric replied.

Bregnest considered Eric's story for some time. Alex also thought about the story, concerned about his own ability to swim upstream against a swift current. Of course, they'd have to find the stream first, before trying to swim up it, so perhaps there was no need to worry just yet.

"Is the stream of water the only entrance to the tunnel?" questioned Bregnest.

"I cannot say for sure," answered Eric. "Though this small map shows no other."

Eric produced an old piece of paper from his pocket and held it up for Bregnest to see. The map showed the city of Varlo, the castle, and the fields around the city. The bottom of the map showed a stream that began south of the city, well away from the city walls.

"This map shows nothing of the tunnel," said Bregnest after looking carefully at the paper. "If it showed the tunnel or the inside of the castle, it might be of value."

"I have no such map to offer," said Eric. "Though I daresay my story has been worth its promised price."

"Perhaps," said Bregnest. "But perhaps this story is of your own making. Have you any proof that what you've said is true?"

"Only my word," replied Eric in a defiant tone. "I am old and have nothing of value but my word. I give you my word and a promise to repay the story's price if it should prove false."

"And if we should return to claim payment," commented Bregnest with a slight smile. For several minutes Bregnest remained silent, then he spoke again. "Your story is a good one and worth the price."

"You are most kind," said Eric, bowing slightly. "I will take my leave of your company then, as it is late."

Bregnest nodded to the old man and handed him five gold coins, motioning for each in the company to do the same. Eric moved around the room, collecting his fee and bowing to each of the adventurers in turn.

"Where will we find you, if we return?" asked Bregnest as Eric moved toward the door.

"Here at the inn," answered Eric. "I oversee the stables for Tantic, though there is little to do these days."

"And if we do not return for many years? Who shall we pay in your place?" Bregnest questioned as Eric opened the door to leave.

"If it takes you that long, you may keep the payment," Eric replied with a smile. "You still have far to go before ever reaching Varlo, and you may never get there. I will wait for your return as long as I can."

Bregnest nodded as Eric left the room, closing the door behind him.

"I don't trust him," said Halfdan after several minutes of silence. "How did he know we were going to Varlo at all?"

"He believed the story," commented Arconn in a thoughtful tone. "It may not be a true story, but he believes it."

"True story or not, Bregnest is right: a secret entrance once used is no longer secret," said Thrang sounding as angry as Halfdan. "Though the old man was right to say it's better than the front gate."

"Not better if it leads us straight to the dragon's den," said Tayo.

"Better to surprise the dragon in his den than to have him surprise us some place else," said Skeld with a smile.

"And do our youngest members have nothing to say on this matter?" Bregnest asked.

"Youth should speak when spoken to," replied Andy with a bow.

"That may do in your father's house," said Bregnest with a slight smile. "You and Alex are part of this company and may speak or remain silent as you see fit."

"I have little to say," said Andy. "Though if there is a secret way, it would be worth a look."

"But if it's blocked, we may waste time looking," said Alex, following Andy's lead. "And if the dragon knows about it, won't he watch it closely?"

"All have made good points," said Bregnest, rubbing his chin thoughtfully. "We have a long road before reaching Varlo. We will have time to consider Eric's story and what course we should take as we travel. Though I am of the opinion that we should at least look for this secret path."

"How far is it to Varlo?" Alex asked.

"A good distance," Bregnest answered. "If we take the straightest road, we must still ride to the Brown Hills and then past the ruins of Aunk."

"And then there is the dark forest. We must pass that no matter which road we take," Thrang added.

"The dark forest should not be difficult to cross if we take the right paths," Arconn commented.

"And meet the right people," said Bregnest, looking up at Arconn. "But nothing is sure, except that tomorrow we must ride on. We will discuss this again when we are closer to Varlo."

"To Varlo," said Halfdan, raising his mug.

"To Varlo indeed," Bregnest replied without toasting.

Chapter Thirteen

Dwarf Realm

Morning came sooner than Alex would have liked after the company's late night. It was wet and windy outside, though surprisingly warm. Skeld laughed at the weather in his usual manner, but the rest of them did not feel so happy. Halfdan complained loudly and asked more to himself than to his companions if it would be better to stay another day. Alex looked around the stable as he saddled Shahree, but there was no sign of Eric Von Tealo.

"A poor day to start, as Halfdan has noted," Bregnest commented as they led their horses out of the stable.

"Poor or fair, Halfdan would rather have another drink than ride," said Skeld, laughing merrily as he looked up at the sky.

Halfdan gave Skeld an evil look. The others saw the look and smiled at each other, knowing that Halfdan had consumed a large amount of the fine spiced ale of Techen the night before. Now his words and mood showed he was paying the price for his over-indulgence.

Ignoring the weather, they mounted their horses and Bregnest led them back to the city's gates. The guards allowed them to pass with only a nod, obviously preferring their dry watch hut to asking questions in the rain. The company headed east, leaving the mud-colored city of Techen behind.

The rain continued to fall all day, but as night approached, the rain finally slowed to only a few drops. There had been little talk on the road, and Alex had spent the time thinking about his studies. He had learned the elfin letters and could read most of the book Iownan had given him.

Arconn was pleased with Alex's progress, but each night, he insisted Alex spend some time with the magic book. Alex did what Arconn told him to do, though he worked much slower with the magic book than he did with the book Iownan had given him.

Alex had mixed feelings about magic, and a lot of questions as well. He didn't doubt that magic worked; it was more that it seemed too easy. He worried that if things were too easy he wouldn't appreciate them, that he might start to think of magic as a common thing.

Of course he was pleased that he could start fires and put them out with a simple command, and he was also pleased that the same magic had allowed him to defeat a troll. He could see that magic might be very useful, and he knew that learning more magic would be helpful. The voice at the back of his mind, however, warned him that magic could also be danger-ous. Alex thought he should understand magic better before learning too much of it.

By the next morning, the rain had stopped completely, though the sky was still cloudy and dark. The winds had died down as well, and even Halfdan seemed to be in a better mood. The road was slick and muddy so they moved slowly. Arconn continued his practice of riding ahead or off to the side, returning with some item for Alex to identify.

This routine went on for a week, and on the eighth night after leaving Techen, Alex finally asked Arconn, "How much further is it to the Brown Hills?" He was supposed to be studying his magic book, but his heart wasn't in it.

"Tired of the journey already?" Arconn asked with a smile.

"No," Alex replied. "I was just wondering how far away the hills are. Bregnest made it sound like the journey might take years, but I don't see how it could."

"If we could journey directly and without incident from the great arch to Varlo, it would take us four months, maybe five," said Arconn. "However, we cannot ride directly to Varlo, and as you know from our encounter with the bandits and the troll, we cannot go far without meeting some kind of trouble."

"Then why would it take years to travel from Techen to Varlo and back again?"

"As I said, we cannot go untroubled," answered Arconn. "Though trouble might not be the best choice of words."

"Is there a better word?" Alex asked, closing the magic book.

"Burdened might be better. After all, I would not call our visit to the White Tower trouble, but it was a burden."

"How can you say that?" Alex questioned. He didn't consider their visit to Iownan a burden.

"The Oracle gives knowledge, and with knowledge comes

responsibility," said Arconn. "Knowledge and responsibility are always a burden, even if we accept them willingly."

"I understand," replied Alex. "And will there be other places, like the tower, where we must stop before we reach Varlo?"

"Indeed there will be, though to say we *must* stop is not entirely accurate. Perhaps it is better to say that we *choose* to stop. There are many places ahead of us where we may choose to stop—not least of which is the dark forest. Many of my kinsmen still live in this land after all and the dark forest is their home."

"Your kinsmen?" Alex asked, surprised and delighted.

"Of course," replied Arconn with a smile. "And we shall meet some of Thrang and Halfdan's kinsmen as well when we reach the Brown Hills. Though dwarfs are not always as friendly with other dwarfs as elves are with other elves."

"Dwarfs aren't friendly with their own families?"

Arconn laughed happily. "Are you so friendly with your own family?"

"I have no real family," Alex answered softly. "I only have a stepfather and a stepbrother."

"Are not all men of the same family?" Arconn questioned thoughtfully. "Men live but a short time in most lands. They soon forget their own past."

"Is it different with elves and dwarfs?"

"It is very different, especially for elves," replied Arconn. "Dwarfs live many hundreds of years. Elves do not grow old at all, as I have told you."

"So you remember your own past better," Alex said.

"Yes, we do. Perhaps it is because we live so long that we remember so much more."

"Will you live forever?"

"Perhaps," Arconn replied thoughtfully. "Though as I told you, elves can die as surely as any other living thing."

"It seems sad, in a way, that you go on living for so long," said Alex.

"To many of us it is. And many of my race have left the known lands to find peace."

"I remember you mentioned fading," said Alex, thinking back to when he and Arconn had talked about this before. "Is fading like asking to die?"

"Nothing like that," answered Arconn, his smile flickering slightly. "Those who choose to fade . . . well, it is hard to explain. I would say they seem to sleep and slowly vanish from the land. They are waiting for the lands to be renewed, and then they will wake once more."

"And the dwarfs, can you tell me about them?" Alex asked.

"Ah, well," Arconn began. "Perhaps Thrang or Halfdan should tell you about their own people, as I see things as an elf and not as a dwarf."

"Please," Alex persisted.

"Very well, I will tell you as I see it," Arconn consented. "As I said, dwarfs do not live forever and to an elf their lives seem short."

"But much longer than a man's."

"Much longer than *most* men," Arconn corrected. "The

dwarfs were once one people, living in one land. As time passed, they have spread to most of the known lands, and perhaps to a few lands that are not known to any but themselves."

"So they have forgotten that they are one people?"

"Not at all," Arconn replied, pausing for a moment to think. "Dwarfs know that they are one people, unlike men. However, they do not give their trust easily to strangers, even of their own kind. They are true in their friendships, but it is a hard-won friendship."

"Will the dwarfs in the Brown Hills be unfriendly to us?"

"Perhaps. Though I think they will be kind enough. I don't think they will hinder our journey."

"How closely are Thrang and Halfdan related to the dwarfs here in Vargland?" Alex questioned.

"Closer than they might think. Though it has been a long time since any of Thrang's people have come to Vargland."

Alex and Arconn sat in silence for a time, watching the campfire burn down. It seemed incredible to Alex that elves could live forever, provided they weren't killed. He wondered what it would be like to live so long, but it was hard to imagine.

"Your watch has passed," said Arconn as the last flames of the fire fell into glowing embers.

"One more question, please," said Alex, getting up.

"What more could you ask?"

"You said that dwarfs live longer than most men," said Alex. "Are there men who live longer than dwarfs?"

"A few."

"Can you tell me about them?" Alex pried.

"There are some men and women scattered through the known lands who live much longer than others. It is said some of them are like the elves. I have met a few of them myself, but I do not think they are like elves," answered Arconn, his smile fading to a frown.

"Do you know why they live so long?" Alex asked.

"You said one more question, and now you have asked three," said Arconn, his smile returning.

"But this is so interesting," Alex argued. "I know so little, and things I thought I knew now seem to be wrong."

"Very well," Arconn replied. "I will tell you this one last thing for tonight, then you must sleep."

"I promise."

"The men who live so long are not like other men," said Arconn. "Most of them are wizards of great power. A few are oracles like your friend Iownan. Others . . . others are neither wizard nor oracle, but live on just the same. Some of these men and women are good, some are evil, and some simply are."

"Do all wizards live so long?" Alex asked, forgetting his promise.

"No, not all," answered Arconn, his troubled look returning. "Only the most powerful, or the most evil. Now you must rest. We will talk of this again tomorrow if you wish."

Alex left his friend sitting beside the glowing embers of the fire and made his way to his tent, his mind buzzing with additional questions. Alex's feelings about magic were no longer as confused as they had been. And a part of him was actually beginning to like the idea of magic, even if he didn't really understand it yet.

◆ ◆ ▶

The next morning dawned clear and bright, and the company made good time across the open grasslands. By mid-afternoon, they could see the outline of the Brown Hills on the far horizon, and seeing the hills seemed to please both Thrang and Halfdan.

"A few more days and we should reach the dwarf realm," said Thrang while they ate dinner that night.

"I hope the stories of its greatness are true," Halfdan added, a strange light in his eyes.

"And what are these stories?" Bregnest questioned.

"It is said that the halls of the Brown Hills are a wonder among dwarfs," Halfdan replied reverently. "There are great halls carved from the living rock, and vast cities hidden from view. It is rumored that some of the old dwarf magic remains here in Vargland and that true silver is still found here in abundance."

"Halfdan!" Thrang said loudly, an angry look on his face. "You should learn to hold your tongue."

"Keeping secrets from the company?" asked Skeld, smiling slyly at Thrang.

"Not at all," Thrang replied, embarrassed. "It's just that . . . well, we don't speak openly about the true silver of the Brown Hills. Not even among ourselves."

"There is great wisdom in that," said Arconn. "If half of

what I have heard is true, the dwarf cities would soon be over-whelmed with traders seeking true silver."

"And I daresay you've heard less than I have," replied Thrang.

"What is true silver?" Alex asked.

Thrang looked around nervously before answering. "True silver is different than common silver. For one thing, it is much harder to find and thus worth much more—even more than gold. Once found and polished, true silver will never lose its shine."

"It doesn't turn black like normal silver?" Alex asked.

"No, it doesn't," answered Thrang. "But that has little to do with the value of true silver. It can be worked and forged into armor and weapons that are harder and stronger than any iron or steel. I suspect your wonderful sword is made of true silver, though it is difficult to tell. I don't know why the blade is so dark, but I would guess it has something to do with the elf magic in it."

"Dwarfs are keen on keeping true silver to themselves," said Halfdan as Thrang fell silent. "Not so much for its value, but because of its beauty."

"That's true enough," said Thrang with a smile. "True silver can be shaped into wonderful things that never tarnish or break. It can also be used in cunning ways that others some-times call dwarf magic."

"Dwarf magic?" Alex questioned.

"Nothing like a wizard's magic," Halfdan said quickly.

"Dwarf magic is more for making things like strong doors and tools that won't break."

"There are other kinds of dwarf magic as well," Thrang added. "And not just any dwarf can do magic. Like starting and putting out fires, you have to have some magic in you to make it work."

"But magic is magic, isn't it?" Alex asked.

"Perhaps it all comes from the same place," replied Thrang. "But dwarf magic is just used for things that dwarfs find helpful or pleasing. It's normally not as strong as, say the magic in your sword or anything like that."

"Do you think we will be able to see some true silver when we reach the Brown Hills?" Andy asked in a hopeful tone.

"Perhaps," Thrang replied, sounding slightly worried. "But I would ask that none of you mention it to the dwarfs there. They'll not be happy if they knew how much information we've shared. Too many questions will test any friendship they may offer us."

"Then I will make it a command," said Bregnest, looking at each member of the company in turn. "When we reach the dwarf realm, none of us will speak of true silver—except of course Thrang and Halfdan, who will know what to say and to whom."

"A kind gesture," said Thrang, getting to his feet and bowing to Bregnest.

There was little more talk before Bregnest and the others began rolling into their blankets for the night. Alex sat with Arconn by the campfire to keep his watch.

"You seem much more interested in your magic book tonight," Arconn commented.

"A bit," Alex replied with a smile.

"So you've decided you like the idea of magic now?"

"I'm still not sure," answered Alex slowly. "I've been a little afraid of it. You know, after what you said about power and responsibility. I've also worried that magic can be dangerous if you don't really understand it."

"But your fear is starting to fade?" Arconn pressed.

"Yes, it is," replied Alex. "I think it might be useful to know a bit more magic than I do now. When Thrang and Halfdan were talking about dwarf magic being used to help the dwarfs with things, I thought maybe I could learn some magic that would help us as we travel. You know, something more than just how to start and put out fires."

"Indeed," said Arconn. "But don't forget the responsibility that comes with your knowledge and power, Alex. Any use of power has to be accounted for."

"I'll remember," said Alex, closing his book and moving toward his blankets as his watch ended.

The next day remained sunny and the Brown Hills grew larger as the days passed. Arconn continued to bring Alex items from the roadside, though now there were very few of them that Alex could not name.

"Your knowledge has grown quickly," said Arconn, glancing quickly at Alex and then back to the road. "Soon you will know all the plants in the book the Oracle gave you."

"The plants, maybe," said Alex, smiling at Arconn.

"Though I know little of the potions and less about the animals."

"That will come in time," said Arconn, laughing. "It seems another fire has been lit inside of you—a fire of learning."

Alex did not reply, happy to ride along and watch the Brown Hills grow into mountains in front of them. Arconn was right, he thought. His desire to learn was like a fire inside him. His nightly watch always seemed too short, and he would often stay into Arconn's watch to ask questions of his friend.

"Here is a sign," said Thrang loudly, interrupting Alex's thoughts.

Thrang pointed to a large stone pillar standing by the side of the road. Hundreds of small, neatly cut markings covered the pillar, and Alex realized that the markings were some kind of writing.

"We are now entering the lands of the dwarf realm of Vargland," said Thrang happily. "The pillar says we should ride forward until sunset. We will be met as the sun sinks into the west."

"Met by whom?" Bregnest questioned, looking at the pillar.

"It doesn't actually say," answered Thrang. "If they follow custom, though, we should be met by soldiers and a warden of the king."

"Soldiers?" Andy questioned nervously.

"Not to trouble us," said Halfdan. "But as a sign of respect."

"And in case we're troublemakers, I would guess," Thrang

added. "If we look like trouble, they may attack, but they would probably give us the chance to withdraw first."

"Are you sure it's safe to go forward?" Bregnest asked, sounding unhappy about the soldiers and Thrang's words.

"'Course it is," said Thrang with a grunting laugh. "It's not as if we're here to make trouble."

"But will your cousins know that?" Skeld asked slyly.

Bregnest didn't wait for Thrang's reply. He asked Arconn and Thrang to change places in line before the company continued. Arconn smiled at the request, though Thrang seemed a bit put out by it.

"It's really not necessary," Thrang protested loudly. "It's not as if we're in any danger."

"But you should have a place of honor," said Arconn. "And most dwarfs are not overly fond of elves in any event."

"You're right about that," Thrang admitted, taking his place as the company rode forward. "But I'm sure you'll be well received, and if you're not, I'll have something to say about it."

"Then let us hurry to the reception," said Skeld loudly.

Following Bregnest and Thrang, the group rode past the stone pillar, heading for the Brown Hills. As the sun began to drop behind them, they suddenly came to a halt.

"Declare yourselves," a loud voice called out.

Alex looked, but he could not see where the voice came from.

"Silvan Bregnest and company," Bregnest called back. "We are a company of adventurers, traveling to the east."

For a few moments there was silence, then the voice called back again.

"We see two of our kinsmen among your company. Have them come forward."

Slowly, and with Bregnest's approval, Thrang and Halfdan moved away from their companions toward the voice. For several minutes, the rest of them heard nothing, and then the voice called again.

"Your companions have vouched for you. You may approach," the voice called.

They all moved forward, following the road and looking around as they went. Alex spotted several dwarfs standing in the shadows of large rocks on either side of the road now that he was closer. The fading light made them difficult to see.

"Hold and dismount," the voice commanded as the company rode into the shadow of a large hill.

They did as instructed, moving forward to stand in a line with their horses behind them.

"Welcome," said a round dwarf, stepping out of the shadows. "We seldom see such a company in these times. Your companions have spoken well of you. If you will come with us, we will lead you to the city of King Osrik."

"You are most kind," said Bregnest, bowing. "My companions and I are grateful for the hospitality of the great dwarf realm."

"My lord, King Osrik, will wish to welcome you himself. I am sure he will wish to speak with you about many things," the round dwarf said, returning Bregnest's bow.

"We would be honored to greet your king," replied Bregnest, bowing once more.

The dwarf smiled and then turned and started walking away. Bregnest and the others followed on foot; Thrang and Halfdan rejoined the company after a few hundred yards, beaming with happiness.

"We are in luck," said Thrang to Bregnest. "King Osrik is an old friend of my father, from years back."

Alex looked around and saw that the dwarfs he'd spotted earlier were following them. They were moving quietly a short distance behind the company, and they seemed to be watching Alex and his friends closely.

"You may leave your horses here," said the round dwarf as they approached a large barn concealed near the mountainside. "We have few horses of our own, and they are not allowed inside the city."

"Sorry, Shahree," Alex said, leading her into the barn. "I'm sure the dwarfs will look after your needs."

Shahree nuzzled his shoulder softly as a sign that she understood him, and Alex smiled. He patted her neck gently before turning to follow his companions out of the barn. The dwarfs who were in the barn had noticed Alex speaking to Shahree, and they all smiled broadly at him as he left.

Alex and his companions followed the round dwarf along a wide path that led up into the mountains. The path seemed to flow along the side of the mountain like a strange river, climbing gently upward. The path twisted back on itself several times as they climbed high above the foothills. As they walked around the side of the mountain, the main gates to the dwarf city came into view.

Alex was surprised by what he saw. The two huge stone doors of the main gate were at least thirty feet tall. They were open, folded back against the mountainside. On either side of the giant doorway stood a dozen well-armed guards in bright silver armor. A warm light shone from the large cavern behind the main doors, and it felt very welcoming as the shadows of night covered the valley behind them.

Their guide led them through the giant gates and into the cavern, nodding to the guards as they passed. Alex was impressed with the smooth stone walls and floors of the cavern; the wonderfully carved pillars lining the passageway were beyond description. The roof of the cavern was at least fifty feet high and expertly carved with all kinds of decorations, just like the pillars.

After a short walk, the company entered another vast stone hall, which was lit by hundreds of gold and silver lamps. The stone floor was so well polished it reflected the light like a mirror. At the far end of the hall, the floor rose several feet, forming a large stone pedestal, which was surrounded by neat stone circles that served as wide steps leading up to it. At the top of the steps, sat a very old-looking dwarf in a large stone chair. Alex knew without being told that this was King Osrik. As they approached the pedestal, the dwarf who had been their guide motioned for them to stop and form a line. Climbing the first three steps toward the king, their guide began to speak.

"My Lord Osrik," the dwarf said loudly. "This company of

adventurers has come at your goodwill. Among their number are two of our kinsmen from far off Thraxon. They speak well of their comrades and vouch for their honor. They await your pleasure, King Osrik, as they stand before you—"

"Enough," said Osrik, waving his hand impatiently. "You are as long-winded as ever, and the feast is nearly prepared."

Alex smiled at Osrik's words, but bowed his head so no one would see.

"Tell me your names," said Osrik, standing and moving down the stairs toward Alex and his companions.

"Silvan Bregnest," Bregnest answered, bowing to the king. "I am the leader of this company."

"And an able leader, I daresay," Osrik replied with a smile.

"Thrang Silversmith," said Thrang, also bowing to the king.

"Ah, yes, Thrang," said Osrik in a happy tone. "I knew your father well. You look very much like him."

"You are most kind," Thrang replied with another bow.

The king continued down the line until he came to Alex. Alex was nervous, having never met a king before. He started to bow before he told the king his name, then catching himself, he blushed bright red.

"Alexander Taylor," he managed to say as he finished his bow.

"Don't worry," said Osrik, smiling at Alex. "I do hate formalities, but the chamberlain insists."

Alex returned the king's smile, liking the old dwarf immediately. Osrik seemed pleased with Alex as well; he took

him by the arm and started to walk back through the hall with
him.

"Come along, then, one and all," he said in a jaunty tone.
"The feast will be ready shortly, and we can have a good long
talk while we eat."

The king smiled brightly at Alex as they walked, and he
would nod now and then to one of the dwarf guards who all
bowed as they passed.

"The guards are a custom," Osrik said in a lowered tone,
as if speaking privately to Alex. "Personally, I think all this
bowing and nodding is more trouble than it's worth. But I suppose we have to keep up appearances."

Osrik led them into another hall, which was almost overflowing with dwarfs. The dwarfs sat at long, low tables, talking
happily and loudly. As the king and his guests entered the hall,
all of the dwarfs stood up, waiting for Osrik to take his own seat
at the head of the hall.

"Well, now," said Osrik, looking at Alex and his companions. "It seems you have traveled far in coming here. I do hope
you have some good tales to tell."

"As many as you may wish to hear, Lord Osrik," Bregnest
replied from his seat at the king's left.

Alex thought the king seemed like a kindly old man, and
he had to remind himself that Osrik was a dwarf. Osrik was
polite to each of the company as the feast was served, asking
them about their own lands and travels. He spoke for a long
time with Thrang and Halfdan, asking about people he knew

from long ago and events in far-off Thraxon. Alex felt comfortable sitting next to Thrang and listening to all the talk.

"I suppose we should all get some sleep," Osrik said at last. "I've had chambers prepared for you all. I hope you'll be comfortable."

"You show us great kindness, Lord Osrik," Bregnest replied for the group.

"Yes, well, we don't often see travelers, and I do miss the news they bring," said Osrik. "However, tomorrow we have more serious matters to talk about. You will be summoned to the great hall after breakfast."

The entire hall rose again as Osrik stood to leave. Alex and his companions stood and bowed to the king to show their respect and thanks. As soon as Osrik had left, the other dwarfs began to wander off as well, though some of them remained and watched Alex and his friends. While Alex was looking around the hall, a young-looking dwarf appeared at Bregnest's side and bowed to him.

"The king has asked that I show you to your sleeping chambers and supply you with whatever you may need," said the young dwarf.

"And what may we call you?" asked Bregnest.

"I am called Thrain," the dwarf replied with a broad smile. "It is my great honor to meet you," he added with a deep bow.

Bregnest returned the dwarf's bow. "We are pleased to know you, Thrain, and will follow where you lead."

Thrain blushed slightly at Bregnest's words, obviously happy with his duty of leading the adventurers through the dwarf city.

"Are you really adventurers then?" Thrain asked in a reverent tone as he led them out of the feasting hall. "I mean, if you don't mind saying."

"We are," Bregnest replied with a kindly smile.

"I've never met any real adventurers before," Thrain said breathlessly. "It must be amazing and wonderful to go on adventures."

"And often sad, dangerous, and uncomfortable," replied Thrang, walking beside Bregnest. "It's not a path any may follow, as I'm sure you have been told."

"Indeed, yes, Master Silversmith, I have," answered Thrain. "But like many others here, I hope to be chosen when the time comes."

"Why would any wish to leave the beauty and comfort of this dwarf realm?" Halfdan questioned.

"The hearts of the young are often restless," Thrang commented. "You should remember how you felt before you were chosen, Halfdan."

Thrain led them along the well-lit corridors of the dwarf city and after turning many corners and climbing several stairways, they entered another large chamber. Several small alcoves had been cut into the rock walls of the chamber, and each alcove contained a bed and a lamp.

"I hope you will be comfortable here," said Thrain. "If you need anything in the night, simply ring the bell. I, or one of my friends, will come directly."

"Our thanks, Master Thrain," Bregnest replied with a slight bow. "We are in the king's debt for so fine a guide."

Thrain smiled and bowed almost to the floor, then turned and left the company alone in the chamber.

"The king has been very kind," commented Thrang, testing one of the beds. "And not least of all to our young wizard."

"What do you mean?" Alex questioned.

"When the king took your arm and walked with you into the feasting hall," answered Halfdan with a smile. "Among dwarfs, that is a great show of respect."

"Why did he take my arm and not Bregnest's or Thrang's?" Alex asked quickly.

"Perhaps he saw something in you that we all have begun to see," Thrang replied. "Or perhaps his dislike of pomp and ceremony made him choose you, our youngest member. I know little about Osrik, though I think he sees things better than most."

"And now we should all take advantage of the king's kindness and get some sleep," said Bregnest before Alex could ask any more questions.

"That would be best. It's likely that we'll be called early in the morning," replied Thrang.

Alex selected a bed of his own. He was concerned that Osrik had shown him so much respect, and had not chosen Bregnest, Thrang, or even Halfdan to walk with. He put off his worries by remembering Osrik's dislike for ceremony, hoping that was the reason for Osrik's attention.

CHAPTER FOURTEEN
THE FIRST BAG

W hen Alex woke the next morning, there were at least a dozen dwarfs moving about the chamber. Thrang and Halfdan were talking happily to some dwarfs who appeared to be their long-lost cousins, and their enthusiastic chatter made Alex smile. The rest of Alex's companions were dressing and listening to the dwarfs' conversation.

Thrang and Halfdan were telling their relatives about their adventures and how the company had come to the Brown Hills. As they spoke, several more dwarfs brought trays of food into the chamber for the company. A large round table in the center of the chamber was soon holding their breakfast, and most of the dwarfs were leaving.

"Is he really a wizard then?" Alex heard one of the dwarfs ask Halfdan in a lowered voice as he moved toward the door.

Alex didn't look up, but continued pulling his boots on, listening to Halfdan's reply.

"'Course he is," said Halfdan, turning his head slightly to look at Alex. "Hasn't been trained yet, but he's very magical just the same."

"It seems your fame will continue to grow," said Skeld as Alex joined him at the table. "Your friends here have been telling all kinds of stories about you."

"Nothing that isn't true," replied Thrang defensively, throwing a dirty look at Skeld.

"You are too kind, my friend," said Alex. He felt too happy to let Skeld's joke or Thrang's and Halfdan's storytelling bother him today.

"And the storytelling should be cut short," said Bregnest. "We will be called before King Osrik soon."

The dwarfs who had brought the food bowed to the company and swiftly departed. Alex noticed a few of them glanced back at him as they left, but he didn't let their glances trouble him.

"Why am I so interesting to them?" Alex asked as Thrang took a seat beside him. "Are wizards really so rare?"

"There have never been many wizards," answered Thrang, filling his plate with waffles and bacon. "And few wizards have ever visited the dwarf realm of Vargland."

"I hope I won't disappoint your friends," said Alex, smiling at Thrang while elbowing Skeld in the ribs.

Skeld choked on some eggs, coughing too much to say anything back. The rest of the company laughed at Alex and Skeld before attacking their own breakfasts. The dwarf food was not as grand as the food in Techen or at the White Tower, but it was good just the same.

As they finished, Bregnest stood and spoke. "When we meet with the king, remember not to speak of our final goal."

"It's likely Osrik has already guessed our quest," commented Thrang. "However, you are correct, none of us should speak openly of our final destination."

The company agreed that, if anyone asked, they would direct the question to Bregnest. Then, as they had done at the White Tower, they each placed their weapons and magic bags on their beds, waiting for the king's summons. Alex started to feel nervous again, wondering what Osrik might say about his being an untrained wizard, when Thrain appeared at the chamber door.

"You have been called to the counsel of King Osrik," said Thrain in as commanding a voice as he could manage. "I am to lead you to the king."

"Lead on," replied Bregnest with a formal bow to Thrain.

Thrain blushed, as he seemed to do every time Bregnest bowed to him. He led the company through the city, walking slightly in front of them and trying to look official. He didn't speak to them as they walked, though Alex could see it was a struggle for him to stay quiet. They followed Thrain back to the king's hall. Nine large chairs had been placed in a circle at the foot of the stone pedestal and Osrik was waiting for them in one of the chairs.

"I thought we should all be comfortable," said Osrik as the company approached. "It's such a bother talking to people from the throne. This seems so much friendlier."

"Your kindness overwhelms us, great king," answered Bregnest as the entire company bowed.

"A kindness to you, or to me?" Osrik replied, a playful grin on his face. "But come and join me, we have much to discuss."

Osrik directed each of the company to a chair, calling them by name one at a time. Bregnest sat to the king's left, while Thrang was again on Osrik's right. Alex sat between Thrang and Halfdan, which seemed to please both dwarfs very much.

"You have traveled far and through dangerous lands," Osrik began, looking at Bregnest. "Will you tell me the story of your journey?"

"Perhaps your kinsman would be best at telling the story," Bregnest replied, looking at Thrang. "I am sure he will know which points will interest you much better than I would."

"You speak well, Master Bregnest," said Osrik, still smiling. "Thrang, will you tell this tale?"

"As you command, Lord Osrik," replied Thrang, standing and bowing to both Osrik and Bregnest.

Thrang began with the gathering of the company. He explained to Osrik how each member had been chosen and asked to join the adventure. Osrik nodded as Thrang spoke, but asked no questions.

When Thrang told Osrik about how Alex became the eighth man, Alex listened closely. It appeared that his joining the company had not been as big a chance as he had thought. Thrang and Arconn had gone to Mr. Clutter's shop on the advice of an oracle, which came as a surprise to Alex. Thrang also told Osrik about the sign in the adventurer's shop, and how Alex had applied to join the adventure without knowing what he was doing. Osrik laughed at this but said nothing.

Then Thrang told how, to everyone's surprise, Alex had been told he could use a staff.

"A wise choice I would say," Osrik observed, glancing at Alex. "Or perhaps a lucky chance."

Alex was sure the story of his being an untrained wizard had already reached Osrik, and he smiled weakly at Osrik's words.

Thrang continued the story, including the first time Alex had used the inferno command and nearly set his beard on fire. When he told how Alex had defeated the three-legged troll, Osrik chuckled to himself and Alex turned pink.

"These seven bags you recovered, do you carry them with you?" Osrik questioned, glancing at Alex and then at Bregnest.

"Indeed, yes," answered Thrang. "Master Taylor carries the burden of the seven."

Osrik nodded thoughtfully and motioned for Thrang to continue the story.

Thrang told of the Oracle's invitation and how Iownan had named Alex a friend. He told of the discovery of Alex's magical sword, Moon Slayer.

Alex squirmed slightly in his chair, embarrassed because his own part of the story seemed very impressive the way Thrang told it.

When Thrang told Osrik about Alex's sudden magical change during the bandit attack, Osrik took a deep breath.

"I have heard of such swords, though I have never seen one," Osrik commented, sounding almost as excited as Thrain had the night before.

Thrang finished the story, leaving out the part about the old man in Techen and his secret map to the dragon's lair. For a few minutes, Osrik did not speak, lost in his deep thoughts.

"It is nearly time for the midday meal," said Osrik at last, glancing around the circle. "Before we eat, I would ask something of you."

"We will do what we can for you," Bregnest answered, noncommitally.

"These seven bags you recovered," said Osrik, glancing at Alex. "Will you show them to me?"

"May I ask why, Lord Osrik?" Bregnest questioned, still looking a little worried.

"One of my cousins went on an adventure. It has been almost twenty years now, and we have heard nothing of his fate," answered Osrik, an uneasy look on his face.

"You fear his bag is among the seven," said Bregnest.

"I do," said Osrik in a sad and troubled tone. "We were very close, and in the last few years, his family has fallen on hard times. If his bag is among the seven, whatever treasure is inside may help to repair their fortunes."

"Then they will be brought before you immediately," said Bregnest, turning to look at Alex.

"Thrain will lead you back to your chambers," said Osrik, motioning for Thrain to come forward. "And if you don't mind, I would dearly love to see this wondrous sword of yours as well."

"As you wish, Lord Osrik," replied Alex with a bow.

The rest of the company remained seated as Alex followed

Thrain out of the hall. As soon as they were out of the main hall, Thrain began to ask Alex questions.

"Are you really a wizard then?"

"Untrained and untried," answered Alex with a smile. "Though everyone says that I can be a true wizard, in time."

"And you killed a three-legged troll all by yourself?" Thrain continued, almost bubbling over with excitement.

"With a great deal of luck."

Thrain asked questions during the entire walk through the city and back to the chamber where Alex picked up his magic bag and sword. Alex answered him as well as he could, always trying to make his own part in the adventure seem smaller than Thrang had made it out to be.

"I'd love to be an adventurer," said Thrain, as he led Alex back through the city toward the great hall. "But so few of us are ever chosen. I'll probably end up being a silversmith like my father."

"A noble profession, and far less dangerous than adventures," said Alex. Then he asked, "How are your people chosen as adventurers?"

"Oh, that's simple," said Thrain, sounding pleased that Alex had shown interest. "When we come of age at fifty, we can seek your friend, the Oracle." Thrain seemed happy to refer to the Oracle as Alex's friend, and Alex had to smile. "Then, if she tells us we should be adventurers, we go to Telous to find an adventure to join."

Alex was a bit puzzled by the idea of Iownan telling someone they should be an adventurer. She had spoken plainly to him, but he knew that was not her normal way.

"Few of us ever seek the White Tower these days though," Thrain said, sounding a bit sad. "The roads are hard, and as you know, there are bandits. Most of my people prefer to remain here in the Brown Hills to make their fortunes."

"When will you come of age?" Alex questioned.

"I'll be fifty next spring," said Thrain happily. "If I can find a few others who are willing, I'm going to find the White Tower."

"You should think long before taking that road," Alex advised. "The Oracle may not tell you what you wish to hear."

"I'd like to see the White Tower anyway," said Thrain, his smile still in place. "At least that would be an adventure, even if I never got to go on another."

They had returned to the great hall and Alex thanked Thrain for leading him through the city. Thrain bowed deeply to Alex and quickly returned to his post at the edge of the hall.

"The sword Moon Slayer, Lord Osrik," said Alex, holding his sword out for Osrik to see.

"Will you remove it from the scabbard?" Osrik asked, twitching slightly with excitement.

Alex drew the sword and held it in his hands so Osrik could see it better. The king bent over the sword to look closely at it, but he did not touch it. Alex remembered how Arconn had not touched the sword either, once he had discovered what it was. He wondered if there was some reason for their caution.

"A most excellent weapon," said Osrik, leaning back into

his chair. "The dark elves were always the best swordmakers, after all."

"There is more to it than swordmaking," commented Arconn.

"I'm sure there is, my friend," Osrik replied, smiling at Arconn. "If dwarfs had the magic of elves, then such swords might be more common."

"And of less worth," Thrang added in a thoughtful way.

"Return your sword to your side," said Osrik, seeming to take no note of Thrang's comment. "You shall all be free to carry weapons in the dwarf realm of Vargland, for I name you all friends of my kingdom."

"Your kindness overwhelms us," replied Bregnest.

"And now for the bags," said Osrik.

Alex spoke softly into his own magic bag, withdrawing the seven recovered magic bags one at a time. As he produced the bags, Alex heard Thrain gasp behind him. Osrik carefully examined each of the bags as Alex handed them to him. When Alex handed him the fifth bag, the color drained out of Osrik's face and he let out an audible moan.

"It is as I feared," said Osrik, his head sinking to his chest, his hands clutching the bag tightly. "Poor Umbar, he shall never return."

"You recognize his bag then?" Thrang asked softly.

"As if it were my own," answered Osrik, shaking his head in sorrow. "I will send for his heir and order the preparations made. The ceremony of returning the bag will take place this evening."

Osrik gently handed the bag back to Alex, his hands shaking with emotion as he waved for Thrain to come forward.

"Forgive me, my friends, my sorrow is too great. I cannot join you for the midday meal," said Osrik, looking incredibly old and sad.

"You have our sympathy," said Bregnest as they all stood and bowed to Osrik.

Thrain motioned for the company to follow him. He led them back to their sleeping chamber without speaking, a troubled and worried look on his face. Alex wondered if Thrain was reconsidering his desire to become an adventurer, now that he realized how dangerous it could be.

After Thrain left, Alex turned to Arconn. "What is the ceremony for returning a lost bag?"

"It's a little different, depending on where you are," said Arconn.

"The Handbook doesn't say anything about a ceremony," said Alex nervously.

"You'll be fine," said Bregnest, breathing a heavy sigh and putting one hand on Alex's shoulder. "I should not have let you carry this burden on your first adventure."

"It was his right and his choice," said Thrang, taking a seat next to Alex. "Besides, it's not that difficult really."

"Will you explain it, please?" Alex asked. "I don't want to upset the ceremony, or make a fool of myself."

"Among dwarfs, the ceremony is almost always the same." Thrang stopped to gather his thoughts before continuing. "The ceremony will take place in the feasting hall. You will be called to the front of the hall by the king. He will ask if you are the bearer of the lost bag, stating the name of the adventurer who was lost. You simply reply, 'I am.'"

"And then what happens?" Alex questioned.

"Well, you'll hold up the lost bag so everyone can see it," Thrang went on. "Then the king will call the adventurer's heir forward and ask him to state his name and titles. Then the king will ask you if you believe that the person is the rightful heir."

"It will be, won't it?" Alex asked in a worried tone. "I mean, I don't think Osrik would call the wrong person forward."

"It has been known to happen," said Arconn, listening closely to Thrang's explanation.

"So what should I say?"

"Say that you accept the heir and his claim, but that the lost adventurer requires proof," answered Thrang, stroking his beard. "Then the heir will whisper the bag's passwords in your ear."

"But I thought those words were secret," Alex interrupted.

"They are," said Thrang. "But the heir will know what they are and be able to tell you. Use the passwords to go in and then come out of the bag. Once you've done that, you will say the lost adventurer is satisfied. The king will ask what payment the heir will give for the return of the bag and the heir will make an offer. If the offer sounds good to you, say, 'It is fair,' and then hand the bag to the heir."

"What do you mean, payment?" Alex questioned.

"Reward may be a better word," said Arconn with a smile.

"A reward is always offered for the return of a lost bag. You should know that from your reading, Alex."

"What if the offer—sorry, reward—doesn't sound good?" Skeld asked with a wicked smile.

Thrang looked slightly worried. "Then you say, 'It is unjust,' and the king will ask the heir to make another offer."

"Is the offer likely to be unjust?" Alex asked, trying hard to remember everything Thrang was saying.

"It might be," said Thrang. "Normally the heir will offer part of the treasure in the bag. Sometimes the heir will offer something else as well as part of the treasure. You know, in case there isn't much treasure in the bag. Or, if they think there's a lot of treasure in the bag, they might offer something else and a smaller share of the bag's treasure."

"What would you consider a fair offer?" Alex questioned.

"It's not my place to say," said Thrang, shrugging his shoulders. "I'd say, if the heir offers you one-in-ten or one-in-twelve of the bag's treasure, you should consider it fair. Anything less than that, though, would be an insult."

"What if I forget what to say?"

"You'll be fine," said Thrang, smiling. "And if you don't think the offer is fair, feel free to say so."

"What if the offer seems like too much?" Alex asked, wondering if that ever happened.

"Then you say, 'You are too generous,' and say what you will accept instead," Thrang replied. "But be careful because if you offer a lot less than the heir has offered, he may take it as an insult."

"Right," said Alex, rubbing his hands together and trying to remember what to say and when to say it. He remembered what Andy told him about dwarfs and their money and he hoped he wouldn't insult the heir to the bag. Then another thought came to him.

"What happens if the heir doesn't know the passwords?"

"I've never heard of that happening, so I'm sure you don't need to worry about it."

"But what if he doesn't know?" Alex persisted.

"Well, then, I suppose the lost adventurer can't be satisfied and you can't give the bag back," said Thrang. "And if that happens, the heir will need to visit either the Oracle or the bag maker in Telous to find out what the passwords are."

"And I'd have to carry the bag until he does?"

"Yes," said Thrang.

"What, and wait here until the heir finds out what the passwords are?"

"Not at all," said Arconn with a soft laugh. "You would be free to go. If the heir doesn't know the passwords, he will have to find out what they are and then wait until you come back again."

"But don't worry," said Thrang, slapping Alex on the shoulder. "The heir will know the words, and you'll do fine. Just remember not to insult him by asking too little for the bag. After all, the return of a lost bag is about more than the treasure in the bag. Among dwarfs, the return of a lost bag to the adventurer's heir is also a return of lost honor."

As the afternoon wore on, Alex thumbed through his

Adventurer's Handbook without reading any of it. He was worried and nervous about the upcoming ceremony, and he hoped everything would work out all right. The idea of accepting a reward for returning a lost bag troubled him, and he was concerned about how much the heir would offer. He really hoped the heir's first offer would be fair. More than anything else, he hoped the heir would know the bag's passwords.

All too soon, the company was summoned back to the feasting hall. Alex carried the lost adventurer's bag over his shoulder and walked quietly beside Thrang. He was still nervous, but Thrang's instructions returned to his mind and that calmed him a little. When they entered the hall, they were seated at a table to the king's right.

Alex could see several richly dressed and important-looking dwarfs seated around the king, and he hoped that his clean but plain clothes would be acceptable.

"Master Taylor, please come forward," Osrik called loudly.

Alex hadn't been paying attention to what was going on as he worried about his appearance. Thrang nudged him gently and nodded toward the king. Alex stood up and walked forward nervously, carrying the lost magic bag in his hands.

"Are you the bearer of the magic bag that once belonged to Umbar, son of Olin, the adventurer who was lost?" questioned Osrik.

"I am," Alex replied and held the bag high above his head so everyone in the hall could see it.

The ceremony proceeded, and Alex was relieved he didn't forget anything Thrang had told him. He worried a little when the heir—Umbar, son of Umbar—told him the bag's passwords. The words were obviously dwarfish, and Alex was afraid he wouldn't be able to pronounce them correctly. He managed to get in and out of the bag without too much trouble, though he had to repeat the exit password twice to get it right. Then it was time for the heir to say what he would offer for the bag's return.

"I will give one hundred true silver pennies and one-half of all the bag contains for its return," Umbar said loudly.

Alex was stunned. Even with his limited understanding of treasure, he had not expected such an extravagant offer.

"You are too generous," Alex replied slowly, thinking that one-in-ten of all the treasure would perhaps be a better number.

As this thought went through his mind, Alex saw Thrang out of the corner of his eye. Thrang was mouthing "one-third" wildly, while trying not to attract too much attention to himself. Alex considered again Andy's words about dwarfs and their money, and what Thrang had said about not asking for too little. Not wanting to offend Umbar, he decided to take Thrang's advice.

"I will ask for one-third of the treasure in the bag," said Alex, looking Umbar in the eye.

"It is acceptable," said Umbar, bowing low to Alex, a look of relief and happiness on his face.

Alex presented the bag to Umbar and bowed as well. The ceremony complete, both Alex and Umbar bowed to Osrik and returned to their seats.

"The payment for the bag's return will begin tomorrow after the midday meal," said Osrik in a commanding voice. "Now, let us feast in memory of Umbar, who was lost."

"You did very well," said Thrang as Alex returned to his chair. "I was afraid you'd ask too little and insult the heir."

"I could see you saying one-third," replied Alex with a smile. "And knowing very little about what might offend a dwarf, I took your advice."

"You've done very well for yourself," Thrang laughed. "A hundred true silver pennies and one-third of the bag's treasure. That could be a fair amount."

"We get the silver pennies as well?" Alex questioned.

"You do," said Thrang, taking a long drink from his mug. "Your treasure room could be a respectable size once payment is made."

"You mean, all of our treasure rooms," Alex corrected. "After all, we are to share the reward."

"We shall see," said Bregnest, smiling at Alex.

Alex didn't say anything, but it sounded to him like Bregnest and the others would not be willing to accept a share of the reward for returning the lost bag. This annoyed Alex, but there was a feast going on, so he held his tongue.

◆ ◆ ◆

The next day, Alex asked Thrang about the true silver pennies.

"Long ago, true silver pennies were the standard currency in the dwarf realms, but true silver is too rare these days,"

Thrang commented thoughtfully. "And not many of the pennies are left now anyway, so they're quite valuable."

"Every penny would be worth at least twenty gold coins," said Halfdan, taking a seat next to Alex. "Quite a bit more than that in some places."

"Then Umbar has been extremely generous," said Alex.

"As he should be," Thrang replied with a smile. "You've done him a great service after all. The return of the lost bag is also a return of his family's lost honor, as I told you."

Alex sat quietly, thinking. He knew he had done a service for Umbar by returning his father's bag, and he also knew his own honor had increased because of what he'd done. Still, he didn't really understand what his friends meant when they talked about honor. Things they said were honorable seemed odd to him because Alex simply thought of them as the right thing to do.

After they had finished their midday meal, Alex tried to say something to his friends about dividing the reward, but he didn't get a chance to say anything. One of Osrik's officers appeared and led them all to a large room deep inside the dwarf city. When they arrived, Osrik was waiting for them with Umbar at his side. Both dwarfs smiled brightly as the company entered, and Osrik winked at Alex.

"You have done me a great kindness," said Umbar, stepping forward and bowing to Alex. "You have been both kind and generous."

"It has been my honor," replied Alex, having been told in

advance what to say by Thrang. "I am pleased to have been of service."

"Then let the payment begin," commanded Osrik, still smiling.

Umbar nodded and walked to Alex, handing him a leather pouch. Alex took the pouch without opening it, knowing that it held the one hundred true silver pennies that were part of the reward; he bowed to Umbar in thanks.

"The wardens have been up all night sorting and counting the wealth of Umbar," Osrik said. "Now they will bring one-in-three of all the treasure the bag held."

Alex bowed to the king and stood with his companions to wait. The wait was not long as several dwarfs soon began carrying all kinds of treasure into the room. The dwarfs piled the treasure in one corner of the room and continued to go in and out of the room in a seemingly endless stream.

The room filled quickly with gold and silver bars and coins. Several of the dwarfs carried large bags into the room and placed them in separate piles against one wall, the piles growing nearly as high as Alex was tall. Each bag had a tag attached to it, and Alex guessed the tag identified the bag's contents. There had to be at least three or four times more treasure here than they had taken from the troll. Alex was stunned.

"It appears Umbar was a successful adventurer," said Thrang, standing beside Alex and watching the room fill around them.

"Indeed he was," said Osrik with a laugh.

Alex thought he should say something about this being too

much treasure, but a look from Thrang told him not to speak. He looked around at the enormous mounds of treasure; the room was almost too crowded to stand in. Alex wondered how long it would take to divide everything eight ways.

Finally the dwarfs brought the last bag into the room, bowing at Osrik before leaving. Osrik and Umbar turned to Alex.

"Do you accept your payment?" asked Osrik.

"I . . . I do," Alex replied, his voice shaking slightly.

"Then we will leave you to sort your treasure," said Osrik with a smile. "We will see you this evening at the heir's feast."

Osrik and Umbar walked out of the room, leaving Alex and his companions alone. Alex looked around in disbelief at the piles of treasure around him. He didn't think he and his companions could possibly have it all sorted and divided before the feast began, and not going to the feast was out of the question.

"You'd better make a start then," Skeld laughed, dropping onto a pile of bags in one corner.

"We all had," said Alex.

"No," replied Bregnest softly but firmly. "You had."

"But we are to share equally," Alex protested. "I said when I took the lost bags that all rewards would be shared equally between us."

"But that is not the custom, as you should know from your reading," replied Bregnest with a smile. "You are the winner of the bags. The reward is yours alone."

"But I—" Alex began.

"It will do no good arguing the point," Bregnest interrupted, holding up his hand. "We have decided on this, and I will not be moved."

"You must take something," Alex insisted. "I mean, what will I do with all of this?"

"You are kind and generous," said Bregnest with a slight bow and a smile. "However, you do not know what your future holds, or how much treasure you may need some other day."

"And you've not seen any really large treasures yet," said Halfdan with a laugh. "What we took from the troll was a fair amount compared to what trolls normally have, but it was hardly a dragon's hoard."

Alex continued to object loudly as Skeld and Andy took him by the arms and led him to a pile of treasure.

"Best get started or you'll miss the feast for sure," said Skeld laughing.

"It will take days to get all this in my bag," said Alex, hoping that would force the others to take some of the treasure.

"Nonsense," Thrang replied. "Just hold your bag next to a pile and say, 'treasure room.'"

Alex did as he was told, though with some doubts. He had only put single items in his bag before, and he'd never tried anything as large as the pile of treasure in front of him. To his surprise, the command worked and the entire pile of treasure vanished into his bag.

Alex approached one of the tagged bags and saw that the bag contained diamonds. He wondered how many thousands of diamonds were in the pile of labeled bags in front of him. He looked around at his companions once more, trying to talk them into taking something. They simply laughed at him and refused to accept any of his treasure.

Finally, after what seemed like hours, only one pile of bags remained in the room. Alex looked at the tag to see what was inside. There was a single dwarfish letter on the tag.

"What does this mean, Thrang?" Alex asked, carrying one of the bags to his friend.

"Oh, my!" Thrang exclaimed, looking at the tag and then at the large pile of bags on the floor. "It's . . . it's true silver."

CHAPTER FIFTEEN
HAUNTED RUINS

Alex and his friends remained in the halls of King
Osrik for a week, feasting and talking each night with
the king. They wandered the dwarf city freely, often
getting lost and having to ask directions from one of the passing dwarfs. The dwarfs were always happy to help them find
their way, and many of them would take the time to lead the
members of the company back to their chambers.

"Now I know what dwarf cities are like," said Skeld, smiling at Thrang and Halfdan as they ate breakfast on their final
day in the city.

"And what do you think about them now?" Halfdan
questioned.

"I think they are different than I imagined them to be,"
answered Skeld, still smiling. "Though not as green and open
as I have been told."

Alex chuckled to himself, remembering the comment
Skeld made in Techen about "dwarf caves." Alex had been
happy in Osrik's city and was sorry to be leaving.

Alex had another reason to be happy because, in the end,
each of his companions had agreed to take a bag of the true

silver Alex had received in payment for returning Umbar's lost bag. They had each thanked him so many times that Skeld started teasing them about it, laughing at himself as well as the others.

"Our last breakfast in the city," said Halfdan sadly. "I hope we will be able to return here one day."

As they finished their breakfast and prepared to leave, Thrain appeared in the doorway. Alex and Andy had become good friends with Thrain during their short stay, and they were happy to see him again.

"The king wishes to bid you farewell," said Thrain. "He awaits you in the great hall."

"Then we will follow you to the king, Master Thrain," replied Bregnest.

Thrain led the way, trying hard once again to look official. The company followed him, smiling and nodding to the dwarfs they passed along the way. There seemed to be a lot of dwarfs along their way this morning, smiling and waving good-bye to the company or wishing them good luck on their journey.

"Ah, at last," said Osrik, walking down the steps from his throne as Alex and his friends approached. "A final meeting before you go—though I hope this will not be the last time we meet."

"You have shown us great kindness, King Osrik. We will not soon forget you or your people," said Bregnest as the company bowed to the king.

"Nor will we forget the happiness you and your company

have brought to us," Osrik replied. "You are all free to come and go in this kingdom whenever you may wish. And now my kinsman Umbar asks permission to give you each a gift."

"A token of thanks from the house of Lanoch," said Umbar, stepping forward. He handed each of them a small package. When Umbar came to Alex, he handed him a larger package.

"These are but small tokens of thanks for your kindness in returning the lost bag of my father," said Umbar in a low voice to Alex. "If ever I, or any of my family, may be of service to you, please, feel free to call on us."

"You are both kind and generous," replied Alex with a bow.

"And now you must go," Osrik said sadly. "I wish you a safe journey and a speedy return to my halls."

"You have our thanks, great king," said Bregnest. "If ever we can be of service to you or your kingdom, we will do all that we can."

Alex and the others waited until Osrik was back on his throne before bowing one last time.

As they left the great hall, Thrain fell into step beside Alex and Andy, walking with them out of the main gates and toward the path to the valley below.

"I hope I will see you both again," Thrain said brightly. "Perhaps we will be able to go on an adventure together."

"That would be nice," said Andy. "But you have not been chosen as an adventurer. At least not yet."

"Perhaps you will return in time to go with me to the White Tower," said Thrain hopefully.

"Perhaps we will," said Alex in a cheerful tone. "Then I would have the pleasure of introducing you to my friend, the Oracle."

Thrain beamed with happiness at Alex's words.

When they approached the large barn, they saw that their horses were already saddled and waiting for them.

"Farewell, my friends," Thrain called as they mounted their horses. "May you find your goal and return quickly to our city."

"Farewell, Master Thrain," answered Bregnest. "May the best of your hopes come to pass."

Alex and Andy waved good-bye to Thrain, falling into line behind Skeld and Tayo as they rode off into the east.

"It would be nice to ride with Thrain to the White Tower," said Andy, taking one last look at the dwarf city behind them.

"I doubt we will return to the tower soon," said Tayo grimly.

"Always a ray of sunshine, aren't you?" said Skeld with a laugh and a smile.

They rode quickly across the open lands beyond the city of King Osrik, leaving the Brown Hills behind them. There was little talking as they went along, and it seemed to Alex a shadow had fallen over the company's mood. The weather was warm and dry, and as the sun began to sink behind them, they stopped to make camp. After they had eaten their evening meal, they took out the packages Umbar had given them. Inside each package was a chain made of true silver with a large white diamond set in the center. In addition to the chain, there was also a true-silver brooch, which bore the emblem of the dwarf realm of Vargland. Alex's package also contained a long dagger in a silver-and-black scabbard. When he drew the blade, he saw several dwarfish letters engraved on it.

"A blade made of true silver," said Thrang, looking at the dagger in Alex's hands. He pointed to the engraving. "And a charm to keep it sharp and unbroken. It will serve you well."

"Umbar has been most generous," Halfdan commented, putting his chain around his neck.

"The return of his father's bag has made him richer than many dwarf lords," said Thrang with a wide smile. "He can afford to be generous."

"Still, it is a kind gift," said Arconn, pinning his brooch to his tunic. "That he has been generous to us all and not just to the bringer of the bag is strange."

"I think he heard our young friend trying to share his reward with us," said Skeld. "Perhaps he is trying to make up for what we would not take."

"Perhaps," Bregnest agreed, looking at his own brooch. "But whatever the reason, he has been most kind."

They were all in good spirits as they drank a toast to Umbar, son of Umbar, but Alex still felt as if some shadow was hanging over them.

During his watch, Alex wondered when and if they would ever reach the end of their journey, and then remembering that a dragon waited for them, he wasn't sure if he was really in such a hurry for the adventure to end. Thinking about what had happened so far, he had to admit the adventure had been a great deal of fun. The attack of the bandits and fighting the three-legged troll seemed almost like dreams now, and not something to be afraid of.

"So you've decided you like your adventure," Arconn said with a smile, as Alex shared his feelings that night.

"It's different than I thought it would be," replied Alex with a smile of his own.

"But it is not over yet, and it may be very different again before we reach the end."

"That's true," Alex admitted. "But I'm not as worried about the end as I once was."

"Perhaps you've spent too much time with Skeld," said Arconn, laughing.

"I don't think I'm as bad as that," Alex replied, laughing as well.

Alex spent the rest of his watch studying his books while Arconn sat quietly by the fire. Alex's ability to read the magic book was improving, though he still occasionally asked Arconn about the meaning of some of the words.

The days passed quickly as they followed the road east, and it wasn't long before the weather turned wet again. Afternoon thunderstorms became an almost daily event, and they spent most of their evenings trying to dry their clothes. It was during one of these afternoon storms that Bregnest called them to a sudden halt.

"We will camp here tonight," he said, a worried look on his face.

"Perhaps we should move further away," suggested Arconn, looking through the rain at the road ahead.

"It has been a long day and we need rest," said Bregnest, sounding both nervous and troubled. "We should be far enough away—though not as far as I had hoped."

Alex wondered why Bregnest and Arconn kept looking at the road ahead of them; Alex couldn't see anything but rough-looking ground. That night during his watch, Alex asked Arconn about Bregnest's troubled look and words.

"We are close to the ruins of Aunk," said Arconn. "Bregnest had hoped to reach them early tomorrow so we could pass them in the daylight."

"Why? Are there bandits there?"

"No, not bandits," replied Arconn slowly. "The ruins are said to be haunted by the ghosts of men, but I do not think that is true."

"Yet there is something you fear about the ruins," said Alex.

"Aunk has become an evil place, and I do not think it is because of ghosts. I feel great anger and hatred coming from there, though I do not know the source of it," replied Arconn.

"Do you think we are in danger?" Alex asked, looking into the darkness around the camp.

"I cannot say for sure. But I feel both watchful and nervous."

Alex put his books away, troubled and uneasy. He looked to the east and felt the mysterious shadow that had been following them since leaving the Brown Hills draw closer.

"Rest, my friend," said Arconn. "Tomorrow we will pass the ruins, and soon we will meet my kinsmen in the dark forest."

Alex turned slowly back to the camp. He walked to his tent, glancing east once more, before ducking inside. The nervous feeling continued to grow in his mind, and he remained fully dressed as he lay down on his blankets.

It was still dark when Alex woke with a start. The sound of Andy snoring next to him was comforting, but his thoughts remained troubled. He rolled over and tried to go back to sleep, but his mind buzzed with strange thoughts and he didn't feel tired anymore.

Quietly, Alex got up and stepped out of the tent. The clouds in the sky blocked any light from the moon or the stars. The ashes of the campfire were gray and cold, and when Alex looked around, he couldn't see any of his companions on watch. Sensing trouble, he wondered if he should wake Bregnest when a soft voice broke the silence.

"Your companions are tired," the voice whispered. "They have failed to keep the watch."

Alex turned toward the voice and saw a tall, dark figure standing a short distance from the dead fire. He opened his mouth to warn his friends, but something inside kept him from speaking.

"You have chosen strange companions," the figure continued. "I would not think that one as great as yourself would be seen in such company."

"I didn't choose them, they chose me," replied Alex. "And I am not great, I'm only a first-time adventurer."

Soft laughter came from the dark figure, but it was like nothing Alex had ever heard. His skin crawled at the sound of it, making him feel like hundreds of tiny pins were sticking him.

"If they chose you," the voice continued, "it was only so they could use your power."

"What do you mean?" Alex questioned.

"I mean you could be great—far greater than any of these who call you friend," the voice sneered. "You need only find your true self and your true friends. Friends who will help you to greatness."

"These are my friends," Alex replied defiantly.

"Friends," the voice scoffed. "Friends who take treasure that should be yours. Friends who laugh at you behind your back."

"They have taken nothing but their fair share—less than that at times," said Alex, anger building inside of him.

"But it was *you* who killed the troll," the voice replied softly. "It was *you* who defeated the bandits, and it was *you* who returned the lost bag to its heir."

"We have an agreement," Alex said. "I only did what had to be done. As any of them would have done."

"Do not be deceived, my young friend," said the voice in a soothing tone. "None of them could have done what you did. When you faced the troll, where were they? Hiding in the bushes, no doubt, waiting to see if you would survive."

"They were searching for our horses," said Alex, his thoughts returning to the night he'd fought the troll. He remembered now that the others had appeared suddenly, once he'd defeated the troll.

"And did not your leader offer to take the so-called burden of the bags from you?" the voice asked. "Did not this leader seek to take your honor and glory?"

"He did it as a favor to me," answered Alex, only half-believing his own words. "He said the reward would be mine, even if he carried the bags."

"He has said many things, but that does not make them so," the voice hissed. "Did not the elf say that Bregnest is seeking to fulfill a prophecy? Yet the company has not heard what this is."

Alex thought for a moment, confused. Bregnest had said the company would have no secrets, yet he knew nothing of Bregnest's prophecy. Were the others using him for their own purposes? Could it be they were only pretending to be his friends? His mind felt clouded and he was having difficulty focusing his thoughts.

"Your true friends would be more open," the voice continued. "We would tell you what we seek, and what we could do for you."

"And what is that?" Alex questioned. He felt a coldness creeping into him, like ice-cold claws tearing at his insides.

"We want you to be great," said the voice. "We know you can be the greatest wizard who has ever lived. You can be the greatest king in all the known lands."

"And what price would you ask for this greatness?" Alex asked, more to himself than to the shadow.

"A small thing that another has asked of you," replied the voice. "The simplest of things to look at, though it is strong in magic."

"What?" Alex demanded.

"The crystal the Oracle would claim as her own," the voice hissed. "It was not stolen as she pretends, it was taken by its rightful owner."

"But I have sworn an oath," said Alex. He remembered Iownan's face, her kind words and her smile that made him feel safe and happy.

"An oath to a liar has no meaning," said the voice. "And with the crystal we can show you the way to greatness. The Oracle saw what is in you, but she said nothing. We will tell you all."

"The others have sworn an oath as well. They believe what the Oracle told them," said Alex, his mind feeling more confused and muddled. Was it possible the Oracle had lied to them? Could an oracle tell a lie? Alex didn't know.

"You do not need the others," answered the voice. "Your true friends will take care of them. Then you can recover the crystal for us. When we have the crystal, we will tell you why you are so great."

"What do you mean—take care of?"

"We will drive them away. Once they are gone, you can fulfill your destiny," said the voice urgently. "It is your destiny to slay the dragon. Only you can do this. We will help you. We will guide you to victory and greatness."

For a moment, Alex could see himself in a strange dream, sitting on a beautiful golden throne, crowds of people bowing and cheering for him. He could see every wild wish he'd ever had coming true, his every desire fulfilled.

"Leave the others and come with us," the voice said, low and persuasive. "We are your true friends. We are the ones who want to see you become all that you can be."

"But the others . . ." Alex said. "What will become of them? What will they think?"

"They will think whatever you tell them to think," the voice replied coldly. "They will do as you command, or they will die."

Alex's hand automatically grabbed his sword. The cold feel of Moon Slayer under his hand helped focus his mind, and the magical fire began to burn inside of him, clearing his thoughts as the dreams of greatness slipped away.

"Slay your enemies," the cold voice said softly. "They mean nothing. Only your greatness matters. We will help you. All creatures will know you as their king."

The words rang inside Alex's head as the heat of the sword grew more intense. Bregnest and the others were not his enemies, they were his friends. They had not taken advantage of him, but had shown him great kindness.

"Slay them and join us," the dark voice screamed in Alex's mind. "Together we will rule all the known lands."

Alex drew his sword, looking around as the magic heat

burned like a raging fire inside of him. There was not one dark figure standing beyond the cold ashes of the campfire, but many. They stood motionless, watching Alex as though they were made of stone. But the sound of their evil laughter filled the air around him.

"I will slay my enemies!" Alex yelled back at the dark figures, the flaming heat of his magic sword burning away his clouded thoughts and doubts. "I will destroy them all!"

Jumping across the cold ashes at the dark figures in front of him, Alex saw Moon Slayer shining like a blue flame in his hands. He swung the sword at the figures closest to him, and as the blade passed through them, they melted away like mist. Terrible screams and howls of pain filled the air as he moved forward, swinging his sword at any movement.

Alex felt like he was on fire, but the power of the sword kept him on his feet, moving and hacking at the dark figures that surrounded him. The screaming grew louder, though the figures did not try to fight back or run away. Soon only one figure remained. One last shadow standing tall, waiting for Alex in a dark mist blacker than any night.

"Join us," the cold voice begged. "We are your path to fame and glory. If you stay with them, you will become nothing. There is much more in you than you know. Only we can show you what you really are."

"You lie!" Alex yelled back in anger. "You are full of hate and lies!"

Alex rushed forward, swinging Moon Slayer with all his strength at the last of his enemies. As the sword passed through the last shadow, a terrible shriek ripped through the air, filling Alex's mind completely. The heat that had been burning inside him went out like a light, and he felt like his insides had turned to ice. He was so cold—so very cold and tired.

Alex tried to remain standing, but his legs felt weak and unsteady. He remembered the dream that had scared him out of sleep in Telous so long ago, the painful cold that had filled him. Struggling to turn back to camp and his friends, Alex stumbled and fell forward with his sword under him. He remembered nothing more.

CHAPTER SIXTEEN
THE DARK FOREST

Alex," a voice called from far away.

He was so comfortable and didn't want to answer, but the voice kept calling. Maybe if he ignored it, the voice would go away.

"Alex, can you hear me?"

"Yes," Alex answered reluctantly.

The voice seemed to be coming from the strange light behind him. Alex didn't want to look at the light because his eyes were tired and the softly shaded land in front of him looked so pleasant. If he moved forward, across that low stone wall, then perhaps the voice would leave him alone.

"Alex, you need to open your eyes," said the voice, desperate and worried. "Turn to the light."

"Very well," Alex said slowly, his brain struggling to remember the words as he spoke.

He turned away reluctantly from the gray lands and the low wall. Facing the light, he discovered it wasn't as bad as he thought it would be. The light was gentle, soft and warm. Perhaps he would feel warmer if he moved toward the light.

"Alex, open your eyes," the voice pleaded.

Slowly Alex obeyed, blinking several times to bring things into focus. He saw Arconn's worried face above him. He looked old and sad, not at all like himself.

"Can you sit up?" asked Arconn wearily.

"I think so," Alex answered, the words coming slowly.

With a great effort he tried to sit up, but his body felt so heavy. It would be easier to go back to sleep—back to the gray lands, the strange wall, and what was beyond.

"You need to get up," said Arconn, lifting Alex to his feet. "You need to move around."

"Very well," said Alex, forcing himself to think about standing. For a moment he felt dizzy, and then he felt sick. His stomach lurched as he tried to move his feet, and he would have fallen if Arconn had not caught him.

"Come," said Arconn softly. "Over to the fire, then you can rest for a bit."

Alex struggled to walk, dragging his legs and feet forward as his stomach churned inside of him. He shook his head, try-ing to clear the cobwebs from his mind, but everything still seemed blurry.

"Drink this," said Arconn, pressing a cup to his lips. "It will help with your dizziness."

Alex sipped the sweet liquid and after a moment he felt steadier and less dizzy. His mind cleared a little as he sat down near the fire and wiped cold sweat from his forehead with his shirtsleeve. Things slowly returned to focus, and he could see the worried faces of his friends all around him.

"What happened?" Alex asked.

"We were hoping you could tell us," said Thrang, looking at Alex in concern.

Alex suddenly lurched forward, his stomach retching and his whole body shaking with cold. The memory of the shadow figures returned to him, and a sudden cold stabbed at his insides.

"Shadows," Alex managed to say through clenched teeth. "Shadows of darkness were here last night."

"Wraiths," said Arconn, nodding grimly. He wrapped a blanket around Alex's shoulders, gently pulling him back into a sitting position.

Alex could see that his companions' faces had gone white when Arconn had named the shadows, and they looked afraid.

"They are gone now," said Alex, trying to cheer his friends. "They are gone, forever."

"Can you tell us what happened?" Bregnest asked, deep concern for Alex showing in his face.

"I woke up in the night," said Alex, shaking so hard his teeth chattered. "Nobody was on watch. I was about to wake you when they spoke to me."

"You spoke with the wraiths?" Arconn questioned softly, his voice troubled.

"They wanted me to join them," Alex said, nodding. "They wanted me to bring the Oracle's crystal to them and join them."

"And you refused," said Arconn, looking into Alex's eyes.

"They said if I joined them I could be great," Alex stammered. "They said you were not my friends and that they would drive you all away so I could get the crystal from the dragon. They told me that you would do as I said or you would die. When they said that, I reached for Moon Slayer. I was on fire. I knew they were lying to me. I attacked them. They didn't even try to run away. When I attacked the last one, the fire inside me went out, and I . . . I felt like I had turned to ice."

"Enough," said Arconn. "We will not speak of this here. We must press on to the dark forest at once."

Bregnest nodded, motioning for the others to finish packing up their camp.

Alex remained by the fire with the blanket wrapped tightly around him. He felt cold and weak, and he was having trouble focusing his thoughts. Arconn remained with him, silent and watchful.

"Will he be able to ride?" Bregnest asked in a worried tone.

"I think so," Arconn replied. "And I think the rest of us have little to fear from Aunk now. The darkness that I felt has gone."

"Where has it gone?" Tayo asked from behind Bregnest.

"It is simply gone," answered Arconn. "I believe that Alex has driven it out completely."

Alex wanted to ask what Arconn meant, but he couldn't remember the words. His mouth felt dry and empty. His stomach continued to turn and twist inside of him. He couldn't seem to focus on anything. He was so tired. So cold.

"Drink a little more of this," said Arconn, lifting the cup to Alex's lips again. "It will help with the cold."

Arconn carefully helped Alex onto Shahree's back, wrapping the blanket tightly around him. Even though the sun was bright and warm, Alex shivered under the blanket. He thought Skeld and Andy rode next to him, but he couldn't be sure. He wanted to tell them not to worry, that Shahree wouldn't let him fall, but the words disappeared before he could speak.

The day passed in fits and starts. Every time Alex managed to look around, the landscape had changed, his vision blurring and all the colors turning to gray.

As the sun began to set, Alex felt his insides growing colder. The blanket was an icy weight around his neck, and he could feel his legs shaking wildly. He wondered if he would ever be warm again.

"The forest is near," said Arconn as darkness covered the land. "We must press on quickly and hope to find my kinsmen."

"If they are there, we will find them," said Bregnest, sounding determined.

Alex felt so tired. All he wanted to do was sleep. Sleep so the cold would go away. Maybe he would dream of the gray lands, the shadowlands that beckoned. It would be nice to sleep, to dream, to be warm.

He didn't know when the dream took him away into darkness.

———◆◆———

A soft breeze blew and Alex turned slowly, standing high on a hill, looking out over the soft gray lands that spread out in front of him. The low stone wall stood at the bottom of the hill, promising rest and relief.

Slowly he made his way down the hill, the wall growing larger before him as he studied the land beyond. How pleasant it would be to explore those lands, to find a spot to rest and leave all of his troubles and worries behind.

"Alex," a voice called from behind him. "Alex, please stop."

Alex turned to see who had spoken. To his surprise, the most beautiful woman he had ever seen was walking down the hill toward him.

"Who are you?" Alex asked as the woman drew closer.

"I am Calysto. I have come to call you back to the land of light."

"Why would I want to go there?" Alex asked, turning to look at the wall. "The land beyond the wall looks so nice. The light isn't very bright, but you can see for miles and miles just the same."

"It is the land of shadows, Alex," said Calysto. "If you go there, you can never return to the world of light."

"If I go there, all of my troubles will be forgotten," Alex answered.

"All the good that you may do will be lost," said Calysto in a worried tone. "Come. Return to life. There will be time for the shadowlands another day."

"No," said Alex. "I want to go beyond the wall. Come with me. Let's explore this new world together."

"I do not belong there."

"Come with me," Alex repeated, turning to look back at Calysto. "Together we will find a peaceful place to rest."

Slowly Calysto moved forward, her feet dragging across the ground as if reluctant to do as Alex asked. Calysto looked beyond him into the shadowlands, and he could see the fear crossing her face.

"Come," Alex commanded.

Calysto took a few quick steps toward him and then slowed once more.

"I . . . I do not wish to go there," Calysto said as she finally came to a halt. "If you will not return to the world of light and life, then please, do not ask me to join you in the shadow-lands."

"Light and life." Alex considered the words. "Warmth and friendship as well."

"Yes, those as well."

"The lands beyond the wall look so inviting," said Alex. "So restful."

"It is not your time," answered Calysto. "You have things to do in the world of light. You have promises to keep."

"Yes. I do."

"Then come," said Calysto. "Please, return with me."

"I . . . I will come," replied Alex, suddenly tired. "I have promises to keep."

Alex slowly climbed up the hill toward Calysto. When he reached her, he paused and looked back over his shoulder toward the shadowlands. Calysto reached out and quickly took his hand in hers. At her touch, he felt stronger and warmer as well. He knew he had made the right choice to return with Calysto, and he didn't look back at the shadowlands again as they climbed the hill toward the light.

"Return," Calysto's voice said softly. "Return and find happiness."

And then the light swallowed the dream.

When Alex woke again he was lying in a soft bed covered with a warm, green blanket. Looking around, he saw he was alone in a low-roofed room, his sword and his magic bag sitting on the table beside his bed. Pushing back the covers, he tried to sit up, but his body was too weak.

"Not yet," a soft voice said from the doorway. "You do not have your strength back."

Alex looked up and saw a beautiful woman smiling at him. She walked into the room, her long golden hair shining in the sunlight and her bright green eyes full of happiness.

"You gave us quite a scare," she said with a warm smile. "We thought we might lose you to the shadowlands, but it seems you have returned."

"The shadowlands?" Alex questioned.

"The gray lands you saw in your dreams," the woman answered. "You were close to crossing the wall when I called you back."

"I . . . I know you," Alex whispered.

"I am Calysto," answered the woman. "I am the queen of the dark woods, and your very happy—and relieved—host."

"The elves of the dark wood—Arconn's kinsmen," murmured Alex, more to himself than Calysto.

"Indeed," Calysto replied softly. "And fortunate you were to find us so quickly. You would not have lasted the night without our care."

"Where are the others?" Alex asked, feeling more awake with Calysto in the room.

"They are close," said Calysto. "They will be happy to hear you are awake; they have been worried."

"How long have I been here? I don't remember reaching the forest."

"You have slept for five days," answered Calysto, looking into Alex's eyes. "You spoke many things in your sleep, but that trial is behind you."

"What . . . what did I say?"

"You should rest," Calysto replied soothingly. "You have suffered much, and dark tales are best left for another time."

"But I'm not tired," said Alex. "And I wish to know what happened after . . . after I fell asleep," he added haltingly.

Calysto moved to the far side of the room. She mixed something in a goblet as she hummed softly to herself.

"Drink this," she said, returning to Alex's bedside. "It will help you rest. Tomorrow, all of your questions will be answered."

Alex took the goblet from Calysto's hand, smiling weakly. The liquid seemed to warm him from the inside as he drank it, and he suddenly felt tired once more.

"Rest, my young friend," he heard Calysto say as his eyes closed. "Rest and dream happy dreams."

———— ◆•► ————

When Alex woke again, he felt wonderful. Sunlight flooded the room and his heart felt light inside of him. The memory of the shadowy figures at Aunk had lost its terror, and the cold he had felt was completely gone.

"You look much better," commented Calysto, entering the room. "Though you will still be weak from lack of food."

"I feel wonderful," said Alex, sitting up and smiling at Calysto.

"After six days and nights of sleep you should," said Arconn from the doorway.

"Arconn!" Alex exclaimed happily. "I'm so glad to see you."

"I have never been far," replied Arconn, smiling and bowing at Alex's warm greeting.

"And he would have been closer, if I'd allowed it," added Calysto, smiling at both Alex and Arconn.

"Only your word could keep me from his side," said Arconn, bowing to Calysto.

"More like my word and a few threats," replied Calysto with a happy laugh. "Though the threats were more for the others than you."

"You are most kind, lady, and even your threats are music to my ears," said Arconn, laughing.

"You may rejoin your friends," said Calysto, handing Alex

a goblet to drink. "They will be pleased to see you feeling so well."

"Thank you," said Alex, draining the goblet. "You have been very kind." Calysto smiled and left the room so Alex was alone with Arconn.

"She seems so strange," Alex commented, after Calysto had gone.

"How so?"

"I don't know. It's like happiness flows out of her."

Arconn laughed and agreed with Alex's comments. He helped Alex pull on his boots and walked close beside him as they left the room and the small house.

Alex was glad Arconn was close because he felt a little awkward on his feet. More than once he stumbled and Arconn had to catch him before he fell. Arconn led him slowly across a green meadow to another wooden house close by. Alex felt much better after the short walk, and even his legs felt stronger.

"Alex!" Thrang's voice boomed as Alex and Arconn entered the house. "Thought we were going to lose you." He rushed over and gathered Alex into a bear hug.

The rest of his companions crowded around, slapping Alex on the back and hugging him warmly as he moved into the room.

"Thought we'd lost you that time, little brother," Skeld laughed, lifting Alex off his feet in yet another hug. "But our elf friends seem to have cured you."

Alex felt truly happy as he returned the hugs of his companions and laughed with them. They all made a great fuss about making him comfortable and then rushed around the room, bringing out food and something for him to drink.

"That was close," said Bregnest, sounding relieved. "We were lucky to find Arconn's kinsmen so quickly."

"You all seem to know what happened to me, can you tell me what happened to you?" Alex asked as he started to eat the food Thrang placed before him.

"On the night you fought the shadows, we were all overpowered by sleep," said Thrang, eager to tell the story. "Even the noble Arconn succumbed to the wraith's spell. That's why there was no watch when you woke up."

"I wonder why they didn't use the same magic on me?" Alex questioned, slightly puzzled.

"I think they must have tried to put the spell on you as well," said Arconn, taking a seat across from Alex. "But for some reason you were able to shake it off."

"How many wraiths were there?" Andy asked. "I mean, if you can remember and don't mind talking about it."

Alex closed his eyes and thought for a moment. "I'm not really sure. At first I only saw one, but the voice kept saying, 'join *us*,' and, '*we* are your friends.' After I touched Moon Slayer, I saw there were several of them—maybe a dozen? I didn't take the time to count."

Andy looked surprised. "I've only ever heard of one or two wraiths together."

"I would have been much happier with only one or two," Alex said, shuddering at the memory.

"Once you'd defeated them, we all woke up," Thrang went

on. "We found you pretty quickly, but your body was stone cold. We were worried we were already too late."

"I remember hearing you call," said Alex, looking at Arconn. "I could hear your voice calling from a long way off."

"If your spirit had traveled much further, you wouldn't have heard me or been able to return," said Arconn. "You were nearly to the wall, and I was afraid you wouldn't answer."

"The wall," said Alex, thinking back to his dreams. "Yes, I remember the wall and the soft gray lands around it."

"We're all glad you did not cross that wall," Thrang said. "If you had, we wouldn't be talking now."

"What did you see beyond the wall?" Tayo asked in a slow, quiet tone, his expression troubled. "Did you see people there? Friends? Family?"

"I don't remember seeing anyone on the other side of the wall," Alex replied after a short pause. "I only remember feeling that if I crossed the wall, all my troubles would disappear."

"We should not speak of such things," said Bregnest. "It will bring worry and darkness to us all."

"I don't know," said Alex, thinking about it. "The wall didn't seem like a place of worry. It was more like a place to start a new adventure."

Tayo's troubled look seemed to fade a little at Alex's words.

Alex continued to eat. The food tasted wonderful and he could feel his strength returning with every bite. He could see how happy his friends were that he had recovered and that reassured him the wraiths had been lying to him.

"Once you had answered my call and had come partway

back, we rode as quickly as we could toward the dark forest," said Arconn, continuing the story. "I knew that when darkness returned, you would be tempted to go back to the shadowlands. I had called you back once, but just barely. I feared I would not be able to do so a second time."

"I remember you saying something about the forest being near," said Alex. "But everything was dark, and all I wanted to do was sleep."

"Yes, the sun had gone down and you were returning to the shadowlands and the wall," replied Arconn. "Luckily, we found some of Calysto's people as soon as we entered the forest. I explained what I could about your battle with the wraiths, and they rushed you to Calysto without asking questions.

"At first they tried to put you on one of their own horses, but Shahree wouldn't let them," Arconn continued. "She was determined to carry you herself, as though she was afraid they would not get you here fast enough. In the end, my kinsmen took Shahree's reins and led the two of you here as quickly as they could."

"And it was lucky they did, because you were almost gone when you arrived. You were speaking softly in your dreams about the gray land and wanting to see what was beyond the wall," Thrang interjected.

"And then Calysto called me back," Alex said quietly.

"It was more like a demand than a call," said Arconn, looking suddenly grim. "I have never seen so much power used to call someone back from the wall. For a time . . ."

"For a time, what?" Alex questioned.

"For a time it seemed that you would take Calysto across the wall with you." Arconn's face was grim.

"I almost did," Alex said, remembering his insistence that Calysto come with him.

"Indeed you did. I do not know how it was possible," Arconn said, his eyes distant, "but it seems that in the end you wanted to come back and Calysto seems happy that you did."

"As are all the elves," said Thrang with a laugh and a smile. "Gives them a reason to hold a feast."

"There's going to be a feast?" Alex asked happily.

"Tonight," Arconn replied. "In your honor."

"My honor? Why?"

"You defeated the wraiths," said Thrang, refilling Alex's mug. "You're something of a hero around here. Not to mention the elves are all impressed with your sword."

"But you'll need to take a bath first," said Skeld, laughing. "Or the elves will be disappointed in their hero, and the rest of us will need to stay upwind of you."

Alex laughed and threw a bit of bread at Skeld before asking where he could take a bath. Skeld led him to a smaller room at the back of the house where a huge tub was already filled with hot water. Fine new clothes and polished boots were sitting to one side of the tub.

The hot water felt wonderful and Alex relaxed, alone with his thoughts. He wondered how Calysto had managed to call him back, and why Arconn had said that her call had been more like a demand. The food and the bath helped clear his thoughts, but he couldn't seem to remember exactly what had happened after the company reached the forest. He felt like he should remember, and the fact that he couldn't troubled him.

The sun was sinking into the forest when Alex returned to his friends once more. They all seemed excited for the feast to start, and pleased that the feast was in Alex's honor. Alex was slightly embarrassed by it all, thinking that he hadn't really done anything worthy of a feast. As shadows covered the meadow, a tall elf appeared in the doorway of the house. He smiled and asked them to follow him to the celebration.

"It will be a grand feast," said the elf as they walked into the woods. "Our people have been arriving all day. From what I hear, the kitchens have pulled out all the stops as well."

Alex laughed at the elf's excitement, which reminded him a great deal of his young friend, Thrain. He wondered how old this elf might be, before remembering that elves did not age like men or dwarfs. He glanced at Arconn who was walking beside him, remembering how old his friend had looked after calling him back from the wall the first time.

"Are you troubled?" Arconn asked, noticing Alex's glance.

"Not really," Alex replied. "I was just wondering why you looked so old the morning after the wraiths attacked me."

"It was not age you saw," said Arconn with a faint smile. "You saw me after a great effort, an effort that took me to a place few elves ever go."

"I am sorry I took you there," Alex said softly so only Arconn could hear him.

"Do not be," said Arconn. "I have long wanted to see the

wall, and now I have. Though having seen it, I would not willingly return. Enough of this talk, we have arrived."

They walked into a vast meadow lit by hundreds of silver lamps. The meadow was crowded with elves sitting at long tables or carrying serving trays. Off to one side, a choir of elves sang happily, while more elves appeared from the trees around the clearing.

"The lady Calysto bids you all to her table," said the tall elf, bowing.

Alex and his companions followed the elf through the crowded meadow toward Calysto's table. As they walked, many of the elves stopped what they were doing and bowed to the company, while others simply smiled and nodded.

Calysto's table sat above the others on a raised wooden platform so that it overlooked the other tables. Chairs ran alongside one side of the table, and in the center chair sat Calysto, smiling as her guests approached.

"Welcome, my friends," said Calysto in her musical voice. "We are pleased you could join us."

"The honor is truly ours," replied Bregnest, beginning to bow but then stopping himself.

Alex barely had time to wonder about Bregnest's unfinished bow before he and his companions were shown to their places at Calysto's table. Alex sat on Calysto's right; an important-looking elf sat to his right. Calysto introduced him as Delinus, the chamberlain of the dark forest.

"Let the feast begin," said Calysto as soon as Alex had taken his seat.

The feast was as good as any he'd ever attended, and it was not only the food that took away his troubled thoughts and worries. The happiness on the faces of the elf host, mixed with their singing and fair voices laughing, left Alex feeling like nothing bad could ever happen again.

Looking along the table, Alex saw Skeld joking loudly with the elves beside him. Andy was trying to sing an elfin song, and even Tayo smiled as he sat listening to the elf choir singing. All too soon the feast ended, the plates and food cleared away, and the elves grew quiet.

"A final toast," said Calysto, rising from her chair. "To he who vanquished the shadows!"

"To he who vanquished the shadows!" the elf host shouted, raising their cups and drinking.

Alex turned bright red at the toast, but managed to hide his embarrassment by drinking from his own cup. The elves all cheered again and started to sing as the feast ended. Alex remained seated, listening to the happy voices all around him and wishing that this night could go on forever.

"Will you walk with me?" asked Calysto, leaning close so that only Alex could hear her.

"As you wish," said Alex, rising from his chair.

Calysto smiled and, taking Alex's hand, led him away from the meadow. They walked in silence for a time, and the happy voices faded behind them.

"You are still troubled," said Calysto softly as they walked through the trees. "You feel that something is missing. That you have forgotten something important."

"You see much," answered Alex, looking at Calysto.

Her face seemed to shine with an inner light, as though a hidden fire or power burned inside of her.

"So, it seems, do you," she replied. "Do you remember what has passed between us?"

"Do you mean after I woke, or before?" Alex asked, afraid of what her answer would be.

"Before," said Calysto, her smile still in place.

"I do not remember everything," answered Alex. "Though I feel that I should."

Calysto stopped walking and turned to face Alex. For what seemed like a long time there was no sound at all, just Calysto looking deeply into Alex's eyes. Then Alex felt as if a light had suddenly been turned on inside his head, a light that showed him the darkest corners of his own mind.

Alex blinked several times before speaking. He felt like he'd just woken up, but he knew he had not. He looked at Calysto's face, remembering her as he had seen her before, when she met him at the edge of the shadowlands.

"Your memories have returned," Calysto said at last, breaking the spell of silence. "I hope they will not be a burden to you."

"I am sorry I forced you to come there," said Alex, shaking slightly. "I did not . . . I did not mean for that to happen."

"It was a near thing," said Calysto, smiling again. "Almost you convinced me to cross the wall with you. But it seems your bonds here were stronger than your desire to leave." She placed a gentle hand on Alex's shoulder. "Do not be troubled. I came of my own free will, and place no blame for what happened on you."

Alex nodded his thanks, unable to speak.

Calysto took his hand again and began walking. "You have great power in you, my young friend," she said at last. "Greater than of anyone I have ever met."

"A power I can't control," replied Alex. "And as long as I do not control it, it is a danger to others, as it was to you."

"Then you know the path you must take," said Calysto. "A wizard's path is often a lonely one, but know that you will always find friends here."

"May I ask you something?"

"Of course," Calysto answered, smiling, her face beaming in the moonlight.

"Why did Bregnest stop himself from bowing to you?"

"Oh," said Calysto, and laughed softly in surprise. "Your friends have forgotten to tell you—you have all been named elf friends. And as elf friends, there is no need for bows, though I think Bregnest finds this practice troublesome."

"Among adventurers, bowing is a way of showing respect," said Alex, smiling.

"Among elves and elf friends, respect is already known so there is no need for the show. Though as you saw, some of my own people have adopted your custom. I think your friend Bregnest was trying to show his respect by not bowing tonight."

They walked in silence for a time, Alex's thoughts less troubled than they had been since the start of his adventure.

He knew now exactly what he had to do, and what he had to become. He also knew that, with time, he would make his friends proud.

"I will leave you here," said Calysto. "Your friends are waiting for you inside."

Alex noticed for the first time that they had come back to the wooden house the company was staying in. He smiled at Calysto, trying to think of a way to thank her for all she had done.

"I am in your debt," he said at last. "If ever you have need, I will always answer your call."

Calysto bowed slightly, a smile in her bright eyes. Then looking up into the star-filled sky, she said, "You are more like an elf than any human I have ever met."

With a last look at Calysto, Alex turned and entered the wooden house.

How long the company remained in the dark forest, Alex was never sure. He remembered many feasts and long nights of singing and laughing with the elves. He remembered walking and talking with Calysto several times, but the days seemed to blend together and he could not count them. When at last the company prepared to leave the forest, the trees were changing color. Summer had passed and soon fall would be arriving.

"We have stayed too long," said Bregnest the night before they were to leave. "Though it is difficult to say good-bye, we must press on."

"Sad will be the parting," said Arconn softly. "Though the return will be more welcome for it."

"You've become more elfin again," said Thrang in a disgruntled tone. "We need to get you away from here so you'll speak plainly again."

Arconn laughed at Thrang's comment, though Alex could see the deep sorrow in his friend. He knew how Arconn felt, leaving the dark forest behind and facing an unknown future. It would be a sad parting for them all, but Alex knew that they all had hopes for a quick return.

The next morning as they were saddling the horses, Calysto came to say good-bye to them. She was smiling, though Alex could see that she, too, was sad to see them leave.

"May good fortune ride with you," Calysto called as they rode into the trees. "And may you return safely to our happy land."

CHAPTER SEVENTEEN
SLATHBOG

None of the company looked back as they rode into the woods. They were all sad to be leaving, and even the hope of successfully finishing their quest did not brighten their thoughts. They followed the path the elves had told them about, a path that would lead them quickly to their final goal.

As the days passed, Alex noticed that the trees had completely changed color from lively greens to bright yellows and reds. There was a chill in the air as well, and each morning seemed a little colder than the one before.

"It will be difficult to cross the wastes in winter," said Tayo one morning.

"It would be difficult at any time," replied Halfdan grimly. "The wastelands around the dragon will test our resolve."

"Then let's make sure we pass that test," said Bregnest as he climbed into his saddle and led them forward.

Slowly the thick forest changed back to meadows, then to open grassland. After a week of hard riding, the grasslands ended suddenly in front of them. The land was bare, empty of grass or trees; only gray rock and brown dirt could be seen.

ADVENTURERS WANTED: SLATHBOG'S GOLD

"We will have to leave the horses here," said Bregnest, unhappy. "We do not have enough food for them, and there is little or nothing that grows in the wasteland."

"I have spoken with them. They know where we are going," Arconn replied. "They will remain close, waiting for our return."

"I hope their wait will be a short one," said Skeld with a smile.

The mood around camp that night was grim and solemn. Now that they were so close to their goal, everyone's thoughts seemed to be on the danger that waited for them, a danger they could almost taste. Even Skeld found little to joke about so close to the wasteland of the dragon.

"We should each add some dry wood to our bags," said Thrang softly, taking his seat next to the fire. "We may need it before we return."

"A fire in the wasteland would be dangerous," said Bregnest. "Though, with winter coming, we may have to risk it."

"And when we slay the dragon, we'll need light to sort the hoard," added Skeld in a positive tone.

"Cold food from here to Varlo," commented Halfdan, picking at his dinner. "Not a happy thought, even for Skeld."

"It need not all be cold," said Arconn, glancing at Alex. "Our young wizard has learned to conjure up fire. If we use his magical fire only in daylight, we should be safe enough."

Alex smiled weakly. Since they'd left the dark forest, he had been practicing spells from his magic book. He was surprised how easy some of them seemed to be. One of the spells could conjure up a bright blue flame, and he was already good at working the magic.

"We should rest," said Bregnest. "Tomorrow we will gather wood and fill our water bags. Then we will begin our journey into the wastelands."

The next morning, Alex spent some time with Shahree. She didn't seem to like the idea of being left behind.

"It's only for a short time," said Alex soothingly. "And I'll be happier knowing you're safe. I know what you did for me in the dark forest, and I will return for you as soon as I can."

Shahree whinnied loudly and nuzzled Alex's shoulder. His words seemed to pacify her, though he could still see a sad look in her eyes.

They put their saddles inside their magic bags, letting the horses wander freely on the open grass. Arconn whispered something into each of the horses' ears and they seemed to understand what he said. Then, with one look back, Alex and his friends walked into the wasteland of Varlo.

Their road was not a difficult one to follow because no plants had grown over it. In fact, Alex couldn't see anything growing at all in the wasteland around them. The land for miles around them appeared completely dead. Alex felt a great sadness inside as he walked through the barren and empty land.

"Dragons usually destroy everything for miles around their lairs," said Andy as he walked beside Alex. "It makes it difficult for anyone to sneak up on them."

"Like we're trying to do," replied Alex with a half-smile.

"It has been many years since anyone has dared bother Slathbog's rest," said Skeld from in front of them. "Perhaps he has grown less watchful over time."

"And perhaps he has grown more," replied Tayo, looking unhappy as he walked beside Skeld.

"If he is watching, perhaps he will meet us on open ground," said Skeld, with a note of hope in his voice. "That would be to our advantage."

"Why?" Alex asked, shifting his bag on his shoulder.

"Slathbog will know the tunnels and ruins of Varlo well," replied Skeld. "On open ground, our chances would improve."

"Time will not have made him so foolish," said Tayo in a grim tone. "He will wait for us in a place of his choosing."

"Wherever he is, we will find him soon enough," said Andy, sounding worried and nervous.

They quit talking and continued to walk. The dead land seemed to press in on them, and their movements seemed loud in the overpowering silence. Alex caught himself looking at the road ahead several times, as if expecting to see the dragon waiting for them. He wasn't the only one. They all seemed to be nervous and watchful, even though there was nothing to see for miles around.

For three days they walked, but there was no sign of the dragon. At mealtimes, Alex would conjure up a bright blue fire for Thrang to cook on, putting it out as soon as the cooking was done. There was little talk as they traveled, and no laughter at all. On the fourth day into the wasteland, it began to rain softly, turning the road into a muddy stream.

"We should turn south," said Bregnest as they slipped and sloshed along the road. "We are near the city. If there is any truth to old Eric's tale, we should look for it."

Alex knew that even if Slathbog knew about the secret passage and was watching the tunnel, a surprise attack was better than waiting for the dragon to find them.

The next morning, they left the road, moving south and east through the empty fields. The fields were far muddier than the road had been and their progess slowed. It was hard work for them to keep moving forward, and they had to stop and rest several times during the day.

As they made their way across the muddy fields, Alex thought that Varlo would have been a pretty land if not for the dragon. Low walls neatly divided the fields, and here and there the burnt stumps of what had once been orchards could still be seen. Alex spent the day thinking about how the land might have looked—before the dragon came.

That night, the rain turned to snow but the fields did not freeze. The company continued to move south, slowed by both mud and snow. It was cold and wet, and even the hot meals Thrang prepared on Alex's magical fire did little to warm them. Alex wondered how many more days they would have to trudge through the sloppy fields of an endless wasteland.

As darkness closed in on the seventh day of their march, Alex heard running water. They soon came to a stream, moving swiftly over broken stones. In the stillness of the wasteland, the sound was incredibly loud.

"This must be the stream the old man told us about," said Thrang as they approached the water. "If ever a stream ran from a dragon's lair, this is it."

Alex agreed. The water in the stream was a sickly pale green, and it looked oily. There was also the nasty smell of rotten fruit in the air, and it turned Alex's stomach. Bregnest ordered them to make camp away from the stream so they wouldn't have to sleep in the stench. Alex walked away from the stream, thinking that there had been some truth to Eric Von Tealo's tale after all. Alex knew that soon they would have to find some way to enter the dragon's lair.

"We will follow this stream to the mountain," Bregnest said the next morning. "Though I don't think any of us like the idea of swimming in its filth to get inside the mountain."

"Perhaps the stream has worn away the stone and we will not need to swim," said Skeld, a note of hope in his voice.

With no other path or plan to follow, they walked beside the smelly stream toward the mountains. They marched all day and most of the next before finally reaching the mountainside. As they approached the mountain, they could clearly see a dark, partly caved-in tunnel next to the spot where the stream emerged. Their spirits lifted when they saw that Skeld's hopes had come true.

"We should rest," said Bregnest as they gathered around the dark opening. "Tomorrow, we will seek our fate in the dragon's den."

The weary adventurers nodded and began setting up camp. Alex conjured up fire for Thrang to cook on, but nobody except Skeld seemed to be hungry.

"If I meet my end tomorrow, I'll do it on a full stomach," Skeld said with a smile.

Alex wandered around the camp feeling uneasy and nervous. He had felt all day that they were being watched. His companions must have felt the same way because they would often glance up at the mountain or out into the wasteland, looking for something that wasn't there.

As the sun sank into the west, its last rays broke free of the clouds. Alex watched the sunbeams with a smile because they lightened his worries and reminded him of the sunny meadows of the dark forest. Alex let his gaze follow the sunbeam's path to the ground. Growing where the light hit the ground was the first plant he'd seen since entering the dragon's wasteland. He looked at the plant in wonder and surprise for several minutes. Partly covered with snow, the small plant seemed odd and out of place growing in the hard soil. Brushing the snow away to get a better look, Alex caught his breath. The plant's broad, dark green leaves were covered at the base with blood-red flecks—Dragon's Bane. Alex was sure of it; he recognized it from Iownan's book.

As carefully as he could, Alex dug the rare plant out of the rocky soil. He filled a large empty sack with soil and gently placed the plant into it. The Dragon's Bane looked like it was barely alive, and Alex feared it might die. He hoped it would not because the next morning they were going inside the dragon's lair. He might need the plant and its healing powers soon.

That night, as the rest of the company slept, Alex kept watch with Arconn. If the dragon caught them unawares and asleep, there would be no chance at all to fight or escape.

As the darkness became complete, Alex felt a small twinge in his mind. It was more than his nervous feelings of being watched. There was something about his feelings that made them more real to him, something he couldn't find a name for. He pondered on his feelings for several minutes, and then he spoke.

"He is close," Alex said softly to Arconn. "I can feel him."

"What?"

"The dragon," Alex replied. "I can feel him."

"You can sense what he is thinking?" Arconn asked in a slightly surprised tone.

"Confusion. Dark thoughts. Hate, and a terrible longing for . . . for something."

"Turn your thoughts away," Arconn warned. "If he sleeps, you may wake him. If he is awake, he may sense you and try to find you through your thoughts. His thoughts may drive you to madness."

"Madness," Alex repeated softly. "That would be a good way of describing what I'm feeling." For a moment, he felt like he was inside the dragon's mind.

"Close your mind to him," Arconn warned again. "Think of happier things."

With some effort, Alex forced himself to think of other

things. He focused his mind on the camp and Arconn sitting beside him in the darkness.

"Are dragons mad?" Alex asked after a few minutes had passed.

"I do not know what you mean by mad," answered Arconn. "If you mean, are they mad like a man who does foolish things for no reason, I would say no. But there is something in them, something that drives them to be the way they are."

"You told me once that some dragons weren't evil."

"That is true. Some of them are free of evil and greed. I have met only one that seemed to be free, and that was long ago."

"You were friendly with a dragon?" Alex questioned.

"We spoke of many things, but I do not think I could call him a friend," said Arconn softly as if remembering something from the distant past.

"What happened to him?"

"I do not know," Arconn sighed. "Perhaps he found a place to live away from the known lands. Or perhaps he has simply hidden himself from all who seek him."

"Could Slathbog hide himself from us?" Alex asked.

"I do not think so, but then, I do not know all the ways of dragons."

They sat in silence for a long time, looking into the darkness around them.

"Go to sleep," Arconn said eventually. "You will need your strength."

Alex walked to his tent, wondering if he would ever meet a

dragon that was not evil, before he remembered that he had never met any dragons at all. That would change in the morning however, and he had to be prepared.

He fell asleep with thoughts of an uncertain future filling his mind.

⸻ ◆ ▸ ⸻

Alex dreamt of dragons. Some of the dragons were good and kind, but most were evil. He dreamt of Slathbog as well, a great red monster that spoke to him the same way the wraiths had spoken to him. He knew Slathbog was lying to him, just like the wraiths had lied to him. In his dream, he was not tempted by Slathbog's words, and Alex woke feeling a strange sort of comfort.

As the sky began to grow light, it was clear that nobody had slept very much during the night. Everyone looked tired in the pale sunlight and worried about what they were going to do. The clouds had blown away during the night, and the dark cave beside the stream looked unpleasant to them all.

Alex and his friends gathered around the small opening, preparing for what they had to do. His eyes fixed on the darkness in front of him and a shiver ran down his back. The darkness didn't bother him, but the smell coming from the cave did. It was a nasty mix of rotten eggs and meat that had been left out too long, and it turned his stomach. Looking away, he tried to think of something happy, but nothing came to him.

Everything that had happened to him in the past few months seemed like a dream, a dream that was fast becoming a nightmare. They had reached the goal of their great quest. Alex had thought this day would never come, and for a moment he wondered why he was here.

"In we must go, or give up our quest," said Bregnest in a grim tone.

"To some this would seem foolish, but let us seek our fate and trust to luck," Skeld added, looking as serious as Alex had ever seen him.

Foolish, thought Alex. That was a good word for what they were about to do. Foolish or incredibly brave, he couldn't decide which. It didn't really matter though, because Alex knew he would go into the dark cave with his friends. He looked around at his seven companions and smiled.

They all checked their weapons, nervously gripping them as if fearing the dragon would attack at any moment. Alex drew Moon Slayer from his side and the pale winter light glimmered bright blue on its sharp edges. He could feel the sword's power enter him, but it was not as violent as before. He knew he would not feel the burning heat until his enemy was much closer.

"A single torch," Bregnest ordered as he bent down to look into the cave. "We will need some light, even if it proves fatal."

Thrang quickly retrieved a torch from his bag. Lighting it with a word, he handed the torch to Bregnest.

Bregnest took a deep breath, looked around at the company, and then slipped into the cave. Arconn followed him with Thrang right behind him.

"After you, master wizard," said Skeld with a brave smile.

"Perhaps your luck will flow behind you and I may catch some of it."

Alex smiled and followed Thrang into the darkness. The smell was even worse inside the cave, and the floor seemed to be covered with slime. He slipped slightly and touched the wall to balance himself, discovering the walls were also covered with greenish slime.

"The dragon's filth is all around us," said Thrang in a hushed whisper.

"Silence," Bregnest whispered back.

Alex could see Bregnest's worried face in the torchlight ahead of him. He knew they needed to surprise the dragon if they could, and the smallest sound might mean their doom. As quietly as he could, Alex moved forward with his friends, keeping close to the slimy wall. The idea of slipping and falling into the dirty stream was far worse than touching the filth on the wall beside him.

They moved along the tunnel slowly, quietly. The water rushed past them, covering any noises they made, including the sound of their breathing. Fortunately, the path was level and fairly wide, running straight into the heart of the mountain.

To Alex, time seemed to crawl by, but in the darkness, it was difficult to tell. Bregnest's torch moved forward, its light flickering against the walls. With every step, Alex became more nervous, sure they would emerge in the dragon's lair. Suddenly the torch stopped, and he could see Bregnest motion for the company to gather around.

"We are close," Bregnest whispered so softly that Alex wasn't sure if he'd heard him or only imagined it. "There is no light ahead. I don't know what that means."

Alex remembered what Arconn had told him about dragons, how their fire made them glow in the darkness. The fact there was no glow from in front of them meant Slathbog wasn't there. And if Slathbog wasn't there, where was he?

Bregnest shifted nervously, looking around at the darkness. He seemed to be thinking the same thing as Alex, and was just as unsure of his answer. Slowly he began to move forward, holding the torch high above his head. The others stayed close behind him, moving quietly along the passage.

They finally came to a wide set of stairs, and Alex knew that these would lead into the great hall of Varlo. This was where they had hoped to find Slathbog. They moved forward in pairs: Arconn beside Bregnest, Thrang beside Alex. The deep darkness and quiet was almost painful, and Alex would have welcomed the dragon, if only to break the silence. Then they would no longer have to wonder and worry about where he was.

When they reached the top of the stairs, two things happened at once. For a second, the torchlight blazed, reflecting back at them from thousands of gold and silver objects in the hall. And then the torch went out.

"*Inferno*," Thrang commanded in the darkness. The torch sputtered and died once more. "*Inferno*," he tried again, but the torch would not stay lit.

"This is some dragon's spell," Thrang muttered. "What do we do?"

There was no time to answer his question. A sudden crash in the tunnel behind them made them jump. Alex felt the touch of the dragon in his mind. Slathbog had found them.

"Cunning worm," spat Halfdan. "He must have seen us entering, and now we are boxed in. He can attack us at his leisure."

"And in this darkness, we can't find our way out of his lair," Thrang complained.

"We must do something," said Bregnest urgently. "If we wait here for the dragon to return, we are doomed."

"Just a moment," said Alex, slipping Moon Slayer back into its scabbard. "I think I remember something that might help."

"If you can do anything at all, do it quickly," Arconn urged. "We have little time before the dragon returns."

Alex moved forward in the darkness, softly speaking the magic words he had learned from his book. He focused all his thoughts on remembering the brightly lit caves of the dwarf city as he worked his spell. He raised his hands to shoulder level as he forced the magic out of himself and into the darkness. He felt suddenly weak once he had finished speaking the words, but he was happy to see his spell had worked.

Hundreds of torches and lamps around the chamber, including the torch in Thrang's hands, sprang to life. Their bright flames were reflected a thousand times over by the vast piles of treasure that filled the gigantic hall. Alex and his friends stood still for a moment, dumbstruck by the incredible size of Slathbog's hoard. Alex had thought his payment from Umbar was large, but it was a drop in a bucket compared to what he saw before him.

"Quickly," said Arconn, regaining his thoughts faster than the others. "We must find a better place than this to face the dragon."

At the sound of Arconn's voice, they began to struggle forward through the piles of treasure blocking their way. The hall was much larger than Alex had first thought, and it took some time to make their way across it. When they finally reached the far side of the hall, they found a wide staircase leading up into the ruined city.

"If we can catch Slathbog where he thinks we won't be, we have a chance," said Bregnest, breathing hard.

"And if he catches us in a narrow passage, we are as good as done," Tayo commented darkly. "Higher up in the ruins would be better than here."

Bregnest didn't wait for any more discussion, turning quickly and starting up the stairs. The stairway was slick with greenish slime, but they all reached the top without falling. Bregnest rushed down another passageway, and then up another set of stairs. Alex noticed that all the torches in Varlo were burning brightly, and he hoped it was because of his spell and not some magic of Slathbog's.

Hurrying through the castle, looking for a good spot to ambush the dragon, he had little time to worry. Alex knew that

Tayo was right: If Slathbog caught them in a narrow passageway, one blast of flame would finish them all.

"Here," said Bregnest, entering a wide hall after the third long stairway. "This is as good a spot as any we will find."

The others nodded, too breathless to speak. Bregnest ordered them to various places in the hall, each man well out of sight of the main entrance. If Slathbog was hasty in his return, they would be able to take him by surprise.

"Behind this pillar, Alex," said Bregnest, pointing. "When the dragon comes, be careful of his wings. The edges are like razors and can cut clean through a man if hit squarely. And remember, do not look into Slathbog's eyes for any reason."

Bregnest rushed off to take his own hiding place. Alex leaned against the pillar, trying to catch his breath while listening for any sound of the dragon's return but all he could hear was the ragged breathing of his friends.

Minutes passed and everyone's breathing grew softer until Alex could hear the torches burning on the walls. The waiting was painful, as every ear strained to hear the slightest sound of Slathbog's return.

Alex started to think there must be some other passageway the dragon could use. If so, Slathbog would be able to come at them from behind, and that would surely mean their death. Alex glanced nervously toward the main doorway they had come through. He hadn't seen any other hallway on their journey here that looked large enough for a dragon, so he tried not to worry.

Alex's thoughts were broken by a sudden, terrible sound—

a roar of pure fury as Slathbog descended through the ruins of Varlo to his hoard. The floor under Alex's feet shook with the dragon's rage.

It wasn't long before Alex heard a loud scraping noise coming closer as Slathbog's armored skin ground against the walls of the passageway. Alex felt nervous and afraid because it sounded like Slathbog was enormous. Shaking slightly, he drew Moon Slayer from his side and prepared to meet his destiny.

As soon as the sword was in his hand, he felt the power of the sword enter, the heat growing fast in his chest. Strange flames of happiness filled Alex's mind, consuming his fears and worries. It felt as though the sword was excited to meet the dragon, almost longing for the battle to begin. It was a wonderful feeling, and at the same time terrible and frightening.

A huge ball of flame shot through the chamber doors. Slathbog had arrived. The fireball hit the wall behind Alex and his friends, scattering bits of burning plaster and rock around the chamber. Everyone held their positions, waiting for Bregnest's order to attack.

Slathbog entered the chamber with a cloud of smoke and flame around him. He rushed wildly to his hoard, blind to his surroundings, afraid his enemies were already stealing his wealth.

"Attack!" Bregnest yelled, rushing forward with his two-handed sword.

Alex stepped from behind the pillar, sword at the ready, but then stopped, staring up at the dragon. Slathbog was a creature of incredible beauty and power, and Alex stood frozen at the sight of the great red dragon.

Bregnest's sword clanged loudly against Slathbog's hind leg, but it bounced off the hard scales, causing no real harm. Arconn's arrows snapped against Slathbog's long neck, unable to pierce the metallic red flesh. Halfdan rushed in with his ax. Swinging with all his strength, he struck at Slathbog's side, but he might as well have attacked the wall for all the good it did.

Slathbog faced his attackers, his great tail swinging around, forcing Halfdan to retreat. The tail hit the pillar next to Alex. The force of the impact knocked Alex off his feet, but it also broke the thoughts holding him motionless. Jumping up, Alex ran forward and slashed at the dragon's tail. Unlike Bregnest's sword and Halfdan's ax, Moon Slayer cut a deep gash in Slathbog's tail, spraying Alex with burning hot dragon blood.

Slathbog roared in pain. Alex moved to attack again. Ignoring the others, Slathbog faced Alex. As the beast turned, Alex could hear a strange hissing noise. It sounded like some kind of language, but the words were too quick and Alex couldn't understand them.

The dragon moved slowly toward him, and Alex looked around at the others, hoping they could distract Slathbog from his deadly mission. His friends were frozen in place, unmoving. Alex guessed the strange hissing he heard had been one of Slathbog's spells.

"You have come far, little one," Slathbog hissed at Alex. "I hope you have enjoyed your journey, as it will be your last."

"I have enjoyed my journey, and I will enjoy many more,"

answered Alex, in a voice he hoped sounded braver than he felt.

Slathbog let out a low laugh and continued to move forward.

"I will enjoy killing you," said Slathbog, stopping a short distance in front of Alex. "It has been a long time since any have dared approach me. Once you are gone, none will ever seek me again."

Alex could feel the fire of his magic sword burning inside him, but he did not raise Moon Slayer to strike at the dragon. Instead of attacking the monster in front of him, he did the one thing he'd been told not to do for any reason: Alex looked into the dragon's eyes.

Everything around him melted away like mist until all he could see was the dragon. Slathbog seemed to freeze as well, still and silent, as he and Alex looked deeply into each other's eyes and minds.

Alex could clearly see the dragon's thoughts and his lust for carnage and destruction. All Slathbog wanted was to hoard wealth and cause pain. There were no happy thoughts in Slathbog's mind. Alex saw, though, that there was a terrible longing for happiness inside of Slathbog because joy was the one desire the dragon did not know how to fill. Looking deeper, Alex saw something he had not expected. Fear was at the center of Slathbog's mind and heart—fear of Alex and his friends, fear that he would lose his hoard, and fear that his evil was at an end.

Alex felt Slathbog's fear working through the dragon's heart and mind. He realized he was stronger than Slathbog. He knew he and his friends would claim the dragon's hoard. He also knew, without a doubt, that Slathbog was about to die.

In a rage of anger and hate, Slathbog coiled, preparing to throw himself at Alex. Slathbog would crush his enemy, even if it meant his own death, but as his fear took hold of him, the spell over Alex's friends was broken.

Tayo suddenly charged at the dragon with a wild yell, driving his long spear into Slathbog's side. The spear sank into Slathbog's body where his great wing met his coiled body.

Slathbog roared in pain, flexing his wings wildly. One wing caught Tayo in the chest, knocking him across the chamber. Slathbog turned away from Alex, trying to dislodge Tayo's spear. Alex saw his chance. Raising Moon Slayer, he ran forward, driving the sword into Slathbog's side just behind his front leg. A second, even more terrible roar filled the hall, followed by mad thrashing as Slathbog struggled to free himself from the burning sword in his side.

Alex held onto his sword with all his strength. Hot dragon blood covered him, but Alex continued to drive his sword deeper into Slathbog's body. He could feel the power of Moon Slayer working inside of him, and he felt like he was on fire. His heart filled with a terrible joy more powerful than anything he had ever felt before, and he almost laughed out loud.

Then as suddenly as it had started, it was over. Slathbog lay motionless at Alex's feet. The fire that had burned inside of Alex was cooling. He pulled his sword from Slathbog's body, feeling that at last he had done something worthy of praise and honor.

The others stood dumbfounded, looking at Alex who was covered in dragon's blood. Skeld finally broke the silence.

"Tayo," he cried, rushing to their fallen comrade. "Tayo, are you still alive?"

Tayo mumbled something unintelligible. They crowded around their friend, not knowing what—if anything—they could do to help him.

"Help me wash this filth off," Alex said, thinking quickly. "And boil some water."

The others sprang into action. Bregnest and Arconn helped Alex wash off most of the dragon's blood that covered him. Thrang quickly lit a fire and started water boiling. Skeld, Halfdan, and Andy tended to Tayo, trying to make him as comfortable as possible.

Alex knelt at Tayo's side, dripping wet and white-faced. Tayo's cut was shallow, but his face was already deathly pale. The edges of his wound seemed burned from the heat of the dragon, and Alex worried the wound might be poisoned.

Thrang brought the boiling water over as Alex retrieved the Dragon's Bane from his bag. To his surprise, the plant seemed to have grown overnight. Carefully, he plucked two of the dark green and red leaves and crushed them in his hands. The fresh leaves crumbled into powder as he rubbed his hands together, and Alex carefully added them to the boiling water.

The fresh, clean smell of springtime filled the hall, bringing hope to Alex's heart. Taking a clean rag from his bag, Alex began cleaning Tayo's wound with the mixture he'd made.

"What is this plant?" Arconn asked, looking at the small plant Alex had set aside.

"It's called Dragon's Bane," answered Alex, without looking away from Tayo. "I found it yesterday, just outside our camp."

When Alex had finished, Skeld stitched Tayo's wound closed and put a dressing on it.

Alex retrieved Iownan's book from his bag and started flipping through the pages. He asked Thrang to boil some more water.

"Do we have black tea, milk, and honey?" Alex asked the others hopefully.

"Plenty of honey, but very little milk," said Thrang, retrieving the items from his bag.

"We only need a little," Alex replied, taking the milk and honey from Thrang.

"I only have green tea, will that do?" Thrang said.

"I have some black tea," said Halfdan, quickly reaching for his own magic bag.

Alex sat down beside the fire Thrang had started and brewed the black tea from Halfdan. He crushed two more Dragon's Bane leaves and added them to the tea along with the milk and honey. He checked his book to make sure he was doing everything right, muttering the spell that went along with the potion that he was trying to make. When he had finished, he returned to Tayo, a full cup of the potion in his hands.

"He needs to drink this," said Alex, looking at the others nervously.

"Let me," said Skeld, holding out his hands for the cup. "I've force-fed sleeping men before."

Alex handed Skeld the potion. Skeld forced Tayo's mouth open and held his nose. Halfdan sat on Tayo's legs, while Skeld used his knees to pin Tayo's arms down. Then Skeld carefully but forcefully poured the tea into Tayo's mouth.

Tayo coughed a little as he swallowed, but did not open his eyes. Alex thought he saw some color return to Tayo's face, but couldn't be sure. "All we can do now is wait," he said.

"Do not be sad," said Skeld with a faint smile. "Tayo knew this might happen, yet still he came."

"We all knew that this might happen," Bregnest added. "Few were as prepared for it as Tayo."

"He's not dead yet," Alex said loudly, an angry edge in his voice.

"You are correct, my friend," agreed Arconn, putting a hand on Alex's shoulder. "And we all hope for his recovery, but dragon wounds are deadly. Even your growing skill with magic may not be enough to cure him."

Alex nodded, feeling sadness dragging him down like a great weight hanging around his neck. Even his companions' happiness about the treasure that was theirs did not cheer him, nor did their retelling of how he slew the dragon. He remembered Tayo's interest in the wall between life and death, but, unlike

Bregnest and Skeld, Alex did not think Tayo was prepared to meet death. If anything, he thought Tayo feared the wall and what was beyond it.

Alex's sorrow changed to anger as he looked at Slathbog's dead body on the chamber floor. Tayo had saved his life, attacking when he did. Tayo had made it possible for him to destroy Slathbog without losing his own life in the battle. Now Alex could do nothing for Tayo but wait to see if his friend would live or die. Slathbog and his evil were to blame for all of this, and as Alex thought about it, his anger began to burn inside of him.

Alex stood up, a deadly rage growing inside of him as he walked toward the smoldering body of the dragon. His anger was hotter than the power of his magic sword had ever been. All he could think about was his hate for Slathbog and his evil. The others were focused on Tayo and did not see the terrible look of pure rage on Alex's face. They could not feel the great sorrow he was feeling.

"*Inferno!*" Alex screamed, his feelings pouring out of him with the word, his eyes fixed on the body of the dragon.

Slathbog's dead body instantly burst into blue-white flames, lighting the entire chamber. There was no noise or smoke as Slathbog incinerated in the intense heat of Alex's anger. The rest of the company watched with open mouths and wide eyes as Alex walked back to them and dropped to the ground beside Tayo.

Chapter Eighteen
The Wall

———◄•►———

Days passed but Tayo remained unchanged. If anything he was growing even more pale and weak, and Alex would seldom leave his side for any reason. The rest of the company spent their time sorting through the dragon's hoard. When they returned in the evenings, they would tell Alex about the vast piles of treasure they had searched through and the wonderful things they had found. Alex smiled at their stories, but a deep sorrow had settled inside of him, and he wondered if he would ever feel happy again.

Sometimes Andy would sit with Alex at night, watching Tayo, worried and troubled. After the third night of Andy's vigil, Alex asked him what was wrong.

"There is a custom among adventurers of our land that if one saves another, there is a debt of honor," Andy said. "The debt can only be repaid in one of two ways. Either the adventurer in debt—or a member of his family—must save the life of the honor holder, or a member of the family in debt must offer the honor holder their share in the primary treasure collected on another adventure." Andy looked down at Tayo's pale face. "My family owes Tayo a debt of honor," he said softly.

"Long ago he saved my father's life, and we have not been able to repay him."

"Tayo is the honor holder, and you fear he will die before you can repay him," said Alex, feeling Andy's sorrow.

"It is more than that," said Andy, his eyes remaining on Tayo. "If the debt is not repaid, my family will lose honor forever. A black mark will be placed against us in the records of our land."

"He has not crossed the wall yet," said Alex, trying to sound hopeful.

"But he is near it," Andy replied. "I had hoped to repay my father's debt on this adventure. But I fear I have failed."

Alex could see by the troubled look on Andy's face that the idea of losing both Tayo and his family's honor were of great concern to him.

The next day, Arconn forced Alex to come up into the sunlit ruins of Varlo with him. The fresh air was pleasant, but the cold winter sun did little to warm the desolate city or to burn away Alex's sadness.

"I fear Tayo is moving toward the wall," said Arconn, looking at Alex. "I do not think I can call him back."

"Would you try?"

"Not willingly," replied Arconn, looking over the ruined city. "Though I have nothing to fear at the wall, I do not wish to see the shadowlands again."

Alex remembered his talks with Calysto and what had happened when she had called him back from the wall. He had not shared the details of the experience with his friends, but he understood Arconn's words and feelings.

"How long will the dragon's wasteland last?" Alex questioned, changing the subject.

"With Slathbog dead and reduced to ashes, his hold over the land will begin to fade," answered Arconn. "The fields will turn green again this spring, I think."

"I would like to see that," said Alex, looking across the bleak and empty lands.

"You may have the chance," said Arconn. "The treasure is far greater than even legend says. It will be some time before it is all sorted and divided. Plus, with so much snow, it would be difficult for us to travel anywhere." Arconn nodded to the three feet of snow that covered the ground.

"Has anyone found the crystal of the White Tower yet?" Alex asked, a strange thought forming in his mind.

"Not yet. Though it has only been four days."

"I will come and look for it," said Alex, his thoughts taking a definite shape.

"A noble task, though dangerous. Perhaps more for you than any of the others."

"What's an adventure without a little danger?" said Alex, laughing grimly.

That afternoon, after checking on Tayo, Alex went with the others to search Slathbog's hoard. While the others were happy that he was doing something besides watching Tayo, Arconn was nervous and worried.

"I believe I know what you are thinking," said Arconn, as

he helped Alex sort through a large pile of treasure. "I should warn you that the crystal might show you things you do not wish to see."

"I have already seen things I have not wanted to see," Alex replied. "I will risk seeing more, if it will help me find the answers I need."

"Then I will do all I can to help you," said Arconn in a firm tone, but his worried look remained.

The two of them searched through the hoard, seeking the treasure Iownan had asked them to return. Alex quickly realized the search could take weeks—weeks he did not have if he wanted to save Tayo. The great chamber was larger than he remembered and every corner was covered with treasure of some kind.

They searched for three more days, and Alex grew more worried and troubled as each day passed. Tayo had started coughing in the night; his time was running out. Skeld said something about him traveling to the other side, and the others all seemed sad and depressed. Alex knew that if he didn't find the crystal—and the answers it held—soon, it would be too late to help Tayo.

As the rest of the company moved around the great hall, sorting different treasures into different piles or carrying it up to the first hall to be sorted, Alex sat down on a pile of gold coins. He was beginning to lose hope of finding the crystal in time, and as his hope fell, so did his mood.

Rubbing his knuckles into his eyes, Alex wondered if Slathbog had known what the crystal was. Would he have put it someplace special? Or would the crystal have been just one more treasure to keep hidden in his dark home?

Alex looked up at the pile of treasure in front of him. He shook his head; it was more like a small mountain of treasure. It would take him weeks to sort through it all, even with everyone's help. It was hopeless to think he could find the crystal in time.

Dropping his head into his hands, Alex felt despair wash over him. He was lost in a sea of treasure, and trying to find the one single item he needed more than anything else appeared to be an impossible task.

"I need to find it," Alex whispered in frustration. "I need to find it before time runs out for Tayo."

Looking back at the mountain of gold in front of him, Alex wondered if there was some magic spell that would help him find the Oracle's crystal. He didn't remember anything from his studies, and he shook his head in frustration. He started to turn away from the pile of treasure when something caught his eye.

At the very top of the massive pile of wealth a strange ball of light glittered brightly. Alex knew the ball was only reflecting the torches around the hall, but it was amazing to look at just the same. The ball of light had not been there a moment ago—he was sure of that—but now it was as clear as the sun on a cloudless day.

Alex climbed the mound in front of him, slipping and sliding as the loose treasure moved under him. He kept his eyes fixed on the crystal as he climbed, afraid it might vanish as suddenly as it had appeared.

Stretching up and forward, Alex grasped the globe of light with both hands. It was feather-light in his hands despite its large size. Carefully lowering himself into a sitting position, he looked into the depths of the crystal. There was no time to worry about what might happen to him or what he might see.

What had been a glowing, fiery surface turned milky white. Alex stared into the crystal, willing it to show him what he desperately needed to know. The orb seemed to come alive with a thousand tiny sparks, and then the face of Iownan appeared, smiling at him from far away, giving him hope.

Alex concentrated on the crystal as Iownan's face faded away, replaced by others he did not know. The faces started changing faster and faster. Alex's eyes began to water, but he did not blink, afraid of breaking the spell. Somehow he knew if he could hold on long enough, the crystal would show him the answers he was looking for.

Alex didn't know how much time had passed before he felt Arconn's touch on his shoulder.

"Alex? Alex, are you all right?"

"I'm fine," said Alex, drawing a deep breath and blinking several times to clear his vision.

"I see you've found what you were looking for," commented Arconn, pointing at the crystal in Alex's hands.

"And it has shown me what I need to know," replied Alex, standing up and carefully climbing down the pile of treasure with Arconn's help.

"Then you must use what you have learned," said Arconn. "I do not think Tayo will last another night."

"Quickly then," said Alex, hurrying across the chamber floor.

As they were leaving the great hall, Alex handed the crystal of Iownan to Bregnest and hurried past without explanation, ignoring the surprised looks from his friends.

"I'm going to call him back," said Alex, as he and Arconn climbed the stairs out of the great hall. "Either that, or help him to cross the wall."

"It will be dangerous," Arconn warned, looking worried. "It has not been long since you almost crossed the wall yourself. What lies beyond will call to you again, and you are not a trained healer."

"I will be fine," replied Alex, smiling at Arconn in a reassuring way. "I know what to expect, and I know how to get back."

When they reached Tayo, Alex knelt at his friend's side. He picked up Tayo's right hand with both of his. He paused for a moment, preparing his thoughts for what he was about to do. He knew it was dangerous and possibly even foolish, but he also knew he had to try. Somehow, he already knew he would be safe.

"If it looks like you are fading, I will break your hold," said Arconn in a determined tone.

"There will be no need, my friend," Alex replied confidently. "I will be safe."

Arconn nodded. He looked worried sitting there in the

torchlight, but Alex had no more time to reassure him. He took a deep breath and focused his thoughts.

"Tayo," he called softly. "Tayo."

It happened faster than Alex expected. Suddenly he felt himself leaving the torchlit chamber, even though he knew he was still sitting next to Arconn. He was walking up a gray, grass-covered hill, a soft breeze blowing in his hair. At the top of the hill, Tayo stood as still as a statue. Alex was surprised that Tayo had waited on the hill for so long.

"Why do you wait here, my friend?" Alex asked, walking up beside Tayo.

"The Oracle told me to wait for a sign," Tayo replied, not looking at Alex.

"What sign?"

"I do not know," said Tayo in a dreamy voice. "I had hoped she would give me a sign, but she has not."

"Who?" Alex questioned, watching Tayo's face as he spoke.

"She who waits beyond the wall," answered Tayo, raising his hand and pointing down the hill to the stone wall below them.

Alex looked and saw a woman standing on the far side of the wall. He wondered who she might be and why she was waiting for Tayo. At first he thought he should ask Tayo who the woman was, but then quickly changed his mind.

"Wait here," commanded Alex.

He turned away from Tayo and walked slowly down the hill to the wall. He felt slightly nervous, remembering the last time he had been this close to the wall. But this time, he felt like he knew what he was doing. This time, he had a different reason for being here.

As Alex approached the wall he could see the woman more clearly. She was tall, with long dark hair that hung loosely around her face. She was pretty, and although she was smiling at Alex, there were tears in her eyes.

"Do you wait for Tayo?" Alex asked the woman when he reached the wall.

"I do," she answered in a voice that sounded far away.

"Why do you not call to him? Or show some sign?"

"It is not his time," she said, her eyes leaving Alex and returning to Tayo.

"Then why do you not send him back?"

"Because I long to speak with him again," she replied in a desperate, longing voice.

"I will speak to him for you—if you will allow me to."

The woman slowly looked away from Tayo once more, her eyes resting on Alex. Her smile faded and she looked lost and confused.

"You would . . . you would do that for me?" she asked in disbelief.

"For you, and for my friend Tayo, who has waited here for many days."

The woman smiled, as if Alex had given her more than she had ever dared to hope for. Tears of joy ran down her face as her eyes returned to Tayo.

"Will you tell him that his time is not yet, but that Elsa waits for him," she said. "Tell him I do not blame him for what happened, or for him not being there when I crossed the wall. Please tell him that he should seek life and happiness while he remains beyond the wall."

"I will tell him for you, Elsa," said Alex, bowing to the woman.

"Bless you, friend of Tayo," replied Elsa, smiling and bowing to Alex.

Without saying anything more, Elsa turned away, walking back into the shadowlands. She vanished from sight before Alex could even look away.

Alex turned away from the wall. He could feel the call of the shadowlands behind him, pulling at him as he walked away, but he did not look back. He slowly climbed up the hill to where Tayo waited. When he reached his friend, he took Tayo's hand in his own.

"Elsa sends word," Alex said softly.

Tayo turned to look at Alex for the first time. Tears poured down his rugged face as Alex gave him Elsa's message.

"I . . . I was away when she died," said Tayo. "She had been sick, but she was getting better. She said I should go on the adventure, and I foolishly went."

"There was no way for you to know she would die," said Alex.

"What kind of man would leave his sick wife to go on an adventure?" asked Tayo.

"You are not to blame for what happened to Elsa."

"Perhaps not, but I should have been there for her," Tayo said. "I should have stayed home until I was sure she was well.

If I'd been there she might have lived. She might still be in the world of light."

"Let go," Alex whispered. "Let go of your anger and doubts. It is the past, and hating the choice you made will not change what happened."

"I should have stayed," Tayo murmured.

"Come," said Alex, taking Tayo by the arm. "You have been here too long, and your friends are worried about you."

Tayo allowed Alex to turn him away from the shadowlands and lead him down the far side of the hill. Neither of them spoke as they walked, and Alex did not look at Tayo.

The gray lands slowly faded around them and Alex could see the glimmering light of the torches growing brighter.

"Alex?" he heard Bregnest say his name softly, nervous and worried.

Alex opened his eyes and looked into the faces of his friends.

They had gathered around Tayo and himself. Each of them looked worried, even afraid, and Alex understood why.

"Tayo," Alex called softly. "Tayo, can you hear me?"

"Yes," answered Tayo in a quiet and tired voice.

"Would you like something to eat?" Alex asked.

"Yes, I am hungry," Tayo answered weakly, opening his eyes to look around. "I feel as if I haven't eaten in days."

"That's because you haven't," said Skeld with a laugh as tears of happiness filled his eyes. "We thought you were going to leave us, now that the dragon is dead and his hoard is ours."

"What?" Tayo blinked several times. "The dragon is dead?"

Alex leaned close and spoke a few words into Tayo's ear. Then, leaning back and looking into Tayo's eyes, he simply said, "Remember."

For a moment, Tayo looked puzzled, but as the memories flooded back, he burst into tears. The others quickly busied themselves around the chamber, not wanting to embarrass Tayo by seeing his outburst of emotion. As Alex turned to move away, Tayo caught his arm.

"I am forever in your debt," he said through his tears. "I can never repay your kindness."

"Your happiness will be payment enough," replied Alex with a smile, and walked over to see what Thrang was cooking.

Over the next several days, Tayo's spirits and health improved greatly. He would laugh and joke with the rest of the company at mealtimes, and would often outdo even Skeld with his joking ways.

"I do not doubt your power, master wizard," Skeld said to Alex one night. "But are you sure you've brought back the right man?"

They all laughed loudly at Skeld's question, and Alex realized his own sad feelings had melted away with Tayo's recovery.

Their days were filled with the toil of sorting and dividing treasure, and enjoying the happiness of completing their quest. They had already moved a large amount of the treasure into the first hall above the great hall to be sorted, but there were still mountains of treasure left.

"Let's all just pick a spot and start filling our bags," said Skeld one night after a long day of sorting. "It will be winter again before we get through all of this."

"I never thought I'd hear Skeld say he was tired of counting treasure," said Tayo, slapping the back of Skeld's head as he walked behind him.

"Now I *am* sure you brought back the wrong man," said Skeld, looking at Alex and laughing hysterically.

Weeks passed and finally they were able to start dividing the treasure into individual piles for each of them. Alex noticed that his pile seemed to be growing quickly and one night at dinner, he asked Bregnest about it.

"Well," Bregnest began in his businesslike tone, "three shares for being a wizard, two for being a warrior, and one for killing the dragon, of course."

"But I did not sign on as a wizard or a warrior," Alex said loudly, but with a smile. "I signed on—as you know very well—as a first-time adventurer."

"Yes," Bregnest agreed. "However, I have modified the Bargain to take certain events into consideration. This is my right, as your leader. You would not break the agreement, would you?"

"It is your right," said Alex, his smile fading. "However, I ask that you not change the agreement. I have gained much more than treasure on this adventure, and feel that I have already been very well paid."

Bregnest looked stern for a moment, but then he smiled and laughed out loud.

"Very well, as you seem so determined to give your treasure away. Hear what I say concerning the division of this treasure." Bregnest spoke loudly so the entire company could hear him. "That portion of the treasure which has already been divided will remain as it is. From now on we will return to the original agreement, by which young Master Taylor will receive two shares out of twenty."

Alex smiled, but Bregnest went on.

"Also, I will use my right as leader to insist that anything which cannot be divided equally go into our young friend's share. Further, I will insist that all rewards from the six remaining lost bags he carries will be his alone. I will insist on this, in spite of his desire to share his treasure with the rest of us. How say you all?"

A great cheer went up from the group, and though Alex was not entirely comfortable having so much treasure given to him, he nodded his acceptance to Bregnest.

"Also," said Bregnest, holding up his hands for silence. "I would ask that Alex accept the honor of carrying the crystal of the White Tower back to the Oracle. Will you accept this honor?"

"I will," Alex said, bowing.

The rest of the company cheered again as Bregnest handed the crystal of Iownan to Alex. Alex carefully placed the crystal, wrapped in a blue velvet cloth, in his bag and bowed to Bregnest once more.

Sorting the treasure had taken months and dividing it was taking weeks more. As they continued working, Alex noticed that all the crowns, necklaces, scepters, and other items that were obviously one of a kind were added to his pile. Once again he protested to Bregnest, but Bregnest simply smiled slyly.

"Well, they are all of different values and cannot be divided equally," he said.

Alex tried to argue, but in the end he was forced to accept all of the items as part of his share, though he remained unhappy about it.

When they had finally divided the hoard and were ready to start transferring it to their magic bags, Andy asked the company to gather by his pile. He looked serious, though he smiled at Alex when he stepped up with the rest of the company.

"Tayo Blackman," Andy began. "You hold the honor of my family. I wish to repay the debt my family owes to you."

"How will you repay?" Tayo questioned, stepping forward.

"As payment, I offer you my share of this adventure's primary treasure."

"Do you do this of your own free will?"

"I do."

"I will accept only part of what you offer," said Tayo, bowing to Andy. "Let all here know that the debt of honor owed to myself is now paid by Anders Goodseed. Will you all witness that it is so?"

"We will," six voices replied.

"Then witness what I accept, and know that the debt of honor is paid."

The company watched as Tayo removed a small amount of treasure from Andy's pile and added it to his own.

"The debt is paid. Your family honor is whole," said Tayo, smiling and bowing to Andy.

The company cheered and clapped as the ceremony ended.

"A moment, Master Taylor," said Tayo as Alex turned away. "Another ceremony is in order as I am now in your debt."

"What?" Alex asked nervously.

"You called me back from the wall," Tayo replied. "You now hold the honor of my family."

"Ah, yes," said Alex, thinking quickly. "However, I only had to call you back because you saved my life. If you had not attacked Slathbog when you did, I would be dead. So I would say the debt is paid, and your family honor is whole."

"Well-spoken," said Bregnest with a nod and a smile.

Tayo stood quietly, the old, grim look back on his face. For a moment, Alex wondered what Tayo would say, but then he smiled and laughed.

"Very well, my friend," he replied. "We will call this debt even."

The entire company cheered once more, and then they each returned to their own piles of treasure and started filling their magic bags. Alex thought about the honor ceremony. He didn't understand why Andy had to offer all of his treasure and why Tayo had taken so little. When they took a break from storing treasure, Alex asked Andy to explain.

"Because it was a debt of honor," Andy replied. "Honor demanded I offer my entire share, but Tayo did not have to take it all. In fact, Tayo increased his honor by taking only a small amount."

"Then wouldn't it increase Tayo's honor even more if he did not accept anything?" Alex asked, still confused.

"He has to take something or it would be an insult," Andy laughed. "It would be saying that my father's life meant nothing to him."

"I guess I understand," said Alex slowly, knowing he had more thinking to do about honor and what it meant. "I'm happy your family honor is whole."

They spent days storing their piles of treasure in their bags, laughing and joking as they worked. There was so much treasure Alex began to wonder how big his expanding room could possibly get, and then laughed at himself for wondering.

Once they had all stored their shares, they went down for one last look at the great hall. It seemed even larger now that it was empty, and when the company cheered one last time, their voices echoed wildly around the empty hall. Collecting the rest of their gear, Alex and his friends slowly climbed into the bright afternoon light.

"Your wish is almost fulfilled," Arconn said to Alex as they walked away from Varlo. "Already the snows are melting. Soon the green of spring will be on this land."

Arconn was correct as usual. As they marched down the muddy road each day, Alex could see small shoots of green dotting the ground where the snow had melted. By the third day, the snow had almost disappeared, and new green plants were springing up everywhere.

"We still have a long walk back to the horses," commented Halfdan as they ate their evening meal.

"And a long ride back to Telous," Thrang added.

"And many happy places to visit, now that we have found success," said Tayo with a smile.

"And what will you do with your great hoard?" Skeld asked Thrang, laughing. "Young Alex and Andy can't help you spend it or they'll never manage to spend any of their own."

"Retire, perhaps," said Thrang thoughtfully, then laughed at the worried looks on Skeld's and Tayo's faces. "Though perhaps my adventuring days are not over just yet."

They spent a happy night joking and telling stories, not bothering to keep watch in the wastelands of the dragon. Alex wished they could stay in this newly reborn land forever, but he knew that, like Thrang, he had many more adventures before him.

CHAPTER NINETEEN
THE JOURNEY HOME

Alex and his companions walked along the road out of the wastelands, happy to see that the countryside was returning to life. There was no need to hurry, and they enjoyed laughing and singing together as they traveled. One afternoon, as they approached the edge of the wastelands, they heard horses galloping toward them.

"Shahree!" Alex called out as the horses came into view.

Shahree whinnied loudly at Alex's call and trotted quickly to his side. He stroked her silver-gray neck happily, and the rest of the company laughed with joy. The other horses galloped up behind Shahree, and Arconn made a point of personally thanking each horse.

"She has been worried since you parted," Arconn told Alex as he rubbed Shahree's forehead.

"That makes us even because I have been worried about her as well," said Alex with a laugh.

They made camp for the night, happy with their success and excited to be going home. Thrang prepared an excellent dinner, and Alex amused his friends by turning the campfire different colors and twisting the smoke into various shapes as it floated into the darkening sky.

The next day, Skeld and Tayo sang several strange and happy songs as they rode. They even managed to convince Andy to join them on a few of the songs, though it took a lot of teasing to do it. Alex was as amazed as the rest of the company to see the great change that had come over Tayo. Alex was glad that Tayo seemed to have taken Elsa's advice to find joy and happiness in his life.

When they eventually returned to the dark forest, Calysto was waiting to greet them in the same meadow they had left months before. It seemed she had known they were coming long before they arrived.

"You left before the first snows fell and already you have returned," she said with a smile. "It seems fortune has favored you greatly."

"Indeed," replied Bregnest. "It has allowed us to return quickly to your happy land."

As before, Alex was unsure how long they stayed in the dark forest with the elves. He remembered many feasts and long walks in the sunny meadows. He felt at peace in the dark forest and was sad that they would have to leave eventually, but he knew his future was not here.

While they remained in the forest, each member of the company exchanged many fine gifts with the elves. Alex gave Calysto a true silver necklace set with hundreds of small, bright green emeralds. It was one of the many items Bregnest had added to his share from the dragon's hoard.

"A gift for some great lady," said Calysto, admiring the necklace.

"Then it is well given," Alex replied.

Calysto wore the necklace at their parting feast, which made Alex happy. At the end of the feast, Calysto and many of the other elves walked with the company to their wooden house. They were all laughing and singing songs Alex had never heard before. No one wanted the night to end, but like all things, it eventually did.

The next morning, as the company prepared to depart, Calysto came to say her final farewell. Alex could see the sadness of their parting behind her usually happy smile.

"May your fortunes be bright," she called after them as they rode to the edge of the meadow. "And if ever you come this way again, the meeting will be a merry one."

Alex turned Shahree before entering the trees, looking back at Calysto. He didn't have words to thank Calysto for all she had done. He simply waved a final farewell, somehow knowing he would return to the dark forest someday.

When they reached the edge of the forest, the sun was setting. They made camp and told stories late into the night. Skeld and Tayo managed to force Andy into telling them about his own first adventure. Andy insisted it was a long and boring story, but they all wanted to hear it just the same.

"You'll have better tales to tell on your next adventure, won't you?" Tayo laughed, slapping Andy's knee as they prepared to sleep.

The next day they started early, pressing forward and passing the ruins of Aunk before the sun set. Alex shivered slightly as he remembered his battle with the wraiths. He knew the wraiths could not harm him now, but he still felt a shadow of darkness as they rode past. He quickly forced himself to think of his friend Thrain and the wonderful halls of Osrik that lay ahead of them.

It was clear the elves had sent word to Osrik while Alex and his friends were still in the dark forest because a troop of dwarf warriors on horseback met them on the road with orders to escort them to Osrik's halls. Osrik was exactly the same as Alex remembered—uncomfortable with too much ceremony and happy to listen to all the stories they had to tell.

"Quite an adventure," said Osrik after Thrang had told their story. "Never thought we'd see the end of Slathbog in my days."

Alex and his friends remained with the dwarfs for almost three weeks, trading treasure for items made of true silver and giving gifts to Osrik and his officers. When it came time to leave the dwarf realm, Osrik asked them to meet with him in his throne room.

"I have a favor to ask," said Osrik, looking at Bregnest.

"Ask what you will, Lord Osrik," replied Bregnest. "Nothing would please us more than to be of service to you."

"It's about my grandson, Thrain," said Osrik, looking past the company at Thrain who was standing at attention at the edge of the great hall. "He's seen your success and heard your stories and he thinks he'd like to be an adventurer."

"Adventurers do not choose themselves, as you know," said Bregnest, glancing toward Thrain.

"No, they don't," agreed Osrik with a smile. "But he and a couple of his friends want to see the Oracle. I have forbidden them to go on their own, but if you were going that way, I thought perhaps they could accompany you. If it is too great a favor, please say so. To be honest, I'm not too happy with the idea myself."

"It would be our pleasure to have their company," said Bregnest happily. "Though we will not be returning this way. How will they get back?"

"I suspect all sorts of people will start traveling east again once the news of your adventure is well-known," said Osrik, winking at Bregnest. "I think the way back will be less troubled, then—fewer bandits and the like around."

"Then we will happily accept their company," said Bregnest, bowing to Osrik. "And we will try not to encourage your grandson's desire too much as we travel."

Osrik laughed at Bregnest's reply, waving for Thrain to come forward.

"It seems you have your wish, my fine young dwarf," Osrik said to Thrain. "You'd best be off and tell your friends. You'll be leaving in the morning."

Thrain was too happy to even speak. He ran forward and hugged his grandfather tightly, and then turned and ran full speed out of the hall.

"I hope he is happy with what the Oracle tells him," Osrik commented, watching Thrain depart. "But even if he gets his wish, I've made him promise to return here before going on any adventures."

"Wise counsel," said Bregnest. "And if he is chosen, my company and I will be happy to help him in any way we can."

"Thank you, my friends," replied Osrik. He smiled wryly. "And you know, there is a part of me that hopes he does get his wish, even if the rest of me does not."

The company all laughed with Osrik before saying good night to the king.

The next morning, Alex and his friends assembled in front of the main gates of the dwarf city. Thrain and his two friends, Melnoch and Nitek, were waiting nervously to one side, away from the company.

Alex was happy Thrain would be traveling with them to the White Tower because it meant he would not have to say good-bye just yet. He had not met Thrain's friends, but he knew if they were anything like Thrain, the journey would be a happy one.

Osrik came out to the gate to say a final good-bye.

"I'm placing the three of you in Master Bregnest's care," Osrik said sternly to Thrain, Melnoch, and Nitek. "If any of you misbehave or fail to follow his orders, I'll throw you all in the dungeon for a hundred years."

Alex and Andy tried not to laugh as Osrik turned his back to Thrain and his friends and winked at the company.

"Good-bye, my friends. If ever you come this way again, you will be most welcome," Osrik said.

"Good-bye, great king," replied Bregnest. "Your kindness will remain with us always."

They all bowed to Osrik and then started down the slopes of the Brown Hills. Thrain and his friends brought up the rear, which made Alex and Andy feel a little strange at first because they were used to being the last in line. As they turned their horses west, though, Thrain rode up beside Alex and Andy and started talking happily with them.

As they traveled from the Brown Hills to the city of Techen, Thrain, Melnoch, and Nitek adapted, as well as they could, to the adventuring lifestyle. However, they were still a little unsure of how to deal with Skeld and Tayo's constant teasing and joking.

"You get used to it in time," said Andy in a low voice to the dwarfs. "And they don't mean any harm."

"Because if we did mean harm, our wizard friend would turn us into toads," Skeld laughed, overhearing Andy's words anyway.

"I may do that anyway," replied Alex, laughing along with the rest of his companions.

When they arrived at Techen, Alex saw that the city had changed a great deal since they had left it. A vast array of tents had sprung up around the mud-brown walls. Hundreds of horses and carts crowded the roads, and a great number of people were selling all kinds of things just outside the main city gates. Bartholomew the gatekeeper was still there, but he looked tired and a bit thinner than Alex remembered.

"You seem to have some new friends," Bregnest commented with a smile.

"I don't know about friends, but there are a lot of them," replied Bartholomew. "Been turning up in droves over the last couple of weeks."

"Why would that be?" Bregnest asked.

"Well, it's the dragon, isn't it?" said Bartholomew, looking at the tents and carts along the road. "Story is out that old Slathbog has finally died, or been killed, or gone away, depending on which story you choose to believe. This lot is off to look for the dragon's treasure, and in my opinion, the sooner they go, the better."

They all had to suppress their laughter because they knew these treasure hunters would find little in Varlo, unless they were looking for land.

"The magistrate must be happy with all the trade," said Bregnest with a short laugh.

"I suppose he is," Bartholomew replied thoughtfully. "Though it's hard to tell what makes him happy. I suppose you'll be spending the night then?"

"If we can find a room in the city," said Bregnest.

"Oh, you needn't worry about that," Bartholomew called, as the company started moving through the gate. "Not many of these will pay for a room. I believe old Tantic has plenty of space."

Tantic greeted the company as if they were old friends he hadn't seen in years. Before they could even climb off their horses, he had brought out a tray of drinks for them and was toasting to the good fortunes of Techen. After their drinks and a few words with Tantic, Alex and the others took their horses into the stable for the night. There was no sign of Eric Von Tealo, so Bregnest asked Tantic where he could be found.

"Ah, a sad story that," answered Tantic. "A good man he was with horses, though perhaps not so good with people."

"You say *was*," Bregnest interrupted. "Is he no longer here?"

"Old Eric turned sick this last winter," said Tantic, shaking his head sadly. "We tried to care for him, but there was only so much we could do. He crossed the wall just as spring was coming in."

"I am sorry to hear that," Bregnest said. "We owed him a debt. Can you tell us where he is buried? The least we can do is pay our respects."

"That's very kind of you," said Tantic with a smile. "Though I doubt you'll be happy with his resting place."

The company followed Tantic's directions to Techen's graveyard to pay their last respects to Eric. They noticed that there were many fine headstones scattered about the graveyard, but on Eric's grave was only a small wooden marker with his name on it. When they returned to Tantic's inn, Bregnest questioned Tantic about it.

"The magistrate didn't much like old Eric," Tantic said, an unhappy look on his face. "Eric was always telling him off for the poor way his soldiers took care of their horses, and for anything else that didn't seem right. The magistrate wouldn't let me put a stone on his grave, only that small wooden marker."

"Can you send word to the magistrate that we would like to see him?" Bregnest asked in a calm voice.

"'Course I can," said Tantic, a slightly wicked grin spreading over his face. "It would do my heart good if you lot told him off."

Bregnest motioned for the others to follow him into the inn's common room. The company sat around a large table, leaving the chair to Bregnest's right empty. Thrain, Melnoch, and Nitek sat at the bar, watching with a great deal of interest. It wasn't long before the magistrate appeared, walking up to their table and frowning.

"You wished to speak with me?" he asked, in an unfriendly tone as though their request to see him was a great inconvenience.

"We do," replied Bregnest and motioned for him to be seated.

"What can I do for you?" asked the magistrate brusquely.

"We wish to discuss the grave of Master Eric Von Tealo," Bregnest replied calmly.

"What about it?" The magistrate's face turned slightly red.

"Well, you see," said Bregnest. "We all owe a debt to the late Master Von Tealo. Now that he has crossed the wall, we would like his final resting place to be honored with something more than a piece of wood." Bregnest's words were spoken softly, but there could be no doubt of the power and anger behind them.

"I'm sure some arrangement can be made," said the magistrate, hardly bothering to conceal the greed in his voice.

"It will be made," Bregnest replied coldly. "We will pay for a large stone to be placed on the grave. Further, we will pay the city of Techen for upkeep of the stone and the grave so that weeds do not grow over it. We will also pay for fresh flowers to be placed on the grave twice a week. We will require these services to be performed for the next one hundred years."

"That is quite a lot for an old man who worked in a stable," the magistrate sneered.

"Perhaps, but we are willing to pay the price you name for these services," Bregnest replied. "Draw up an agreement and we will all sign it."

The magistrate thought for a moment and then called for Tantic to bring him pen and paper. He wrote out the agreement and offered the pen to Bregnest so he could sign it.

"You first," said Bregnest, looking the magistrate in the eye.

The magistrate signed the document and placed the seal of Techen beside his name.

"What price will you ask?" Bregnest questioned.

"The city of Techen asks five thousand gold coins for this service," said the magistrate coldly, a wicked smile on his face.

"Outrageous!" said Tantic from behind the magistrate.

"We accept," said Bregnest, signing his name to the document. The rest of the company each signed his name.

Bregnest pulled out his magic bag. "But know this my fine, greedy magistrate," he said in an ice-cold tone. "If ever I, or any of my companions, hear that you or your city have failed in this agreement, we will return. One of our company is a wizard and we all have many friends close to your city. If you fail to keep this agreement, we will know. If you choose to run, we will hunt you from here to the wall to claim our revenge."

The magistrate's face paled at Bregnest's words. "Of course it will be done," he said nervously, his upper lip trembling slightly. "No need for threats or violence. I have given my word."

"And I'll make sure he keeps it," said Tantic, taking the pen and signing the agreement as witness.

Bregnest handed the magistrate a large bag full of gold and dismissed him with a wave of his hand. The others could barely control their laughter as the magistrate rushed, stumbling more than once, out of the room.

"Let us share in this expense," Skeld laughed. "The price is small compared to the look on his sour face."

"You already have," replied Bregnest. "The five thousand came out of the share for expenses, and I think it was well spent. So Tantic, my friend, can you arrange for a stone?"

"Of any size and style you request," replied Tantic. "And I'll pin this up in the bar so the whole city will know what the magistrate has agreed to." He held up the agreement the magistrate had left behind in his rush to leave.

"And you might have fun reminding him from time to time that we have many friends not too far from Techen," Tayo laughed.

They spent a merry night in Techen, and Alex wished they could stay longer. Bregnest, however, wished to move on as soon as possible. After discussing the stone for Eric's grave with Tantic, and leaving him more than enough money to pay for it, the company rode away the following morning.

They traveled northwest along the ancient road, meeting a few companies of people who were traveling east to Varlo. They tried hard not to laugh as the people told them that Slathbog was dead and that piles of gold were lying everywhere for anyone who wished to take them.

"Well, they're half right," laughed Skeld as they left one of the groups behind.

They met no bandits as they rode toward the White Tower, but they set a watch each night just in case. Alex, having finished reading his books, now spent his watch practicing spells from his magic book. Sometimes Andy, Thrain, Melnoch, and Nitek would sit up with him, talking about adventures, and watching Alex practice his magic.

The journey was pleasant, but Alex was beginning to worry that it soon would be over. He didn't really want to go home, and the idea of going back to his stepfather's tavern and his old life made him more than a little sad. He felt more like starting another adventure right away.

One morning, Alex woke to a strangely familiar dinging sound. Sitting up, he saw a bottle-necked geeb standing beside his blankets.

"Do you have a message for me?" Alex asked politely.

"Ding," the geeb replied.

"May I have it please?"

"Ding! Ding! Ding!" answered the geeb, producing a letter for Alex.

"What's that noise?" said Skeld, sitting up in his own blankets.

"It's a geeb," replied Alex as he opened the letter. "Only just arrived."

Dear friend,

    I am happy to hear of your success and your safe return. Please accept this invitation for you and your company, including your three new traveling compan-ions, to dine with me on your arrival at the White Tower tomorrow evening.

                       Your friend,
                       Iownan

"It seems we've been invited to dinner," said Alex happily, handing the letter to Bregnest. "I suppose you will all wish to accept the invitation," he added, grinning at his friends.

"Good thing too," Skeld said loudly. "Thrang's cooking has been going downhill since he's become so rich."

"Shut your gob," replied Thrang, throwing a dirty pair of socks at Skeld.

They all laughed at this exchange, and then laughed even harder when Tayo suggested that the dirty socks were what Thrang had been using to make soup.

"Indeed, yes, we will accept," said Bregnest with a smile.

"Can you take a reply back to the Oracle?" Alex questioned the waiting geeb.

"Ding," the geeb replied.

Alex took out his writing things and thought for a moment before he started writing.

My friend,

We are overwhelmed by your kindness, and I am happy to accept your invitation on behalf of our company and friends. We will be looking forward to our arrival, and place ourselves at your service.

Your friend,

Alex

"I believe Calysto was right about you," said Arconn, reading Alex's note over his shoulder. "You are very much like an elf."

"Careful," Tayo warned. "He might take that as an insult."

They all laughed at Tayo's joke as Alex folded the letter and placed it in an envelope.

"Here is your payment," Alex said to the geeb, tossing a bright blue sapphire into the air.

The geeb bounced up and caught the sapphire quickly and then left several gold and silver coins on Alex's blanket.

"Please take this letter to the Oracle. If you require additional payment, please return," Alex said to the geeb.

With a final ding and a slight popping sound, the geeb disappeared. Alex collected the coins from his blanket and put them in his small moneybag, then asked about breakfast.

When Thrain, Melnoch, and Nitek heard that they were included in the Oracle's invitation, they were overcome with joy. They had been worried the Oracle wouldn't see them right away, and had started to wonder where they would stay while they waited for her call.

"When we dine with Iownan, she is not the Oracle," Alex

explained to the three young dwarfs as they rode along that day.

"She addresses you as friend," said Thrain in admiration.

"We are friends," Alex replied.

"Do you think you could put in a good word for us?" Thrain asked sheepishly.

"I doubt very much that the Oracle will be influenced by anything I say," replied Alex with a slight laugh.

It was almost noon the next day when a rider carrying a green flag with a white tower on it approached them. He asked them to follow him to the western houses, and they all happily agreed. Once again, the second house was filled with fine food when they arrived and the bathhouse now held eleven large brass tubs full of hot water. When the sun touched the western hills, a young woman appeared to lead them to Iownan's table.

"You have traveled far, my friends," said Iownan, beaming at them as she entered the room.

"Yes, we have," said Bregnest, standing and bowing to Iownan.

"And now you have many new tales to tell," said Iownan, taking her seat between Alex and Bregnest.

Their dinner was full of lively talk and long tales, and when they were finished and Iownan had said good night, they returned to the sleeping house tired and happy. Alex slipped away to the stables to check on Shahree.

"In this fine stable again," said Alex as he stroked Shahree's neck. His thoughts returned to when he had first entered this stable at night and spoken to Iownan. Could it really have been more than a year ago?

"I see that you are not yet broken," Iownan said from behind him.

"Not yet," replied Alex, turning to face her.

"And I see you have gazed into the crystal."

"Only because need forced me to," said Alex with a bow. "I ask your forgiveness. The crystal was not mine to use."

"Though it served you well."

"It did," Alex said.

"Come," said Iownan, taking his hand. "You need your rest. Tomorrow I will speak with your company about your pledge."

"The pledge is fulfilled," said Alex happily.

"Not quite," Iownan replied. "You still hold the crystal, though I do not doubt its return. I know what you had to go through to reclaim this treasure for me."

"You told me I would be tested," replied Alex, his thoughts returning to the night he'd fought the wraiths.

"You are troubled by something," said Iownan, turning to look into his eyes.

"It was something the wraiths said," Alex answered, meeting her eyes. "I didn't think about it at the time because I knew they were full of lies."

"But now you wonder if they did not speak at least a little truth," Iownan finished for him.

"They said you saw something in me—something that made me different."

"I told you that I could see many things in you," replied Iownan. "But you were not ready then to know everything I saw."

"Am I ready now?"

"I believe you are," Iownan replied after a short pause. "What I saw, but did not tell you, was that you are not completely human as you believe yourself to be."

"Then what am I?" Alex asked in surprise.

"You are a blend, a mixture of many races," said Iownan thoughtfully. "I cannot say how much of each race is in you, but I see in you human, elf, and dwarf. And other things as well."

"What other things?" Alex questioned, worried.

"It is difficult to say for sure," replied Iownan, turning away from Alex. "It is strange. I have never met anyone like you before."

"If you do not wish to say—"

"I would tell you if I could," said Iownan, cutting him off, a troubled look on her face. "But it is beyond even my powers to see all that you are, or all that you might become."

"Forgive me for asking," said Alex.

"Come," said Iownan, her smile returning. "You need your rest."

Alex didn't ask any more questions. He knew Iownan spoke the truth and that if she could have told him more she would have. He accepted her hand, and together they left the stable, walking back to the sleeping house.

The next morning, a young man named Thomas appeared

as they were finishing breakfast. He told them the Oracle would like to meet with Bregnest and his company in the gardens by the fountain. He also said that Thrain, Melnoch, and Nitek would be called to the Oracle after the midday meal. Alex quickly retrieved the crystal in its blue-velvet wrapping from his bag and followed Bregnest to the gardens.

"You have returned from your quest successfully," said the Oracle as they approached.

"We have," Bregnest replied, bowing to her.

"And are you prepared to fulfill your pledge?"

"We are," eight voices answered.

"Who among you carries the crystal?"

"Master Taylor has the honor," said Bregnest, gesturing to Alex.

"Let him come forward," the Oracle commanded.

Alex walked forward, carrying the crystal carefully in both hands. When he reached the Oracle, he bowed, then removed the velvet cover and held up the crystal for all to see. Once more it was like a ball of light, shining in the morning sun.

"Do you return this of your own free will?" she questioned, looking at Alex.

"I do," replied Alex.

"Do any here make a claim on this crystal?"

"We do not," eight voices replied.

"Then as the Oracle of the White Tower, I accept this crystal from you. Your pledge is fulfilled and your honor is enlarged," she said solemnly, taking the crystal from Alex's hand as he dropped to one knee and offered it to her.

The Oracle turned and walked away from them, returning to the White Tower without another word.

"There is great power in the Oracle," said Arconn, as they watched her walk away.

They all murmured their agreement, slowly filing out of the garden and returning to the second house.

"It seems strange," said Alex as they sat around the central table. "She asked us as Iownan to return the crystal, but then accepted it from us as the Oracle."

"Not so strange," said Thrang. "As Iownan, she could ask us to return the crystal. As the Oracle, she would have had to command us."

"Would anyone say no to an oracle?" Alex wondered out loud.

"Perhaps not," Arconn answered. "Though by making it a request and not a command, she allowed us to choose."

They said nothing more about the crystal, because Thrain, Melnoch, and Nitek walked in, dressed in their finest clothes and looking nervous. They hardly ate anything of the midday meal, and Skeld and Tayo took great pleasure in teasing all three of them.

After the meal, Thomas arrived to take the three dwarfs to the Oracle. He told the company that Iownan would not be able to join them for dinner that night, but would come the following night.

When Thrain, Melnoch, and Nitek rejoined the company for the evening meal, Alex could tell they were happy with what they had learned. Thrain seemed ready to burst with excitement. He looked like he was hoping someone would ask him what the Oracle had said, but nobody did, and as he ate, his excitement seemed to cool, but only slightly.

The three young dwarfs said they would be leaving in the morning and were disappointed that they couldn't stay another day.

When morning arrived however, the excitement and happiness of the three dwarfs had returned in full strength. They thanked Bregnest and the others for allowing them to travel with them to the White Tower and then said their farewells.

"Perhaps we will ride together again some day," said Thrain, winking at Alex and Andy as he mounted his horse.

"Perhaps so," replied Andy with a knowing smile and a final farewell.

The next night, the company dined with Iownan and their meal was mixed with laughter and talking. Arconn told of Alex's encounter with the wraiths, his recovery, and the feast the elves held in his honor. Alex was glad Arconn left out the part about how he almost took Calysto with him across the wall, though he suspected Iownan already knew about it. After all the stories had been told, Iownan wished them all good night and then asked Bregnest for a private word.

"What were you two whispering about?" Skeld asked when Bregnest rejoined his companions in the sleeping house.

"Planning another adventure already?" Tayo guessed.

"Nothing so grand as that," Bregnest replied with a secretive smile.

"What then?" Thrang questioned.

"When we were last here, I sent a letter," replied Bregnest. "Iownan wished to tell me that an answer had come."

"What was this letter about?" Halfdan asked.

"No secrets among the company," Andy added loudly.

"You will find out tomorrow morning," said Bregnest, acting suddenly tired and laying down on his bed. "Now, I think I will get some sleep."

The others yelled and demanded an answer, but Bregnest would say no more. As Skeld and Tayo tried to wrestle an answer from Bregnest, Alex left the sleeping house to say good night to Shahree. He knew before he reached the stables that Iownan would not be there.

The next morning they all resumed questioning Bregnest about the mysterious letter. He seemed unwilling to answer any questions until after he had eaten, which meant he had to endure Skeld and Tayo throwing bits of food at him while he ate.

"Very well," said Bregnest as a piece of toast hit him on the nose.

He stood up, rubbing his nose, and rang the gong in the second house. Thomas soon appeared, carrying a large package wrapped in brown paper. He set the lumpy package down on one of the main tables and departed as quickly as he had come.

"The letter I sent was to Whalen Vankin, a wizard I know of some reputation," Bregnest said.

"Some reputation indeed," said Thrang, as if this did not describe Whalen Vankin properly.

"In any event," Bregnest continued, ignoring Thrang's

comment. "I asked Whalen if he would be willing to take young Alex on as his apprentice. Whalen has agreed, but says he wishes to meet Alex in person before making any final arrangements."

"Wonderful," said Thrang.

"Outstanding," said Skeld.

"Incredible," said Halfdan.

"Yes," said Bregnest, holding up one hand and motioning for silence. "Unfortunately, Whalen is in the middle of an adventure of his own and won't be able to meet Alex for some time. He has, however, sent along this package for Alex, which I believe contains several magic books and other items, including a letter of instructions. Whalen asks that the package not be opened until Alex is safely at home."

"Oh, but that hardly seems fair," Andy complained loudly.

"Fair or not, it is what Whalen asks," Bregnest replied sternly. "And I don't think any of us—Alex included—would like to go against the wishes of Whalen Vankin."

"No, of course not," Andy admitted quickly.

"Very well then," Bregnest said. "Alex, I suggest you put the package in your bag somewhere where you won't be tempted to open it before you get home."

Alex did as Bregnest said, placing the heavy package inside his magic bag in a corner behind some of his old clothes. He was curious about what might be in the package, and he tried to feel anything he could through the paper as he put it in his magic bag.

They remained at the White Tower for three more days, resting, relaxing, and dining each night with Iownan.

The morning of the fourth day, as the company prepared to leave, Iownan arrived to say her farewells. She thanked them all for returning the crystal to the tower and wished them all a safe journey.

Then, bowing to Alex, she spoke in a lowered voice. "I hope we shall meet again," she said softly. "And I hope Whalen Vankin can meet with you soon."

Alex returned her bow, his heart heavy knowing that this adventure would soon be over. He didn't want it to end, but he knew it was time to go home.

CHAPTER TWENTY

HOME AGAIN

As the company rode back to the great arch, Alex thought about everything that had happened to him. The adventure had lasted little more than a year and a half, but almost everything was different now. He wondered when he would be able to find a new adventure to go on, and if any of his friends would be able to join him.

When they rode past the Troll's Stream, Alex looked toward the hills. He knew that the stone troll would still be there, and part of him wanted to see it again.

"You seem strangely quiet, Alex," Arconn observed that night as they ate.

"Oh, just thinking," answered Alex.

"Thinking how you'll spend your fortune, no doubt," Skeld commented with a laugh.

"No," said Alex. "Just wishing the adventure wasn't over."

"It's not really over," said Thrang. "After all, you've still got to meet with Whalen Vankin and learn to be a true wizard."

"I suppose so," Alex admitted. "But it won't be the same."

"Because he won't have Thrang's cooking to keep him going," Tayo laughed happily.

"Nor a pair of jokers who don't know when they're well-off," Thrang replied.

Alex laughed, happy to be with his friends. He tried not to think about leaving them to go back to his old life. He thought it would be the hardest thing he'd done so far.

"Don't worry," said Andy, throwing a biscuit at Tayo. "I'm sure we'll all meet again."

Alex smiled at Andy's words and then joined in the sudden biscuit battle that broke out. Thrang yelled madly at them for wasting food, but that only made him a target for everyone else.

Their last days in Vargland passed quickly and Alex realized Thrang was right—his adventures were only just beginning. He had the package from Whalen Vankin to open when he got home, and he was looking forward to that. He also needed to meet with Whalen, and that might be quite an adventure all by itself.

They finally reached the great arch, and as they rode through it, the dismal colors of fall magically turned into the happy greens of spring. The lands around Telous seemed to be exactly the same as when they'd left.

They arrived in Telous in time for a midday meal at the Golden Swan. After lunch, Bregnest left to arrange for their rooms and to order an evening feast. Andy and Alex wandered into the streets of Telous, leaving the others talking happily in the bar.

"I want to see the bag maker," Andy said. "I need to add a

couple of rooms to my bag. And you can ask him about the six lost bags while we're there."

Alex quickly agreed; the thought of returning the lost bags gave him hope for new adventures.

"Ah, gentlemen," said the bag maker when Alex and Andy walked through the door. "What can I do for you today?"

"Quite a bit, I hope," answered Alex.

"Oh? Had some good fortune on your last adventure, did you?"

"Yes, we did," said Andy. "We both would like to add some rooms to our bags."

"Excellent," replied the bag maker. "Do you know which rooms you would like to add?"

Andy ordered five new rooms for his bag, though he had only planned on three.

The bag maker handed Andy's bag back to him and then turned to Alex. "Now, what can I do for you?"

"I would like a bathroom, a bedroom, an ice room, and a library added to my bag," answered Alex.

"Very good," said the bag maker. "All useful rooms to be sure."

It didn't take long to add the rooms to Alex's magic bag, and Alex wondered how hard it might be to learn that bit of magic.

The bag maker smiled as he accepted his money from Andy and Alex. "Is there anything else I can help you with?"

"Yes, there is actually," said Alex. "On my last adventure, I was able to recover several lost magic bags. I was hoping you could tell me who they belonged to, and where their families or heirs might be found."

"Of course," answered the bag maker. "Returning lost bags is a great honor. I will be happy to tell you all that I can. Please, if I may see the bags you've recovered, I can write you a list of heirs and locations."

"Thank you, that would be most helpful," said Alex.

It didn't take long for the bag maker to identify the owners of the lost magic bags, but it did take him some time to find the named heirs and to write everything down. Alex was happy to wait. At least now he would have some idea of where the heirs of the lost bags might be found and that might lead him to future adventures.

Alex and Andy returned to the Golden Swan in time for the company's final feast, which was a long and happy event. They joked and laughed late into the night until Bregnest finally insisted they all go to bed.

"We will meet as a company in the morning to divide what is left of the share for expenses," Bregnest said. "I have already delivered the share that was set aside for the Widows and Orphans fund, though you may wish to make your own contributions as well. Then we will declare our agreement fulfilled and our adventure at an end."

Alex went to bed both happy and sad, knowing that tomorrow the company would be no more. As he slept, he dreamed of his friends in Vargland. He saw Iownan in her tower, and Osrik on his stone throne. He could hear Thrain pestering Osrik to let him go on an adventure, and he wondered what the Oracle had said to Melnoch and Nitek. Last of all, he dreamed of Calysto in the dark woods. He wondered when he would see her again.

When Andy shook him awake the next morning, his sorrows were gone and he felt happier than he had in weeks. He knew one day he would return to Vargland and see all his friends again.

At breakfast, Tayo and Skeld were already teasing Thrang about his retirement, asking how they could survive their next adventure without such a good cook. Thrang insisted he was too old for adventures and it was time to settle down, but his smile seemed to say he was just joking.

"It is time to divide the last of the share set aside for expenses," said Bregnest loudly so the others would stop making so much noise. "I have decided to divide it evenly between us. There are two reasons for this—first, because you have been a wonderful company and have made this a first-class adventure."

The company exploded in cheers at Bregnest's decision and praise.

"The second reason," Bregnest said, holding up his hands for quiet, "is because I know our young wizard would complain loudly if I tried to give more to him than to the rest of us. So, to keep him happy, we will share equally."

Another cheer went up from all of them, and Alex blushed as Bregnest bowed to him with a smile and a wink.

Bregnest had already sorted and divided the remaining

treasure into eight large piles, which the company found waiting for them in a room at the back of the inn.

After they had stored their treasure, Bregnest led them out of the Golden Swan and across the road to a large building where they could make their donations to the Widows and Orphans fund. Alex had read about the fund in the *Adventurer's Handbook,* so he had a good idea of how much he should give. He hoped it wouldn't be more than Bregnest's donation, because if he gave more than the company's leader it would be an insult. Bregnest was generous and Alex was relieved that he could give as much as he had planned.

The company wandered off through the streets of Telous. There were a few hours left before the midday meal, and Alex asked Arconn and Thrang to come with him to the bookshop. He wanted their advice on some new books about adventures and magic.

When they returned to the Golden Swan for their final meal together the mood was somber and a little sad. There was little joking as everyone was thinking about how much they would miss each other and what they would do next.

"It is time," Bregnest said at last. "If there are no questions or disputes, we will call our agreement complete."

"I have a question," Alex said suddenly, remembering something.

"And what is that?" Bregnest asked.

"Arconn mentioned once that you were trying to fulfill a prophecy on this adventure," Alex said. "Can you tell us what that prophecy was—or is?"

Bregnest smiled and laughed softly to himself. "I wasn't really sure it would be fulfilled on this adventure," he said. "That is why I didn't tell you about it at the beginning of our quest. However, I see that the prophecy has partly come true, so I will tell you what I can."

Bregnest paused for a long moment.

"The prophecy was given to me many years ago, and I was never sure it was a true prophecy," he said slowly.

"Enough," Thrang said loudly. "Just tell us what it is."

"Very well, Master Silversmith," said Bregnest. "I was told that I would find a great wizard on my adventures. A wizard who would also be a warrior, though he would not know of his talents when I found him. The prophecy said I would help him find the path he should follow, and that he would go on to do many great and noble deeds."

"That seems to have come true in part then," said Thrang, smiling at Alex. "And as soon as young Alex goes on another adventure, it may come true completely."

"Indeed," Bregnest agreed, raising his mug to toast Alex. The others all followed his example.

Alex went pink, but smiled and raised his own mug as well.

"I declare our agreement fulfilled and our adventure at an end," said Bregnest after the toast. "Some of you will be leaving when we finish here, and the rest of us will leave in the morning. Until we meet again, I wish you all a fond farewell."

"Until we meet again," the company repeated.

There were many good-byes and promises to visit each other in distant lands. Alex promised to visit everyone, though he had no idea how to find any of his friends once they left Telous.

Andy, Skeld, and Tayo were leaving that afternoon, and Alex joined the others in front of the Golden Swan to say good-bye once more. Tayo pulled Alex to one side as the others crowded around Skeld and Andy to say their farewells.

"I owe you more than the others will ever know," said Tayo. "If ever you have need, please, feel free to call on me."

"You are most kind, my friend," replied Alex. "I hope you find the happiness you deserve."

Tayo pulled Alex into a huge bear hug, squeezing him so tight Alex thought for a moment that his ribs would break. When Tayo released him and pulled away, Alex saw tears of happiness in Tayo's eyes.

"Farewell," Bregnest called as Andy, Skeld, and Tayo rode away. "May we meet again soon."

Once the three warriors were out of sight, Alex went back into the Golden Swan with his remaining companions. He was just wondering when he would see his departed friends again, when he suddenly thought of something else.

"How am I going to get home?" he said out loud as the thought occurred to him.

"Oh, you needn't worry," laughed Thrang. "Bregnest, Arconn, and I will be coming with you to Clutter's shop."

"You will?" Alex asked in surprise.

"'Course we will," Thrang laughed. "Bregnest needs to pay Clutter his share for the adventure, and Arconn and I have to update everyone's files."

"What files?" Alex questioned.

"The Adventure Shop keeps records about all adventurers. After each adventure, one or two of the company are chosen to update the files on themselves and the other adventurers. And I don't mind saying, we'll have a fair bit of work updating your file."

Another thought occurred to Alex. "What about Shahree?"

He didn't want to leave his horse behind, but he had no idea what he would do with a horse back at the Happy Dragon. Not to mention how he would explain how he had gotten a horse if he took Shahree home with him.

"You can stable her here," Thrang suggested. "The Swan keeps a good stable, and the price is fair. And if you leave her here, she'll be waiting when you go on your next adventure."

Alex was relieved, and he left his companions at once to make arrangements for Shahree's care. He stopped by her stall to say good-bye, at least for a little while. She seemed to understand when he told her he was going home but she was staying there. She looked sad, but nuzzled Alex's shoulder in her own farewell.

The next morning, Alex ate breakfast with Bregnest, Arconn, Thrang, and Halfdan. It was a quiet affair without Skeld and Tayo's jokes or Andy's laughter. When they finished, Halfdan said good-bye to Alex and made him promise to come visit as soon as possible. Halfdan would be waiting at the Golden Swan for Thrang to return so the two of them could journey home together.

"If you're ready then," said Thrang.

"I suppose I am," said Alex. "Though I wish I could start another adventure, now that I've been on one."

"I doubt you will have to wait for long," Thrang replied. "Wizards are always wanted on adventures. Plus you've got your meeting with Vankin to look forward to."

"And your home may be different than you remember it, now that you've been on an adventure," said Arconn.

Alex nodded and smiled. He waved good-bye to Halfdan as he and the others made their way along the streets of Telous. Almost before he knew it, they were standing in the same field he had arrived in so long ago. There was no sign of a magic door however, and he wondered how they would get back into the adventurer's shop.

"Mr. Clutter should be opening the door any time now," said Arconn. "I sent him a geeb, telling him what time we'd be arriving."

Almost as soon as Arconn had finished speaking, the silver outline of a door appeared in front of them. The door opened slowly, and the four of them stepped into Mr. Clutter's shop.

"Well, then," said Mr. Clutter, smiling. "Back already, are you?"

"We've had a fair bit of luck," replied Thrang, moving into the room. "Our young first-timer here proved more valuable than we bargained for."

"Ah, Mr. Taylor," said Mr. Clutter happily. "So glad to see you again. I received a message for you just this morning . . . let me see, where did I put that . . ." Mr. Clutter searched his desk and produced an envelope. "Ah, here we are. As I said, just arrived this morning. Very exciting, I must say."

Alex took the letter from Mr. Clutter. His name was written on the front of the envelope in large red letters. Alex wondered if it was an invitation to join another adventure already or perhaps a message from one of his friends in Vargland. The back of the envelope was sealed with dark purple wax and the image of a star. Alex slit the envelope open and read the letter inside.

Master Alexander Taylor, Esq.,
Dear Alex,

I hope you won't mind if I call you Alex as our mutual friend, Bregnest, told me that I should.

Alex, I know that right now you'd like nothing more than to be starting a new adventure. However, I must insist that you return home to your stepfather's house. I don't have time to go into details now, but I will explain everything to you as soon as I can.

Yours in fellowship,
Whalen Vankin

Alex wondered how Vankin had known he would be in the adventurer's shop this morning. He also wondered why the letter was signed, "Yours in fellowship," which didn't mean anything to him.

"I suppose Whalen knows what he's talking about," said Bregnest when Alex showed him the letter. "He may have his own ways, and I'll admit he sometimes acts oddly, but he knows more than most. You should do what he says."

Alex nodded and put Vankin's letter inside his magic bag. Looking toward the door of the shop, he realized it was time to say good-bye.

"You'll want to change then," said Mr. Clutter, carrying a tray of tea and cakes into the room. "No good going home looking like that."

Alex looked down at himself and realized he was still wearing his traveling gear, including the true silver dagger that Umbar had given him. He wondered what Mr. Roberts would say if he turned up looking like this.

"Just in here," said Mr. Clutter, directing Alex to another door. "You can put your old things on and be ready to go."

Alex walked through the door and noticed that his clothes suddenly felt strangely loose. Looking at himself in a nearby mirror, he saw that his hair, which had grown long during his adventure, was as short as it had been when he'd first entered Mr. Clutter's shop. The change had happened so quickly Alex hadn't noticed the magic around him.

Laughing in surprise, Alex changed back into his old clothes. He carefully folded his traveling clothes and stored them in his bag, wondering when he would need them again. For several minutes, he looked at his silver dagger, unwilling to put it away. He thought once more of his friends in Vargland and the amazing adventures he'd had. With a sigh, he slipped the beautiful dagger into his bag, and put this adventure away with it.

Looking at the mirror, he saw himself exactly as he had been the afternoon he'd walked into Mr. Clutter's shop. The only difference was that now he carried a leather bag over one shoulder.

"Well, you do look different," commented Thrang, eyeing him as he emerged from the changing room.

"Not as scared as he looked the first time we saw him," Arconn added.

"And not as doubting either," said Alex. "I'd like to thank you both for choosing me."

"Haven't you learned anything?" Thrang laughed. "We didn't choose you—it was the sign."

"I know, I know," said Alex, laughing as well.

It took a long time for him to say good-bye to Thrang, Arconn, and Bregnest. Alex felt sad as he walked to the front door of the shop alone. His friends waved as he opened the door, and he turned to say one last good-bye.

"Go on, then," Thrang said loudly. "You've got work to do, remember."

Alex raised his hand and then stepped through the door and back onto Sildon Lane. He turned his steps toward the Happy Dragon, wondering if he should tell Mr. Roberts about his adventure. He had no idea how he could possibly explain it all, so in the end, he decided not to say anything at all.

As he walked toward the tavern, Alex realized he was really happy to be home. He would miss his new friends and the fun he'd had on his adventure, but he belonged here too and he was glad to be back. When he reached the back door of the tavern, he wasn't surprised to find Todd waiting for him.

"Sorry about the glasses, Alex," he said, smiling weakly. "Didn't mean for Dad to yell at you."

"It's all right," said Alex, returning the smile.

"Hey, where'd you get this?" Todd asked, noticing Alex's magic bag and reaching his hand out to touch it.

"Leave it!" Mr. Roberts boomed so loudly that both Todd and Alex jumped.

Mr. Roberts stood behind Todd looking at Alex with a stunned expression on his face and rubbing his hands together nervously.

"Todd, go help in the kitchen," Mr. Roberts ordered. "Alex, you come with me."

Alex wondered if Mr. Roberts was still mad about the broken glasses. He remembered how loudly his stepfather had yelled so long ago, and then he reminded himself that it hadn't been that long ago, it had only been earlier today.

Following his stepfather, Alex climbed up the stairs to the second floor of the tavern to Mr. Roberts's study. Alex was uncomfortable, because normally neither he nor Todd was allowed in this room.

Mr. Roberts closed the door behind them, moved to his desk, and turned to look at Alex as he sat down. For what seemed a long time, Mr. Roberts didn't say anything at all.

"So," he finally said. "You've been on an adventure then."

Alex's jaw dropped and his eyes grew to twice their normal size. How could Mr. Roberts possibly know about his adventure?

Mr. Roberts smiled, laughing at Alex's stunned look. He got up and walked to the closet, continuing to chuckle to himself as he went. Unlocking the door, he removed two items from the top shelf—items Alex instantly recognized as magic bags.

"Your mother insisted that I never encourage you," said Mr. Roberts, returning to his seat. "Thought I might give you wild ideas and send you off on dangerous adventures."

"What are you talking about?"

"I suppose I should tell you everything, but it's quite a long story," Mr. Roberts said. "For now, I'll tell you that I was once an adventurer. Never went on many adventures, though, and never had a great deal of luck finding treasure. Your dad . . . now *he* was an adventurer."

"My father was an adventurer?" Alex asked, almost numb from the information Mr. Roberts was telling him.

"Of course," said Mr. Roberts. "A great adventurer if ever there was one. In the end, though, his luck ran out. That's why your mother asked me never to tell you about it."

"She didn't want me to know about my father?"

"Not until you were ready," Mr. Roberts replied. "She didn't know you would be an adventurer, and if you weren't, how could she tell you about your dad?"

"I see," said Alex, a thousand new questions racing through his mind.

"Your dad was sick when he got back from his last adventure. I never thought sickness would get him. Trolls, maybe, or goblins, but never sickness," Mr. Roberts said sadly. "After your dad crossed the wall, your mom came and stayed here. I had been close to both your mom and dad so I agreed to play the part of your stepfather. I knew your mom loved your dad too much to ever marry again. But I also knew she needed someone to help look after you, and well . . . it was the least I could do for my friends."

"But . . ." Alex stammered.

"I know it's a lot to take in all at once," said Mr. Roberts, nodding. "Going on your first adventure, then finding out your dad was an adventurer, too. Now that you've been chosen, I suppose I need to give you this."

Mr. Roberts held out one of the magic bags from the closet. Alex looked at the bag, then at Mr. Roberts, then at the bag again.

"It was your father's," said Mr. Roberts with a smile. "You're his heir, so the bag—and what's in it—belongs to you."

"Shouldn't I be offering you a reward for returning it?" Alex asked.

Mr. Roberts smiled. "I see you've learned about returning lost bags."

"Yes," said Alex.

"That's good," said Mr. Roberts. "But you don't need to offer a reward for this bag because it was never lost. After all, your dad came home and everything. I've just been keeping it for you."

"Do you know what's in it?"

"No, I don't," answered Mr. Roberts, scratching his chin thoughtfully. "The bag didn't belong to me. Your mom told me the passwords before she . . . well . . ."

"Died," Alex said softly.

Mr. Roberts nodded. "It's time for you to accept your father's bag."

"But—" Alex started.

"But nothing. Your parents would be proud to know you had been chosen and have gone on an adventure without any help or encouragement. Your mom only insisted on not telling you because she didn't want you to be disappointed. You know, if you weren't chosen."

Alex smiled at Mr. Roberts as he took his father's bag and listened to the passwords. This was something he had never expected, not even in his wildest dreams. Now he was excited to tell Mr. Roberts everything that had happened to him and everything he had learned on his adventure.

"We've got plenty of time," said Mr. Roberts. "And I have a few tales for you, about your dad and the things he did."

"May I ask you something, sir?" Alex asked.

"Anything at all," Mr. Roberts replied.

"I'm not sure how the choosing works, but since my dad was an adventurer and I was chosen, does that mean that Todd will be an adventurer too?"

"I don't know," replied Mr. Roberts, considering the question. "He doesn't really seem the type, and anyway, it doesn't seem to happen just because your father or mother were adventurers. I don't think anyone knows exactly how the choosing works."

Alex nodded, wondering if Mr. Roberts had ever told Todd about any of his adventures.

"I suspect you've got things to do," said Mr. Roberts as he

moved toward the door. "You'll probably spend the rest of the day taking a look at your father's bag. You can tell me about your adventure another time."

Alex sat thinking for a long time. Of all the surprises he'd had on his first adventure, this was the biggest and the best. Excitement flooded him as he held his father's magic bag in his hands and softly spoke the magic word that would let him enter. He was about to discover something about the father he'd never known, and he thought that this might be an even better adventure than the one he had just finished.

READING GUIDE

1. At the beginning of the story, Alex wishes for a different life. Have you ever wished for a different life? Have you ever wished that you could be somebody else? Who would you like to be?

2. If you suddenly had a chance to go on a great adventure like Alex, would you go? Would you be afraid? Would you want to take someone with you? Who?

3. Arconn tells Alex that if he doesn't go on the adventure he will regret it for the rest of his life. Why do you think he would regret it? Are there things in your life that you regret not doing? How about things that you have done that you regret now?

4. Early in the story, Andy is warned to be careful of his curiosity. Why should we be careful of our own curiosity? Are there things that you are curious about that might be dangerous?

5. Alex is told that where there is power there is also accountability. What kinds of things in your world could be

considered power? What kind of accountability is there for the powers you've been given?

6. It takes a long time for Alex to really believe in magic. Are there things in your world that you find hard to believe in? Are there things you believe now that you didn't believe when you first learned about them?

7. When Alex fights the three-legged troll everything turns out well, but he is still punished. Is it fair for Alex to be punished? Have you ever broken rules to do something you know is right?

8. Iownan tells Alex that she can only see possibilities. Do your friends and families sometimes see your possibilities better than you do?

9. Iownan asks each of the adventurers to promise to return the lost crystal of the tower to her. Why do you think Iownan would make that request? Have you ever had to keep a promise that somebody else made?

10. Eric Von Tealo can only give his word that the story he's told the adventurers is true. Would the people who know you be willing to accept your word? How important is it to have a reputation for being honest?

11. When Alex faces the wraiths at the ruins of Aunk he is tempted to do what they say. Have you ever been tempted by someone? Have you ever been tempted by something you wanted?

12. The wraiths tell Alex that they are his friends and that

they will help him become great if he helps them first. Has anyone ever promised to be your friend if you did something for them first? Are they still your friend?

13. Alex crosses the wall into the dangerous shadow lands to help his friend Tayo. How far would you be willing to go to help your friends? How far would your friends go to help you? Should there be a limit to how far you go?

14. On the journey home, Alex and his friends take the time to remember Eric Von Tealo. They make sure that his grave is marked and that his name will be remembered. How important is it to remember people who have helped you? If the people who helped you aren't around any more, is it still important to remember them? Why?

15. When Alex returns home he is surprised to discover that his own father was once an adventurer. Have you ever discovered things about your parents that surprised you? Have you ever tried to find out about things your parents did when they were your age?

16. Arconn tells Alex that all words have power. Words can sometimes hurt us, and sometimes words can make us feel good. How do you use your words? Have you ever hurt someone with your words?

17. How is reading a book like going on an adventure? How many book adventures have you been on? What have you learned from your adventures?

DO YOU HAVE THE COURAGE, THE WITS, AND THE SKILL TO BE AN ADVENTURER?

If so apply online at
AdventurersWanted.com

- Fill out an Adventurer's application

- Nominate *Slathbog's Gold* for Book of the Year in your state

- Play games

- Access bonus material

- Request M. L. Forman to come to your school

APPLY NOW— POSITIONS ARE LIMITED AND GOING FAST!

ENJOY THIS SNEAK PEEK

OF

BOOK TWO

THE HORN OF
MORAN

CHAPTER ONE
WIZARD IN TRAINING

A cool breeze stirred the curtain by the open window. Alex watched the slow, swaying movement of the cloth for a moment before forcing his tired mind to focus. Standing up with some difficulty, he stretched, then turned off the lamp on the table he used as a desk. It had been a long day, but as tired as he was, Alex didn't want to sleep.

"Foolish," Alex said as he moved toward his bed.

It was foolish not to sleep, foolish not to let his body rest. There was nothing to fear, not here at home. He knew his dreams—even his nightmares—might be important, but he didn't know what, if anything, they meant.

"The dreams won't come tonight," Alex told himself as he dropped onto his bed.

He only half-believed his own words. The dreams had been random, waking him at least once a week. The last one had been only three days before, and Alex hoped for an uneventful night. Reaching out, Alex turned off the light beside his bed. He let himself relax, clearing his mind of worries, and slowly let sleep take him.

Almost immediately, Alex found himself walking along a

familiar, narrow, dark corridor. Shadows danced in the flickering light of the few torches that were hanging from the walls, creating the illusion of movement. For a moment Alex felt that he was inside some living thing, the walls moving around him like some giant creature was breathing. But the dream was entirely silent, and that troubled him.

He knew where he was—this dimly lit corridor had haunted his dreams for months—and he knew where he had to go. Slowly Alex started forward, following the line of torches deeper into the unknown. He walked for what felt like hours, and with each step the silence pressed a little closer, making it harder for him to breathe.

Eventually, a chamber appeared in front of him just as it always did, empty except for an enormous mirror in the center of the room. Reluctantly Alex moved toward the mirror, afraid of what it would show him yet knowing he would look anyway. A reflection appeared slowly, as if it, too, was afraid to look out of the mirror.

This time, though, it wasn't a single image that appeared in front of him, but two. Alex's breath caught in his throat, and he had to force himself to breathe. The two images were both of him, but one image was true, reflecting him as he was, while the other image was different, an older version of Alex. After a moment the two reflections separated, the older to the left side of the mirror, the younger disappearing to the right, out of his line of sight.

Alex stepped closer to the mirror, trying to see where the images had gone, but the surface was blank. He lifted his hand,

and as he touched the mirror, the glass rippled like water under his fingers. Without thinking he pushed himself through the liquid surface of the mirror. As he stepped through, he discovered that the mirror was still in front of him, but now he was surrounded by other mirrors as well.

Panic clawed at the back of Alex's mind, but he couldn't run, he could only turn and look into the mirrors around him. Most were empty, reflecting only darkness back at him, but two mirrors held images of himself. On his left, the older Alex walked slowly away. To his right, his true reflection looked back at him.

Alex faced his true reflection and reached out to touch the mirror. His hand passed through the watery surface, and at his touch all the mirrors around him collapsed, the water dropping to the stone floor and vanishing into the cracks.

Doors appeared on either side of the chamber, and a large double door seemed to emerge out of the floor at the far end.

Alex moved to the middle of the room. Standing with his eyes partly closed, he listened for any sound, anything that would help him understand why he was there or know what to do next. A cold breeze blew across his face. It came from the direction of the double doors, and he took it as a sign. He moved to the doorway, reaching out for the glimmering, gold doorknob. Then he stopped, his hand shaking slightly. He could feel evil and hate waiting behind the doors. Not just waiting, waiting for *him*.

Alex froze. He didn't want to know what was behind those doors, and yet a sudden need filled him, an urgency and the knowledge that time was running out. He feared whatever was waiting for him behind the doors, but something in his mind told him that he had to face his fears. He had to confront the evil that was waiting for him. If he turned back now—if he gave in to his fear—then his future would vanish like the water from the mirrors. It took all the strength he had to lift his hand and push open the doors.

Everything went dark as he moved through the doorway, and his feet found only emptiness. Alex tumbled into the darkness, his voice screaming that it wasn't fair, anger and frustration racing through his mind. Laughter answered his protests, a laughter that filled his mind with rage and his bones with ice. There were no answers here; there was only the laughter and the endless falling into darkness.

Alex woke with a start.

For a moment he was lost, and then he had to fight to get free of his blankets. Alex fumbled with the lamp beside his bed, knocking things over in his hurry to turn on the light. Finally, feeling panicked that he was really still asleep, the light came on.

Rubbing his eyes, Alex twisted around and sat on the edge of his bed. He glanced at the clock on the wall and saw that it was 4:30 A.M. For a minute he sat there, looking around the room, making sure that he wasn't in another dream.

Staggering to his feet, Alex moved to his desk. He dropped into the swivel chair, turned on the lamp, and pulled a large notepad toward him. Checking his calendar, he scribbled the date on the notepad, followed by the time. For a long moment he paused, and then he slowly started to write everything he could remember about the nightmare he'd just had.

Alexander Taylor was not what he appeared to be. Most people thought Alex was a normal sixteen-year-old boy, but they were wrong. Alex was—among other things—an adventurer.

Six months ago, Alex had indeed been what people expected him to be: normal. But that had all changed when he had accidentally wandered into the adventure shop belonging to Mr. Cornelius Clutter. After entering Mr. Clutter's shop, Alex had become part of a great adventure, and that experience had changed everything he thought he knew. While on his adventure he had learned all kinds of new things, but perhaps the strangest thing of all was that he had learned he was an untrained wizard.

When Alex had come home from his first adventure—on the same afternoon that he had left—he was shocked to learn that his stepfather, Mr. Roberts, knew all about adventures and magic. Not only that, but Mr. Roberts told Alex that his father had been an adventurer as well.

That had been six long months ago, and almost everything in Alex's life had changed. His stepbrother, Todd, had gone off to college, and Alex no longer had to wash dishes or help in the kitchen, or even clean up once the customers at the tavern had left. In fact, the only things Alex really had to do were study and practice magic.

Learning magic sometimes required open spaces in order to keep things from getting out of hand. Alex smiled as he remembered the first time he'd tried to summon a magical wind. He'd ended up blowing everything in his old bedroom into a giant mess. To make things easier for Alex, and to help prevent problems like the mess in his bedroom, Mr. Roberts had cleared the third floor of the tavern and given the space entirely to his stepson.

This morning Alex was grateful for the privacy. He leaned back in his chair and reviewed the details he had written down about his dream. His teacher, Whalen Vankin, had told Alex that the dreams he was having might be warnings. "Dreams are often more than they appear to be," Whalen had said in his letters. "As your power grows, you will have many dreams, and many nightmares. You would be wise to pay attention to both."

Alex wondered when he would be able to meet the great wizard face to face. Whalen was perhaps the greatest wizard alive, and he had agreed to take Alex as his apprentice. Unfortunately, Whalen was currently on an adventure of his own, so Alex was stuck at home waiting, learning magic by magical mail.

Whalen had sent Alex several books about magic—some of which could only be read by moonlight—and several small magical objects as well. He had also sent a letter instructing Alex about what he should do and what he should try to learn. Whalen had warned him not to join any more adventures, at least not until they had met in person.

Alex was learning a lot, but he hated waiting for a new

adventure. It was hard for him to imagine what was taking Whalen so long. And apart from waiting, there were other things that annoyed him. Though his first adventure had taken a year and a half, he'd come home as his fifteen-year-old self. He wasn't as strong as he remembered being, or as tall, or anything else. He felt trapped in his own small, weak body.

Being smaller and weaker than he remembered wasn't the worst thing about being home. What really annoyed him was the way people treated him. On his adventure, Alex had been treated as an equal. His fellow adventurers were always willing to listen to his opinions and ideas. Here, at home, there were few people who even pretended to listen to a sixteen-year-old. Some people would smile politely and nod, but if anything that was more frustrating than the people who simply ignored him.

Alex tried hard to push his frustrations away, but it wasn't always easy. He often found himself becoming angry for almost no reason at all. Whalen had warned him it would be hard to control his emotions—anger most of all—and Alex was working hard to keep his emotions from running away with him.

Sighing, Alex realized he wasn't going to be able to go back to sleep. At least not for a while. Pushing aside the notepad, he reached for his magic bag and whispered into the top. As soon as he had finished speaking, a second magic bag appeared in his hand, a bag that had once belonged to his father. Setting his own bag aside, he whispered the password that would allow him to enter his father's bag.

After returning home from his first adventure, Alex had spent a lot of time searching the bag and, with Mr. Roberts to answer his questions, he felt like he was finally getting to know his father.

There were the things he'd expected to find in his father's bag: stored food, a bedroom, clothes, a treasure room that was at least as large as his own, and lots of other things that adventurers would find helpful or useful. But then there were the things he had not expected to find. His father had a surprisingly large library, sculptures of different creatures, maps of places Alex had never heard of or even read about, a kitchen big enough to cook for a hundred people, and a room that was set up like a blacksmith shop.

"Your father was a gifted smith," Mr. Roberts had said when Alex had questioned him about the workroom. "He won lots of awards for the weapons and armor he made. He also made all kinds of jewelry—rings, necklaces, brooches, and such. Never sold any of it as far as I know; he used to give the pretty things away to friends, or sometimes to people who helped him on an adventure."

Once inside the bag, Alex headed directly for the workroom. Whalen had suggested, more than once, that he find a hobby; something to take his mind off waiting. Something that had nothing at all to do with magic. Making things with his hands, not with magic, seemed like a perfect hobby. There were plenty of books in the workroom to get him started, as well as piles of his father's notes.

Alex was walking past the large stone dragon statue that stood next to the workroom door, when he noticed something he was sure he had never seen before. A golden chain was dangling from the dragon's mouth.

Curious, he looked at the chain for a minute, wondering where it had come from. He could feel magic near the dragon's head, an old spell with little power. He'd never felt magic like that before, so he carefully reached out and touched the chain. Nothing happened. He pulled gently on the chain, ready to let go of it if he felt the magic change, and he heard something move inside the dragon's mouth. As the chain moved inch by inch, the mouth of the dragon slowly opened. A pendant attached to the chain dropped out of the dragon's mouth where a rolled-up piece of paper now appeared.

Slowly Alex reached for the paper, half afraid that the mouth would snap shut on his hand, or worse, close before he could get the paper out. The dragon's jaws didn't move, and the old magic he had felt was fading, its purpose fulfilled. Carefully unrolling the paper, his jaw dropped open as he started to read.

My son,

I cannot tell you all that I would wish in this short note. I have left this pendant for you, not to wear, but to study. The ancient symbol on the pendant is an important one, with great meaning to those who know what it is. All I can say is that you may freely trust any person who wears this symbol or a pendant like this one. Do not wear this pendant yourself, but remember it. Do not ask questions about the symbol unless you meet a person who wears it. I hope, in time, that you

will learn more and understand why I cannot explain
more to you.

Your loving father,
Joshua

Alex was dumbfounded. He looked at the pendant, and then read the note again just to make sure he wasn't imagining things. He looked at the dragon, whose mouth remained open as if it had always been that way. His head spun with excitement, and for several minutes he wasn't sure what to do.

Wildly at first, and then with more control, Alex sent his magic searching. If his father had left him one magically hidden message, maybe he had left others. He searched every corner of the bag, and then to make sure he hadn't missed anything, he searched again. There was no magic to be found, no hidden compartments or doors, nothing. If there were other messages for him, his father had hidden them very well, and all he could do was wait until they were ready to be discovered.

Disappointed that he hadn't found more, Alex turned his attention to the pendant in his hand. It was made of gold and silver, and it looked like a small flower or a blossom of some kind. He tried to remember if he'd ever seen anything like it before. Nothing came to mind, but he had never paid much attention to the jewelry that others wore. He focused on the pendant for a few more minutes, promising himself that he would remember it if he ever saw it again.

Finally, Alex looped the chain over the dragon's head, letting the pendant hang around the neck of the statue. His father had left him a message, and he would remember it. He had questions, and in time he hoped he would find the answers, but he wasn't going to find them in his father's bag, and he wasn't going to find them today.

———————◆·◆————————

"You look tired," Mr. Roberts commented when Alex sat down for breakfast.

"Another nightmare," Alex replied.

"I guess that goes with being a wizard."

"It's not so bad," said Alex, trying to be casual.

"Bad enough, it would seem. What does Whalen have to say about it?"

"He says that dreams can sometimes be warnings and that I should try to remember them."

"Well, it's good to have a warning, even if you lose some sleep."

"It would be, if I knew what the nightmare was about," Alex replied in a resentful tone. "The dreams are always so mixed up, it's hard to know what any of it means. Or even if it means anything at all."

"Don't let it get to you, Alex. I'm sure you'll understand the dream in time," said Mr. Roberts. "It takes time to understand most things after all."

"I just hope the warning isn't for something that's going to happen today," said Alex.

"I doubt it," Mr. Roberts replied with a chortle. "Why don't you have some breakfast and then get a few more hours of sleep. If a dragon turns up, I'll be sure to wake you."

It was nearly noon when Alex woke up again. He still felt a little tired, but he rolled off the bed and stretched just the same. There were things he needed to do, and he wasn't going to let his bad dreams stop him.

Sitting down at his table, Alex looked at the notepad he'd used the night before. What he remembered from the nightmare didn't make any more sense to him now than it had when he'd written it down. He was sure it must be a warning, but the broken bits of his dream were impossible to piece together no matter how hard he tried.

"Just have to pay attention and keep my eyes open," Alex said to himself as he tossed the pad back onto the table.

A small popping sound and a loud ding interrupted his thoughts.

Looking around, Alex saw a yellow bowling-pin shaped creature with a red zigzag line around its middle standing on the far edge of the table. The geeb was balancing on its single birdlike leg, waiting for him to say something.

"Hello," said Alex in surprise.

"Ding," the geeb replied, its head changing into the shape of a small bell.

"Do you have a message for me?" Alex questioned.

"Ding!"

"Can I have the message, please?"

"Ding," replied the geeb and an envelope appeared from what Alex always thought of as the geeb's mouth.

"Thank you," said Alex.

"Ding!"

"Have you been paid?"

"Honk." The geeb's head took the shape of a small bicycle horn.

"Hang on a moment," said Alex as he opened the letter. "Let me see what this is, then I'll pay you."

"Ding!"

Alex recognized Whalen's handwriting on the front of the envelope, and he felt certain that this would be another long letter explaining magic, answering questions, and telling him what he should study next. To his surprise, however, the envelope contained only a short message and no instructions at all.

> *Dear Alex,*
>
> *Have just heard about a new adventure our friend Silvan Bregnest is putting together. He is in a bit of a rush and has asked me for permission to take you along. As the adventure is happening in Norsland, I thought you might like to go.*
>
> *I will expect you to keep up with your studies while you're away and to keep me informed of your activities. If you promise to send me a report every two weeks, I think you should join Bregnest on this adventure.*
>
> > *Yours in fellowship,*
> > *Whalen*
>
> *P.S. I believe Bregnest will be sending you a geeb shortly. Good luck, and remember to keep me up to date.*

Alex was stunned for a moment. His chest felt like a large balloon had inflated inside of him, and he thought he might float away with happiness. He had been waiting for months, and now Whalen had said he could go on another adventure. Better yet, Whalen had even picked an adventure for him to join. And best of all, his friend Bregnest would be leading the adventure. It was much more than Alex had dared to hope for. He was so distracted that he almost forgot about the geeb standing on the edge of his table.

"Ding!"

"Oh, sorry. Can you take a reply back to Whalen?" Alex asked as he reached for a piece of paper.

"Ding!"

Alex thought for a moment, and then wrote a quick reply to Whalen. He reviewed the page once before folding it and putting it in a new envelope, writing Whalen's name as neatly as he could on the outside.

"Can you take this to Whalen Vankin?" Alex asked the geeb again, wanting to make sure it would deliver the message to the right person.

"Ding," the geeb answered, but made no move to accept Alex's letter.

"Oh, yes, your payment. Sorry about that."

Alex retrieved a small ruby from his magic bag and tossed it in the general direction of the geeb. The geeb hopped into the air, catching the ruby with ease before landing back on the table. Once on the table the geeb produced eight gold coins and seven silver coins as change for the ruby.

Alex held his letter out for the geeb to take. "If you require more payment, please return."

"Ding." The geeb accepted the letter and then disappeared with a single hop on its birdlike leg and a small popping sound.

Almost immediately, a second geeb appeared with a loud ding.

"Do *you* have a message for me?" Alex asked, surprised.

"Ding!"

"May I have it, please?"

"Ding!"

"Thank you," said Alex, picking up the envelope that the geeb had dropped and tearing it open. He had trouble unfolding the letter and getting it right side up, but once he did, a smile spread across his face.

Master Alexander Taylor, Esq.

Dear Alex,

> *As you may have already heard from our friend, Whalen Vankin, I am putting together another adventure. I've written to Whalen and asked if you might come along. Whalen seems to think that it would be good for you to join the adventure, so I thought that I should send you a message and ask you to at least listen to the details.*

> *This won't be a great quest like our last adventure, but there is a large reward involved. If you are interested in coming, please send me a message. I'd like to*

meet as soon as possible at Mr. Clutter's Adventure Shop to discuss details and the bargain.

Your friend,
Silvan Bregnest

P.S. Andy has informed me that our friends Skeld and Tayo have both decided to get married, and they want you at the weddings. This won't be a problem for our adventure, and shouldn't cause us any delay.

Alex read the letter through twice, wondering when Bregnest wanted to meet at the adventure shop. He bit his lip, worried. Now that he thought about it, he didn't remember seeing Clutter's shop when he'd been in Sildon Lane only a few days ago. In fact, he didn't remember seeing it at all since he'd gotten home. If the shop wasn't still there, how was he going to meet Bregnest and go on this adventure?

"Can you take a reply back?" Alex questioned.

"Ding!"

Alex thought about Bregnest's note and the fact that their friends Skeld and Tayo were both getting married. Missing the weddings was unthinkable; he had to go. If worse came to worst, he would ask Whalen how to travel to Telous using magic.

"Here's your payment for delivering the message," Alex said to the geeb, who was waiting patiently on the table.

He tossed a small diamond in the air. The geeb caught the jewel easily as it fell through the air, and once again left a handful of gold and silver coins as change.

"Please take this message to Silvan Bregnest."

"Ding," the geeb answered, and accepted the message Alex had just written.

The second geeb of the day vanished, and Alex added the coins to his magic bag. He was wondering if he should go ahead and ask Whalen about getting to Telous with magic now, or if he should wait until after he'd tried to find the adventure shop, when another popping sound made him jump. Alex had never seen so many geebs in so short a time, and he wondered what this one might be bringing him.

After asking the geeb for the message and to wait for a reply, Alex sat down and opened the newest envelope. He could see from the writing that it was a second note from Whalen.

Dear Alex,

I've received your promise and intend to hold you to it. I had hoped to meet with you before you went on another adventure, but that has proven impossible. My current adventure is taking much longer than expected, and I have no idea when I'll be able to return.

I know you've been working hard to learn every-thing you can, and I promise you that much of what you have already learned will come in handy on this new adventure. I will warn you, however, not to become overconfident. There are many magical places and people in the known and the unknown lands, and many of them are not as friendly as they might be. To be honest, there are people and powers that would like nothing more than to control you, or failing that, to destroy you.

    This is a dangerous time for you, as you are not yet fully trained; and yet, you are able to use great power when you need to. I must warn you again to be careful when using your powers and remind you to not let your emotions get the best of you. Emotions are powerful things, Alex, and you need to learn to keep them under control. Study hard and keep your eyes open for danger. Remember, you are a wizard in training.

    I will write when I can but will expect a message from you at least every other week.

    Be careful and have fun.

      Yours in fellowship,
      Whalen

Alex thought Whalen sounded worried in his letter, and he wondered what exactly Whalen had meant by saying it was a dangerous time for him. His concerns about the note didn't last long, and thoughts of a new adventure filled his mind.

His first adventure had been so exciting, and he'd had so much fun with his friends. Slowly, however, his happy memories turned to darker thoughts. He considered what new dangers he might have to face. Were the nightmares he'd been having warnings about Bregnest's new adventure? Whalen had said that Bregnest was in a rush to put the company together, and Bregnest had wanted to meet as soon as possible. It seemed that time might be running out, but running out on what, Alex couldn't guess.